Julia QUINN

The Secrets of Sir Richard Kenworthy

PIATKUS

PIATKUS

First published in the US in 2015 by Avon Books,
An imprint of HarperCollins, New York
First published in Great Britain in 2015 by Piatkus
by arrangement with Avon
This paperback edition published in 2021 by Piatkus

13 5 7 9 10 8 6 4 2

A CIP catalogue record for this book
is available from the British Library.

ISBN 978-0-3494-3049-2

Printed and bound in Italy by Elcograf S.p.A.

Papers used by Piatkus are from well-managed forests
and other responsible sources.

Piatkus
An imprint of
Little, Brown Book Group
Carmelite House
50 Victoria Embankment
London EC4Y 0DZ

An Hachette UK Company
www.hachette.co.uk

www.littlebrown.co.uk

For Tillie, sister of my heart.

And also for Paul,
even though I still think you should have gone
for the Jedi Knighthood.

Chapter One

Pleinsworth House
London
Spring 1825

To QUOTE THAT book his sister had read two dozen times, it was a truth universally acknowledged that a single man in possession of a good fortune must be in want of a wife.

Sir Richard Kenworthy was not in possession of a fortune, but he was single. As for the wife . . .

Well, *that* was complicated.

"Want" wasn't the right word. Who *wanted* a wife? Men in love, he supposed, but he wasn't in love, had never been in love, and he didn't anticipate falling in such anytime soon.

Not that he was fundamentally opposed to the idea. He just didn't have time for it.

The wife, on the other hand . . .

He shifted uncomfortably in his seat, glancing down at the program in his hand.

*You are Cordially Welcomed to
the 19ᵗʰ Annual Smythe-Smith Musicale
featuring a well-trained quartet of violin,
violin, cello, and pianoforte*

He had a bad feeling about this.

"Thank you, *again*, for accompanying me," Winston Bevelstoke said to him.

Richard regarded his good friend with a skeptical expression. "I find it unsettling," he remarked, "how often you've thanked me."

"I'm known for my impeccable manners," Winston said with a shrug. He'd always been a shrugger. In fact, most of Richard's memories of him involved some sort of *what-can-I-say* shoulder motion.

"It doesn't really matter if I forget to take my Latin exam. I'm a second son." *Shrug.*

"The rowboat was already capsized by the time I arrived on the bank." *Shrug.*

"As with all things in life, the best option is to blame my sister." *Shrug.* (Also, *evil grin.*)

Richard had once been as unserious as Winston. In fact, he would very much like to be that unserious again.

But, as mentioned, he hadn't time for that. He

had two weeks. Three, he supposed. Four was the absolute limit.

"Do you know any of them?" he asked Winston.

"Any of who?"

Richard held up the program. "The musicians."

Winston cleared his throat, his eyes sliding guiltily away. "I hesitate to call them musicians . . ."

Richard looked toward the performance area that had been set up in the Pleinsworth ballroom. "Do you know them?" he repeated. "Have you been introduced?" It was all well and good for Winston to make his customary cryptic comments, but Richard was here for a reason.

"The Smythe-Smith girls?" Winston shrugged. "Most of them. Let me see, who's playing this year?" He looked down at his program. "Lady Sarah Prentice at the pianoforte—that's odd, she's married."

Damn.

"It's usually just the single ladies," Winston explained. "They trot them out every year to perform. Once they're married, they get to retire."

Richard was aware of this. In fact, it was the primary reason he had agreed to attend. Not that anyone would have found this surprising. When an unmarried gentleman of twenty-seven reappeared in London after a three-year absence . . . One did not need to be a matchmaking mama to know what that meant.

He just hadn't expected to be so rushed.

Frowning, he let his eyes fall on the pianoforte.

It looked well-made. Expensive. Definitely nicer than the one he had back at Maycliffe Park.

"Who else?" Winston murmured, reading the elegantly printed names in the program. "Miss Daisy Smythe-Smith on violin. Oh, yes, I've met her. She's dreadful."

Double damn. "What's wrong with her?" Richard asked.

"No sense of humor. Which wouldn't be such a bad thing, it's not as if everyone else is a barrel of laughs. It's just that she's so . . . obvious about it."

"How is one obvious about a *lack* of humor?"

"I have no idea," Winston admitted. "But she is. Very pretty, though. All blond bouncy curls and such." He made a blond bouncy motion near his ear, which led Richard to wonder how it was possible that Winston's hand movements were so clearly not brunette.

"Lady Harriet Pleinsworth, also on violin," Winston continued. "I don't believe we have been introduced. She must be Lady Sarah's younger sister. Barely out of the schoolroom, if my memory serves. Can't be much more than sixteen."

Triple damn. Perhaps Richard should just leave now.

"And on the cello . . ." Winston slid his finger along the heavy stock of the program until he found the correct spot. "Miss Iris Smythe-Smith."

"What's wrong with her?" Richard asked. Because it seemed unlikely that there wouldn't be something.

Winston shrugged. "Nothing. That I know of."

Which meant that she probably yodeled in her spare time. When she wasn't practicing taxidermy. On crocodiles.

Richard *used* to be a lucky fellow. Really.

"She's very pale," Winston said.

Richard looked over at him. "Is that a flaw?"

"Of course not. It's just . . ." Winston paused, his brow coming together in a little furrow of concentration. "Well, to be honest, that's pretty much all I recall of her."

Richard nodded slowly, his eyes settling on the cello, resting against its stand. It also looked expensive, although it wasn't as if he knew anything about the manufacture of cellos.

"Why such curiosity?" Winston asked. "I know you're keen to marry, but surely you can do better than a Smythe-Smith."

Two weeks ago that might have been true.

"Besides, you need someone with a dowry, do you not?"

"We all need someone with a dowry," Richard said darkly.

"True, true." Winston might be the son of the Earl of Rudland, but he was the *second* son. He wasn't going to inherit any spectacular fortunes. Not with a healthy older brother who had two sons of his own. "The Pleinsworth chit likely has ten thousand," he said, looking back down at the program with an assessing glance. "But as I said, she's quite young."

Richard grimaced. Even he had limits.

"The florals—"

"The florals?" Richard interrupted.

"Iris and Daisy," Winston explained. "Their sisters are Rose and Marigold and I can't remember what else. Tulip? Bluebell? Hopefully not Chrysanthemum, poor thing."

"My sister's name is Fleur," Richard felt compelled to mention.

"And a lovely girl she is," Winston said, even though he had never met her.

"You were saying . . ." Richard prompted.

"I was? Oh, yes, I was. The florals. I'm not sure of their portions, but it can't be much. I think there are five daughters in the family." Winston's lips twisted to one side as he considered this. "Maybe more."

This didn't necessarily mean that the dowries were small, Richard thought with more hope than anything else. He knew little of that branch of the Smythe-Smith family—he knew little of any branch, truth be told, except that once a year they all banded together, plucked four musicians from their midst, and hosted a concert that most of his friends were reluctant to attend.

"Take these," Winston suddenly said, holding out two wads of cotton. "You'll thank me later."

Richard stared at him as if he'd gone mad.

"For your ears," Winston clarified. "Trust me."

"*Trust me*," Richard echoed. "Coming from your lips, words to send a chill down my spine."

"In this," Winston said, stuffing his own ears with cotton, "I do not exaggerate."

Richard glanced discreetly about the room. Winston was making no effort to hide his actions; surely it was considered rude to block one's ears at a concert. But very few people seemed to notice him, and those who did wore expressions of envy, not censure.

Richard shrugged and followed suit.

"It's a good thing you're here," Winston said, leaning in so that Richard could hear him through the cotton. "I'm not sure I could have borne it without fortification."

"Fortification?"

"The pained company of beleaguered bachelors," Winston quipped.

The pained company of beleaguered bachelors? Richard rolled his eyes. "God help you if you attempt to form sentences while intoxicated."

"Oh, you'll have that pleasure soon enough," Winston returned, using his index finger to hold his coat pocket open just far enough to reveal a small metal flask.

Richard's eyes widened. He was no prig, but even he knew better than to drink openly at a musical performance given by teenaged girls.

And then it began.

After a minute, Richard found himself adjusting the cotton in his ears. By the end of the first movement, he could feel a vein twitching painfully in his brow. But it was when they reached a long violin solo that the true gravity of his situation sank in.

"The flask," he nearly gasped.

To his credit, Winston didn't even smirk.

Richard took a long swig of what turned out to be mulled wine, but it did little to dull the pain. "Can we leave during intermission?" he whispered to Winston.

"There is no intermission."

Richard stared at his program in horror. He was no musician, but surely the Smythe-Smiths had to know that what they were doing . . . that this so-called concert . . .

It was an assault against the very dignity of man.

According to the program, the four young ladies on the makeshift stage were playing a piano concerto by Wolfgang Amadeus Mozart. But to Richard's mind, a piano concerto seemed to imply actual playing of a piano. The lady seated at that fine instrument was striking only half the required notes, if that. He could not see her face, but from the way she was hunched over the keys, she appeared to be a musician of great concentration.

Albeit not one of great skill.

"That's the one with no sense of humor," Winston said, motioning with his head toward one of the violinists.

Ah, Miss Daisy. She of the bouncing blond curls. Of all the performers, she was clearly the one who most considered herself a great musician. Her body dipped and swayed like the most proficient virtuoso as her bow flew across the strings. Her movements were almost mesmerizing, and Richard supposed that a deaf man might have described her as being one with the music.

Instead she was merely one with the din.

As for the other violinist . . . Was he the only one who could tell that she could not read music? She was looking anywhere but at her music stand, and she had not flipped a single page since the concert began. She'd spent the entire time chewing on her lip and casting frantic glances at Miss Daisy, trying to emulate her movements.

Which left the cellist. Richard felt his eyes settle on her as she drew her bow across the long strings of her instrument. It was extraordinarily difficult to pick out her playing underneath the frenetic sounds of the two violinists, but every now and then a low mournful note would escape the insanity, and Richard could not help but think—

She's quite good.

He found himself fascinated by her, this small woman trying to hide behind a large cello. She, at least, knew how terrible they were. Her misery was acute, palpable. Every time she reached a pause in the score, she seemed to fold in on herself, as if she could squeeze down to nothingness and disappear with a "pop!"

This was Miss Iris Smythe-Smith, one of the florals. It seemed unfathomable that she might be related to the blissfully oblivious Daisy, who was still swiveling about with her violin.

Iris. It was a strange name for such a wisp of a girl. He'd always thought of irises as the most brilliant of flowers, all deep purples and blues. But this girl was so pale as to be almost colorless. Her hair was just a shade too red to be rightfully called blond, and yet strawberry blond wasn't quite right, either. He couldn't see her eyes from his spot halfway across the room, but with the rest of her coloring, they could not be anything but light.

She was the type of girl one would never notice.

And yet Richard could not take his eyes off her.

It was the concert, he told himself. Where else was he meant to look?

Besides, there was something soothing about keeping his gaze focused on a single, unmoving spot. The music was so jarring, he felt dizzy every time he looked away.

He almost chuckled. Miss Iris Smythe-Smith, she of the shimmering pale hair and too-large-for-her-body cello, had become his savior.

Sir Richard Kenworthy didn't believe in omens, but this one, he'd take.

WHY WAS THAT man staring at her?

The musicale was torture enough, and Iris should know—this was the third time she'd been thrust onto the stage and forced to make a fool of herself in front of a carefully curated selection of London's elite. It was always an interesting mix, the Smythe-Smith audience. First you had family, although in all fairness, they had to be divided into two distinct groups—the mothers and everyone else.

The mothers gazed upon the stage with beatific smiles, secure in their belief that their daughters' display of exquisite musical talent made them the envy of all their peers. "So accomplished," Iris's mother trilled year after year. "So poised."

So blind, was Iris's unsaid response. *So deaf.*

As for the rest of the Smythe-Smiths—the men, generally, and most of the women who had already paid their dues on the altar of musical ineptitude—they gritted their teeth and did their best to fill up the seats so as to limit the circle of mortification.

The family was marvelously fecund, however, and one day, Iris prayed, they would reach a size where they had to forbid the mothers from inviting anyone outside of family. "There just aren't enough seats," she could hear herself saying.

Unfortunately, she could also hear her mother asking her father's man of affairs to inquire about renting a concert hall.

As for the rest of the attendees, quite a few of them came every year. A few, Iris suspected, did so out of kindness. Some surely came only to mock. And then there were the unsuspecting innocents, who clearly lived under rocks. At the bottom of the ocean.

On another planet.

Iris could not *imagine* how they could not have heard about the Smythe-Smith musicale, or more to the point, not been warned about it, but every year there were a few new miserable faces.

Like that man in the fifth row. Why was he staring at her?

She was quite certain she had never seen him before. He had dark hair, the kind that curled when it got too misty out, and his face had a finely sculpted elegance that was quite pleasing. He was handsome, she decided, although not terrifyingly so.

He was probably not titled. Iris's mother had been very thorough in her daughters' social educations. It was difficult to imagine there was an unmarried nobleman under the age of thirty that Iris and her sisters could not recognize by sight.

A baronet, maybe. Or a landed gentleman. He must be well connected because she recognized his companion as the younger son of the Earl of Rudland. They had been introduced on several occasions, not that that meant anything other than the fact that the Hon. Mr. Bevelstoke could ask her to dance if he was so inclined.

Which he wasn't.

Iris took no offense at this, or at least not much. She was rarely engaged for more than half the dances at any given assembly, and she liked having the opportunity to observe society in full swirl. She often wondered if the stars of the ton actually *noticed* what went on around them. If one was always at the eye of the proverbial storm, could one discern the slant of the rain, feel the bite of the wind?

Maybe she *was* a wallflower. There was no shame in that. Especially not if one enjoyed being a wallflower. Why, some of the—

"*Iris,*" someone hissed.

It was her cousin Sarah, leaning over from the pianoforte with an urgent expression on her face.

Oh, blast, she'd missed her entrance. "Sorry," Iris muttered under her breath, even though no one could possibly hear her. She never missed her entrances. She didn't care that the rest of the players were so mind-numbingly awful that it didn't really matter if she came in on time or not—it was the principle of the matter.

Someone had to try to play properly.

She attended to her cello for the next few pages of the score, doing her best to block out Daisy, who was wandering all over the stage as she played. When Iris reached the next longish break in the cello part, however, she could not keep herself from looking up.

He was still watching her.

Did she have something on her dress? In her hair? Without thinking, she reached up to brush her coiffure, half expecting to dislodge a twig.

Nothing.

Now she was just angry. He was trying to rattle her. That could be the only explanation. What a rude boor. And an idiot. Did he really think he could irritate her more than her own sister? It would take an accordion-playing minotaur to top Daisy on the scale of bothersome to seventh circle of hell.

"Iris!" Sarah hissed.

"Errrrgh," Iris growled. She'd missed her entrance again. Although really, who was Sarah to complain? She'd skipped two entire pages in the second movement.

Iris located the correct spot in the score and leapt back in, relieved to note that they were nearing the end of the concerto. All she had to do was play her final notes, curtsy as if she meant it, and attempt to smile through the strained applause.

Then she could plead a headache and go home and shut her door and read a book and ignore Daisy and pretend that she wasn't going to have to do it all over again next year.

Unless, of course, she got married.

It was the only escape. Every unmarried Smythe-Smith (of the female variety) had to play in the quartet when an opening at her chosen instrument arose, and she stayed there until she walked down a church aisle and claimed her groom.

Only one cousin had managed to marry before she was forced onto the stage. It had been a spectacular convergence of luck and cunning. Frederica Smythe-Smith, now Frederica Plum, had been trained on the violin, just like her older sister Eleanor.

But Eleanor had not "taken," in the words of Iris's mother. In fact, Eleanor had played in the quartet a record seven years before falling head over heels for a kindly curate who had the amazing good sense to love her with equal abandon. Iris rather liked Eleanor, even if she did fancy herself an accomplished musician. (She was not.)

As for Frederica . . . Eleanor's delayed success on the marriage mart meant that the violinist's chair was filled when her younger sister made her debut. And if Frederica just happened to make certain that she found a husband with all possible haste . . .

It was the stuff of legend. To Iris, at least.

Frederica now lived in the south of India, which Iris suspected was somehow related to her orchestral escape. No one in the family had seen her for years, although every now and then a letter found its way to London, bearing news of heat and spice and the occasional elephant.

Iris hated hot weather, and she wasn't particularly fond of spicy food, but as she sat in her cousins' ballroom, trying to pretend that fifty people weren't watching her make a fool of herself, she couldn't help but think that India sounded rather pleasant.

She had no opinion one way or the other on the elephants.

Maybe she could find herself a husband this year. Truth be told, she hadn't really put in much of an effort the two years she'd been out. But it was so hard to make an effort when she was— and there was no denying it—so unnoticeable.

Except—she looked up, then immediately looked down—by that strange man in the fifth row. *Why* was he watching her?

It made no sense. And Iris *hated*—even more than she hated making a fool of herself—things that made no sense.

Chapter Two

Iᴛ ᴡᴀs ᴄʟᴇᴀʀ to Richard that Iris Smythe-Smith planned to flee the concert the moment she was able. She wasn't obvious about it, but he'd been watching her for what seemed like an hour; by this point, he was practically an expert on the expressions and mannerisms of the reluctant cellist.

He was going to have to act quickly.

"Introduce us," Richard said to Winston, discreetly motioning toward her with his head.

"Really?"

Richard gave a curt nod.

Winston shrugged, obviously surprised by his friend's interest in the colorless Miss Iris Smythe-Smith. But if he was curious, he did not show it past his initial query. Instead he maneuvered through the crowd in his usual smooth manner. The woman in question might have been standing awkwardly by the door, but her eyes were sharp, taking in the room, its inhabitants, and the interactions thereof.

She was timing her escape. Richard was sure of it.

But she was to be thwarted. Winston came to a halt in front of her before she could make her move. "Miss Smythe-Smith," he said, everything good cheer and amiability. "What a delight to see you again."

She bobbed a suspicious curtsy. Clearly she did not have the sort of acquaintance with Winston as to warrant such a warm greeting. "Mr. Bevelstoke," she murmured.

"May I introduce my good friend, Sir Richard Kenworthy?"

Richard bowed. "It is a pleasure to meet you," he said.

"And you."

Her eyes were just as light as he'd imagined, although with only the candlelight to illuminate her face, he could not discern their precise color. Gray, perhaps, or blue, framed by eyelashes so fair they might have been invisible if not for their astonishing length.

"My sister sends her regrets," Winston said.

"Yes, she usually attends, doesn't she?" Miss Smythe-Smith murmured with the merest hint of a smile. "She's very kind."

"Oh, I don't know that kindness has anything to do with it," Winston said genially.

Miss Smythe-Smith raised a pale brow and fixed a stare on Winston. "I rather think kindness has everything to do with it."

Richard was inclined to agree. He could not imagine why else Winston's sister would subject herself to such a performance more than once. And he rather admired Miss Smythe-Smith's acuity on the matter.

"She sent me in her stead," Winston went on. "She said it would not do for our family to be unrepresented this year." He glanced over at Richard. "She was most firm about it."

"Please do offer her my gratitude," Miss Smythe-Smith said. "If you'll excuse me, though, I must—"

"May I ask you a question?" Richard interrupted.

She froze, having already begun to twist toward the door. She looked at him with some surprise. So did Winston.

"Of course you may," she murmured, her eyes not nearly as placid as her tone. She was a gently bred young lady and he a baronet. She could offer no other response, and they both knew it.

"How long have you played the cello?" he blurted out. It was the first question that came to mind, and it was only after it had left his lips that he realized it was rather rude. She knew the quartet was terrible, and she knew that he must feel the same way. To inquire about her training was nothing but cruel. But he'd been under pressure. He couldn't let her leave. Not without some conversation, at least.

"I—" She stammered for a moment, and Richard felt himself floundering inside. He hadn't meant to—Oh, bloody hell.

"It was a lovely performance," Winston said, looking as if he'd like to kick him.

Richard spoke quickly, eager to rehabilitate himself in her eyes. "What I meant was that you seemed somewhat more proficient than your cousins."

She blinked several times. Bloody hell, now he'd gone and insulted her cousins, but he supposed better them than her.

He plowed on. "I was seated near to your side of the room, and occasionally I could hear the cello apart from the other instruments."

"I see," she said slowly, and perhaps somewhat warily. She did not know what to make of his interest, that much was clear.

"You're quite skilled," he said.

Winston looked at him in disbelief. Richard could well imagine why. It hadn't been easy to discern the notes of the cello through the din, and to the untrained ear, Iris must have seemed just as dreadful as the rest. For Richard to say otherwise must seem the worst sort of false flattery.

Except that Miss Smythe-Smith knew that she was a better musician than her cousins. He'd seen it in her eyes as she reacted to his statement. "We have all studied since we were quite young," she said.

"Of course," he replied. Of course that would be what she'd say. She wasn't about to insult her family in front of a stranger.

An awkward silence descended upon the trio, and Miss Smythe-Smith made that polite smile again, with the clear intention of excusing herself.

"The violinist is your sister?" Richard asked, before she could speak.

Winston shot him a curious look.

"One of them, yes," she replied. "The blond one."

"Your younger sister?"

"By four years, yes," she said, her voice sharpening. "This is her first season, although she did play in the quartet last year."

"Speaking of that," Winston put in, thankfully saving Richard from having to think up another exit-preventing question, "why was Lady Sarah seated at the pianoforte? I thought the quartet was for unmarried ladies only."

"We lack a pianist," she answered. "If Sarah had not stepped up, the concert would have been canceled."

The obvious question hung in the air. Would that have been such a bad thing?

"It would have broken my mother's heart," Miss Smythe-Smith said, and it was impossible to tell just what emotion colored her voice. "And those of my aunts."

"How very kind of her to lend her talents," Richard said.

And then Miss Smythe-Smith said the most astonishing thing. She muttered, "She owed us."

Richard started. "I beg your pardon?"

"Nothing," she said, smiling brightly . . . and falsely.

"No, I must insist," Richard said, intrigued. "You cannot make such a statement and leave it unclarified."

Her eyes flitted to the left. Maybe she was making sure her family could not hear. Or maybe she was simply trying not to roll her eyes completely. "It is nothing, really. She did not play last year. She withdrew on the day of the performance."

"Was the concert canceled?" Winston asked, brow furrowed as he tried to recall.

"No. Her sisters' governess stepped in."

"Oh, right," Winston said with a nod. "I remember. Jolly good of her. Remarkable, really, that she knew the piece."

"Was your cousin ill?" Richard inquired.

Miss Smythe-Smith opened her mouth to speak, and then at the last moment changed her mind about what she was going to say. Richard was sure of it.

"Yes," she said simply. "She was quite ill. Now if you will excuse me, I'm afraid there is a matter I must attend to."

She curtsied, they bowed, and she departed.

"What was that about?" Winston asked immediately.

"What?" Richard countered, feigning ignorance.

"You practically threw yourself in front of the door to prevent her from leaving."

Richard shrugged. "I found her interesting."

"Her?" Winston looked toward the door through which Miss Smythe-Smith had just exited. "Why?"

"I don't know," Richard lied.

Winston turned to Richard, then back to the

door, and then back to Richard again. "I must say, she's not your usual type."

"No," Richard said, even though he'd never thought of his preferences in those terms. "No, she's not."

But then again, he'd never needed to find himself a wife. In two weeks, no less.

THE FOLLOWING DAY found Iris trapped in the drawing room with her mother and Daisy, waiting for the inevitable trickle of callers. They *had* to be at home for visitors, her mother insisted. People would want to congratulate them on their performance.

Her married sisters would stop by, Iris imagined, and most likely a few other ladies. The same ones who attended each year out of kindness. The rest would avoid the Smythe-Smith home—any of the Smythe-Smith homes—like the proverbial plague. The last thing anyone wanted to do was make polite conversation about an aural disaster.

It was rather as if the Dover cliffs crumbled into the sea, and everyone sat about drinking tea, saying, "Oh yes, ripping good show. Too bad about the vicar's house, though."

But it was early still, and they had not yet been graced by a visitor. Iris had brought down something to read, but Daisy was still aglow with delight and triumph.

"I thought we were splendid," she announced.

Iris lifted her eyes from her book just long enough to say, "We weren't splendid."

"Perhaps *you* weren't, hiding behind your cello,

but I have never felt so alive and in tune with the music."

Iris bit her lip. There were so very many ways she could respond. It was as if her younger sister was *begging* her to use every sarcastic word in her arsenal. But she held her tongue. The concert always left her feeling irritable, and no matter how annoying Daisy was—and she was, oh, she was—it wasn't her fault that Iris was in such a bad mood. Well, not entirely.

"There were so many handsome gentlemen at the performance last night," Daisy said. "Did you see, Mama?"

Iris rolled her eyes. Of course their mother had seen. It was her job to notice every eligible gentleman in the room. No, it was more than that. It was her vocation.

"Mr. St. Clair was there," Daisy said. "He's so very dashing with his queue."

"He'll never look twice at you," Iris said.

"Don't be unkind, Iris," their mother scolded. But then she turned to Daisy. "But she's right. And nor would we wish him to. He's far too rakish for a proper young lady."

"He was talking with Hyacinth Bridgerton," Daisy pointed out.

Iris swung her glance over to her mother, eager—and, truth be told, amused—to see how she'd respond to that. Families didn't get more popular or respectable than the Bridgertons, even if Hyacinth—the youngest—was known as something of a terror.

Mrs. Smythe-Smith did what she always did

when she did not wish to reply. Her brows rose, her chin dipped, and she gave a disdainful sniff.

Conversation over. At least that particular thread.

"Winston Bevelstoke isn't a rake," Daisy said, tacking a bit to the right. "He was seated near the front."

Iris snorted.

"He's gorgeous!"

"I never said that he wasn't," Iris replied. "But he must be nearly thirty. And he was in the fifth row."

That seemed to mystify their mother. "The fifth—"

"It's certainly not the front," Iris cut in. Blast it all, she hated when people got the little details wrong.

"Oh, for heaven's sake," Daisy said. "It doesn't matter where he was sitting. All that matters is that he was *there*."

This was correct, but still, so clearly not the salient point. "Winston Bevelstoke would never be interested in a girl of seventeen," Iris said.

"Why wouldn't he be?" Daisy demanded. "I think you're jealous."

Iris rolled her eyes. "That is so far from the truth I can't even begin to say."

"He was watching me," Daisy insisted. "That he is as yet unmarried speaks to his selectiveness. Perhaps he has simply been waiting for the perfect young lady to come along."

Iris took a breath, quelling the retort tickling at her lips. "If you marry Winston Bevelstoke," she said calmly, "I shall be the first to congratulate you."

Daisy's eyes narrowed. "She's being sarcastic again, Mama."

"Don't be sarcastic, Iris," Maria Smythe-Smith said, never taking her eyes from her embroidery.

Iris scowled at her mother's rote scolding.

"Who was that gentleman with Mr. Bevelstoke last night?" Mrs. Smythe-Smith asked. "The one with the dark hair."

"He was talking to Iris," Daisy said, "after the performance."

Mrs. Smythe-Smith fixed a shrewd stare upon Iris. "I know."

"His name is Sir Richard Kenworthy," Iris said.

Her mother's brows rose.

"I'm sure he was being polite," Iris said.

"He was being polite for a very long time," Daisy giggled.

Iris looked at her in disbelief. "We spoke for five minutes. If that."

"It's more time than most gentleman talk to you."

"Daisy, don't be unkind," their mother said, "but I must agree. I do think it was more than five minutes."

"It wasn't," Iris muttered.

Her mother did not hear her. Or more likely, chose to ignore. "We shall have to find out more about him."

Iris's mouth opened into an indignant oval. Five minutes she'd spent in Sir Richard's company, and her mother was already plotting the poor man's demise.

"You're not getting any younger," Mrs. Smythe-Smith said.

Daisy smirked.

"Fine," Iris said. "I shall attempt to capture his interest for a full quarter of an hour next time. That ought to be enough to send for a special license."

"Oh, do you think so?" Daisy asked. "That would be so romantic."

Iris could only stare. *Now* Daisy missed the sarcasm?

"Anyone can be married in a church," Daisy said. "But a special license is special."

"Hence the name," Iris muttered.

"They cost a terrific amount of money," Daisy continued, "and they don't give them out to just anybody."

"Your sisters were all properly married in church," their mother said, "and so shall you be."

That put an end to the conversation for at least five seconds. Which was about how long Daisy could manage to sit in silence. "What are you reading?" she asked, craning her neck toward Iris.

"*Pride and Prejudice,*" Iris replied. She didn't look up, but she did mark her spot with her finger. Just in case.

"Haven't you read that before?"

"It's a good book."

"How can a book be good enough to read twice?"

Iris shrugged, which a less obtuse person would have interpreted as a signal that she did not wish to continue the conversation.

But not Daisy. "I've read it, too, you know," she said.

"Have you?"

"Quite honestly, I didn't think it was very good."

At that, Iris finally raised her eyes. "I beg your pardon."

"It's very unrealistic," Daisy opined. "Am I really expected to believe that Miss Elizabeth would refuse Mr. Darcy's proposal of marriage?"

"Who is Miss Elizabeth?" Mrs. Smythe-Smith asked, her attention finally wrenched from her embroidery. She looked from daughter to daughter. "And for that matter, who is Mr. Darcy?"

"It was patently clear that she would never get a better offer than Mr. Darcy," Daisy continued.

"That's what Mr. Collins said when he proposed to her," Iris shot back. "And then Mr. Darcy asked her."

"Who is Mr. Collins?"

"They are fictional characters, Mama," Iris said.

"Very foolish ones, if you ask me," Daisy said haughtily. "Mr. Darcy is very rich. And Miss Elizabeth has no dowry to speak of. That he condescended to propose to her—"

"He loved her!"

"Of course he did," Daisy said peevishly. "There can be no other reason he would ask her to marry him. And then for her to refuse!"

"She had her reasons."

Daisy rolled her eyes. "She's just lucky he asked her again. That's all I have to say on the matter."

"I think I ought to read this book," Mrs. Smythe-Smith said.

"Here," Iris said, feeling suddenly dejected. She

held the book out toward her mother. "You can read my copy."

"But you're in the middle."

"I've read it before."

Mrs. Smythe-Smith took the book, flipped to the first page and read the first sentence, which Iris knew by heart.

It is a truth universally acknowledged, that a single man in possession of a good fortune, must be in want of a wife.

"Well, that's certainly true," Mrs. Smythe-Smith said to herself.

Iris sighed, wondering how she might occupy herself now. She supposed she could fetch another book, but she was too comfortable slouched on the sofa to consider getting up. She sighed.

"What?" Daisy demanded.

"Nothing."

"You sighed."

Iris fought the urge to groan. "Not every sigh has to do with you."

Daisy sniffed and turned away.

Iris closed her eyes. Maybe she could take a nap. She hadn't slept very well the night before. She never did, the night after the musicale. She always told herself she would, now that she had another whole year before she had to start dreading it again.

But sleep was not her friend, not when she couldn't stop her brain from replaying every last moment, every botched note. The looks of derision, of pity, of shock and surprise . . . She supposed she could almost forgive her cousin Sarah for feigning illness the year before to avoid playing. She understood. Heaven help her, no one understood better than she.

And then Sir Richard Kenworthy had demanded an audience. What had that been about? Iris was not so foolish to think that he was interested in her. She was no diamond of the first water. She fully expected to marry one day, but when it happened, it wasn't going to be because some gentleman took one look at her and fell under her spell.

She had no spells. According to Daisy, she didn't even have eyelashes.

No, when Iris married, it would be a sensible proposition. An ordinary gentleman would find her agreeable and decide that the granddaughter of an earl was an advantageous thing to have in the family, even with her modest dowry.

And she did have eyelashes, she thought grumpily. They were just very pale.

She needed to find out more about Sir Richard. But more importantly, she needed to figure out how to do that without attracting attention. It wouldn't do to be seen as chasing after him. Especially when—

"Callers, ma'am," their butler announced.

Iris sat up. *Time for good posture,* she thought with false brightness. Shoulders up, back straight . . .

"Mr. Winston Bevelstoke," the butler intoned.

Daisy straightened and preened, but not before tossing an *I-told-you-so* glance at Iris.

"And Sir Richard Kenworthy."

Chapter Three

"YOU KNOW," WINSTON said to him as they paused at the bottom of the steps to the Smythe-Smith home, "it will not do to raise the girl's hopes."

"And here I thought it was an accepted custom to pay a call upon a young lady," Richard said.

"It is. But these are the Smythe-Smiths."

Richard had started to climb the stairs, but at this he halted. "Is there something exceptional about this family?" he inquired in a mild tone. "Other than their unique musical talents?" He needed to marry quickly, but he also needed gossip—and—God forbid, scandal—to be kept to a minimum. If the Smythe-Smiths had dark secrets, he had to know.

"No," Winston said with a distracted shake of his head. "Not at all. It's just . . . Well, I suppose one would say . . ."

Richard waited. Eventually Winston would spit it out.

"This particular branch of the Smythe-Smith family is somewhat . . ." Winston sighed, unable to finish the sentence. He really was a good sort, Richard thought with a smile. He might stuff his ears with cotton and drink from a flask during a concert, but he could not bring himself to speak ill of a lady, even if his only insult was that she was unpopular.

"If you court one of the Misses Smythe-Smith," Winston finally said, "people will be curious why."

"Because I'm such a catch," Richard said in a dry voice.

"Aren't you?"

"No," Richard said. It was just like Winston to be oblivious to such a thing. "I'm not."

"Come now, things can't be as bad as that."

"I've only just managed to save Maycliffe's lands from my father's neglect and mismanagement, there is an entire wing of the house that is presently uninhabitable, and I have two sisters of whom I am the sole guardian." Richard gave him a bland smile. "No, I would not say I'm a splendid catch."

"Richard, you know I—" Winston frowned. "Why is Maycliffe uninhabitable?"

Richard shook his head and went up the steps.

"No, really, I'm curious. I—"

But Richard had already brought down the knocker. "Flood," he said. "Vermin. Probably a ghost."

"If you're that hard up," Winston said quickly,

eyeing the door, "you're going to need a bigger dowry than you'll find here."

"Perhaps," Richard murmured. But he had other reasons to seek out Iris Smythe-Smith. She was intelligent; he had not needed long in her company to assure himself of that. And she valued family. She must. Why else would she have participated in that wretched musicale?

But could she value *his* family as well as she did her own? She would need to, if he married her.

The door was swung open by a somewhat portly butler who took his and Winston's cards with a stiff bow. A moment later they were ushered into a small but elegant drawing room, decorated in shades of cream, gold, and green. Richard immediately noticed Iris on the sofa, quietly watching him through her lashes. On another woman the expression might have been flirtatious, but on Iris it was more watchful. Assessing.

She was taking his measure. Richard wasn't certain how he felt about that. He *ought* to be amused.

"Mr. Winston Bevelstoke," the butler announced, "and Sir Richard Kenworthy."

The ladies rose to greet them, and they gave their attention first to Mrs. Smythe-Smith, as was proper.

"Mr. Bevelstoke," she said, smiling at Winston. "It has been an age. How is your dear sister?"

"Very well. She is nearing the end of her confinement, else she would have attended last night." He motioned to Richard. "I do not believe you have been introduced to my good friend, Sir Richard Kenworthy. We were at Oxford together."

She smiled politely. "Sir Richard."

He bowed with his head. "Mrs. Smythe-Smith."

"My two youngest daughters," she said, motioning to the two ladies behind her.

"I had the honor of making Miss Smythe-Smith's acquaintance last night," Richard said, honoring Iris with a small bow.

"Yes, of course you did." Mrs. Smythe-Smith smiled, but it didn't quite reach her eyes, and once again Richard had the distinct impression that he was being weighed and measured. Against what yardstick, however, he could not know. It was damned unsettling, and not for the first time he found himself thinking that Napoleon might have been defeated well before Waterloo if only they'd sent the London mamas out to take care of strategy.

"My youngest," Mrs. Smythe-Smith said, tilting her head toward Daisy, "Miss Daisy Smythe-Smith."

"Miss Daisy," Richard said politely, bowing over her hand. Winston did the same.

Once the necessary introductions were made, the two gentlemen took their seats.

"How did you enjoy the concert?" Miss Daisy asked.

She seemed to be directing her question to Winston, for which Richard was immeasurably grateful.

"Very much," he said, after clearing his throat six times. "I can't remember the last time I, er . . ."

"I imagine you have never heard Mozart played with such fervor," Iris said, coming to his rescue.

Richard smiled. There was a cleverness to her that was quite appealing.

"No," Winston said quickly, relief evident in his voice. "It was a singular experience."

"And you, Sir Richard?" Iris asked. He met her eyes—a very, very light blue, he finally deduced—and to his surprise he saw a flash of impertinence. Was she baiting him?

"I find that I am most grateful that I decided to attend," he replied.

"That's no sort of an answer," she said, her voice too low to be properly heard by her mother.

He quirked a brow. "It's as much of one as you're going to get."

Her mouth opened as if to gasp, but in the end she just said, "Well met, Sir Richard."

The conversation ambled through predictable topics—the weather, the King, and then the weather again—until Richard took advantage of the banality of their discussion by suggesting a walk in nearby Hyde Park.

"Because the weather is so fine," he concluded.

"Yes, it is just as I said," Daisy exclaimed. "The sun is shining uncommonly well. Is it warm outside, Mr. Bevelstoke? I have not yet left the house."

"Tolerably warm," Winston replied before shooting Richard a quick but lethal glance. They were even now, or perhaps he was in Winston's debt. The Smythe-Smith musicale could not be nearly as trying as an hour on the arm of Miss Daisy. And they both knew that Winston would not be the one escorting Iris.

"I was surprised to see you so soon after the

concert," Iris said once they were outside and headed toward the park.

"And I am surprised to hear you say so," he countered. "Surely I gave no impression of disinterest."

Her eyes widened. Normally he would not be so forward, but he did not have time for a subtle courtship.

"I am not certain," she said carefully, "what I have done to earn your regard."

"Nothing," he admitted. "But then, regard is not always earned."

"Is it not?" She sounded startled.

"Not in its immediacy." He smiled down at her, pleased that the brim of her bonnet was shallow enough for him to see her face. "Isn't that the purpose of courtship? To determine whether an initial regard is worthy?"

"I believe what you call regard, I call attraction."

He chuckled. "You are of course correct. Please accept my apologies and my clarification."

"Then we are agreed. I do not have your regard."

"But you do hold attraction," he murmured daringly.

Her cheeks colored, and he realized that when Iris Smythe-Smith blushed, she did so with every inch of her skin. "You know that's not what I meant," she muttered.

"You have my regard," he said firmly. "If you had not earned it last night, you have done so this morning."

Her eyes took on a bewildered expression, and

she gave her head a little shake before turning her gaze back to the path ahead.

"I have never been a man who values stupidity in females," he said lightly, almost as if he was remarking on a shop display.

"You hardly know me well enough to measure my intelligence."

"I can measure it well enough to know you're not stupid. Whether you can speak German and do sums in your head I can learn soon enough."

She looked as if she was trying not to smile, then she said, "Yes to one, no to the other."

"German?"

"No, sums."

"Pity, that." He gave her a knowing look. "The language would come in so handy with the royal family."

She laughed. "I believe they all speak English by now."

"Yes, but they keep marrying Germans, don't they?"

"More to the point," Iris said, "I don't expect an audience with the King any time in the near future."

Richard chuckled, enjoying her quick wit. "There is always little Princess Victoria."

"Who likely *doesn't* speak English," Iris conceded. "Her mother certainly doesn't."

"You've met?" he asked dryly.

"Of course not." She gave him a bit of a look, and he had a feeling that had they known each other better, she might have accompanied it with a friendly elbow in the ribs. "Very well, I am convinced. I must find a German tutor posthaste."

"Have you an aptitude for languages?" he inquired.

"No, but we were all forced to study French until Mama declared it unpatriotic."

"Still?" Good gracious, the war had been over for nearly a decade.

Iris gave him a pert look. "She can hold a grudge."

"Remind me not to cross her."

"I wouldn't recommend it," she murmured distractedly. Her head tilted just a bit to the side, and she grimaced. "I fear we might need to save Mr. Bevelstoke."

Richard looked over toward Winston, who was about twenty feet ahead of them on the path. Daisy was clutching his arm and talking with such vigor that her blond curls were indeed bouncing about.

Winston was putting on a good front, but he looked vaguely ill.

"I love Daisy," Iris said with a sigh, "but she's an acquired taste. Oh, Mr. Bevelstoke!" With that, she detached herself from Richard's arm and hastened toward Winston and her sister. Richard picked up the pace and followed.

"I meant to ask you," he heard Iris say, "what is your opinion of the Treaty of St. Petersburg?"

Winston looked at her as if she were speaking another language. German, perhaps.

"It was in yesterday's newspaper," Iris continued. "Surely you read about it."

"Of course," Winston said, quite clearly lying.

Iris smiled brightly, turning away from her sister's scowl. "It does sound as if it's been worked out to everyone's satisfaction. Wouldn't you agree?"

"Er . . . yes," Winston said, with rising enthusiasm. "Yes, indeed." He understood what Iris was about, even if he had no idea what she was saying. "Quite right."

"What are you talking about?" Daisy demanded.

"The Treaty of St. Petersburg," Iris said.

"Yes, you said as much," Daisy said irritably. "But what *is* it?"

Iris froze. "Oh, well, it's, ehrm . . ."

Richard choked down a laugh. Iris didn't know. She'd jumped into the breach to save Winston from her sister, but she didn't know the answer to her own question.

One really couldn't help but admire her brazenness.

"It's the agreement, you know," Iris continued, "between Great Britain and Russia."

"Indeed," Winston said helpfully. "A treaty. I believe it was signed in St. Petersburg."

"It's quite a relief," Iris put in. "Don't you think?"

"Oh, yes," Winston answered. "We should all sleep more soundly because of it."

"I've never trusted the Russians," Daisy said with a sniff.

"Well, I don't know if I'd go that far," Iris said. She looked over at Richard, but he just shrugged, enjoying himself far too much to intercede.

"My sister almost married a Russian prince," Winston said offhandedly.

"Did she?" Daisy asked, suddenly aglow.

"Well, no, not really," Winston admitted. "But *he* wanted to marry her."

"Oh, how divine," Daisy gushed.

"You just said you don't trust the Russians," Iris reminded her.

"I didn't mean royalty," Daisy said dismissively. "Tell me," she said to Winston, "was he terribly handsome?"

"I'm not really the best judge of that," Winston hedged, then offered, "He was very blond, though."

"Oh, a *prince*." Daisy sighed, one fluttery hand coming to rest over her heart. Then her eyes narrowed. "Why on earth didn't she marry him?"

Winston shrugged. "I don't believe she wanted to. She married a baronet instead. They're quite nauseatingly in love. Good fellow, though, Harry is."

Daisy gasped so loudly Richard was sure they heard it in Kensington. "She chose a baronet over a prince?"

"Some women aren't swayed by titles," Iris said. She turned to Richard, and said in a low voice, "Believe it or not, this is the second time we've had this conversation today."

"Really?" His brows rose. "Who were you talking about before?"

"Fictional characters," she explained, "from a book I was reading."

"Which one?"

"*Pride and Prejudice*," she said with a wave of her hand. "I'm sure you haven't read it."

"I have, as a matter of fact. It is a favorite of my

sister, and I thought it prudent to acquaint myself with her reading choices."

"Do you always take such a paternal view with respect to your siblings?" she asked archly.

"I am her guardian."

Her lips parted, and she hesitated a moment before saying, "I am sorry. That was rude of me. I did not know."

He accepted her apology with a gracious nod. "Fleur is eighteen and a bit of a romantic. If she had her way, she'd read nothing but melodramas."

"*Pride and Prejudice* is not a melodrama," Iris protested.

"No," he said with a laugh, "but I have no doubt that Fleur has managed to turn it into one in her head."

She smiled at that. "Have you had her guardianship for very long?"

"Seven years."

"Oh!" Her hand came to her mouth, and she stopped walking. "I'm so sorry. That is an unimaginable burden on such a young man."

"I regret to say that I did consider it a burden at the time. I have two younger sisters, in fact, and after my father died, I sent both of them away to live with our aunt."

"You could hardly have done otherwise. You must have still been in school."

"University," he confirmed. "I am not so harsh on myself that I think I should have tended to them myself at that point, but I should have been a more involved guardian."

She placed her hand on his arm in a gesture of comfort. "I am sure you did your best."

Richard was sure he had not, but he said, "Thank you."

"How old is your other sister?"

"Marie-Claire is almost fifteen."

"Fleur and Marie-Claire," Iris murmured. "How very French."

"My mother was a fanciful woman." He flashed her a smile, then added a little half-shrug. "And she was also half-French."

"Are your sisters now at home?"

He gave a nod. "Yes. In Yorkshire."

She nodded thoughtfully. "I have never been so far north."

This surprised him. "Have you not?"

"I live year-round in London," she explained. "My father is the fourth of five sons. He did not inherit land."

Richard wondered if she was issuing a warning. If he was a fortune hunter, he should look elsewhere.

"I visit with my cousins, of course," she continued lightly, "but they are all in the south of England. I don't believe I have ever traveled past Norfolk."

"It's a very different landscape in the north," he told her. "It can be quite desolate and bleak."

"You are not proving yourself an enthusiastic ambassador for your county," she chided.

He chuckled at that. "It's not all desolate and bleak. And the parts that are are beautiful in their own way."

She smiled at the description.

"At any rate," he continued, "Maycliffe sits in a rather pleasant valley. It's quite tame compared to the rest of the county."

"Is that a good thing?" she asked with an arch of her brow.

He laughed. "We're actually not too far from Darlington, and the railway that is being built there."

Her blue eyes lit up in wonder. "Are you? I should love to see that. I read that when it is completed, one might be able to travel at fifteen miles per hour, but I cannot credit such a speed. It sounds frightfully dangerous."

He nodded absently, glancing over at Daisy, who was still interrogating poor Winston about the Russian prince. "I suppose your sister thought that Miss Elizabeth should not have refused Darcy's first proposal."

Iris stared at him blankly before blinking, and saying, "Oh, yes, the book. Yes, you're correct. Daisy found Lizzy to be most foolish."

"What do you think?" he asked, and he realized that he truly wished to know her opinion.

She paused, taking the time to choose her words. Richard did not mind the silence; it gave him the opportunity to watch her as she thought. She was prettier than he'd supposed at first sight. There was a pleasing symmetry to her features, and her lips were far rosier than one might guess, given how pale the rest of her was.

"Given what she knew at the time," Iris finally said, "I don't see how she could possibly have accepted him. Would you wish to marry someone you could not respect?"

"Certainly not."

She nodded officiously, then frowned as she regarded Winston and Daisy again. Somehow, they had managed to get quite a bit ahead. Richard couldn't hear what they were talking about, but Winston had the look of a man in trouble.

"We will have to save him again," Iris said with a sigh. "But this time you must do it. I've exhausted my knowledge of Russian politics."

Richard allowed himself to lean toward her, close enough so that he could murmur in her ear. "The Treaty of St. Petersburg defined the boundary between Russian America and the North Western Territory."

She caught her lip between her teeth, clearly trying not to smile.

"Iris!" Daisy called out.

"It appears we won't have to stage an interruption," Richard said as they closed the gap between the two couples.

"I have invited Mr. Bevelstoke to the poetry reading at the Pleinsworths' next week," Daisy said. "Do insist that he attend."

Iris stared at her sister in horror before turning to Winston. "I . . . insist that you attend?"

Daisy gave a petulant snort at her sister's lack of resolve and turned back to Winston. "You must attend, Mr. Bevelstoke. You simply must. It is sure to be uplifting. Poetry always is."

"No," Iris said, with a pained frown, "it's really not."

"Of course we will be there," Richard announced.

Winston's eyes narrowed dangerously.

"We wouldn't miss it," Richard assured Daisy.

"The Pleinsworths are our cousins," Iris said with a pointed look. "You might recall Harriet. She played violin—"

"*Second* violin," Daisy cut in.

"—in the concert last night."

Richard swallowed. She could only be talking about the one who could not read music. Still, there was no reason to think this boded ill for a poetry reading.

"Harriet's a bore," Daisy said, "but her younger sisters are darling."

"I like Harriet," Iris said firmly. "I like her a great deal."

"Then I am certain it will be a most pleasant evening," Richard said.

Daisy beamed and looped her arm once again through Winston's, leading the way back to the Cumberland Gate through which they'd entered. Richard followed with Iris, setting their pace more slowly so that they might be able to speak privately.

"If I were to call upon you tomorrow," he asked in a quiet voice, "would you be at home?"

She did not look at him, which was a pity, because he would have liked to see her blush again.

"I would," she whispered.

That was the moment he decided. He was going to marry Iris Smythe-Smith.

Chapter Four

Later that evening
A London ballroom

"THEY'RE NOT HERE yet," Daisy said.

Iris pretended to smile. "I know."

"I've been watching the door."

"I know."

Daisy fussed with the lace on her minty green dress. "I do hope Mr. Bevelstoke likes my gown."

"I do not see how he could find it anything less than charming," Iris said quite honestly. Daisy drove her utterly mad most of the time, and Iris did not always have kind words for her younger sister, but she was willing to give compliments when they were deserved.

Daisy was lovely. She had always been lovely, with her bright golden curls and rosebud mouth. Their coloring really wasn't too terribly different, but what shone like gold on Daisy left Iris rather bleached and washed-out.

Her nanny had once said that Iris could vanish in a bucket of milk, and really, she wasn't too far off the mark.

"You shouldn't have worn that color," Daisy said.

"And just when I was having benevolent thoughts," Iris muttered. She liked the ice blue silk of her gown. She rather thought it brought out her eyes.

"You should be wearing darker colors. For contrast."

"Contrast?" Iris echoed.

"Well, you need *some* color."

One of these days, she was going to kill her sister. She really was.

"Next time we go shopping," Daisy continued, "let me pick out your gowns."

Iris stared at her for a moment, then started to walk away. "I'm getting some lemonade."

"Fetch some for me, would you?" Daisy called out.

"No." Iris didn't think Daisy heard her, but she didn't much care. She'd figure out eventually that no refreshment was forthcoming.

Like Daisy, Iris had been watching the door all evening. Unlike Daisy, she'd been trying to do it surreptitiously. When Sir Richard had returned her to her home earlier in the day, she had mentioned that she would be at the Mottram ball that evening. It was an annual affair, and always well attended. Iris knew that if Sir Richard did not have an invitation, he would be able to procure one with ease. He had not said that he would be in attendance, but he had thanked her for the information. Surely that meant something?

Iris skirted around the perimeter of the ballroom, doing what she did best at events such as these—watching everyone else. She liked standing at the periphery of the dance floor. She was an avid observer of her friends. And her acquaintances. And the people she didn't know, and the people she didn't like. It was entertaining, and truly, most of the time she enjoyed it more than she did dancing. It was just that tonight . . .

Tonight there was someone she actually wanted to dance with.

Where was he? Granted, Iris had arrived unfashionably on time. Her mother was a stickler for punctuality, no matter how often she was assured that the time listed on a ball invitation was merely a guideline.

But the ballroom was now bustling, and anyone concerned about arriving too early would have no cause to worry. In another hour, it would be—

"Miss Smythe-Smith."

She whirled around. Sir Richard stood before her, strikingly handsome in his evening clothes.

"I didn't see you come in," she said, and then proceeded into mental self-flagellation. *Stupid stupid.* Now he'd know she'd been—

"Were you watching for me?" he asked, his lips curving into a knowing smile.

"Of course not," she stammered. Because she'd never been a good liar.

He bowed over her hand and kissed it. "I would be flattered if indeed you were."

"I wasn't *watching* for you exactly," she said, trying not to let her embarrassment show. "But I did look about from time to time. To see if you were here."

"Then I am flattered by your 'looking about.'"

She tried to smile. But she was not *good* at flirtation. Put her in a room of people she knew well, and she could carry her end of a conversation with flair and wit. Her deadpan sarcasm was legend in her family. But put her before a handsome gentleman, and her tongue twisted in knots. The only reason she had performed so well that afternoon was that she had not been sure that he was pursuing her.

It was easy to be oneself when the stakes were low.

"Dare I hope you have set aside a dance for me?" Sir Richard asked.

"I have many unclaimed dances, sir." As she usually did.

"That cannot be."

Iris swallowed. He was gazing down at her with an unnerving intensity. His eyes were dark, almost black, and for the first time in her life she understood what people meant when they said they could drown in someone's eyes.

She could drown in *his* eyes. And she'd enjoy the descent.

"I find it difficult to believe that the gentlemen

of London are so foolish as to leave you at the side of the room."

"I do not mind," she said, then added, "Truly," when she saw that he did not believe her. "I very much like to watch people."

"Do you?" he murmured. "What do you see?"

Iris looked out over the ballroom. The dance floor was a swirl of color as the ladies spun about. "There," she said, motioning toward a young lady about twenty feet away. "She is being scolded by her mother."

Sir Richard leaned slightly to the side for a better view. "I see nothing out of the ordinary."

"One could argue that being scolded by one's mother is not out of the ordinary, but look more carefully." Iris pointed as discreetly as she could. "She's going to be in much more trouble later. She's not listening."

"You can tell this from twenty feet away?"

"I have some experience with being scolded myself."

He laughed aloud at that. "I suppose I must be too much of a gentleman to inquire what you did to warrant such a scolding."

"Certainly, you must," she said with an arch smile. Maybe she was finally learning how to flirt. It was rather nice, actually.

"Very well," he said with a gracious nod, "you are most observant. I shall count that among your many positive attributes. But I will not believe that you do not like to dance."

"I did not say I do not like to dance. I merely said I do not like to dance every dance."

"And have you danced every dance yet this evening?"

She smiled up at him, feeling bold and powerful and quite unlike herself. "I am not dancing *this* dance."

His dark brows rose at her impertinence, and he immediately gave a gracious bow. "Miss Smythe-Smith, will you do me the very great honor of dancing with me?"

Iris smiled widely, quite incapable of feigning sophisticated nonchalance. She placed her hand in his and followed him to the dance floor, where couples were lining up for a minuet.

The steps were intricate, but for the first time in her life, Iris felt as if she were moving through the dance without having to think about what to do. Her feet knew where to go, and her arms reached out at precisely the right moments, and his eyes—oh, his eyes—they never left hers, even when the dance sent them to different partners.

Iris had never felt so treasured. She had never felt so . . .

Desired.

A shiver ran through her, and she stumbled. Was this what it felt like, to be wanted by a gentleman? To want one in return? She had watched her cousins fall in love, shaken her head in dismay as infatuation made fools of them all. They had spoken of breathless anticipation, of searing kisses, and then, after their marriages, it had all dropped to a low whisper among themselves. There were secrets—very pleasant ones, it seemed—that were not spoken of among unmarried ladies.

Iris had not understood. When her cousins had spoken of that perfect moment of desire, right before a kiss, she could only think that it sounded dreadful. To kiss someone on the mouth . . . Why on earth would she wish to do that? It seemed rather sloppy business to her.

But now, as she circled through the dance, taking Sir Richard's hand and allowing him to spin her about, she could not help but stare at his lips. Something awakened within her, a strange yearning, a hunger from deep inside that stole her breath.

Dear God, this was desire. *She* wanted *him*. She, who had never even so much as wished to hold a man's hand, wanted to *know* him.

She froze.

"Miss Smythe-Smith?" Sir Richard was immediately at her side. "Is something amiss?"

She blinked, and then finally remembered to breathe. "Nothing," she whispered. "I feel a bit faint, that is all."

He led her away from the other dancers. "Allow me to get you something to drink."

She thanked him, then waited in one of the chaperones' chairs until he returned with a glass of lemonade.

"It's not cold," he said, "but the other choice was champagne, and I don't think that would be wise if you're feeling light-headed."

"No. No, of course not." She took a sip, aware that he was studying her intently. "It was very warm out there," she said, feeling the need to explain herself, however falsely. "Don't you think?"

"A bit, yes."

She took another sip, glad to have something in her hands upon which to focus her attention. "You don't need to remain here and watch over me," she told him.

"I know."

She had been trying not to look at him, but the pleasant simplicity of his words caught her attention.

He gave her a mischievous half smile. "It's quite agreeable here at the edge of the ballroom. So many people to watch."

She turned quickly back to her lemonade. It was a sly sort of compliment, but a compliment, indeed. No one would have understood it but they two, and for that reason it was all the more wonderful.

"I shall not be sitting here long, I'm afraid," she said.

His eyes seemed to sparkle. "Such a statement can only demand explanation."

"Now that you have danced with me," she told him, "others will feel the need to follow suit."

He chuckled at that. "Really, Miss Smythe-Smith, do you find we men so lacking in originality?"

She shrugged, still keeping her gaze fixed ahead. "As I told you, Sir Richard, I am very fond of observation. I cannot say *why* men do as they do, but I can certainly tell you *what* they do."

"Follow one another like sheep?"

She bit back a smile.

"I suppose there is some truth in that," he acknowledged. "I shall have to congratulate myself on having noticed you all on my own."

She looked over at him at that.

"I am a man of discerning tastes."

She tried not to snort. Now he was really laying it on too thick. But she was glad of it. It was easier to remain indifferent when his compliments felt too deliberate.

"I have no reason to doubt your observations," he continued, leaning back in his chair as he watched the crowds milling about. "But as I am a man, and therefore one of your unknowing subjects—"

"Oh, *please*."

"No, no, we must call a spade a spade." He tilted his head toward hers. "All in the name of science, Miss Smythe-Smith."

She rolled her eyes.

"As I was saying," he continued, in a voice that brazenly dared her to interrupt, "I believe I can shed some light upon your observations."

"I do have a hypothesis of my own."

"Tsk tsk. You said you could not say why men act as they do."

"Not conclusively, but I would be appallingly lacking in curiosity if I did not ponder the matter."

"Very well. You tell me. Why are men such sheep?"

"Well, now you've boxed me into a corner. How am I meant to answer that without giving offense?"

"You can't, really," he admitted, "except that I will promise that my feelings will not be hurt."

Iris let out a breath, hardly able to believe she was having such an irregular conversation. "You, Sir Richard, are not a fool."

He blinked. Then said, "As promised, my feelings are not hurt."

"And as such," she continued with a smile—because really, who could have not smiled at that?—"when you take an action, other men will not immediately think you foolish. I imagine there are even a few young gentlemen out there who look up to you."

"You are too kind," he drawled.

"To continue," she said, brooking no interruption, "when you ask a young lady to dance . . . More specifically, a young lady who is not known for dancing, others will wish to know why. They will wonder if you have seen something in her that they have not. And even if they look more closely and still find nothing of interest, they will not wish to be thought ignorant. So they will ask her to dance, too."

He didn't say anything right away, so she added, "I suppose you think me cynical."

"Oh, without a doubt. But that's not necessarily a bad thing."

She turned toward him in surprise. "I beg your pardon?"

"I think we should conduct a scientific experiment," he announced.

"An experiment," she repeated. What on earth was he about?

"Since you have observed my fellow gentlemen as if we were specimens in a rather grandly decorated laboratory, I propose that we make the experiment more formal." He looked to her for reply, but she was speechless, utterly speechless.

"After all," he continued, "science requires the gathering and noting of data, does it not?"

"I suppose," she said suspiciously.

"I shall lead you back toward the dancing. No one will approach you here in the chaperones' chairs. They'll suppose you injured. Or ill."

"Really?" Iris drew back in surprise. Maybe that was part of the reason she was not often asked to dance.

"Well, it's what I've always thought, at any rate. Why else would a young lady be over here?" He glanced in her direction, causing Iris to wonder if perhaps his question had not been hypothetical, but the moment she opened her mouth, he continued with: "I shall lead you back, and leave you be. We shall see how many men ask you to dance."

"Don't be silly."

"And you," he continued, as if she had not said a word, "must be honest with me. You must tell me truthfully if you are engaged for more dances than usual."

"I promise to tell the truth," Iris said, stifling a laugh. He had such a way about him, of saying the silliest thing as if it were of grave importance. She could almost believe this was all in the pursuit of science.

He stood and held out his hand. "My lady?"

Iris set down her empty lemonade glass and stood.

"I trust you are no longer suffering the effects of light-headedness," he murmured as he led her across the ballroom.

"I believe I shall manage for the rest of the evening."

"Good." He bowed. "Until tomorrow, then."

"Tomorrow?"

"We are walking, are we not? You did grant me permission to call on you. I thought we might stroll about town if the weather cooperates."

"And if it doesn't?" she asked, feeling just a bit saucy.

"Then we shall discuss books. Perhaps"—his head dipped closer to hers—"something your sister has not read?"

She laughed, loud and true. "I am almost hoping for rain, Sir Richard, and I—"

But she was cut off by the approach of a sandy-haired gentleman. Mr. Reginald Balfour. She'd met him before; his sister was good friends with one of hers. But he'd never done more than greet her politely.

"Miss Smythe-Smith," he said, bowing to her curtsy. "You look exceptionally fine this evening."

Iris's hand was still on Sir Richard's arm, and she could feel him tensing as he tried not to laugh.

"Are you engaged for the next dance?" Mr. Balfour asked.

"I am not," she said.

"Then may I lead you out?"

She glanced over at Sir Richard. He winked.

Ninety minutes later, Richard stood near the wall, watching Iris as she danced with yet another gentleman he did not recognize. For all her talk about never dancing every dance, she appeared to be well on her way to that goal tonight. She seemed honestly surprised by the attention. Whether she was enjoying herself, he was not certain. He supposed that even if she weren't, she would view the evening as an interesting experience, one worthy of her particular brand of observation.

Not for the first time, it occurred to him that Iris Smythe-Smith was highly intelligent. It was one of the reasons he'd chosen her. She was a rational creature. She would understand.

No one seemed to notice him in the shadows, so he took advantage of the moment by mentally ticking through his list. He'd drawn one up when he'd found himself racing back to London a few days earlier. Well, not drawn. He wasn't so foolish as to write such a thing down. But he'd had ample time on the journey to reflect upon what he needed in a wife.

She could not be spoiled. Or the sort who liked to draw attention to herself.

She could not be stupid. He had good reason to marry quickly, but whomever he chose, he was going to have to live with the lady for the rest of his life.

It would be nice if she was pretty, but it was not imperative.

She ought not be from Yorkshire. All things considered, it would be much easier if she was a stranger to the neighborhood.

She probably could not be rich. He needed someone for whom he might be considered an advantageous match. His wife would never need him as much as he needed her, but it would be easier—at least at the beginning—if she did not realize this.

And above all, she must understand what it

meant to value one's family. That was the only way this was going to work. She had to understand *why* he was doing this.

Iris Smythe-Smith fit his needs in every way. From the moment he saw her at her cello, desperately wishing that people were not looking at her, she had intrigued him. She'd been out in society for several years, but if she'd received any marriage proposals, he had not heard of them. Richard might not be rich, but he was respectable, and there was no reason for her family to disapprove of him, especially when no other suitors were forthcoming.

And he liked her. Did he wish to throw her over his shoulder, spirit her away, and ravish her? No, but nor did he think it would be unenjoyable when the time came.

He liked her. And he knew enough of marriage to know that this was more than most men had when they went to the altar.

He just wished he had more time. She was too sensible to accept him so soon after their first meeting. And honestly, he didn't want to be married to the type of female who would act so rashly. He was going to have to force the issue, which was unfortunate.

But, he reminded himself, there was nothing to be done that evening. His only task was to be polite and charming so that when the time came, no one would put up much of a fuss.

He'd already had enough fuss to last a lifetime.

Chapter Five

The following day

"Not Daisy," Iris pleaded. "Please, anyone but Daisy."

"You cannot walk about London with Sir Richard without a chaperone," her mother said, adjusting her hairpins as she examined her reflection in her vanity mirror. "You know that."

Iris had rushed to her mother's bedchamber the moment she'd learned that Daisy had been asked to accompany her for the day's outing with Sir Richard. Surely her mother would realize the foolishness of such a plan. But no, Mrs. Smythe-Smith seemed perfectly content with the idea and was acting as if it was all settled.

Iris scooted around to her mother's other side, positioning herself too close to the mirror to be ignored. "Then I'll take my maid. But not Daisy. She won't hang back. You know she won't."

Mrs. Smythe-Smith considered this.

"She will insert herself into every conversation," Iris pressed. Her mother still looked unconvinced, though, and Iris realized she would need to approach this from a different angle. The *your-daughter-is-quite-on-the-shelf-and-this-might-be-her-last-chance* angle.

"Mama," Iris said, "please, you must reconsider. If Sir Richard wishes to know me better, he will certainly meet with no success if Daisy is with us all afternoon."

Her mother let out a little sigh.

"You know it's true," Iris said quietly.

"You do have a point," Mrs. Smythe-Smith said with a frown. "Although I don't want Daisy to feel left out."

"She's four years younger than I am," Iris protested. "Surely there is time enough for her to find a gentleman of her own." And then, in a very small voice, she said, "It's my turn."

She liked Sir Richard, even if she did not quite trust him. There was something so odd, so unexpected about his attentions toward her. He had quite clearly sought an introduction at the musicale; Iris could not recall the last time that had happened. And then to call upon her the very next day, and to spend so much time at her side at the Mottram ball . . . It was unprecedented.

She did not believe his intentions were less than

honorable; she liked to think herself a good judge of character, and whatever his aims, her ruination was not one of them. But nor could she believe that he had been struck by a grand passion. If she were the sort of female who inspired men to fall in love at first sight, surely someone else would have done so by now.

But there could be no harm in seeing him again. He had asked her mother for permission to call upon her, and he had treated her with every courtesy. It was all very proper, and very flattering, and if she'd gone to sleep that night with a picture of him in her mind, surely there was nothing uncommon in that. He was a handsome man.

"Are you certain he does not plan to bring Mr. Bevelstoke with him?" her mother asked.

"Quite. And I shall be honest, I do not think Mr. Bevelstoke has any interest in Daisy."

"No, I suppose not. She's far too young for him. Very well, you may take Nettie. She did the same for your sisters on several occasions so she'll know what to do."

"Oh, thank you, Mama! Thank you so much!" Surprising even herself, Iris threw her arms around her mother and hugged her. It lasted but a second before they both stiffened and stepped back; theirs had never been a demonstrative relationship.

"I'm sure this will all amount to nothing," Iris said, because it would not do to get her hopes up anywhere but in her own mind. "But it will *certainly* go nowhere with Daisy in attendance."

"I do wish we knew a little more about him,"

her mother said with a frown. "He hasn't been to town for several years now."

"Were you acquainted with him when Marigold was out?" Iris asked. "Or Rose or Lavender?"

"I believe he was in town when Rose made her debut," her mother said, referring to Iris's eldest sister, "but we did not move in the same circles."

Iris wasn't sure what to make of that.

"He was young," her mother said with a flip of her hand. "Matrimony was not on his mind."

In other words, Iris thought wryly, he'd been a bit wild.

"I did speak to your aunt about him, though," her mother continued, not bothering to clarify which aunt. Iris supposed it didn't really matter; they all tended to be equally good sources of gossip. "She said that he came into the baronetcy some years ago."

Iris nodded. She knew as much.

"His father lived beyond his means." Mrs. Smythe-Smith's mouth pinched disapprovingly.

Which likely made Sir Richard a fortune hunter.

"But," Iris's mother mused, "that does not seem to be the case with the son."

A well-principled fortune hunter, then. He had not accrued his own debts; he'd merely had the misfortune of inheriting them.

"He is clearly looking for a wife," Mrs. Smythe-Smith continued. "There is no other reason a gentleman of his age would return to town after an absence of several years."

"He has the guardianship of his two younger sisters," Iris told her. "Perhaps he is finding it dif-

ficult without a female influence in the house."
As she said it, though, she could only think that
the future Lady Kenworthy would be thrust into
quite a challenging position. Hadn't he said that
one of his younger sisters was already eighteen?
Old enough so that she would likely not appreciate guidance from her brother's new wife.

"A sensible man," Mrs. Smythe-Smith mused.
"It does him credit that he can recognize when he
requires help. Although one can only wonder why
he did not do so years earlier."

Iris nodded.

"We can only speculate upon the condition of
his estate if his father was as much a spendthrift
as rumored. I do hope he does not think you have
a grand dowry."

"Mama," Iris said with a sigh. She didn't want
to talk about this. Not now, at least.

"He wouldn't be the first to make that error,"
Mrs. Smythe-Smith said blithely. "With all of our
connections to the aristocracy—close connections, mind you—people do seem to think we
have more than we do."

Wisely, Iris held her tongue. When her mother
was pontificating on a topic of social importance,
it was best not to interrupt.

"We ran into this with Rose, you know. Somehow it got about that she had fifteen thousand.
Can you imagine?"

Iris could not.

"Perhaps if we'd had but one daughter," her
mother said. "But with five!" She let out a little
laugh, the sort that sounded of disbelief and wish-

ful thinking. "We shall be lucky if your brother inherits anything by the time we get all of you married off."

"I'm sure John will be very comfortable," Iris said. Her only brother was three years younger than Daisy and still away at school.

"If he's lucky, *he* shall find a girl with fifteen thousand," her mother said with a caustic laugh. She stood abruptly. "Well. We can sit here all morning speculating over Sir Richard's motives or we can get on with the day." She glanced at the clock on her vanity. "I don't suppose he mentioned when he might arrive?"

Iris shook her head.

"You should make sure you're ready, then. It will not do to keep him waiting. I know that some women think it best not to appear eager, but you know that I think it's rude."

A knock at the door forestalled Iris's exit, and they both looked up to see a housemaid in the doorway. "Begging your pardon, milady," she said. "But Lady Sarah is in the drawing room."

"Ah, well, that's a pleasant surprise," Mrs. Smythe-Smith said. "I'm sure she's here to see you, Iris. Run along."

Iris headed downstairs to greet her cousin, Lady Sarah Prentice, née Lady Sarah Pleinsworth. Sarah's mother and Iris's father were siblings, and as they were reasonably close in age, so were their children.

Sarah and Iris were but six months apart and had always been friendly, but they had grown closer since Sarah's marriage to Lord Hugh Prentice the previous year. They had another cousin who was also their age, but Honoria spent most of her time with her husband in Cambridgeshire, whereas both Sarah and Iris lived in London.

When Iris reached the drawing room, Sarah was sitting on the green sofa, leafing through *Pride and Prejudice,* which Iris's mother had obviously left there the day before.

"Have you read this?" Sarah asked without preamble.

"Several times. It's lovely to see you, too."

Sarah pulled a face. "We all must have someone with whom we need not stand on ceremony."

"I tease," Iris said.

Sarah glanced at the door. "Is Daisy about?"

"I'm sure she's making herself scarce. She still hasn't forgiven you for threatening to run her through with her own violin bow before the musicale."

"Oh, that wasn't a threat. It was an honest attempt. That girl is lucky she has good reflexes."

Iris laughed. "To what do I owe this visit? Or are you simply starved for my sparkling company?"

Sarah leaned forward, her dark eyes gleaming. "I think you know why I'm here."

Iris knew exactly what she meant, but nonetheless, she leaned forward, meeting her cousin's gaze dead-on. "Illuminate me."

"Sir Richard Kenworthy?"

"What about him?"

"I saw him chase after you at the musicale."

"He did not chase after me."

"Oh, yes, he did. It was all my mother could talk about afterward."

"I find that difficult to believe."

Sarah shrugged. "I'm afraid you're in a very sticky spot, dear cousin. With me married and none of my sisters old enough to be out, my mother has determined to fix all of her energies on you."

"Dear heavens," Iris remarked, with no sarcasm whatsoever. Her aunt Charlotte took her duties as a matchmaking mother very seriously.

"Not to mention . . ." Sarah went on, her words laced with great drama. "*What* happened at the Mottram ball? I did not attend, but clearly I should have done."

"Nothing happened." Iris fixed her best *what-nonsense!* expression upon her face. "If you refer to Sir Richard, I simply danced with him."

"According to Marigold—"

"When did you speak with Marigold?"

Sarah flicked a hand in the air. "It doesn't matter."

"But Marigold wasn't even there last night!"

"She heard it from Susan."

Iris sat back. "Good Lord, we have too many cousins."

"I know. Really. But back to the matter at hand. Marigold said that Susan said that you were practically the belle of the ball."

"That is an exaggeration beyond compare."

Sarah jabbed her index finger toward Iris with the speed of a practiced interrogator. "Do you deny that you danced every dance?"

"I do deny it." She had sat out quite a few before Sir Richard had arrived.

Sarah paused, blinked, then frowned. "It's not like Marigold to get her gossip wrong."

"I danced more than I usually do," Iris allowed, "but certainly not every dance."

"Hmmm."

Iris eyed her cousin with considerable suspicion. It never boded well when Sarah looked to be in deep thought.

"I think I know what happened," Sarah said.

"Pray, enlighten me."

"You danced with Sir Richard," Sarah went on, "and then you spent an hour with him in private conversation."

"It wasn't an hour, and how do you *know* this?"

"I know things," Sarah said flippantly. "It's best not to inquire how. Or why."

"How does Hugh live with you?" Iris asked to the room at large.

"He does very well, thank you." Sarah grinned. "But back to last night. However much time you spent in the company of the exceedingly handsome Sir Richard—no, don't interrupt, I saw him myself at the musicale, he's quite pleasing to the eye—it left you feeling . . ."

She stopped then, and did that odd thing with her mouth she did whenever she was trying to think of something. She sort of moved her lower jaw to one side so that her teeth no longer lined up, and her lips did a funny little twist. Iris had always found it disconcerting.

Sarah frowned. "It left you feeling . . ."

"Feeling what?" Iris finally asked.

"I'm trying to think of the right word."

Iris stood. "I'll ring for tea."

"Breathless!" Sarah finally exclaimed. "You felt breathless. And all aglow."

Iris rolled her eyes as she gave the bellpull a stiff yank. "You need to find a hobby."

"And when a woman *feels* all aglow, she *looks* all aglow," Sarah continued.

"That sounds uncomfortable."

"And when she looks—"

"All prickly skin and sweaty brows," Iris plundered on. "Sounds a bit like a sun rash."

"Will you stop being such a spoilsport?" Sarah huffed. "I declare, Iris, you are the least romantic person I know."

Iris paused on her way back to the seating area, resting her hands on the back of the sofa. Was that true? She knew she was not sentimental, but she was not completely without feelings. She'd read *Pride and Prejudice* six times. That had to count for something.

But Sarah was oblivious to her distress. "As I was saying," she went on, "when a woman feels beautiful, she has a way about her."

It was on the tip of Iris's tongue to say, "I wouldn't know," but she stopped herself.

She didn't want to be sarcastic. Not about this.

"And when that happens," Sarah said, "men flock to her side. There is something about a confident woman. Something . . . I don't know . . . *je ne sais quoi*, as the French say."

"I'm thinking of switching to German," Iris heard herself say.

Sarah stared at her for a moment, her expression baffled, then carried on as if she had not even paused. "And that, my dear cousin," she said with great flair, "is why every man in London wanted to dance with you last night."

Iris came back around the sofa and sat down, folding her hands in her lap as she thought about what Sarah had said. She was not sure she believed it, but nor could she dismiss it without consideration.

"You're very quiet," Sarah remarked. "I was certain you'd argue the point."

"I don't know what to say," Iris admitted.

Sarah eyed her with open curiosity. "Are you all right?"

"Perfectly. Why do you ask?"

"You seem different."

Iris gave a little shrug. "Perhaps it is my glow, as you termed it."

"No," Sarah said bluntly, "that's not it."

"Well, that was a short-lived glow," Iris quipped.

"*Now* you sound like yourself."

Iris just smiled and shook her head. "How are *you*?" she asked, in a not-so-subtle attempt to change the subject.

"Very well," Sarah said with a broad smile, and it was then that Iris noticed . . . something.

"You seem different, too," she said, eyeing her more closely.

Sarah blushed.

Iris gasped. "Are you expecting?"

Sarah nodded. "How did you know?"

"When you tell a married woman she looks different, and she blushes . . ." Iris grinned. "It can be nothing else."

"You really do notice everything, don't you?"

"Almost everything," Iris said. "But you have not allowed me to congratulate you yet. This is wonderful news. Please do tell Lord Hugh that I wish him joy. How are you feeling? Have you been ill?"

"Not at all."

"Well, that's fortunate. Rose threw up every morning for three months straight."

Sarah winced in sympathy. "I feel splendid. Perhaps a little fatigued, but not terribly so."

Iris smiled at her cousin. It seemed so strange that Sarah would soon be a mother. They had played as children together, moaned about the musicale together. And now Sarah had moved on to the next phase of her life.

And Iris was . . .

Still here.

"You love him very much, don't you?" she said quietly.

Sarah did not reply right away, regarding her cousin with an expression of curiosity. "I do," she said solemnly. "With everything I am."

Iris nodded. "I know." She thought Sarah would speak then, perhaps to ask her why she'd made such a silly query, but Sarah remained silent, until Iris could not help but ask, "How did you know?"

"Know?"

"That you loved him."

"I—" Sarah stopped, pausing to think. "I'm not sure. I can't really remember the exact moment.

It's funny, I always thought that if I did fall in love, I would do it in a grand flash of insight. You know, bolts of lightning, angels singing on high . . . that sort of thing."

Iris grinned. That did sound like Sarah. She'd always had a penchant for drama.

"But it wasn't like that at all," Sarah continued wistfully. "I remember feeling very strange and wondering about it, trying to determine if what I felt was love."

"So someone might not *know* while it's happening?"

"I suppose not."

Iris caught her lower lip between her teeth, then whispered, "Was it when he first kissed you?"

"Iris!" Sarah smiled in shock and delight. "What a question!"

"It's not so improper," Iris said, glancing at a spot on the wall that was decidedly to the left of Sarah's face.

"Oh, yes it is." Sarah's chin drew back in her surprise. "But I love that you asked it."

That was not what Iris expected her to say. *"Why?"*

"Because you always seem so . . ." Sarah waved a hand through the air, swirling it about as if that might draw out the correct word. " . . . untouched by these things."

"By what things?" Iris asked suspiciously.

"Oh, you know. Emotions. Infatuations. You're always so calm. Even when you're furious."

Iris bristled defensively. "Is there something wrong with that?"

"Of course not. It's simply who you are. And quite frankly, it's probably the only reason Daisy has reached the age of seventeen without your killing her. Not that she'll ever appreciate it."

Iris couldn't stop a wry smile. It was nice to know *some*one appreciated her forbearance with her younger sister.

Sarah narrowed her eyes and leaned forward. "This is about Sir Richard, isn't it?"

Iris knew there was no point in denying it. "I just think—" She pressed her lips together, almost worried that if she didn't, a whole string of nonsense would burst forth. "I like him," she finally admitted. "I don't know why, but I do."

"You don't need to know why." Sarah squeezed her hand. "It sounds as if he likes you, too."

"I believe that he does. He's paid me quite a bit of attention."

"But . . . ?"

Iris's eyes met her cousin's. She should have realized Sarah would hear the silent "but" at the end of the sentence. "But . . . I don't know," Iris said. "Something isn't quite right."

"Is it possible that you are searching for problems where they do not exist?"

Iris took a long breath and then let it out. "Perhaps. It's not as if I have anyone with whom to compare."

"That's not true. You've had suitors."

"Not many. And none I liked well enough to care if they continued in their attentions."

Sarah sighed, but she did not argue the point.

"Very well. Tell me what seems 'not quite right,' as you put it."

Iris tipped her head to the side, and she looked up, momentarily mesmerized by the way the sunlight danced upon the crystal chandelier. "I think he likes me too well," she finally said.

Sarah let out a loud bark of laughter. "*That's* what is not quite right? Iris, do you have any idea how many—"

"Stop," Iris interrupted. "Hear me out. This is my third season in London, and while I admit I have not been the most eager of debutantes, I have never been the subject of such warm attentions."

Sarah opened her mouth to speak, but Iris held up her hand to forestall her. "It's not even that they are so *warm* . . ." She felt herself blushing now. What a stupid choice of words. "It's that they were so instant."

"Instant?"

"Yes. You probably did not notice him at the musicale, as you were facing away from much of the audience."

"I was trying to jump into the pianoforte and close the lid is what you mean," Sarah joked.

"Quite right," Iris said with a little laugh. Of all her cousins, Sarah was the one who most shared Iris's loathing of the musicale.

"I'm sorry," Sarah said. "I couldn't resist. Pray, continue."

Iris pursed her lips, remembering. "He was watching me the entire time," she said.

"Maybe he found you beautiful."

"Sarah," Iris said frankly, "no one finds me beautiful. At least not at first glance."

"That's not true!"

"You know it is. It's fine. I promise."

Sarah looked unconvinced.

"I know I am not *ugly*," Iris assured her. "But it's as Daisy said—"

"Oh no," Sarah cut in forcefully, "*don't* quote Daisy."

"No," Iris said, trying to be fair. "Occasionally she says something that makes sense. I lack color."

Sarah held her gaze for a long moment, and then said, "That is the most asinine thing I have ever heard."

Iris lifted her brows. Her pale, colorless brows. "Have you ever met anyone quite so pale?"

"No, but that signifies nothing."

Iris let out a frustrated breath, trying to articulate her thoughts. "I'm trying to say that I'm used to being underestimated. Overlooked."

Sarah just stared at her. And then—"What are you *talking* about?"

Iris let out a frustrated little puff of a breath. She knew Sarah would not understand. "People rarely notice me. And that's—no, I swear it!—all right. I don't want to be the center of attention."

"You're not shy," Sarah pointed out.

"No, but I like being able to watch people, and"—she shrugged—"if I'm honest, mock them inside my own head."

Sarah sputtered a laugh.

"Once people get to know me, it's different," Iris continued, "but I do not stand out in a crowd.

And that is why I do not understand Sir Richard Kenworthy."

Sarah was silent for a full minute. Every now and then she'd open her mouth as if to speak, but her lips would just hang in an oval, and then she'd shut them again. Finally she asked, "But you like him?"

"Were you not listening?" Iris practically exploded.

"Every word!" Sarah insisted. "But I do not see how any of it is relevant, at least not yet. For all we know, he *did* take one look at you and fall desperately in love. His behavior is certainly consistent with such a thing."

"He's not in love with me," Iris insisted.

"Maybe not *yet*." Sarah let her words hang in the air for some time before asking, "If he asked you to marry him, this very afternoon, what would you say?"

"That's ridiculous."

"Of course it is, but I still want to know. What would you say?"

"I wouldn't say anything, because he would not ask."

Sarah scowled. "Will you stop being so stubborn for one moment and indulge me?"

"No!" Iris was ready to throw up her arms in exasperation. "I fail to see the point in attempting to determine my reply to a question that will not be asked."

"You would say yes," Sarah said.

"No, I wouldn't," Iris protested.

"Then you would say no."

"I did not say that, either."

Sarah sat back and nodded slowly, a very smug look washing over her features.

"What now?" Iris asked.

"You won't even ponder the question because you're afraid to examine your own feelings."

Iris did not reply.

"I'm right," Sarah said triumphantly. And then, as an aside: "I love being right."

Iris took a deep breath, although whether this was to rein in her temper or summon her courage she did not know. "If he asked me to marry him," she said, each word enunciated with precision, "I would tell him that I needed time to give him an answer."

Sarah nodded.

"But he's not going to ask me."

Sarah let out a loud peal of laughter. "You have to have the last word, don't you?"

"He's not going to ask me."

Sarah just grinned. "Oh, look, tea has arrived. I'm famished."

"He's not going to ask me." Iris's voice had taken on a singsong quality.

"I shall leave directly after tea," Sarah said officiously. "Much as I'd love to make his acquaintance, I wouldn't want to be here when he arrives. I might get in the way."

"He's not going to ask me."

"Oh, do have a biscuit."

"He's not going to ask me," Iris said again. And then, because she had to, she added, "He's not."

Chapter Six

Five days later
Pleinsworth House

IT WAS TIME.

It had been but a week since Richard had first laid eyes on Iris Smythe-Smith, right here in this very house. And now he was going to make her a proposal of marriage.

Of sorts.

He had called upon her every day since the Mottram ball. They had strolled in the park, ordered ices at Gunther's, shared a box at the opera, and visited Covent Garden. In short, they had done everything a courting couple in London was supposed to do. He was full certain that Iris's family expected him to ask her to marry him.

Just not quite yet.

He knew that Iris held him in some affection. She might even wonder if she was falling in love. But if he asked for her hand tonight, he was almost certain she would not be prepared to give an immediate answer.

He sighed. This was not how he had imagined getting himself a wife.

He'd come alone this evening; Winston had flatly refused to attend any artistic endeavor produced by the Smythe-Smith family, regardless of Richard's previous acceptance on his behalf. Now Winston was home with a false head cold, and Richard was standing in the corner, wondering why a piano had been brought into the drawing room.

And why it appeared to have been decorated with twigs.

A quick perusal of the room told him that Lady Pleinsworth had made up programs for the evening, although he did not seem to have been handed one, even though he had arrived nearly five minutes earlier.

"There you are."

He turned at the soft voice and saw Iris standing before him in a simply adorned gown of pale blue muslin. She wore that color frequently, he realized. It suited her.

"I'm sorry to have left you unattended," she said. "My assistance was required backstage."

"Backstage?" he echoed. "I thought this was meant to be a poetry reading."

"Ah, that," she said, her cheeks turning a rather guilty shade of pink. "There has been a change of plans."

He tipped his head in question.

"Perhaps I should get you a program."

"Yes, I don't seem to have been given one when I arrived."

She cleared her throat about six times. "I believe it was decided not to hand them out to the gentlemen unless requested."

He considered that for a moment. "Dare I ask why?"

"I believe," she said, glancing up at the ceiling, "there was some concern that you might not choose to remain."

Richard looked in horror at the piano.

"Oh, no," Iris quickly assured him. "There will be no music. At least not that I know of. It's not a concert."

Still, Richard's eyes widened with panic. Where was Winston and his little balls of cotton when he needed him? "You're frightening me, Miss Smythe-Smith."

"Does that mean you don't want a program?" she asked hopefully.

He leaned very slightly toward her. It wasn't enough to breach the rules of propriety, but still, he knew she noticed. "I think it's best to be prepared, don't you?"

She swallowed. "Just a moment."

He waited as she crossed the room and approached Lady Pleinsworth. A moment later she returned with a sheet of paper. "Here," she said sheepishly, holding it out.

He took it and looked down. Then looked back up. *"The Shepherdess, the Unicorn, and Henry VIII?"*

"It's a play. My cousin Harriet wrote it."

"And we're to watch," he confirmed warily.

She nodded.

He cleared his throat. "Do you, ah, have any idea of the length of this production?"

"Not as long as the musicale," she assured him. "At least I don't think so. I have seen only the last few minutes of the dress rehearsal."

"The piano is part of the set, I assume?"

She nodded. "It's nothing compared to the costumes, I'm afraid."

He could barely bring himself to ask.

"It was my job to affix the horn to the unicorn."

He tried not to laugh, he really did. And he almost managed.

"I'm not sure how Frances is going to get it off," Iris said with nervous expression. "I glued it to her head."

"You glued a horn to your cousin's head," he repeated.

She winced. "I did."

"Do you *like* this cousin?"

"Oh, very much. She's eleven and really quite delightful. I'd trade Daisy for her in a heartbeat."

Richard had a feeling she would trade Daisy for a badger if given the option.

"A horn," he said again. "Well, I suppose one can't be a unicorn without one."

"That's just the thing," Iris said with renewed enthusiasm. "Frances loves it. She adores unicorns. She's quite convinced they are real, and I think she would become one if she were so able."

"It appears she has taken the first step toward that noble goal," Richard said. "With your kind assistance."

"Ah, that. I'm rather hoping no one tells Aunt Charlotte that I was the one to wield the glue."

Richard had a feeling she was out of luck there. "Is there any chance it will remain a secret?"

"None whatsoever. But I shall cling to my false hope. With any luck, we shall have a terrible scandal tonight, and no one will notice that Frances has gone to bed with her horn still attached."

Richard started to cough. And then kept coughing. Good Lord, was that dust in his throat or a boulder of guilt?

"Are you all right?" Iris asked, her face drawn with concern.

He nodded, unable to voice his answer. Dear God, a scandal. If she only knew.

"Shall I fetch you something to drink?"

He nodded again. He needed to pour liquid down his throat almost as much as he needed not to look at her for a moment.

She would be happy in the end, he told himself. He would be a good husband to her. She would want for nothing.

Except the choice in marrying him.

Richard groaned. He had not expected to feel so bloody guilty about what he was going to do.

"Here you are," Iris said, holding out a crystal goblet. "A bit of sweet wine."

Richard nodded his thanks and took a fortify-
ing sip. "Thank you," he said hoarsely. "I don't
know what came over me."

Iris made a sympathetic noise and motioned
to the woodsy piano. "The air is probably dusty
from all those twigs Harriet brought in. She was
out collecting them in Hyde Park for hours yesterday."

He nodded again, draining his glass before
setting it down on a nearby table. "Will you sit
with me?" he asked, realizing that while he had
assumed she would, he owed her the politeness of
an invitation.

"I would be delighted," she said with a smile.
"You shall probably need someone to translate, in
any case."

His eyes grew wide with alarm. "Translate?"

She laughed. "No, no, don't worry, it's in English.
It's only . . ." She laughed again, her smile wide in
her face. "Harriet has her own singular style."

"You're very fond of your family," he observed.

She started to make a reply, but then something
caught her attention behind him. He turned to see
what she was looking at, but she'd already started
saying, "My aunt is signaling. I think we're meant
to take our seats."

With some trepidation, Richard sat next to her
in the front row and regarded the piano, which he
assumed marked the stage. The audience's voices
dimmed to whispers, and then to silence as Lady
Harriet Pleinsworth stepped out of the shadows
dressed as a humble shepherdess, crook and all.

"O beautiful, brilliant day!" she proclaimed,

pausing to bat away one of the ribbons on her wide-brimmed bonnet. "How blessed am I with my noble flock."

Nothing happened.

"My noble flock!" she repeated, quite a bit louder.

There was a crashing noise, followed by a grunt and a hissed "Stop it!" and then five small children dressed as sheep ambled forth.

"My cousins," Iris whispered. "The next generation."

"The sun shines down," Harriet went on, spreading her arms wide in supplication. But Richard was too fascinated by the sheep to listen. The largest of the lot was bleating so loudly, Harriet finally had to give him a little kick, and one of the smaller ones—good God, the child could not be more than two—had crawled over to the piano and was licking the leg.

Iris clamped her hand over her mouth, trying not to laugh.

The play continued in this vein for several minutes, with the fair shepherdess extolling the wonders of nature until somewhere someone crashed a pair of cymbals and Harriet shrieked (as did half the audience).

"I *said*," Harriet ground out, "that we are lucky it's not likely to rain for the next week."

The cymbals crashed again, followed by a voice yelling, "Thunder!"

Iris gasped, and a second hand flew up to cover the first, which was still wrapped over her mouth. Eventually he heard her utter the word, "Elizabeth" in horrified whisper.

"What's happening?" he asked her.

"I think Harriet's sister has just changed the script. All of act one will be lost."

Luckily, Richard was saved from having to stifle his smile by the arrival of five cows, which on closer inspection appeared to be the sheep with brown splotches of fabric pinned onto their wool.

"When do we get to see the unicorn?" he whispered to Iris.

She shrugged helplessly. She didn't know.

Henry VIII trundled forth a few minutes later, his Tudor tunic stuffed with so many pillows the child within could barely walk.

"That's Elizabeth," Iris whispered.

Richard nodded sympathetically. If he were forced to wear that costume, he'd want to skip the first act, too.

But nothing compared to the moment the unicorn burst onto the scene. Its whinny was terrifying, its horn tremendous.

Richard's jaw went slack. "You glued that to her brow?" he whispered to Iris.

"It was the only way it would stay on," she whispered back.

"She can't hold her head up."

They both stared at the stage in horror. Little Lady Frances Pleinsworth was stumbling about like a drunkard, not quite able to keep her body erect under the weight of the horn.

"What is that made out of?" Richard whispered.

Iris held up her hands. "I don't know. I didn't think it was *that* heavy. Maybe she's acting."

Richard watched, aghast, half expecting he'd have to leap forward to stop the girl from accidentally goring someone in the first row.

An eternity later, they reached what he thought might be the end, and King Henry waved his turkey leg in the air, loudly proclaiming, "This land shall be mine, henceforth and forevermore!"

And indeed, it seemed that all was lost for the poor, sweet shepherdess and her strangely changeable flock. But just then, there was a mighty roar—

"Is there a lion?" Richard wondered.

—and the unicorn burst onto the scene!

"Die!" the unicorn shrieked. "Die! Die! Die!"

Richard looked to Iris in confusion. The unicorn had not thus demonstrated an ability to speak.

Henry's scream of terror was so chilling, the woman behind Richard murmured, "This is surprisingly well acted."

Richard stole another look at Iris; her mouth was hanging open as Henry leapt over a cow and ran behind the piano, only to trip over the littlest sheep, who was still licking the piano leg.

Henry scrambled for purchase, but the (possibly rabid) unicorn was too fast, and it ran headfirst (and head down) toward the frightened king, plunging its horn into his large, pillowed belly.

Someone screamed, and Henry went down, feathers flying.

"I don't think this was in the script," Iris said in a horrified whisper.

Richard could not take his eyes off the gruesome spectacle on stage. Henry was on his back with the unicorn's horn stuck in his (thankfully fake) belly. Which would have been bad enough, except that the horn was still very much attached to the unicorn. Which meant that every time Henry thrashed about, the unicorn was jerked about by the head.

"Get off!" Henry yelled.

"I'm *trying*," the unicorn growled in return.

"I think it's stuck," Richard said to Iris.

"Oh, my heavens!" she cried, clapping her hand over her mouth. "The glue!"

One of the sheep ran over to help, but it slipped on a feather and got tangled in the unicorn's legs.

The shepherdess, who had been watching everything with as much shock as the audience, suddenly realized she needed to save the production and jumped forward, bursting into song.

"O blessed sunlight," she sang. "How your warmth doth shine!"

And then Daisy stepped forth.

Richard turned sharply to Iris. Her mouth was hanging open. "No no no," she finally whispered, but by then Daisy had launched into her violin solo, presumably a musical representation of sunshine.

Or death.

Daisy's performance was cut blessedly short by Lady Pleinsworth, who rushed onto the stage when she realized her two youngest children were hopelessly stuck together. "Refreshments in the other room, everyone!" she trilled. "We have cake!"

Everyone stood and applauded—it was a play,

after all, no matter how startling the finale—and began to file out of the drawing room.

"Perhaps I ought to help," Iris said, casting a wary glance at her cousins.

Richard waited while she approached the melee, watching the proceedings with no small amusement.

"Just remove the pillow!" Lady Pleinsworth directed.

"It's not that easy," Elizabeth hissed. "Her horn goes right through my shirt. Unless you want me to disrobe—"

"That will be enough, Elizabeth," Lady Pleinsworth said quickly. She turned to Harriet. "Why is it so sharp?"

"I'm a unicorn!" Frances said.

Lady Pleinsworth absorbed that for a moment, then shuddered.

"She wasn't supposed to ride me in the third act," Frances added petulantly.

"Is that why you gored her?"

"No, that was in the script," Harriet said helpfully. "The horn was supposed to come off. For the purpose of safety. But, of course, the audience wasn't supposed to see that."

"Iris glued it to my brow," Frances said, twisting her head in an attempt to look up.

Iris, who was standing at the edge of the small crowd, immediately took a step back. "Perhaps we should get something to drink," she said to Richard.

"In a moment." He was having far too much fun to leave.

Lady Pleinsworth grabbed the horn by both hands and pulled.

Frances screamed.

"Did she use *cement?*"

Iris's hand wrapped around his arm like a terrified vise. "I really need to go *now.*"

Richard took one look at Lady Pleinsworth's face and hurriedly guided Iris out of the room.

Iris sagged against the wall. "I'm going to be in so much trouble."

Richard knew he should try to reassure her, but he was laughing too hard to be of any use.

"Poor Frances," she moaned. "She's going to have to sleep with that horn on her head tonight!"

"She will be fine," Richard said, his laughter still peeking through his words. "I promise you, she will not walk down the aisle at her wedding with a horn on her head."

Iris looked up at him in momentary alarm, and he could only imagine what was racing through her imagination. And then she burst out laughing. She laughed so hard she doubled over right there in the hall.

"Oh my goodness," she gasped. "A horned wedding. It could only happen to us."

Richard started to chuckle again, watching in amusement as Iris's face turned red from her exertions.

"I shouldn't laugh," she said. "I really shouldn't. But the wedding—Oh my heavens, the wedding."

The wedding, Richard thought, and it all slammed back to the forefront of his mind. Why he was here tonight. Why he was with her.

Iris wasn't going to have much of wedding. He needed to get back to Yorkshire too quickly for that.

Guilt pricked along his spine. Didn't all ladies dream about their weddings? Fleur and Marie-Claire used to spend hours imagining theirs. For all he knew, they still did.

He took a breath. Iris wasn't going to get her dream wedding, and if all went according to plan, she wasn't even going to get a proper proposal.

She deserved better.

He swallowed, tapping his hand nervously against his thigh. Iris was still laughing, oblivious to his suddenly serious mien.

"Iris," he said suddenly, and she turned toward him with surprise in her eyes. Maybe it was the tone of his voice, or maybe the fact that it was the first time he called her by her given name.

He put his hand at the small of her back and led her away from the still-open doorway to the drawing room. "Might I have a moment of your time?"

Her brows came together, and then they rose. "Of course," she said, somewhat haltingly.

He took a breath. He could do this. It wasn't what he'd planned, but it was a better way. This one thing, he thought, he could do for her.

He dropped down to one knee.

She gasped.

"Iris Smythe-Smith," he said, taking her hand in his, "will you make me the happiest man alive and consent to be my wife?"

Chapter Seven

Iris was struck dumb. She opened her mouth, but apparently it wasn't to say anything. The back of her throat tightened and closed, and she just stared down at him, thinking—

This can't be happening.

"I imagine this is a surprise," Richard said in a warm voice, stroking the back of her hand with his fingers. He was still on bended knee, gazing up at her as if she were the only woman in all creation.

"Ahdebadeba . . ." She couldn't speak. She well and truly could not speak.

"Or perhaps it isn't."

No, it is. It really is.

"We have known each other but a week, but you must be aware of my devotion."

She felt her head shaking, but she had no idea

if that meant yes or no, and either way, she wasn't sure which question she was answering.

It wasn't supposed to happen this fast.

"I could not wait any longer," he murmured, coming to his feet.

"I—I don't—" She wet her lips. She'd found her voice, but she still could not manage a complete sentence.

He brought her fingers to his lips, but instead of kissing the back of her hand, he turned it gently over and laid a featherlight kiss on the inside of her wrist.

"Be mine, Iris," he said, his voice husky with what she thought might be desire. He kissed her again, allowing his lips to brush along her tender skin. "Be mine," he whispered, "and I will be yours."

She couldn't think. How could she think when he was staring at her as if they were the only two souls left on earth? His midnight eyes were warm—no, hot, and they made her want to melt into him, to throw over everything she knew, all good sense. Her body quivered, and her breath quickened, and she could not look away from his mouth as he kissed her yet again, this time moving to her palm.

Something tightened within her. Something she was sure it was not proper to feel. Not here in her aunt's hallway, not with a man she'd only just met.

"Will you marry me?" he asked.

No. Something was wrong. It was too soon. It did not make sense that he would love her so quickly.

But he did not love her. He had not said he loved her. And yet, the way he looked at her . . .

Why did he want to marry her? Why could she not trust him?

"Iris?" he murmured. "My darling?"

And she finally found her voice.

"I need time."

DAMN IT.

This was exactly what he had thought would happen. She wasn't going to agree to marry him after only a weeklong courtship. She was far too sensible for that.

The irony just killed him. If she weren't the intelligent, sensible creature she was, he wouldn't have chosen her.

He should have stuck to his original plan. He'd come here tonight with every intention of compromising her. Nothing extreme; it would be the worst sort of hypocrisy if he stole anything more than a kiss.

But a kiss was all he needed. One witnessed kiss, and she was as good as his.

But no, she'd mentioned the word *wedding*, and then he'd felt guilty, and he knew he damn well *should* feel guilty. A romantic proposal was his way of making it up to her, not that she knew there was anything for which he must atone.

"Of course," he said smoothly, rising to his feet. "I spoke too soon. Forgive me."

"There is nothing to forgive," she said, stumbling on the words. "It was just so surprising, and I hadn't considered, and you've only met my father just once, and in passing at that."

"I will, of course, ask his permission," Richard said. It wasn't exactly a falsehood. If he could get Iris to say yes in the next few minutes, he would happily seek a private audience with her father and do things in the proper manner.

"May I have a few days?" she asked, her expression hesitant. "There are so many things I don't know about you. And at least as much you do not know about me."

He let his eyes burn hot into hers. "I know enough to know that I shall never find a more worthy bride."

Her lips parted, and he knew that his compliments were well aimed. If he only had had more time, he could have wooed her the way a bride ought to be wooed.

He took both of her hands in his and gave them a gentle squeeze. "You are so precious to me."

She appeared not to know what to say.

He touched her cheek, stalling for time as he tried to figure out how to salvage this. He needed to marry her, and he could not afford a delay.

Out of the corner of his eye, he saw a flash of movement. The door to the drawing room was still open. He was at an odd angle to it; he could see only a sliver of the interior. But he had a feeling that Lady Pleinsworth would exit at any moment, and—

"I must kiss you!" he cried out, and he pulled Iris roughly into his arms. He heard her gasp with shock, and it tore painfully through him, but he had no choice. He had to go back to his original plan. He kissed her mouth, her jaw, her lovely exposed neck, and then—

"Iris Smythe-Smith!"

He jumped back. Strangely, he did not have to feign surprise.

Lady Pleinsworth rushed over. "What in the name of God is happening here?"

"Aunt Charlotte!" Iris stumbled back, trembling like a frightened deer. Richard saw her eyes go from her aunt to someone behind her, and with an increasing sense of dread he realized that the Ladies Harriet, Elizabeth, and Frances had also come into the hall and were staring at them with openmouthed shock.

Dear God, now he was responsible for the corrupting of children.

"Get your hands off my niece!" Lady Pleinsworth thundered.

Richard thought it best not to point out that he had already done so.

"Harriet," Lady Pleinsworth said, never taking her eyes off Richard. "Go fetch your aunt Maria."

Harriet gave a jerky nod and did her bidding.

"Elizabeth, summon a footman. Frances, go to your room."

"I can help," Frances protested.

"Your room, Frances. *Now!*"

Poor Frances, who was still wearing her horn, had to hold it with both hands as she ran off.

When Lady Pleinsworth spoke again, her voice was deadly. "Both of you, in the drawing room. This instant."

Richard stepped aside to allow Iris to pass. He had not thought she could possibly look more pale than normal, but her skin was positively bloodless.

Her hands were shaking. He hated that her hands were shaking.

A footman arrived just as they entered the drawing room, and Lady Pleinsworth pulled him aside and spoke to him in a low voice. Richard presumed she was sending him with a message for Iris's father.

"Sit," Lady Pleinsworth ordered.

Iris sank slowly into a chair.

Lady Pleinsworth turned her imperious stare on Richard. He clasped his hands behind his back. "I cannot be seated while you remain standing, your ladyship."

"I give you leave," she bit off.

He took a seat. It went against everything in his nature, to sit meekly and silent, but he knew this was what had to happen. He just wished Iris didn't look so hollow, so troubled and ashamed.

"Charlotte?"

He heard Iris's mother's voice coming from the hall. She stepped into the room, followed by Harriet, still holding her shepherdess's crook.

"Charlotte, what is going on? Harriet said . . ." Mrs. Smythe-Smith's words trailed off as she took in the tableau. "What has happened?" she asked, her voice low.

"I have sent for Edward," Lady Pleinsworth said.

"Father?" Iris said tremulously.

Lady Pleinsworth whirled to face her. "You did not think you could act as you did without repercussion?"

Richard shot to his feet. "She is blameless in this."

"What. Happened?" Mrs. Smythe-Smith said again, each word sharply pronounced.

"He has compromised her," Lady Pleinsworth said.

Mrs. Smythe-Smith gasped. "Iris, how could you?"

"This is not her fault," Richard cut in.

"I am not speaking to you," Mrs. Smythe-Smith snapped. "At least not yet." She turned to her sister-in-law. "Who knows?"

"All three of my youngest."

Mrs. Smythe-Smith closed her eyes.

"They won't say anything!" Iris suddenly exclaimed. "They are my cousins."

"They are children!" Lady Pleinsworth roared.

Richard had had enough. "I must ask you not to speak to her in that tone of voice."

"I don't think you are in any position to be making demands."

"Nevertheless," he said softly, "you will speak to her with respect."

Lady Pleinsworth's brows rose at his impertinence, but she said nothing more.

"I cannot believe you would behave so foolishly," Iris's mother said to her.

Iris didn't speak.

Her mother turned to Richard, her mouth cut into a firm, furious line. "You will have to marry her."

"There is nothing that would please me more."

"I doubt your sincerity, sir."

"That's not fair!" Iris cried out, jumping to her feet.

"You defend him?" Mrs. Smythe-Smith demanded.

"His intentions were honorable," Iris said.

Honorable, Richard thought. He was no longer sure what that meant.

"Oh, really," Mrs. Smythe-Smith nearly spat. "If his intentions were so hon—"

"He was in the middle of asking me to marry him!"

Mrs. Smythe-Smith looked from her daughter to Richard and back, clearly not sure what to make of this development. "I will say nothing more on the subject until your father arrives," she finally said to Iris. "It should not be long. The night is clear, and if your aunt"—she tipped her head toward Lady Pleinsworth—"has made clear the import of the summons, he will likely come on foot."

Richard agreed with her assessment. The Smythe-Smith home was a very short distance away. It would be much faster to walk than to wait for a carriage to be readied.

The room remained in tense silence for several seconds until Mrs. Smythe-Smith abruptly turned to her sister-in-law. "You must go to your guests, Charlotte. With neither of us there, it will appear very suspicious."

Lady Pleinsworth nodded grimly.

"Take Harriet," Iris's mother continued. "Introduce her to some of the gentlemen. She is nearly of age to be out. It will seem the most natural thing in the world."

"But I'm still in costume," Harriet protested.

"This is no time to be missish," her mother declared, grabbing her arm. "Come."

Harriet stumbled along behind her mother, but not before shooting a sympathetic last glance at Iris.

Mrs. Smythe-Smith closed the door to the drawing room and then let out a breath. "This is a fine mess," she said, and not with compassion.

"I will make arrangements for a special license immediately," Richard said. He saw no need to tell them that he had already procured one.

Mrs. Smythe-Smith crossed her arms and began to pace.

"Mama?" Iris ventured.

Mrs. Smythe-Smith held up a shaking finger. "Not now."

"But—"

"We will wait for your father!" Mrs. Smythe-Smith snarled. She was shaking with fury, and the expression on Iris's face told Richard that she had never seen her mother thus.

Iris stepped back, hugging her arms to her body. Richard wanted to comfort her, but he knew her mother would fly into a rage if he took even one step in her direction.

"Of all my daughters," Mrs. Smythe-Smith said in a furious whisper, "you are the last one I would have thought might do something like this."

Iris looked away.

"I am so ashamed of you."

"Of me?" Iris said in a small voice.

Richard took a menacing step forward. "I said your daughter is blameless."

"Of course she is not blameless," Mrs. Smythe-Smith snapped. "Was she alone with you? She knows better than that."

"I was in the middle of a marriage proposal."

"May I assume you have not yet requested a private meeting with Mr. Smythe-Smith to obtain his consent?"

"I thought to do your daughter the honor of asking *her*, first."

Mrs. Smythe-Smith's mouth pressed together in an angry line, but she did not respond. Instead she looked vaguely in Iris's direction and let out a frustrated "Oh, where is your father?"

"I'm sure he will be here soon, Mama," Iris replied quietly.

Richard prepared himself to jump to Iris's defense again, but her mother held her tongue. Finally, after several more minutes passed, the door to the drawing room opened, and Iris's father walked in.

Edward Smythe-Smith was not an exceptionally tall man, but he carried himself well, and Richard imagined that he had been quite athletic when he was younger. Certainly, he was still strong enough to damage a man's face, should he decide violence was appropriate.

"Maria?" he said, looking to his wife as he entered. "What the devil is going on? I received an urgent summons from Charlotte."

Mrs. Smythe-Smith wordlessly motioned to the two other inhabitants of the room.

"Sir," Richard said.

Iris looked at her hands.

Mr. Smythe-Smith did not speak.

Richard cleared his throat. "I would very much like to marry your daughter."

"If I am reading this situation correctly," Mr. Smythe-Smith said with devastating calm, "you don't have much choice in the matter."

"Nevertheless, it is what I desire."

Mr. Smythe-Smith tipped his head toward his daughter but did not look at her. "Iris?"

"He did ask me, Father." She cleared her throat. "Before . . ."

"Before *what*?"

"Before Aunt Charlotte . . . saw . . ."

Richard took a breath, trying to hold himself back. Iris was miserable; she could not even finish her sentence. Couldn't her father see this? She did not deserve such an interrogation, and yet Richard instinctively knew that if he were to intercede, he would only make it worse.

But he could not do nothing. "Iris," he said softly, hoping she would hear his support in his voice. If she needed him, he would take over.

"Sir Richard asked me to marry him," Iris said resolutely. But she didn't look at him. She did not even flick her eyes in his direction.

"And what," her father asked, "was your reply?"

"I—I had not yet made one."

"What was your reply going to be?"

Iris swallowed, clearly uncomfortable with all eyes on her. "I would have said yes."

Richard felt his head jerk. Why was she lying? She had told him she needed more time.

"Then it is settled," Mr. Smythe-Smith said. "It

is not how I would have liked to have seen it come about, but she is of age, she wants to marry you, and indeed, she must." He looked to his wife. "I assume we will need a speedy wedding."

Mrs. Smythe-Smith nodded, letting out a relieved breath. "It is perhaps not so dire. I believe Charlotte has the gossip under control."

"Gossip is never under control."

Richard could only agree with that.

"Still," Mrs. Smythe-Smith persisted, "it is not as dire as it could be. We can still give her a proper wedding. It will look better if it is not so rushed."

"Very well." Mr. Smythe-Smith turned to Richard. "You may marry her in two months' time."

Two months? No. That would not do.

"Sir, I cannot wait two months," Richard said quickly.

Iris's father's brows slowly rose.

"I am needed back at my estate."

"You should have considered this before you compromised my daughter."

Richard wracked his brain for the best excuse, the one that would most likely give Mr. Smythe-Smith reason to relent. "I am the sole guardian of my two younger sisters, sir. I would be remiss if I did not soon return."

"I believe you spent several seasons in town a few years back," Mr. Smythe-Smith countered. "Who had charge of your sisters, then?"

"They lived with our aunt. I lacked the maturity to properly fulfill my duties."

"Forgive me if I doubt your maturity now."

Richard forced himself to hold silent. If he had

a daughter, he would be just as livid. He thought of his own father, wondered what he would think of this night's work. Bernard Kenworthy had loved his family—Richard had never doubted that—but his approach to fatherhood could best be described as benign neglect. If he were alive, what would he have done? Anything?

But Richard was not his father. He could not tolerate inaction.

"Two months will be perfectly acceptable," Iris's mother said. "There is no reason you cannot go to your estate and then return for the wedding. To be honest, I would prefer it that way."

"I wouldn't," Iris said.

Her parents looked at her in shock.

"Well, I wouldn't." She swallowed, and Richard's heart ached at the tension he saw in her small frame. "If the decision is made," she said, "I would rather move forward."

Her mother took a step toward her. "Your reputation—"

"—might very well already be in tatters. If that's the case, I would much rather be in Yorkshire where I don't know anyone."

"Nonsense," her mother said dismissively. "We will wait to see what happens."

Iris met her mother's eyes with a remarkably steely gaze. "Have I no say in the matter?"

Her mother's lips trembled, and she looked to her husband.

"It shall be as she wishes," he said after a pause. "I can see no reason to force her to wait. The Lord knows she and Daisy will be at each other's throats the entire time." Mr. Smythe-Smith turned to Richard. "Iris is not pleasant to live with when she is in ill humor."

"Father!"

He ignored her. "And Daisy is not pleasant to live with when she is in good humor. The planning of a wedding will make this one"—he jerked his head toward Iris—"miserable and the other one ecstatic. I should have to move to France."

Richard did not so much as smile. Mr. Smythe-Smith's humor was of the bitterest sort and did not want laughter.

"Iris," the older gentleman said. "Maria."

They followed him to the door.

"I shall see you in two days' time," Iris's father said to Richard. "I expect you will have a special license and settlements prepared."

"I would do no less, sir."

As she left the room, Iris looked over her shoulder, and their eyes met.

Why? she seemed to ask him. *Why?*

In that moment, he realized she knew. She knew that he had not been overcome with passion, that this forced marriage had been—albeit poorly—orchestrated.

Richard had never felt so ashamed.

Chapter Eight

The following week

Iris woke up to thunder on the morning of her wedding, and by the time her maid arrived with breakfast, London was awash with rain.

She walked to her window and peered out, letting her forehead rest against the cool glass. Her wedding was in three hours. Maybe the weather would clear by then. There was an odd little patch of blue off in the distant sky. It looked lonely. Out of place.

But hopeful.

It didn't really matter, she supposed. She wasn't going to get wet. The ceremony was to be held by special license in her family's drawing room. Her

journey to marriage consisted of two corridors
and a flight of stairs.

She did hope that the roads would not be
washed-out. She and Sir Richard were due to
depart for Yorkshire that very afternoon. And
while Iris was understandably nervous about leaving her home and all that was familiar to her, she'd
heard enough of wedding nights to know that she
did *not* wish to spend hers under her parents' roof.

Sir Richard did not maintain a home in London,
she had discovered, and his rented apartments
were not suitable for a new bride. He wanted to
take her home, to Maycliffe Park, where she would
meet his sisters.

A nervous laugh bubbled through her throat.
Sisters. It figured he'd have sisters. If there was
one thing in her life that had never been lacking,
it was sisters.

A knock on her door jolted her from her
thoughts, and after Iris bid her enter, her mother
came into the room.

"Did you sleep well?" Mrs. Smythe-Smith asked.

"Not really."

"I would be surprised if you had. It does not
matter how well she knows her groom. A bride is
always apprehensive."

Iris rather thought that it *did* matter how well
a bride knew her groom. Certainly she'd be less
nervous—or at least nervous in a different way—
if she'd known her intended for more than a fortnight.

But she did not say this to her mother, because
she and her mother did not talk about such things.

They spoke of minutiae and the events of the day, of music and sometimes of books, and most of all, of her sisters and cousins and all their babies. But they did not speak of feelings. That was not their way.

And yet Iris knew she was loved. Her mother might not be the sort to say the words or visit her room with a cup of tea and a smile, but she loved her children with all the fierceness in her heart. Iris had never doubted that, not for a moment.

Mrs. Smythe-Smith sat on the end of Iris's bed and motioned for her to come over. "I do wish you had a lady's maid for your journey," she said. "It's not at all how it should be."

Iris stifled a laugh at the absurdity of it all. After everything that had happened in the past week, it was the lack of a *lady's maid* that was not how it should be?

"You've never been good with hair," her mother said. "To have to dress it yourself . . ."

"I will be just fine, Mama," Iris said. She and Daisy shared a lady's maid, and when given the choice, the young woman had opted to remain in London. Iris thought it prudent to wait to hire a new maid in Yorkshire. It would make her seem less of an outsider in her new home. Hopefully it would make her *feel* less of an outsider, too.

She climbed back onto her bed and leaned against the pillows. She felt very young, sitting here like this. She could not recall the last time her mother had come into her bedchamber and sat upon her bed.

"I have taught you everything you need to

know to properly manage a house," her mother said.

Iris nodded.

"You will be in the country, so that will be a change, but the principles of management will be the same. Your relationship with the house-keeper will be of the utmost importance. If she does not respect you, no one will. She need not *fear* you—"

Iris glanced down at her lap, hiding her some-what panicked amusement. The thought of any-one's fearing her was ludicrous.

"—but she must respect your authority," Mrs. Smythe-Smith concluded. "Iris? Are you listening?"

Iris looked up. "Of course. I'm sorry." She managed a small smile. "I don't think Maycliffe Park is terribly grand. Sir Richard has described it to me. I'm sure there will be much to learn, but I believe I will be up to the task."

Her mother patted her hand. "Of course you will."

There was an oddly awkward moment of silence, then Iris's mother said, "What sort of house is it, Maycliffe? Elizabethan? Medieval? Are the grounds extensive?"

"Late medieval," Iris replied. "Sir Richard said it was built in the fifteenth century, although there have been several alterations over the years."

"And the gardens?"

"I'm not sure," Iris said in slow, careful tones. She was certain her mother had not come to her room to discuss the architecture and landscaping of Maycliffe Park.

"Of course."

Of course? Iris was mystified.

"I hope it will be comfortable," her mother said crisply.

"I'm sure I shall want for nothing."

"It will be cold, I imagine. The winters in the north . . ." Mrs. Smythe-Smith gave a little shake. "I couldn't bear it. You shall have to take the servants in hand to make sure all the fires are—"

"Mother," Iris finally interrupted.

Her mother halted her rambling.

"I know you did not come here to talk about Maycliffe."

"No." Mrs. Smythe-Smith took a breath. "No, I did not."

Iris waited patiently while her mother fidgeted in a most uncharacteristic manner, plucking at the light blue counterpane and tapping her fingers. Finally, she looked up, met Iris's eyes dead on, and said, "You are aware that a man's body is not . . . the same as woman's."

Iris's lips parted with surprise. She had been expecting this discussion, but my, that was blunt.

"Iris?"

"Yes," she said quickly. "Yes, of course. I am aware."

"These differences are what makes procreation possible."

Iris almost said, "I see," except she was fairly certain she didn't. At least, not as much as she would need to.

"Your husband will . . ." Mrs. Smythe-Smith let out a frustrated breath. Iris did not think she had ever seen her mother so discomposed.

"What he will do . . ."

Iris waited.

"He will . . ." Mrs. Smythe-Smith paused, and both of her hands spread in front of her like starfish, almost as if she were steadying herself against thin air. "He will place that part of him that is different inside you."

"In"—Iris didn't seem quite able to get the word out—"side?"

Her mother's cheeks flushed to an improbable shade of pink. "His part that is different goes in *your* part that is different. That is how his seed enters your body."

Iris tried to visualize this. She knew what a man looked like. The statues she had seen had not always utilized a fig leaf. But what her mother described seemed most awkward. Surely God, in his infinite wisdom, would have designed a more efficient means of procreation.

Still, she had no reason to doubt her mother. She frowned, then asked, "Does it hurt?"

Mrs. Smythe-Smith's expression grew serious. "I will not lie to you. It is not particularly comfortable, and it does hurt a great deal the first time. But after that it gets easier, I promise. I find it helps to keep one's mind occupied. I usually go over the household accounts."

Iris had no idea what to say to that. Her cousins had never been so explicit when speaking of their wifely duties, but never had she got the impression they might be using the time to do sums in their heads. "Will I need to do this often?" she asked.

Her mother sighed. "You might. It really depends."

"On what?"

Her mother sighed again, but this one was through clenched teeth. She had not wished for further questions, that much was clear. "Most women do not conceive the first time. And even if you do, you won't know right away."

"I won't?"

This time her mother positively groaned. "You will know you are with child when your courses stop."

Her courses would stop? Well, *that* would be a benefit.

"And besides that," her mother continued, "gentlemen find pleasure in the act that ladies do not." She cleared her throat uncomfortably. "Depending on your husband's appetites—"

"Appetites?" There would be *food*?

"*Please* stop interrupting me," her mother practically begged.

Iris closed her mouth instantly. Her mother never begged.

"What I am trying to say," Mrs. Smythe-Smith said in a tight voice, "is that your husband will likely wish to lie with you a great deal. At least in the early days of your marriage."

Iris swallowed. "I see."

"Well," her mother said briskly. She practically jolted to her feet. "We have much to do today."

Iris nodded. The conversation was clearly over.

"Your sisters will wish to help you dress, I'm sure."

Iris gave a wobbly smile. It would be nice to have them all in one place. Rose lived the farthest away, in the west of Gloucestershire, but even with only a few days' notice, she had had plenty of time to make it to London for the wedding.

Yorkshire was so much farther away than Gloucestershire.

Her mother departed, but not five minutes later there was another knock on the door.

"Enter," Iris called out wearily.

It was Sarah, wearing a furtive expression and her best morning frock. "Oh, thank goodness, you're alone."

Iris immediately perked up. "What is it?"

Sarah glanced back into the hall and then shut the door behind her. "Has your mother been in to see you?"

Iris groaned.

"So she has."

"I would rather not talk about it."

"No, that's why I'm here. Well, not to talk about your mother's advice. I'm sure I don't want to know what she said. If it was anything like my mother . . ." Sarah shuddered, then got hold of herself. "Listen to me. Whatever your mother told you about your relations with your husband, ignore it."

"Everything?" Iris asked doubtfully. "She can't have been *completely* wrong."

Sarah let out a little laugh and came to sit by her on the bed. "No, of course not. She does have six children. What I mean is . . . well, did she tell you it was dreadful?"

"Not in so many words, but it did sound rather awkward."

"I'm sure it can be, if you don't love your husband."

"I don't love my husband," Iris said plainly.

Sarah sighed, and her voice lost some of its authority. "Do you at least like him?"

"Yes, of course." Iris thought about the man who would, in just a few short hours, be her husband. She might not be able to say that she loved him, but to be fair, there was nothing really *wrong* with him. He had a lovely smile, and thus far, he had treated her with the utmost respect. But she hardly knew him. "I might grow to love him," she said, wishing she spoke with more authority. "I hope I do."

"Well, that's a start." Sarah pressed her lips together in thought. "He seems to like you, too."

"I'm fairly certain he does," Iris replied. Then, in quite a different tone, she added, "Unless he is a spectacular liar."

"What does that mean?"

"Nothing," Iris said quickly. She wished she hadn't spoken. Her cousin knew why the marriage was taking place in such a hurry—the whole family did—but no one knew the truth behind Sir Richard's proposal.

Even Iris.

She sighed. It was better if everyone thought it had been a romantic declaration of love. Or at least that he'd thought the whole thing through and decided they were well matched. But not this . . . this . . .

Iris didn't know how to explain it, even to herself. She just wished she could shake this nagging suspicion that something was not quite right.

"Iris?"

"Sorry." Iris gave her head a little shake. "I've been somewhat distracted lately."

"I should think so," Sarah replied, seemingly accepting that explanation. "Still, I have spoken to Sir Richard only a few times, but he seems to be a kind man, and I think he will treat you well."

"Sarah," Iris began, "if your intent was to ease my apprehension, I must tell you that you are failing miserably."

Sarah made a rather amusingly frustrated sound and clasped her head in her hands. "Just listen to me," she said. "And trust me. Do you trust me?"

"Not really."

Sarah's expression was beyond comical.

"I'm joking," Iris said with a smile. "Please, I must be allowed my share of humor on my wedding day. Especially after that conversation with my mother."

"Just remember," Sarah said, reaching forward to take Iris's hand. "It can be lovely, what happens between a husband and wife."

Iris's expression must have been dubious, because Sarah added, "It's very special. Truly, it is."

"Did someone tell you of this before your wedding?" Iris asked. "After your mother spoke to you? Is that why you thought to come and tell me this?"

To Iris's great surprise, Sarah flushed a deep pink. "Hugh and I . . . ah . . . we might have . . ."

"Sarah!"

"Shocking, I know. But it was wonderful, truly, and I could not help myself."

Iris was stunned. She knew that Sarah had always been a freer spirit than she was, but she never would have dreamed that she would have given herself to Hugh before marriage.

"Listen," Sarah said, squeezing Iris's hand. "It does not matter if Hugh and I anticipated our vows. We are married now, and I love my husband, and he loves me."

"I don't judge you," Iris said, although she had a feeling she did, maybe a little bit.

Sarah regarded her with a frank expression. "Has Sir Richard kissed you?"

Iris nodded.

"Did you like it? No, don't answer, I can tell from your face that you did."

Not for the first time Iris cursed her fair skin. There wasn't a person in England who blushed with as much vigor and depth as she did.

Sarah patted her hand. "That's a good sign. If his kisses are lovely, then the rest will most likely be, too."

"This has been the strangest morning of my life," Iris said weakly.

"It's about to get stranger"—Sarah stood and gave Iris an exaggerated tip of the head—"*Lady Kenworthy.*"

Iris threw a pillow at her.

"I must away," Sarah said. "Your sisters will be here at any moment to help you get ready." She moved to the door and placed her hand on the knob, glancing back at her cousin with a smile.

"Sarah!" Iris called out, before she could exit the room.

Sarah tilted her head in question.

Iris gazed at her cousin, and for the first time in her life, realized just how much she loved her. "Thank you."

SEVERAL HOURS LATER, Iris was Lady Kenworthy in truth. She had stood before a man of God, and she had said the words that would bind her to Sir Richard for life.

He was still such a mystery. He had continued to court her during the brief time between her compromise and the wedding, and she could not say that he was anything but charming. But she still could not bring herself to trust in him without reservation.

She did like him. She liked him very much. He had a wicked sense of humor, ideally matched to her own, and if pressed, she would have said that she believed him to be a man of good moral fiber and principles.

But it wasn't so much of a belief as it was a supposition, or in truth, just a hope. Her gut told her all would be well, but she didn't really like to trust her gut. She was far too practical for that. She preferred tangibility; she desired proof.

Their courtship had not made *sense.* She simply could not get past that.

"We must make our farewells," her husband— *her husband*!—said to her shortly after the wedding breakfast. The celebration, like the ceremony, had been simple, although not precisely small. The size of Iris's family had made that impossible.

Iris had passed through the events of the day

in a daze, nodding and smiling at what she hoped were the correct moments. Cousin after cousin stepped forth to congratulate her, but with every kiss on the cheek and pat on the hand, she could only think that she was one moment closer to stepping into Sir Richard's carriage and riding away.

Now that time had come.

He handed her up, and she took a seat facing front. It was a nice carriage, well-appointed and comfortable. She hoped it was well sprung; according to her husband it was a four-day journey to Maycliffe Park.

A moment after she was settled, Sir Richard entered the carriage. He gave her a smile, then sat opposite her.

Iris peeked out the window at her family, gathered together in front of her home. No, not her home. Not any longer. She felt the mortifying prick of tears in her eyes and dug hastily in her beaded reticule for a handkerchief. She barely had her bag open, however, before Sir Richard leaned forward, proffering his own.

There was no point in denying her tearfulness, Iris supposed as she took the handkerchief. He could see her well enough. "I'm sorry," she said as she dabbed her eyes. Brides weren't meant to cry on their wedding days. Surely it could not portend anything good.

"You have nothing for which to apologize," Sir Richard said kindly. "I know this has all been quite an upheaval."

She gave him the best smile she could manage, which wasn't much of one, really. "I was just thinking . . ." She motioned to the window. The carriage had not yet begun to move, and if she tilted her head just so, she could see what had once been her bedroom window. "It's no longer my home."

"I hope you will like Maycliffe."

"I'm sure I will. Your descriptions are lovely." He had told her of the grand staircase and secret passageways. A room where King James I had slept. There was an herb garden near the kitchen and an orangery in the back. It wasn't attached to the house, though, and he'd told her that he'd long thought of connecting them.

"I shall do my best to make you happy," he said.

She appreciated that he said that here, where they had no audience. "As shall I."

The carriage began to move, its pace slow in the congested streets of London.

"How long shall we travel today?" Iris asked.

"About six hours in total, if the roads were not too affected by this morning's rain."

"Not such a long day."

He smiled in agreement. "This close to town there are plenty of opportunities to take a rest, should you need one."

"Thank you."

It was by far the most polite, proper, and boring conversation they had ever had. Ironic, that.

"Do you mind if I read?" Iris asked, reaching into her reticule for a book.

"Not at all. I envy you, as a matter of fact. I am wholly unable to read in a moving carriage."

"Even when you are facing forward?" She bit

her lip. Good heavens, what was she saying? He would construe that to mean she wished for him to come sit next to her.

Which was not what she was saying at all.

Not that she would *mind*.

Which wasn't to say that she desired it.

She was completely indifferent. Really. She did not care one way or another where he chose to sit.

"It matters not which way I am facing," Sir Richard answered, reminding Iris that she had indeed asked him a question. "I find that staring out the window at a far-off spot often helps."

"My mother says the same thing," Iris agreed. "She, too, has difficulty reading in carriages."

"I usually just ride alongside," he said with a shrug. "It's easier all the way around."

"Did you not wish to do so today?" Oh, blast. Now he would think she was trying to boot him from the carriage. Which was *also* not what she was saying.

"I might later on," he told her. "In town we move slowly enough that I'm not affected."

She cleared her throat. "Right. Well, I'll just read now, if you don't mind."

"Please."

She opened her book and began to read. In a closed carriage. Alone with her new handsome husband. She read a book.

She had a feeling this was not the most romantic way to begin a marriage.

But then again, what did she know?

Chapter Nine

IT WAS NEARLY eight in the evening when they finally stopped for the day. Iris had been alone in the carriage for some time. They had made one brief stop so that everyone could see to their needs, and upon the resumption of their journey, Sir Richard had elected to ride alongside the vehicle. Iris told herself she did not feel slighted. He suffered from motion sickness; she did not wish him to become ill on their wedding day.

But it did mean she was left alone, and as the evening wore on, and the light grew dimmer, she could not even escape into the pages of her book. Now that they had left London behind, their pace was swifter, and the horses fell into a steady, soothing rhythm. She must have fallen asleep, because one moment she was somewhere in Buckinghamshire, and the next someone was gently shaking her shoulder and calling her name.

"Iris? Iris?"

"Mmmbrgh." She never had woken up well.

"Iris, we've arrived."

She blinked a few times until her husband's face came into focus in the dim evening light. "Sir Richard?"

He smiled indulgently. "I should think you might be able to dispense with the 'Sir.'"

"Mmmmfh. Yes." She yawned, shaking out her hand, which had fallen asleep. Her foot, too, she realized. "All right."

He watched her with visible amusement. "Do you always wake so slowly?"

"No." She pulled herself into a sitting position. At some point during the ride she'd slumped completely onto her side. "Sometimes I'm slower."

He chuckled at that. "I shall take that under advisement. No important meetings for Lady Kenworthy before noon."

Lady Kenworthy. She wondered how long it would take to grow used to it.

"I can usually be relied upon to be coherent by eleven," Iris returned. "Although I must say, the best part of being married is going to be having my breakfast in bed."

"The best part?"

She blushed, and the sudden import of her words finally woke her up. "I'm sorry," she said quickly. "That was thoughtless—"

"Think nothing of it," he cut in, and she breathed a sigh of relief. Her husband was not one to take ready insult. A very good thing that was, as Iris was not always one to consider her words before she spoke them.

"Shall we go?" Richard asked.

"Yes, of course."

He hopped down and held out his hand. "Lady Kenworthy."

That was twice he'd called her by her new name in the same number of minutes. She knew that many gentlemen did such a thing in the early days of marriage as a sign of endearment, but it made her uncomfortable. He meant well, she knew, but it only served to remind her how very much her life had changed in the space of a week.

Still, she must try to make the best of her situation, and that started with making pleasant conversation. "Have you stayed here before?" she asked as she accepted his hand.

"Yes, I—Whoa!"

Iris wasn't quite sure how it happened—maybe she hadn't managed to shake all of the pins and needles from her foot—but she slipped on the carriage step, and she let out a startled cry as her stomach lurched up against her heart, which returned the favor by launching into a full sprint.

And then, before she could even try to catch her balance, she was caught by Richard, who held her securely as he set her down.

"Goodness," she said, glad to have her feet firmly on the ground. She placed one hand on her heart, trying to calm herself.

"Are you all right?" He did not seem to notice that his hands were still on her waist.

"Quite well," she whispered. Why was she whispering? "Thank you."

"Good." He gazed down at her. "I shouldn't want . . ."

His words trailed off, and for a heavy second they stared into each other's eyes. It was the strangest, warmest sensation, and when he stepped abruptly away, Iris felt off-balance and out of sorts.

"I shouldn't want you to injure yourself." He cleared his throat. "Is what I meant to say."

"Thank you." She glanced over at the inn, its hive of activity a stark contrast to the two of them, who were still as statues. "You were saying something," she prompted. "About the inn?"

He stared at her with a blank expression.

"I had asked if you had stayed here before," she reminded him.

"Many times," he answered, but he still seemed distracted. She waited a moment, pretending to straighten her gloves, until he cleared his throat and said, "It's a three-day journey to Maycliffe, there's no getting around that. I always stay at the same two inns on the journey north."

"And on the journey south?" she quipped.

He blinked, his brow furrowed with either confusion or disdain. Honestly, she could not be sure which.

"It was a joke," she started to say, since it only stood to reason that he'd have to take the same route to London as from. But she cut herself off after two words, and just said, "Never mind."

His eyes remained on her face for a penetratingly long moment, then he held out his arm, and said, "Come."

She looked up at the festively painted sign that hung from the inn. *The Dusty Goose.* Really? She was to spend her wedding night in a coaching inn called *The Dusty Goose*?

"I trust it meets with your satisfaction?" Richard asked politely as he led her inside.

"Of course." Not that she could or would have said anything else. She looked about. It was a charming spot, actually, with diamond-crossed Tudor windows and fresh flowers at the desk.

"Ah, Sir Richard!" exclaimed the innkeeper, bustling over to greet them. "You made very good time."

"The roads held up well despite this morning's rain," Richard said congenially. "It was a most pleasant journey."

"I expect that is more due to the company than the roads," the innkeeper said with a knowing smile. "I wish you joy."

Richard tilted his head toward the innkeeper in salute, then said, "Allow me to introduce my new wife, Lady Kenworthy. Lady Kenworthy, this is Mr. Fogg, esteemed proprietor of the Dusty Goose."

"I am honored to meet you, ma'am," Mr. Fogg said. "Your husband is our favorite guest."

Richard gave him a half smile. "A frequent one, at least."

"Your inn is lovely," Iris said. "I see no dust, however."

Mr. Fogg grinned. "We do our best to keep the geese outside."

Iris laughed, and was dearly grateful for it. The sound had become almost unfamiliar.

"Shall I show you to your rooms?" the innkeeper asked. "Mrs. Fogg has prepared supper for you. Her very best roast, with cheese, potatoes, and Yorkshire puddings. I can have it served in the private dining room whenever you wish."

Iris smiled her thanks and followed Mr. Fogg up the stairs.

"Here we are, my lady," he said, opening a door at the far end of the hall. "It is our finest chamber."

It was indeed very fine for a coaching inn, Iris thought, with a large four-poster bed and a window facing south.

"We have but two rooms with private washing chambers," Mr. Fogg continued, "but, of course, we have saved this one for you." He opened another door, displaying a small windowless room with a chamber pot and a copper tub. "One of our maids will draw you a hot bath, should you wish it."

"I will let you know, thank you," Iris said. She wasn't sure why she was so eager to make a good impression on an innkeeper of all people, except that her husband seemed quite fond of him. And, of course, there was no reason to be rude to someone who was so clearly going out of his way to please her.

Mr. Fogg bowed. "Very well. I shall leave you, ma'am. I am sure you wish to rest after your journey. Sir Richard?"

Iris blinked in confusion as he led Richard to the door.

"You're just across the hall," Mr. Fogg continued.

"Very good," Richard said.

"You're—" Iris caught herself before she blurted something embarrassing. Her husband had reserved separate rooms for their wedding night?

"Ma'am?" Mr. Fogg asked, turning back to her in question.

"It's nothing," Iris said quickly. There was no way she was going to let on that she had been surprised by the sleeping arrangements.

Surprised and . . . And relieved. And maybe a little bit hurt, too.

"If you will just open my room for me," Richard said to Mr. Fogg, "I can make my way there myself. In the meantime, I would like a private word with my wife."

The innkeeper bowed and took his leave.

"Iris," Richard said.

She didn't turn toward him, exactly, but she did glance in his direction. And tried to smile.

"I would not do you the dishonor of demanding a wedding night at a roadside inn," he said in a stiff voice.

"I see."

He seemed to be waiting for a lengthier reply, so she added, "That is very considerate of you."

He was silent for a moment, his right hand tapping awkwardly against his thigh. "You have been rushed into this."

"Nonsense," she said crisply, forcing a touch of levity into her voice. "I have known you all of two weeks. I can name half a dozen marriages that have been forged on slighter acquaintances."

He lifted a brow. A very sardonic one, and not for the first time Iris wished she weren't so bloody pale. Even if she could raise a single brow, no one would be able to see it.

He bowed. "I will take my leave."

She turned away, pretending to fuss with something in her reticule. "Please."

There was another uncomfortable silence.

"I shall see you for supper?" he inquired.

"Of course." She had to eat, didn't she?

"Will a quarter of an hour suffice?" His voice was scrupulously polite.

She nodded, even though she was not facing him. He could discern the movement, she was sure. And she no longer trusted her voice.

"I shall knock before I go down," he said, and then she heard the door click behind him.

Iris held herself still, not even breathing. She wasn't sure why. Perhaps some part of her needed for him to be away, farther away than a simple click of the door. She needed him to cross the hall, enter his own chamber, close that door behind him.

She needed all of that between them.

And then she could cry.

RICHARD CLOSED IRIS'S door, walked carefully across the hall, opened his own door, shut it, locked it, and then let out a stream of invective so fluent, so spectacularly creative that it was a wonder lightning did not smite the entire Dusty Goose on the spot.

What the *hell* was he going to do?

Everything had been going to plan. Everything. He'd met Iris, he'd got her to marry him, and they were on their way north. He hadn't exactly told her everything yet—very well, he hadn't really told her much of anything yet, but he'd never planned to do so until they arrived at Maycliffe and met his sisters, anyway.

That he'd found a wife who was so intelligent and agreeable was a relief. That she was attractive was a lovely bonus. He had not, however, anticipated that he would want her.

Not like this.

He'd kissed her in London, and he'd quite liked it—enough to know that bedding her would be no hardship. But enjoyable as the experience was, he'd had no difficulty stopping when the time came. His pulse had quickened, and he'd felt the first stirrings of desire, but it had been nothing that was not easily tamed.

Then Iris had tripped while exiting the carriage. He'd caught her, of course. He was a gentleman; it was instinct. He would have done so for any lady.

But when he touched her, when his hands settled on the curve of her small waist, and her body slid along his as he lowered her to the ground . . .

Something inside of him had caught fire.

He did not know what had changed. Was it something primitive, something deep in the heart of him that now knew she was his?

He'd felt like an idiot, stunned and frozen, unable to remove his hands from her hips. His blood pounded through his veins, and his heart beat so loudly he could not believe she did not hear it. And all he could think was—

I want her.

And it wasn't just the usual *I-haven't-been-with-a-woman-in-a-few-months* sort of want. It was electric, an instant bolt of desire so strong it stole the breath from his body.

He'd wanted to tilt her face toward his and kiss her until she was gasping with need.

He'd wanted to cup his hands on her bottom and squeeze and lift until she had no choice but to wrap her legs around him.

And then he'd wanted to push her back against a tree and *own* her.

Good Lord. He wanted his wife. And he couldn't have her.

Not yet.

Richard swore again as he wrenched off his coat and flung himself onto his bed. Damn! He did not need such a complication. He was going to have to tell her to lock her bloody door when they took up residence at Maycliffe.

He swore yet again. He didn't even know if there was a lock on the connecting door between the master's and mistress's bedrooms.

He'd have to install one.

No, that would cause talk. Who the hell *added* a lock to a connecting bedroom door?

Not to mention Iris's feelings. He had seen in her eyes that she'd been surprised that he did not plan to visit her on their wedding night. He was quite certain she was at least somewhat relieved—he did not flatter himself that she had fallen desperately in love with him in so short a time. Even if she had, she was hardly the sort to approach the marriage bed without trepidation.

But she was also hurt. He had seen that, too, despite her attempts to hide it. And why shouldn't she be? For all she could tell, her husband did not find her appealing enough to take to bed on their wedding night.

He let out a grim laugh. Nothing could have been further from the truth. God only knew how long it was going to take for his traitorous body to settle down enough to escort her to supper.

Oh yes, that would be genteel. *Here, take my arm, but do ignore my raging erection.*

Someone really needed to invent a better pair of breeches.

He lay on his back, thinking unamorous thoughts. Anything to direct his mind to something other than the delicate flare of his wife's hip. Or the soft pink of her lips. It was a color that would have been ordinary on anyone else, but against Iris's pale skin . . .

He swore. Again. This was *not* the way this was supposed to go. Bad thoughts, unappealing thoughts . . . Let's see, there was that time he'd got food poisoning at Eton. Very bad fish, that was. Salmon? No, pike. He'd vomited for days. Oh, and the pond at Maycliffe. It would be cold this time of year. Very cold. Balls-numbingly cold.

Bird-watching, Latin conjugation, his great-aunt Gladys (God rest her soul). Spiders, soured milk, plague.

Bubonic plague.

Bubonic plague on his cold, numb . . .

That did the trick.

He checked his pocket watch. Ten minutes had passed. Possibly eleven. Certainly enough time to warrant hauling his pathetic self off the bed and making himself presentable.

With a groan, Richard pulled his coat back on. He should probably change for supper, but surely such rules could be relaxed while traveling. And besides, he'd already told his valet that he would not need his services until he retired for the evening. He hoped Iris had not thought she must don a more formal gown. It had not occurred to him to tell her so.

At precisely the correct time, he rapped upon her door. She opened it immediately.

"You did not change," he blurted out. Like an idiot.

Her eyes widened as if she feared she had made an error. "Was I meant to?"

"No, no. I'd meant to tell you not to bother." He cleared his throat. "But I forgot."

"Oh." She smiled. Awkwardly. "Well, I didn't. Change, that is."

"I see."

Richard made a note to compliment himself on his sparkling wit.

She stood there.

So did he.

"I brought a shawl," she said.

"Good idea."

"I thought it might get cold."

"It might."

"Yes, that's what I thought."

He stood there.

So did she.

"We should eat," he said suddenly, holding out his arm. It was dangerous to touch her, even under such innocent circumstances, but he was going to have to get used to it. He could hardly refuse to offer her his escort for the next however many months.

He really needed to find out how many months. *Exactly* how many months.

"Mr. Fogg was not exaggerating about his wife's roast," he said, struggling for something utterly innocuous. "She is a splendid cook."

He might have imagined it, but he thought Iris looked relieved that he had initiated a bit of ordinary conversation. "That will be lovely," she said. "I'm quite hungry."

"Did you not eat in the carriage?"

She shook her head. "I meant to, but I fell asleep."

"I'm sorry I was not there to entertain you." He bit his tongue. He knew exactly how he'd have liked to entertain her, even if she was innocent of such activities.

"Don't be silly. You do not do well in carriages."

True. But then again, he had never taken a long carriage ride with *her*.

"I imagine you will wish to ride alongside the carriage again tomorrow?" she asked.

"I think it would be best." *For so many reasons*.

She nodded. "I might have to find another book to read. I'm afraid I shall finish this one up rather more quickly than expected."

They reached the door to the private dining room, and Richard stepped forward so that he might open it for her. "What are you reading?" he asked.

"Another book by Miss Austen. *Mansfield Park*."

He held out her chair. "I am not familiar with it. I do not think my sister has read it."

"It is not as romantic as her others."

"Ah. That explains it. Fleur would not like it, then."

"Is your sister such a romantic?"

Richard started to open his mouth, then paused. How to describe Fleur? She was not exactly his favorite person these days. "I think she is, yes," he finally said.

Iris seemed amused by this. "You *think*?"

He felt himself smile, sheepishly. "It's not the sort of thing she discusses with her brother. Romance, I mean."

"No, I suppose not." She shrugged and stabbed a potato with her fork. "I certainly would not discuss it with mine."

"You have a brother?"

She gave him a startled look. "Of course."

Damn, he should have known that. What sort of man did not know that his wife had a brother?

"John," she said. "He's the youngest."

This was even more of a surprise. "You have a brother named *John*?"

At that she laughed. "Shocking, I know. He should have been a Florian. Or a Basil. It's really not fair."

"What about William?" he suggested. "For Sweet William?"

"That would have been even more cruel. To have a flower's name and still be so utterly normal."

"Oh, come now. Iris isn't Mary or Jane, but it isn't *so* uncommon."

"It's not that," she said. "It's that there are five of us. What is common and ordinary becomes awful in bulk." She looked down at her food, her eyes dancing with amusement.

"What?" he asked. He had to know what was causing such a delightful expression.

She shook her head, her lips pressed together, obviously trying not to laugh.

"Tell me. I insist."

She leaned forward, as if imparting a great secret. "If John had been a girl, he would have been called Hydrangea."

"Good God."

"I know. My brother is a lucky, lucky boy."

Richard chuckled, then suddenly realized that they had been talking quite comfortably for several minutes. More than comfortably—really, she was quite good company, his new wife. Maybe this would all work out. He just had to get past this first hurdle . . .

"Why was your brother absent from the wedding?" he asked her.

She didn't bother to look up from her food as she answered. "He is still at Eton. My parents did not think he should be removed from school for such a small celebration."

"But all of your cousins were there."

"*You* had no family in attendance," she countered.

There were reasons for that, but he wasn't prepared to go into them now.

"And at any rate," Iris continued, "that wasn't *all* of my cousins."

"Good Lord, how many of you are there?"

Her lips pinched together. She was trying not to smile. "I have thirty-four first cousins."

He stared at her. It was an incomprehensible number.

"And five siblings," she added.

"That is . . . remarkable."

She shrugged. He supposed it didn't seem so remarkable if it was all she had known. "My father was one of eight," she said.

"Still." He speared a piece of Mrs. Fogg's famous roast beef. "I have precisely zero first cousins."

"Truly?" She looked shocked.

"My mother's older sister was widowed quite young. She had no children and no wish to remarry."

"And your father?"

"He had two siblings, but they died without issue."

"I'm so sorry."

He paused, his fork halfway to his mouth. "Why?"

"Well, because—" She stopped, her chin drawing back as she pondered her answer. "I don't know," she finally said. "I cannot imagine being so alone."

For some reason he found this amusing. "I do have two sisters."

"Of course, but—" Again, she cut herself off.

"But what?" He smiled to show her he was not offended.

"It's just so . . . *few* of you."

"I can assure you it did not feel that way when I was growing up."

"No, I imagine not."

Richard helped himself to two more of Mrs. Fogg's Yorkshire puddings. "Your home was a hive of activity, I imagine."

"Closer to a madhouse."

He laughed.

"I'm not jesting," she said. But she grinned.

"I hope you will find my two sisters an adequate substitute for yours."

She smiled and cocked her head flirtatiously to the side. "With a name like Fleur, it was predestined, don't you think?"

"Ah yes, the florals."

"Is that what they call us now?"

"Now?"

She rolled her eyes. "The Smythe-Smith bouquet, the garden girls, the hothouse flowers . . ."

"The hothouse flowers?"

"My mother was not amused."

"No, I don't imagine she was."

"It was not always 'flowers,'" she said with a bit of a wince. "I'm told that some gentlemen were fond of alliteration."

"Gentlemen?" Richard echoed doubtfully. He could come up with all sorts of things that began with H, and none of them were complimentary.

Iris speared a tiny potato with her fork. "I use the term loosely."

He watched her for a moment. At first glance, his new wife seemed wispy, almost insubstantial. She was not tall, only up to his shoulder, and rather thin. (Although not, he had discovered recently, without curves.) And then, of course, there was her remarkable coloring. But her eyes, which on first glance had seemed pale and insipid, sharpened and glowed with intelligence when she was engaged in conversation. And when she moved it became clear that her slender frame was not one of weakness and malaise but rather of strength and determination.

Iris Smythe-Smith did not glide through rooms as so many of her peers had been trained to do; when she walked, it was with direction and purpose.

And her name, he reminded himself, was not Smythe-Smith. She was Iris Kenworthy, and he was coming to realize that he had barely scratched the surface of knowing her.

Chapter Ten

Three days later

THEY WERE GETTING CLOSE.

It had been ten minutes since they'd passed through Flixton, the nearest village to Maycliffe Park. Iris tried not to look too eager—or nervous—as she watched the landscape slide by through the window. She tried to tell herself it was just a house, and if her husband's descriptions were accurate, not even a terribly grand one at that.

But it was *his* house, which meant it was now *her* house, and she desperately wished to make a good impression upon her arrival. Richard had told her there were thirteen servants in the house proper, nothing too daunting, but *then* he'd mentioned that the butler had been there since his childhood, and the housekeeper even longer, and Iris could not help but think that it did not matter that her surname was now Kenworthy—*she* was the interloper in this equation.

They would hate her. The servants would hate her, and his sisters would hate her, and if he had a dog (really, shouldn't she know if he had a dog?), it would probably hate her as well.

She could see it now, prancing up to Richard with a silly dog grin, then turning to her, fangs out and snarling.

A jolly homecoming this would be.

Richard had sent word ahead to alert the household of the approximate time of their arrival. Iris was well enough acquainted with country house life to know that a swift rider would be watching for them a few miles out. By the time their carriage arrived at Maycliffe, the entire household would be lined up to greet them.

Richard spoke of the upper servants with great affection; given his charm and amiability, Iris could only imagine that this feeling was returned in equal measure. The servants would take one look at her, and it would not matter if she was trying to be fair-minded and kind. It would not matter if she smiled at her husband and appeared happy and pleased with her new home. They would be watching her closely and would see it in her eyes. She was not in love with her husband.

And perhaps more importantly, he was not in love with her.

There would be gossip. There was always gossip

when the master of an estate married, but she was a complete unknown in Yorkshire, and given the rushed nature of the wedding, the whispers about her would be intense. Would they think she had trapped him into marriage? It could not be further from the truth, and yet—

"Do not worry."

Iris looked up at the sound of Richard's voice, thankful that he had broken the vicious cycle of her thoughts. "I'm not worried," she lied.

He quirked a brow. "Allow me to rephrase. There is no need for you to worry."

Iris folded her hands primly in her lap. "I did not think there was."

Another lie. She was getting good at this. Or maybe not. From Richard's expression, it was clear he did not believe her.

"Very well," she acceded. "I *am* a little nervous."

"Ah. Well, there probably *is* reason for that."

"Sir Richard!"

He grinned. "Sorry. I could not resist. And if you recall, I would prefer that you not call me sir. At least not when we are alone."

She tilted her head, deciding he deserved the ambiguity of such a response.

"Iris," he said, his voice gentle, "I would be a cad if I did not recognize that you have had to make all of the adjustments in our union."

Not all, Iris thought acerbically. And certainly not the biggest. In fact, one might say that a rather important part of her had not been adjusted in the least. The second night of their journey had passed much the same as the first: in separate bedchambers. Richard had repeated what he'd said before, that she did not deserve a wedding night in a dusty inn.

Never mind that the Royal Oak was every bit as spotless as the Dusty Goose had been. The same went for the Kings Arms, where they'd slept the final night of their journey. Iris knew that she should feel honored that her husband held her in such regard, that he would put her comfort and well-being above his needs, but she couldn't help wondering what had happened to the man who had kissed her so passionately at Pleinsworth House barely a week before. He had seemed so overcome by her nearness, so wholly unable to restrain himself.

And now . . . Now that they were married and he had no reason to hold his passions . . .

It made no sense.

But then again, neither had marrying her, and he'd done *that* with alacrity.

She bit her lip.

"I have asked much of you," he said.

"Not so much," she muttered.

"What was that?"

She gave her head a little shake. "Nothing."

He let out a breath, the only signal that this conversation might be even a little difficult for him. "You have moved halfway across the country," he said. "I have taken you away from all you hold dear."

Iris managed a tight smile. Was this meant to reassure her?

"But I do believe," he continued, "that we will suit very well. And I hope that you will come to view Maycliffe as home."

"Thank you," she said politely. She appreciated

that he was making such an effort to make her feel welcome, but it wasn't doing much to soothe her nerves.

"My sisters will be most eager to meet you."

Iris hoped that was true.

"I wrote to them about you," he continued.

She looked up in surprise. "When?" she asked. He would have had to have done so immediately following their engagement if the news was to reach Maycliffe before she did.

"I sent an express."

Iris nodded, even as she returned her gaze to the window. That would have done it. Express riders were dear, but well worth it if one needed a missive to arrive quickly. She wondered what he might have written about her. How might he describe his intended bride after barely a week of acquaintance? And to his sisters, no less?

She turned back, trying to observe Richard's face without being too obvious about it. He was quite intelligent, this much she'd known after less than a week of acquaintance. He was very good with people, too, far better than *she* was, that was for certain. She imagined that anything he wrote of her to his sisters would depend on *them*. He would know what they would wish to learn about her.

"You've told me almost nothing of them," she said suddenly.

He blinked.

"Your sisters."

"Oh. Haven't I?"

"No." And how strange that she was only just realizing it then. She supposed it was because she knew the most important facts—names, ages, a bit of what they looked like. But she knew absolutely nothing else, save for Fleur's fondness for *Pride and Prejudice.*

"Oh," he said again. He glanced out the window, then back to her, his movements an uncharacteristic staccato. "Well. Fleur is eighteen, Marie-Claire three years younger."

"Yes, you've said as much." Her sarcasm was subtle, and from the look on his face, it took him a few seconds to realize it.

"Fleur likes to read," he said brightly.

"Pride and Prejudice," Iris supplied.

"Yes, see?" He gave her a charming smile. "I've told you things."

"I suppose technically that is true," she said with a little nod in his direction. *"Things* being plural, and *two* being plural, and your having told me two things . . ."

His eyes narrowed, mostly with amusement. "Very well, what would you like to know?"

She hated when people asked questions like that. "Anything."

"You haven't told me anything about your siblings," he pointed out.

"You've met my siblings."

"Not your brother."

"You're not going to *live* with my brother," she retorted.

"Point taken," he acknowledged, "although one might say that any further information from me would be superfluous, as you're going to meet them in about three minutes."

"What?" Iris nearly shrieked, whipping back around to the window. Sure enough, they had left the main road and entered a long drive. The trees were thinner here than on the main road, the fields rolling gently to the horizon. It was a lovely landscape, peaceful and serene.

"It's just over the rise."

She could hear the self-satisfied smile in his voice.

"Just a moment now," he murmured.

And then she saw it. Maycliffe Park. It was bigger than she'd imagined, although certainly nothing to Fensmore or Whipple Hill. But those were homes of earls. Her cousins, but still earls of the realm.

Maycliffe had its charms, though. From the distance, it appeared to be red brick, with rather unusual Dutch gables adorning the façade. There was something almost uneven about it, but given what she knew of its history, that made sense. Richard had told her that the house had been modified and added to several times over the years.

"The family rooms face south," he told her. "You'll be glad for it in the winter."

"I don't know which way we're facing now," Iris admitted.

He smiled. "We are approaching from the west. So your rooms will be around that"—he pointed to the right—"corner."

Iris nodded without turning back to her husband. Right now she wanted to keep her attention on her new home. As they pulled closer, she saw that each gable was dotted with a small circular window. "Who has the rooms at the top?" she asked. "With the round windows?"

"It's a bit of a mix. Some are for servants. On the south, it's the nursery. My mother turned one into a reading room."

He hadn't said much about his parents, either, Iris realized. Just that they'd both passed, his mother when he was a student at Eton, his father a few years later.

But this wasn't the right time to press for more information. The carriage was coming to a stop, and sure enough, all of Maycliffe was lined up in the front drive to greet them. It did look to be more than the thirteen servants Richard had mentioned; perhaps he'd meant only those serving in the house itself. From what Iris could see there were gardeners among the group, stable-hands, too. She had never been greeted by such a complete collection of staff before; she supposed it was because she was not a guest, she was the new mistress of the estate. Why had no one warned her? She was nervous enough without feeling she had to make a good impression on the man who tended the roses.

Richard hopped down, then held a hand up for her. Iris took a deep breath and disembarked, regarding the assembled servants with what she hoped was a friendly yet confident smile.

"Mr. Cresswell," Richard said, leading toward the tall man who could only be the butler, "may I present Lady Kenworthy, the new mistress of Maycliffe Park."

Cresswell gave a stiffly proper bow. "We are delighted to have a woman's presence again here at Maycliffe."

"I am eager to learn about my new home," Iris said, using words she had practiced the night before. "I am sure I will rely upon you and Mrs. Hopkins a great deal during these first few months."

"It will be our honor to assist you, my lady."

Iris felt the terrifying knot within her begin to loosen. Cresswell sounded sincere, and surely the rest of the servants would follow his lead.

"Sir Richard tells me that you have been at Maycliffe for many years," Iris continued. "He is most fortunate to . . ."

Her words trailed off as she glanced over at her husband. His normally genial expression had been replaced by one of near rage.

"Richard?" she heard herself whisper. Whatever could have happened to upset him so?

"Where," he said to the butler, his voice as low and tightly wound as she had ever heard it, "are my sisters?"

RICHARD SEARCHED THE small crowd gathered in the drive, but really, what was the point? If his sisters were here, they would have been standing at the front, a burst of color against the black uniforms of the maids.

Damn it, they should have been out here to greet Iris. It was the worst sort of snub. Fleur and Marie-Claire might be used to having the run of the manor, but Iris was now the mistress of Maycliffe, and everyone—even those born with the surname Kenworthy—needed to get used to that.

Fast.

Furthermore, both of his sisters knew damn well how much Iris was giving up for their family. Even Iris didn't know the full extent of it.

Any extent of it, really.

Something burned through Richard's gut, and he really didn't want to determine whether it was fury or guilt.

He hoped it was fury. Because there was guilt enough already, and he had a feeling it would soon turn to acid.

"Richard," Iris said, placing a hand on his arm. "I'm sure there is a good reason for their absence." But her smile was forced.

Richard turned to Cresswell, and snapped, "Why are they not down?" There was no excuse for this. The rest of the household had had time to exit and assemble. His sisters had four good legs between them. They could bloody well have descended the stairs to meet their new sister.

"Miss Kenworthy and Miss Marie-Claire are not at Maycliffe, sir. They're with Mrs. Milton."

They were with his aunt? "What? Why?"

"She arrived yesterday to collect them."

"To collect them," Richard repeated.

The butler's expression remained impassive. "Mrs. Milton declared herself of the opinion that newlyweds deserve a honeymoon."

"If we were having a honeymoon, it wouldn't be *here*," Richard muttered. What, were they to take up rooms in the east of the house and pretend they were at the seashore? The wind coming through would give a good approximation of Cornwall. Or the Arctic.

Cresswell cleared his throat. "I believe they are to return in two weeks' time, sir."

"Two weeks?" That would not do.

Iris's hand on his arm gave a little squeeze. "Who is Mrs. Milton?"

"My aunt," he said distractedly.

"She left you a letter," Cresswell said.

Richard's eyes snapped back to the butler's face. "My aunt? Or Fleur?"

"Your aunt. I placed it atop your correspondence in your study."

"Nothing from Fleur?"

"I am afraid not, sir."

He was going to bloody well strangle her. "Nothing even to pass along?" he pressed the butler. "A verbal message?"

"Not that I am aware."

Richard took a breath, trying to regain his equilibrium. This was not how he had anticipated their homecoming. He'd thought—Well, in truth he hadn't really thought of much, except that his sisters would be here, and he would be able to begin the next phase of his plan.

As horrifying as that was.

"Sir Richard," came Iris's voice.

He turned, blinking. She'd called him *sir* again, something he was coming to detest. It was a gesture of respect, and if he'd done anything to earn that, it would be lost soon.

She tilted her head awkwardly toward the servants, who were still standing stiffly at attention. "Perhaps we should continue with the introductions?"

"Yes, of course." He managed a tightly false smile before turning toward his housekeeper. "Mrs. Hopkins, will you introduce Lady Kenworthy to the maids?"

Hands clasped stiffly behind his back, Richard followed the two ladies as they greeted each maid. He did not intercede; this was Iris's moment, and if she was to assume her proper role at Maycliffe, he could not be seen as undermining her authority.

Iris handled the introductions with aplomb. She looked slight and pale next to the hearty Mrs. Hopkins, but her posture was straight and firm, and she greeted each maid with grace and poise.

She did him proud. But then again, he'd known she would.

Cresswell took over when the ladies had finished, presenting each footman and groom. When they were done, the butler turned to Richard, and said, "Your rooms have been prepared, sir, and a light luncheon awaits at your convenience."

Richard held out his arm to Iris but continued to speak to Cresswell. "I trust that Lady Kenworthy's rooms have been readied?"

"To your specifications, sir."

"Excellent." Richard looked down at Iris. "Everything has been cleaned and aired out, but we have not redecorated. I supposed that you would wish to choose the colors and fabrics yourself."

Iris smiled her thanks, and Richard gave a silent prayer that her tastes did not run to brocades imported from France. Maycliffe was once again profitable, but they were by no means rolling in funds. There was a reason his original plan had been to find a bride with a generous dowry.

Iris had come with but two thousand pounds. Nothing to sneeze at, but also nothing that would restore the estate to its former glory.

She could redecorate her rooms, though. It was the least he could do.

Iris glanced up at Maycliffe, and as her eyes swept over the red brick façade he loved so well, he wondered what *she* saw. Did she see the charm of the Dutch gables or sad state of the glass in their circular windows? Would she love the history of the ancient home or would she find the hodgepodge of architectural styles jarring and unrefined?

It was his home, but could she ever see it as hers?

"Shall we go inside?" he asked her.

She smiled. "I would like that."

"Perhaps a tour of the house?" he suggested. He knew he should ask if she wished to rest, but he was not ready to take her to her rooms. *Her* bedchamber was connected to *his* bedchamber, and both were in possession of large, comfortable beds, neither of which he could use in the manner he would like.

The last three days had been hell.

Or more specifically, the last three nights.

The Kings Arms had been the worst. They'd been given separate rooms, as he'd requested ahead of time, but the proprietor, eager to please the newlyweds, had shown them to his finest suite. "With connecting doors!" he'd proclaimed with a grin and a wink.

Richard hadn't realized a door could be so thin. He'd heard Iris's every movement, every cough and sigh. He'd heard her blaspheme when she'd stubbed her toe, and he'd known the exact moment she climbed into bed. The mattress had groaned, even under her slim frame, and it had not taken his imagination long to leap from his room to hers.

Her hair would be down. He'd never seen it such, and he'd found himself wondering at all hours of the day how long it was. She always wore it in a loose bun at her nape. He'd never given much thought to ladies' hairstyles before, but with Iris, he could see every pin against her soft, pale hair. Fourteen had been required to secure her tresses that morning. It seemed a great number. Did it somehow indicate the length?

He wanted to touch it, to run his fingers through it. He wanted to see it in the moonlight, sparkling silver like the stars. He wanted to feel it whispering across his skin as she brought her lips to—

"Richard?"

He blinked. It took him a moment to remember that they were standing in the courtyard in front of Maycliffe.

"Is something amiss?" Iris asked.

"Your hair," he blurted out.

She blinked. "My hair?"

"It's lovely."

"Oh." She blushed, self-consciously touching the tendrils at the nape of her neck. "Thank you." Her eyes darted to the side and then back up through her pale lashes. "I had to do it myself."

He stared at her blankly.

"I'll need to hire a maid," she explained.

"Oh, yes, of course."

"I've practiced on my sisters, but I'm not very proficient on myself."

He had no idea what she was talking about now.

"It took me a dozen pins to do what my former maid could do with five."

Fourteen.

"I beg your pardon?"

Oh dear God, he had *not* just said that aloud. "We will find a new lady's maid posthaste," he said firmly. "Mrs. Hopkins can help you. You can begin the search today if you like."

"If you don't mind," Iris said, as he finally led her through Maycliffe's front door, "I think I would like to rest before touring the house."

"Of course," he said. She'd been in a carriage for six hours. It only stood to reason she'd wish to lie down.

In her bedroom.

In a bed.

He groaned.

"Are you sure you're well?" she asked. "You seem very strange."

That was one word for it.

She touched his arm. "Richard?"

"Never better," he croaked. He turned to his valet, who had followed them in. "I believe I need to refresh myself as well. Perhaps a bath?"

His valet nodded, and Richard leaned forward, adding in a low voice, "Nothing too warm, Thompson."

"Bracing, sir?" Thompson murmured in response.

Richard gritted his teeth. Thompson had been with him for eight years, long enough to show such cheek.

"Will you show me the way?" Iris asked.

Would he show her the way?

"To my room?" she clarified.

He stared at her. Stupidly.

"Could you show me to my room?" she asked again, looking up at him with a perplexed expression.

It was official. His brain had stopped working.

"Richard?"

"My correspondence," he said suddenly, grasping onto the first excuse he could think of. He desperately needed *not* to be alone in a bedroom with Iris. "I really need to check on that first."

"Sir," Cresswell began, undoubtedly to remind him that he employed a perfectly good secretary.

"No, no, best to get it over with. Must be done, you know. And there's that letter from my aunt. Can't ignore that." He affixed a jolly smile to his face and turned to Iris. "Mrs. Hopkins should be the one to show you your new rooms, anyway."

Mrs. Hopkins did not look as if she agreed.

"She was in charge of the redecorating," Richard added.

Iris frowned. "I thought you said you had not redecorated."

"The airing out," he said, punctuating with a meaningless wave of his hand. "She'll know the rooms better than I, anyway."

Mrs. Hopkins pursed her lips in disapproval, and Richard felt like a young boy, about to be reprimanded. The housekeeper had been as much a mother to him as his own, and while she would never countermand him in front of others, he knew she would make her feelings known later.

Impulsively, Richard took Iris's hand and brought it to his lips for a brief kiss. No one would accuse him of ignoring his wife in public. "You must rest, my darling."

Iris's lips parted with surprise. Had he not yet called her his darling? Bloody hell, he should have done.

"Will an hour be sufficient?" he asked her, or rather, he asked her lips, which were still delightfully pink and parted. Good Lord, he wanted to kiss her. He wanted to slide his tongue in and taste her very essence, and—

"Two!" he blurted out. "You'll need two."

"Two?"

"Hours," he said firmly. "I do not wish to overtax you." He looked over at Mrs. Hopkins. "Ladies are very delicate."

Iris frowned adorably, and Richard bit back a curse. How could she look adorable when she frowned? Surely that was an anatomical impossibility.

"Shall I see you to your bedchamber, Lady Kenworthy?" Mrs. Hopkins inquired.

"I would appreciate that, thank you," Iris replied, her eyes still pinned suspiciously on Richard.

He gave her a wan smile.

Iris followed Mrs. Hopkins down the hall, but before they turned the corner, he heard her say, "Do you consider yourself delicate, Mrs. Hopkins?"

"No indeed, my lady."

"Good," Iris said in a crisp voice. "Neither do I."

Chapter Eleven

By evening, Richard had come up with a new plan. Or rather, a modification. One he really should have considered from the beginning.

Iris was going to be angry with him. Spectacularly angry. There was no getting around that.

But perhaps he could lessen the blow?

Cresswell had said that Fleur and Marie-Claire would be gone for two weeks. *That* wasn't going to work, but a week could be managed. He could have his sisters fetched home after only seven days; that would be easy enough to arrange. His aunt lived but twenty miles away.

And in the meantime . . .

One of Richard's many regrets was that he had not had the time to properly court his new wife. Iris still did not know the reason for their hasty marriage, but she was no idiot; she could see that something was not quite right. If Richard had had just a little more time back in London, he could have wooed her the way a woman ought to be wooed. He could have shown her that he delighted in her company, that she made him laugh, that he could make *her* laugh. He could have stolen a few more kisses and awakened the desire that he was certain lay deep in her soul.

And then, after all that, when he dropped to one knee and asked her to marry him, Iris would not have hesitated. She would have gazed into his eyes, found whatever sort of love she had been longing for, and she would have said yes.

Maybe thrown herself into his arms.

Blinking back tears of happiness.

That would have been the proposal of her dreams, not the shabby, calculated kiss he'd thrust upon her in her aunt's hallway.

But he'd had no choice. Surely, when he explained everything, she would understand that. She knew what it meant to love one's family, to want to protect them at all costs. It was what she did each year when she played in the musicale. She didn't want to be there; she did it for her mother, and her aunts, and even her eternal-thorn-in-the-side sister Daisy.

She'd understand. She had to.

He had been granted a one-week reprieve. Seven full days before he had to come clean and watch her face grow even more pale at his betrayal. Maybe he was a coward; maybe he should use this time to explain it all, to prepare her for what must come.

But he wanted what he could not have before the wedding. Time.

A lot could happen in seven days.

One week, he told himself as he went to collect her for their first supper together at Maycliffe Park.

One week to make her fall in love with him.

IRIS SPENT THE entire afternoon resting in her new bedchamber. She'd never quite understood how sitting in a carriage could leave a body so weary when sitting in a chair in a drawing room required no energy whatsoever, but the three-day journey to Maycliffe had left her utterly exhausted. Maybe it was the jostling of the carriage or the poor state of the roads this far north. Or maybe—probably—it had something to do with her husband.

She did not understand him.

One moment he was charming, and the next he was fleeing her presence as if she carried plague. She could not *believe* he had had the housekeeper show her to her room. Surely that was a new husband's job. But she supposed she should not have been surprised. Richard had avoided her bed at all three inns they'd visited on the journey north. Why should she think he might behave differently now?

She sighed. She needed to learn to be indifferent to him. Not cruel, not unkind, just . . . unaffected. When he smiled at her—and he *did* smile at her, the cur—her whole being seemed to fizz with happiness. Which would have been lovely, except that it made his rejection even more puzzling.

And painful.

Honestly, it would be better if he weren't so nice to her most of the time. If she could dislike him—

No, what was she thinking? It would *not* be better if he were cruel or ignored her completely. Surely a complicated marriage was better than an unpleasant one. She had to stop being melodramatic. It was not like her. She just needed to find some sort of equilibrium and maintain it.

"Good evening, Lady Kenworthy."

Iris started with surprise. Richard was poking his head through the partially open doorway that led to the hall. "I did knock," he said with an amused expression.

"I'm sure you did," she said hastily. "My mind was elsewhere."

His smile grew more sly. "Dare I ask where?"

"Home," she lied, then realized what she'd said. "I mean London. This is my home now."

"Yes," he said, and he entered the room, quietly shutting the door behind him. His head tilted slightly to the side, and he stared at her for just long enough to make her fidget. "Have you done something different with your hair?"

And just like that, all of her vows to remain indifferent went out the window.

Iris nervously touched her head, just behind her right ear. He'd noticed. She had not thought he would. "One of the maids helped me to dress," she said. "She's rather fond of . . ."

Why was he looking at her so intently?

"Fond of . . . ?"

"Little braids," she said in a rush. A ridiculous rush. She sounded like a ninny.

"It looks lovely."

"Thank you."

He gazed at her warmly. "You do have the most marvelous hair. The color is exquisite. I have never seen the like."

Iris's lips parted. She should say something. She should thank him. But she felt almost frozen—not cold, just frozen—and then she felt ridiculous. To be so affected by a compliment.

Richard was thankfully unaware of her torment. "I'm sorry you had to travel without a maid," he continued. "I confess I did not even consider the issue. Typical of the males of our species, I'm sure."

"I-it was not a problem."

His smile deepened, and Iris wondered if it was because he knew he'd flustered her.

"Nevertheless," he said, "I apologize."

Iris didn't know what to say. Which was just as well, because she wasn't sure she remembered how to speak.

"Did Mrs. Hopkins show you your room?" Richard asked.

"Yes," Iris said with a little bob of a nod. "She was most helpful."

"It meets with your satisfaction?"

"Of course," Iris said with complete honesty. It was a lovely chamber, bright and cheerful with its southern exposure. But what she really loved . . .

She looked up at Richard with bliss in her eyes. "You have no idea how delighted I am to have my own washroom."

He chuckled. "Really? That's what you love best?"

"After sharing one with Daisy for the last seventeen years? Absolutely." She tipped her head toward him in what she hoped was a cheeky manner. "And the view from the window isn't bad, either."

His laugh deepened, and he stepped toward the window, motioning for her to join him. "What do you see?" he asked.

"I don't know what you mean," Iris said, carefully positioning herself so that they did not touch.

But he was not so inclined. He looped his arm through hers and gently tugged her closer. "I have lived my entire life at Maycliffe. When I gaze out this window, I see the tree I first climbed when I was seven. And the spot where my mother always wanted a hedgerow maze."

A wistful expression came over his face, and Iris had to look away. It felt almost intrusive to watch him.

"I cannot see Maycliffe through a newcomer's eyes," she heard him say. "Perhaps you would do me the favor of enlightening me."

His voice was smooth and velvety, flowing through her like warm chocolate. She kept her eyes forward, but she knew that he had turned toward her. His breath tickled her cheek, warming the air between them.

"What do you see, Iris?"

She swallowed. "I see . . . grass. And trees."

Richard made a funny noise, like he was swallowing his surprise.

"Bit of a hill," she added.

"You're not very poetic, are you?"

"Not at all," she admitted. "Are you?" She

turned, forgetting that she had intended not to, and she was startled by his nearness.

"I can be," he said softly.

"When it suits you?"

He smiled slowly. "When it suits me."

Iris gave a nervous smile and looked back out the window. She felt terribly jumpy, her feet wiggling about in her slippers as if someone were sparking tiny fires beneath her. "I'd rather hear what you see," she said. "I need to learn about Maycliffe. I want to be a good mistress of the estate."

His eyes flared, but other than that, his expression remained inscrutable.

"Please," she said.

For a moment he seemed lost in thought, but then he straightened his shoulders and regarded the view through the window with renewed purpose. "Right there," he said, motioning with his chin, "in that field, just beyond the trees. We hold a harvest festival there each year."

"We do?" Iris echoed. "Oh, that's lovely. I should like to be involved in the planning."

"I'm sure you will be."

"Is it in the autumn?"

"Yes, November usually. I always—" He stiffened, and then his head jerked a little, almost as if he were dislodging a thought from his head. "There's a path over there, too," he said, quite clearly changing the subject. "It leads to Mill Farm."

Iris wanted to learn more about the harvest festival, but it was clear he wasn't going to say more, so instead she politely asked, "Mill Farm?"

"One of my tenant farms," he explained. "The largest of them, actually. The son recently took over from his father. I hope he makes a good go of it. The father never did."

"Oh." Iris didn't really have anything to add to that.

"You know," Richard said, turning to her quite suddenly, "I might say that of the two of us, your observations are the more valuable. You may be able to see deficiencies I do not."

"I see nothing deficient, I assure you."

"Nothing?" he murmured, and his voice touched her like a caress.

"But of course I know little about the running of an estate," she said quickly.

"How strange to have lived the whole of your life in London," he mused.

She cocked her head to the side. "Not so strange if that is all you've known."

"Ah, but it is not all you've known, is it?"

Iris felt her brow furrow, and she turned toward him. A mistake. He was closer than she'd realized, and for a moment she forgot what she was going to say.

One of his brows rose in question.

"I—" Why was she staring at his mouth? She wrenched her gaze upward, to his eyes, which were crinkled with amusement.

"Did you wish to say something?" he murmured.

"Just that I . . . ah . . . ." What *had* she been going to say? She turned back to the window. "Oh!" She turned back to Richard. Still a mistake, but at least this time she didn't forget what she meant to say. "What do you mean by it's not all I've known?"

He gave a little shrug. "Surely you've spent time in the country at your cousins' homes."

"Well, yes, but it's hardly the same thing."

"Perhaps, but it would be enough to inform an opinion on life in the country versus that in the city, would it not?"

"I suppose," Iris acceded. "To be honest, I'd never really given it thought."

He looked at her intently. "Do you think you will enjoy living in the country?"

Iris swallowed, trying not to notice that his voice had deepened with the question. "I do not know," she replied. "I hope so."

She felt his hand slip down to hers, and before she realized what was happening, she'd turned again to face him as he raised her fingers to his lips. "I hope so, too," he said.

His eyes met hers over their hands, and in a flash she realized—*He's seducing me.*

He was seducing her. But why? Why would he feel the need? She had never given him any indication that she would refuse his advances.

"I hope you are hungry," he said, still holding her hand.

"Hungry?" she echoed dumbly.

"For supper?" He smiled with amusement. "Cook has prepared a feast."

"Oh. Yes. Of course." She cleared her throat. "I am hungry, I think."

"You think?" he teased.

She took a breath. Forced her heart to beat a little more slowly. "I am quite sure," she said.

"Excellent." He tipped his head toward the door. "Shall we?"

By THE TIME Iris retired for the evening she was nearly jumping out of her skin. Richard had been charming all through supper; she could not remember the last time she'd laughed so much. The conversation had been marvelous, the food delicious, and the way he had looked at her . . .

It was as if she were the only woman in the world.

She supposed she was, in a way. She was certainly the only woman in the house. Apart from the servants, they were the only two in residence, and she, who had always allowed herself to stand at the side and observe, could be nothing but the center of attention.

It was disconcerting and marvelous. And now it was terrifying.

She was back in her own room, and surely at any moment he would knock on the door that connected their bedchambers. He would be in his dressing gown, his legs bare, his cravat missing from his neck.

There would be skin. So much more skin than she had ever seen on a gentleman.

Iris still didn't have a lady's maid, so the girl who'd styled her hair had come in to help her prepare for bed. Iris had been mortified when she'd pulled out one of the nightgowns that had been purchased for her trousseau. It was ridiculously thin and alarmingly revealing, and even though Iris had gone to stand by the fire, she could not seem to get rid of the gooseflesh dancing along her arms.

He would come to her tonight. Surely, he would come to her. And she would finally feel like a wife.

ON THE OTHER side of the door, Richard squared his shoulders. He could do this. *He could do this.*

Or maybe he couldn't.

Who was he kidding? If he entered her room, he would take her hand. And if he took her hand, he would bring it to his lips. He would kiss each slender finger before giving them a little tug, and she'd tumble against him, her body warm and innocent and *his*. He'd have to wrap his arms around her; he could not possibly resist. And then he would kiss her the way a woman was meant to be kissed, long and deep, until she whispered his name, her voice a soft plea, begging him to—

He swore viciously, trying to cut his imagination off before it led him to bed. Fat lot of good it did, though. He was *burning* for his wife.

Again.

Still.

The entire evening had been torture. He could not remember anything he'd said at supper, and he could only hope that he'd managed at least a semblance of intelligent conversation. His mind kept wandering to extremely inappropriate places, and every time Iris licked a bit of food from her lips, or smiled at him, or bloody hell, every time she just *breathed*, his body tightened until he was so hard for her he thought he might explode.

If Iris had wondered why they remained at the table for so long after the meal had concluded, she had not said anything. Thank God. Richard didn't really think there was a polite way to say that he needed half an hour just to get his erection to settle down to half-mast.

Good Lord. He deserved this. He deserved every moment of torment for what he was going to do to her, and yet the knowledge wasn't really helping right now. Richard was no sybarite, but nor was he one to deny himself pleasure. And every nerve in his body was begging for it. It was absolutely *insane* how badly he wanted his wife.

The one woman who, by all rights, he ought to be able to take to bed without an ounce of remorse.

It had all seemed so easy when he'd plotted it out that afternoon. He'd charm her all evening, then kiss her passionately good night. He'd make up some romantic nonsense about wanting her to know him better before they made love. One more kiss, and he'd leave her breathless.

Then he'd touch her chin, whisper, "Until tomorrow," and be gone.

As plans went, it was perfect.

As reality went, it was bollocks.

He let out a long, exhausted breath and raked his hand through his already mussed hair. The connecting door between their rooms was not nearly as soundproof as he'd thought. He could hear Iris moving about, taking a seat at her vanity table, perhaps brushing her hair. She expected him to visit her, and why wouldn't she? They were married.

He had to go in. If he did not, she would be confused. She might even feel insulted. He did not wish to hurt her. Not any more than he was going to, at least.

He took a breath and knocked.

The movements coming from inside her room stilled, and after a long, suspended second, he heard her bid him enter.

"Iris," he said, keeping his voice easy and smooth. And then he looked up.

He stopped breathing.

He was fairly certain his heart stopped beating.

She was wearing a thin silken gown, the palest of blue. Her arms were bare, and so were her shoulders, save for the narrow straps that held the silk in place.

It was a garment designed solely to tempt a man—to tempt the very devil. The neckline was no more revealing than a ball gown, but somehow it hinted of so much more. The fabric was so thin as to be almost translucent, and he could see the faint outline of her nipples puckering underneath.

"Good evening, Richard," she said, and it was only then that he realized he'd been struck utterly dumb.

"Iris," he croaked.

She smiled awkwardly, and he saw that her hands were fluttering at her sides, as if she didn't quite know what to do with them.

"You look lovely," he said.

"Thank you."

Her hair was down. It rippled down her back in soft waves, ending just a bit above her elbows. He'd forgotten how badly he wanted to know how long it was.

"It's my first night at Maycliffe," she said shyly.

"It is," he agreed.

She swallowed, obviously waiting for him to take the lead.

"You must be tired," he blurted out, grasping the only excuse he could think of in the heat of his desire.

"A little."

"I will not bother you."

She blinked. "What?"

He stepped forward, steeling himself for what he must do. What he must do, and then what he must *not* do.

He kissed her, but only on the forehead. He knew his limits. "I will not be a brute," he said, trying to make his voice soft and reassuring.

"But—" Her eyes were huge, bewildered.

"Good night, Iris," he said quickly.

"But, I—"

"Until tomorrow, my love."

Then he fled.

Like the coward he was.

Chapter Twelve

As a married lady, it was Iris's prerogative to take her breakfast in bed, but when she woke the following morning, she gritted her teeth determinedly and got herself dressed.

Richard had rejected her.

He had *rejected* her.

This was not some roadside inn, too "dusty" for a wedding night. They were in their home, for heaven's sake. He had flirted with her all evening. He had kissed her hand, charmed her with his witty conversation, and then, after she'd donned a sheer nightgown and brushed her hair until it shone, he told her she looked *tired*?

She had stared at the door between their rooms for untold minutes after he left. She hadn't even realized she was crying until she'd suddenly gulped back a huge, awful sob and realized that her nightgown—the one she now swore she'd never wear again—was wet with tears.

Then all she could think was that he must have heard her through the door. And how that made it so much worse.

Iris had always known that she did not possess the sort of beauty that drove men to passion and poetry. Perhaps in some other land, women were revered for their utterly colorless skin and lightly ginger hair, but not here in England.

But for the first time in her life, she had begun to *feel* beautiful. And it was Richard who had made her feel that way, with his secret glances and warm smiles. Every now and then she would catch him watching her, and she felt special. Treasured.

But that was all a lie. Or she was a fool for seeing things that simply weren't there.

Or maybe she was just a fool, period.

Well. She wasn't going to take this lying down. And she certainly wasn't going to let him see how deeply she'd felt his insult. She was going to go down to breakfast as if nothing had happened. She'd have jam on toast, and she'd read the newspaper, and when she spoke it would be with the sparkling wit for which she'd always intended to be renowned.

And really, it wasn't even as if she was sure that she *wanted* to do all those things married people did in bed, no matter how lovely her cousin Sarah had said it was. But it would have been nice if *he'd* wanted to.

She would at least have given it a try.

The maid who had assisted her the night before

must have had other duties to attend to, so Iris dressed herself. She twisted her hair into as neat a bun as she could manage on her own, jammed her feet into her slippers, and stalked out of her room.

She paused as she passed Richard's door. Was he still abed? She took a step closer, tempted to put her ear against the wood.

Stop it!

She was behaving like a fool. Listening at his door. She had no time for this. She was hungry, and she wanted breakfast, and she had a great many things to do today, none of which concerned her husband.

She needed to find a lady's maid, for one. And learn her way about the house. Visit the village. Meet the tenants.

Have tea.

What, she asked herself. It was important to have tea. She might as well go and become Italian, otherwise.

"I am losing my mind," she said aloud.

"I beg your pardon, my lady?"

Iris nearly jumped a foot. A housemaid was at the far end of the hall, standing nervously with a large feather duster clasped in her hands.

"Nothing," Iris said, trying not to look embarrassed. "I coughed."

The maid nodded. It wasn't the one who'd dressed her hair, Iris saw.

"Mrs. Hopkins wants to know what time you want your breakfast," the maid said. She bobbed a little curtsy and didn't quite meet Iris's eyes. "We didn't get a chance to ask you last night, and Sir Richard—"

"I'll take my breakfast downstairs," Iris interrupted. She didn't want to hear what Sir Richard thought. About anything.

The maid curtsied again. "As you wish."

Iris gave her an awkward smile. It was difficult to feel like the mistress of the house when the master so clearly had other ideas.

She made her way downstairs, trying to act as if she did not notice that all the servants were watching her—and pretending not to. It was a strange little dance they were all doing, herself most of all.

She wondered how long it would take until she was no longer the "new" mistress of Maycliffe. A month? A year? And would her husband spend the entirety of that time avoiding her bedchamber?

She sighed, then stopped walking for a moment, then told herself she was being silly. She'd never expected a passionate marriage, so why was she pining over one now? She had become Lady Kenworthy, as strange as it seemed, and she had a reputation to uphold.

Iris straightened her shoulders, took a deep breath, and entered the breakfast room.

Only to find it empty.

Bloody hell.

"Oh! Lady Kenworthy!" Mrs. Hopkins came bustling into the room. "Annie just told me you'll be wanting your breakfast downstairs this morning."

"Er, yes. I hope that won't be a problem."

"Not at all, my lady. We still have the sideboard laid from when Sir Richard ate."

"He has already been down then?" Iris wasn't

sure whether she was disappointed. She wasn't sure if she *wanted* to be disappointed.

"Not even a quarter of an hour ago," the housekeeper confirmed. "I believe he thought you would be taking your breakfast in bed."

Iris just stood there with nothing to say.

Mrs. Hopkins gave her a bit of a secret smile. "He asked us to put a flower on your tray."

"He did?" Iris asked, hating the way her voice seemed to gulp from her throat.

"It's a pity we have no irises. They bloom so early, they do."

"This far north?" Iris asked.

Mrs. Hopkins nodded. "They come up each year on the west lawn. I like the purple ones myself."

Iris was just about to agree with her when she heard footsteps in the hall, brisk and determined. It could only be Richard. No servant would ever move about a house with so little regard to noise.

"Mrs. Hopkins," he said, "I'm going—Oh." He saw Iris and blinked. "You're awake."

"As you see."

"You had told me you were a late riser."

"Not today, apparently."

He clasped his hands behind his back, then cleared his throat. "Have you eaten?"

"No, not yet."

"You didn't want breakfast in your room?"

"No," Iris said, wondering if she'd ever had such a stilted conversation in her life. What happened to the man who had been so charming the night before? The one she'd *thought* would visit her bed?

He tugged at his cravat. "I was planning to visit tenants today."

"May I come with you?"

Their eyes met. Iris wasn't sure which one of them was more surprised. She'd hardly realized what she was going to say until the words were out.

"Of course," Richard replied. What else could he say, right there in front of Mrs. Hopkins?

"I'll fetch my spencer," Iris said, taking a step toward the door. Spring was still a chilly season this far north.

"Aren't you forgetting something?"

She turned.

He made a motion toward the sideboard. "Breakfast?"

"Oh." She felt her face flush. "Of course. How silly of me." She walked back to the food and took a plate, nearly jumping when she felt Richard's breath near her ear.

"Should I be worried that my presence turns you off your food?"

She stiffened. *Now* he was flirting with her? "Excuse me," she said. He was blocking the sausages.

He stepped aside. "Do you ride?"

"Not well," she admitted. And then, just because she was feeling peevish, she asked, "Do you?"

He drew back, his eyes startled. And vexed. More vexed than startled. "Of course."

She smiled to herself as she took a seat. Nothing got to a gentleman quite like an insult to his horsemanship.

"You needn't wait with me," she said, cutting her sausage with surgical precision. She was trying so hard to appear normal, not that he knew her well enough to *know* what was normal. But still, it was a matter of pride.

He slid into the seat across from her. "I am at your disposal."

"Are you?" she murmured, wishing that such a comment did not make her pulse race.

"Indeed. I was about to leave when I saw you. Now I have nothing to do but wait."

Iris glanced at him as she spread jam on her toast. He was sprawled in his chair in a most informal manner, leaning back with the lazy grace of a natural athlete.

"I should bring gifts," she said, the idea coming to her rather suddenly.

"I beg your pardon?"

"Gifts. For the tenants. I don't know, baskets of food or some such. Don't you think?"

He took a second or two to ponder that, then said, "You're right. It never even occurred to me."

"Well, to be fair, you weren't planning to have me accompany you today."

He nodded, smiling at her as she lifted her toast to her mouth.

She froze. "Is something wrong?"

"Why would something be wrong?"

"You're smiling at me."

"I'm not allowed to?"

"No, I—Oh, for heaven's sake," she muttered under her breath. "Never mind."

He waved this off. "Consider it forgotten."

But he was still smiling at her.

It made her very uneasy.

"Did you sleep well?" he asked.

Really? He was going to ask her *that*?

"Iris?"

"As well as can be expected," she answered. As soon as she found her voice.

"That doesn't sound very promising."

She shrugged. "It's a strange room."

"By that token, you would have had difficulty sleeping the entire journey."

"I did," she confirmed.

His eyes clouded with concern. "You should have said something to me."

If you'd been in my room, you'd have seen for yourself, she wanted to say. Instead she said, "I didn't want to worry you."

Richard leaned forward and took her hand, which was a little awkward as she'd been reaching for her tea. "I hope you will always feel comfortable coming to me with your problems."

Iris tried to keep her face impassive, but she had a feeling she was looking at him as if he were some sort of zoo exhibit. It was lovely that he was acting with such concern, but they were only talking about a few nights of disrupted sleep. "I'm sure I shall," she said with an uneasy smile.

"Good."

She glanced about the room awkwardly. He was still holding her hand. "My tea," she finally said, tipping her head in the direction of the cup.

"Of course. So sorry." But when he let go, his fingers slid along hers like a caress.

A little frisson of awareness danced up her arm. He had that lovely, lazy smile on his face again, the one that made her feel rather warm inside. He was trying to seduce her again. She was sure of it.

But why? Why would he treat her with such warmth only to reject her? He was not that cruel. He could not be.

She took a hasty sip of her tea, wishing he would stop looking at her so intently. "What was your mother like?" she blurted out.

That seemed to disconcert him. "My mother?"

"You've never told me about her." And more to the point, it was not the sort of topic that invited romance. Iris needed a nice innocuous conversation if she was to have any hope of finishing her breakfast.

"My mother was . . ." He seemed not to know what to say.

Iris took another bite of her breakfast, watching him with a serene expression as he wrinkled his nose and blinked a few times. Maybe she was at heart a selfish, petty creature, but she was enjoying this. He flustered her all the time. Surely a little turnabout was fair game.

"She loved to be outside," he finally said. "She cultivated roses. And other plants, too, but the roses were the only ones I could ever remember the names of."

"What did she look like?"

"A bit like Fleur, I suppose." His brow came together as he remembered. "Although her eyes were green. Fleur's are more hazel—a mix of our parents'."

"Your father had brown eyes, then?"

Richard nodded, tipping back in his chair.

"I wonder what color eyes our children will have."

Richard's chair came down with a thunk, and he spewed tea all over the table. "Sorry," he muttered. "Lost my balance."

Iris looked down at her plate, spotted a bit of tea on her toast, and decided she was done with breakfast, anyway. What a strange reaction, though. Surely Richard wanted children? Every man did. Or at least every man who owned land.

"Is Maycliffe entailed?" she wondered.

"Why do you ask?"

"Isn't it the sort of thing I ought to know?"

"It is not. Entailed, that is. But yes, something you ought to know," he acknowledged.

Iris found herself a new teacup and poured some more. She wasn't really thirsty, but she found herself strangely loath to release him from this conversation. "Your parents must have been quite relieved that their firstborn was a boy," she remarked. "They would not want the property to be separated from the title."

"I confess I never discussed it with them."

"No, I imagine not." She added a bit of milk to her tea, stirred, and took a sip. "What happens to the title if you die without children?"

One of his brows rose. "Are you plotting my demise?"

She gave him a bit of a look. "It seems like another sort of thing I ought to know, don't you think?"

He waved a hand dismissively. "Distant cousin. I think he lives in Somerset."

"You think?" How could he not know?

"I've never met him," Richard said with a shrug. "You have to go back to our great-great-grandfather to locate a common ancestor."

Iris supposed he had a point. She might know a prodigious amount about her overabundance of cousins, but they were *first* cousins. She wasn't sure she could locate any of her more distant relations on a map.

"You have nothing to worry about," Richard said. "If something were to happen to me, you will be well provided for. I made sure of that in the marriage settlement."

"I know," Iris said. "I read it."

"You did?"

"Shouldn't I?"

"Most women don't."

"How would you know?"

Suddenly, he grinned. "Are we having an argument?"

Suddenly, his grin turned her insides to mush. "*I'm* not."

He chuckled. "That's a relief, I must say. I should hate to think we were having an argument, and I missed it."

"Oh, I don't think there's a chance of that."

He leaned forward, tilting his head in question.

"I don't raise my voice often . . ." Iris murmured.

"But when you do, it's a sight to behold?"

She smiled her acknowledgment.

"Why do I have the impression that Daisy is the most frequent recipient of your temper?"

She made a motion with her index finger as if to say—*wrong!* "That would be incorrect."

"Do tell."

"Daisy is . . ." She sighed. "Daisy is Daisy. I don't know how else to describe her. I've long thought one of us must have been switched at birth."

"Be careful what you wish for," Richard warned with a smile. "Daisy is the one who looks just like your mother."

Iris felt herself smiling in return. "She does, doesn't she? I favor my father's side of the family. I'm told I have my great-grandmother's coloring. Funny how many generations it managed to skip before finding me."

Richard nodded, then said, "I still want to know who provokes your temper, if not Daisy."

"Oh, I didn't say that she *doesn't* provoke my temper. She does. All the time. But it's rarely something worth getting riled up about in the end. Arguments with Daisy are generally petty things, all snappish and snide."

"Who makes you angry, then?" he asked softly. "Who can make you so furious that you'd jump out of your skin if you were able?"

You, she almost said.

Except that he hadn't done. Not really. He'd vexed her, and he'd hurt her feelings, but he'd never reduced her to the sort of rage he was describing.

And yet, somehow she knew he could.

He would.

"Sarah," Iris said firmly, putting a halt to her dangerous thoughts.

"Your cousin?"

She nodded. "I once had a row with her . . ."

His eyes lit with delight, and he leaned forward, resting his elbows on the table and his chin in his hands. "I must have every detail."

Iris laughed. "No, you don't."

"Oh, I'm quite sure I do."

"I can't believe that women are said to be the bigger gossips."

"This isn't gossip," he protested. "This is my wishing to better understand my bride."

"Oh, if *that's* the case . . ." She chuckled again. "Very well, it was about the musicale. Honestly, I don't think you would understand. I don't think anyone outside my family would."

"Try me."

Iris sighed, wondering how she could possibly explain. Richard was always so confident, so sure of himself. He couldn't possibly know how it felt to get up on a stage and make an utter fool of himself, all the while knowing that there was absolutely nothing he could do to stop it.

"Tell me, Iris," he urged. "I really want to know."

"Oh, all right. It was last year."

"When she was sick," Richard cut in.

Iris looked at him with surprise.

"You mentioned it to me," he reminded her.

"Ah. Well, she *wasn't* sick."

"I had a feeling."

"She faked the whole thing. She said she was trying to get the entire performance canceled, but honestly, she was just thinking of herself."

"You told her how you felt?"

"Oh yes," Iris replied. "I went to her house the

next day. She tried to deny it, but it was clear she wasn't sick. Even so, she insisted that she had been until six months later at Honoria's wedding."

"Honoria?"

Oh, right. He didn't know Honoria. "Another cousin," she told him. "She's married to the Earl of Chatteris."

"Another musician?"

Iris's smile was clearly half grimace. "Depending on your definition of the word."

"Was Honoria—I'm sorry, Lady Chatteris—in the concert?"

"Yes, but she is so lovely and forgiving. I'm sure she still believes that Sarah was ill. She always thinks the best of everyone."

"And you don't?"

She met his gaze dead-on. "I have a more suspicious nature."

"I shall remember that," he murmured.

Iris thought it best not continue this thread of the conversation, so she said, "At any rate, Sarah did eventually admit the truth. The night before Honoria's wedding. I don't know, she said something about being unselfish, and I simply could not contain myself."

"What did you say?"

Iris winced at the memory. She had spoken the truth, but she had not done it kindly. "I would rather not say."

He did not press her to elaborate.

"That was when she claimed she was trying to get the event canceled," she said.

"You don't believe her?"

"I believe she considered it when she was making her plans. But no, I do not think it was her primary motive."

"Does it matter?"

"Of course it matters," she said with a passion that surprised herself. "It matters *why* we do things. It has to matter."

"Even if the results are beneficial?"

She dismissed this out of turn. "Clearly you've moved on to the hypothetical. *I'm* still talking about my cousin and the musicale. And no, the results were not beneficial. At least not to anyone aside from herself."

"But one could say that your experience was unchanged."

Iris just looked at him.

"Consider it this way," he explained. "If Sarah had not feigned illness, you would have played in the musicale."

He glanced at her for confirmation, which she gave.

"But she did, in fact, pretend to be ill," he continued. "And the result was that you still played in the musicale."

"I don't see your point."

"There was no change in outcome for you. Her actions, while underhanded, did not affect you in the least."

"Of course they did!"

"How?"

"If I had to play, she had to play."

He laughed. "You don't think that sounds just a tiny bit childish?"

Iris ground her teeth with frustration. How dare he laugh? "I think *you've* never got up on a stage and humiliated yourself in front of everyone you know. And worse, quite a few you don't."

"You didn't know me," he murmured, "and look what happened."

She said nothing.

"If not for the musicale," he said lightly, "we would not be wed."

Iris had no idea how to interpret that.

"Do you know what I saw when I attended the musicale?" he asked, his voice soft.

"Don't you mean what you heard?" she muttered.

"Oh, we all know what I heard."

She smiled at that, even though she didn't want to.

"I saw a young woman hiding behind her cello," he continued. "A young woman who actually *knew* how to play that cello."

Her eyes flew to his.

"Your secret is safe with me," he said with an indulgent smile.

"It's not a secret."

He shrugged.

"But you know what is?" she asked, suddenly eager to share. She wanted him to know. She wanted him to know *her*.

"What?"

"I *hate* playing the cello," she said with great feeling. "It's not even just that I dislike playing in the concerts, although I do. I *loathe* the concerts, loathe them in a way I could never begin to articulate."

"Actually, you're doing a fairly good job of it."

She gave him a sheepish smile. "I really do hate playing the cello, though. You could set me down in an orchestra of the finest virtuosos—not that they'd ever allow a woman to play—and I'd still hate it."

"Why do you do it?"

"Well, I don't anymore. I don't have to now that I'm married. I shall never pick up a bow again."

"It's good to know I'm good for something," he quipped. "But honestly, why *did* you do it? And don't say you had to. Sarah got out of it."

"I could never be so dishonest."

She waited for him to say something, but he only frowned, glancing to the side as if lost in thought.

"I played the cello," she said, "because it was expected of me. And because it made my family happy. And despite what I say about them, I love them dearly."

"You do, don't you," he murmured.

She looked at him earnestly. "Even after all that, I consider Sarah one of my dearest friends."

He regarded her with a curiously steady expression. "You obviously possess a high capacity for forgiveness."

Iris felt herself draw back as she considered this. "I never thought so," she said.

"I hope you do," he said quietly.

"I beg your pardon?" Surely she could not have heard that correctly.

But he had already got to his feet and was holding out his hand. "Come, the day awaits."

Chapter Thirteen

"You want *HOW* many baskets?"

Richard pretended not to notice Mrs. Hopkins's dumbfounded expression. "Just eighteen," he said jovially.

"Eighteen?" she demanded. "Do you know how long something like that takes?"

"It would be a difficult task for anyone but you," he demurred.

The housekeeper narrowed her eyes, but he could tell she liked the compliment.

"Don't you think it's an excellent idea to bring baskets to the tenants?" he said, before she could come up with another protest. He tugged Iris forward. "It was Lady Kenworthy's idea."

"I thought it would be a nice gesture," Iris said.

"Lady Kenworthy is all that is generous," Mrs. Hopkins said, "but—"

"We'll help," Richard suggested.

Her mouth fell open.

"Many hands make light work, isn't that something you used to say?"

"Not to you," the housekeeper retorted.

Iris stifled a laugh. Charming little traitor, she was. But Richard was in far too good a mood to take offense. "The dangers of having servants who've known you since school days," he murmured in her ear.

"School days!" Mrs. Hopkins scoffed. "I've known you since you were in—"

"I know exactly how long you've known me," Richard cut in. He didn't need Mrs. Hopkins mentioning his time in nappies in front of Iris.

"I would like to help, actually," Iris said. "I am eager to meet the tenants, and I do think that the gifts would be more meaningful if I helped to pack them myself."

"I don't know that we even have eighteen baskets," Mrs. Hopkins grumbled.

"Surely they don't need to be actual *baskets*," Iris said. "Any sort of container would do. And I'm sure you will know the best things with which to fill them."

Richard just grinned, admiring his wife's easy handling of the housekeeper. Each day—no, each hour—he learned something new about her. And with each revelation, he realized just how lucky he was that he had chosen her. It was so strange to think that he probably would not have looked twice in her direction if he hadn't found himself forced to find a bride so quickly.

It was difficult to recall just what he'd thought he'd wanted in a wife. A substantial dowry, of course. He'd had to give that up, but now, as he watched Iris make herself at home in Maycliffe's kitchen, it no longer seemed so urgent. If the repairs he needed to make to the house had to wait a year or two, so be it. Iris was not the sort to complain.

He thought about the women he had considered before Iris. He could not remember much about them, just that they had always seemed to be dancing or flirting or tapping his arm with a fan. They were women who demanded attention.

Whereas Iris earned it.

With her fierce intelligence and her quiet, sly humor, she had a way of sneaking up on his thoughts. She surprised him at every turn.

Who would have thought that he'd *like* her so well?

Like.

Who liked a wife? In his world, wives were tolerated, indulged, and if one was very lucky, desired. But liked?

If he hadn't married Iris, he'd want her for a friend.

Well, he would, except for the complication of wanting so badly to take her to bed he could barely think straight. The night before, when he'd gone in to bid her good night, he'd almost lost control. He'd wanted to become her husband truly, he'd wanted her to know that he wanted *her*. He'd seen her face after he kissed her on the forehead. She was confused. Hurt. She'd thought he didn't desire her.

Didn't desire her?

It was so far from the truth as to be almost laughable. What would she think if she knew he lay awake at night, taut and burning with need as he imagined all the ways he wanted to bring her pleasure. What would she say if he told her how much he longed to bury himself within her, to imprint himself upon her, to make her understand that she was *his*, that he wanted her to be his, and he would gladly be hers.

"Richard?"

He turned at the sound of his wife's voice. Or rather, he turned partway. His wicked thoughts had left their mark upon his body, and he was relieved that he could conceal himself behind the counter.

"Did you say something?" she asked.

Did he?

"Well, you made a sound," she said with a shrug.

He could only imagine. Good Lord, *how* was he going to get through the next few months?

"Richard?" she said again. She looked amused, perhaps a little delighted at having caught him woolgathering. When he did not immediately reply, she shook her head with a smile and turned back to her work.

He watched her for a few moments, then dipped his hands in a nearby bowl of water and discreetly patted his face. When he was feeling sufficiently cooled, he walked over to where Iris and Mrs. Hopkins were sorting through items.

"What are you putting in that one?" he asked, peeking over Iris's shoulder as she placed items into a small wooden crate.

Iris glanced up at him only briefly. She was clearly enjoying her work. "Mrs. Hopkins said that the Millers likely need some new linens."

"Dishcloths?" It seemed a rather plain gift to him.

"It's what they need," Iris said. But then she flashed him a smile. "We're also adding some biscuits just as soon as they come out of the oven. Because it's always nice to get some things you *want*, too."

Richard stared at her for the longest moment.

Self-consciously, she checked her dress, then touched her cheek. "Do I have something on my face? I was helping with the jam . . ."

She had nothing on her face, but he leaned forward and lightly kissed the corner of her mouth. "Right here," he murmured.

She touched the spot where he'd kissed her. She gazed at him with an expression of wonder, as if she wasn't sure what had just happened.

He wasn't sure, either.

"It's all better now," he told her.

"Thank you. I—" A faint blush stole over her cheeks. "Thank you."

"It was my pleasure."

And it was.

For the next two hours Richard pretended to help with baskets. Iris and Mrs. Hopkins had everything well in hand, and when he tried to make a suggestion, it was either waved away or considered and found wanting.

He didn't mind. He was happy to assume the position of biscuit-tester (uniformly excellent, he was happy to inform Cook), and watch Iris assume her role as mistress of Maycliffe.

Finally, they had a collection of eighteen baskets, boxes, and bowls, each carefully packed and labeled with the surname of a tenant family. No two gifts were the same; the Dunlops, with four boys between the ages of twelve and sixteen, were given a hefty portion of food, while one of Marie-Claire's old dolls was placed in the basket for the Smiths, whose three-year-old daughter was recovering from croup. The Millers got their dishcloths and biscuits, and the Burnhams a hearty ham and two books—a study of land management for the eldest son, who had recently taken over the farm, and a romantic novel for his sisters.

And maybe for the son, too, Richard thought with a grin. Everyone could use a romantic novel every now and then.

Everything was loaded into a wagon, and soon Richard and Iris were on their way, bound for all four corners of Maycliffe Park.

"Not the most glamorous of conveyances," he said with a rueful smile, as they bumped along the road.

Iris put her hand on her head as a stiff wind threatened to steal her bonnet. "I don't mind. Goodness, can you imagine trying to transport all this in a barouche?"

He didn't have a barouche, but there seemed little reason to mention this, so instead he said, "You should tie your bonnet strings. You won't have to keep holding your hat."

"I know. I've just always found it uncomfortable. I don't like the feeling of them tight under my chin." She looked over at him with a sparkle in her eye. "You should not be so hasty to offer advice. Your hat is affixed upon your head in no way whatsoever."

As if on cue, the wagon took a bump just as the wind picked up again, and he felt his top hat rising from his head.

"Oh!" Iris yelped, and without thinking she grabbed his hat and pushed it back down. They had been sitting next to each other, but the movement brought them even closer, and when he slowed the horses and allowed himself to look at her, her face was tipped up toward his, radiant and very, very close.

"I think . . ." he murmured, but as he gazed into her eyes, made even more vivid under the bright blue sky, his words fell away.

"You think . . . ?" she whispered. Her hand was still on his head. Her other hand was on her head, and it would have been the most ridiculous position if it weren't so utterly wonderful.

The horses ambled to a stop, clearly confused by his lack of direction.

"I think I might need to kiss you," Richard said. He touched her cheek, the pad of his thumb stroking softly across her milky skin. She was so beautiful. How was it possible he hadn't realized just how beautiful until this very moment?

The space between them melted into nothingness, and his lips found hers, soft and willing, breathless with wonder. He kissed her slowly, languorously, giving himself time to discover the shape of her, the taste, the texture. It was not the first time he'd kissed her, but it felt brand-new.

There was something exquisitely innocent in

the moment. He did not crush her to his body; he did not even wish to. This was not a kiss of possession, nor one of lust. It was something else entirely, something born of curiosity, of captivation.

Softly, he deepened the kiss, letting his tongue glide along the silken skin of her lower lip. She sighed against him, her body softening as she welcomed his caress.

She was perfect. And sweet. And he had the strangest sense that he could stay there all day, his hand on her cheek, her hand on his head, touching nowhere else but at their lips. It was almost chaste, almost spiritual.

But then a bird cawed loudly in the distance, its sharp call piercing the moment. Something changed. Iris grew still, or maybe she simply breathed again, and with a shaky exhale, Richard managed to pull himself a few inches away. He blinked, then blinked again, trying to bring the world into focus. His universe had shrunk to this one woman, and he could not seem to see anything but her face.

Her eyes were filled with amazement, the same expression, he thought, that must be in his own. Her lips were gently parted, offering him the tiniest peek at her pink tongue. It was the strangest thing, but he felt no urge to kiss her. He wanted just to look at her. He wanted to watch the emotions wash across her face. He wanted to watch her eyes as the pupils adjusted to the light. He wanted to memorize the shape of her lips, to learn how quickly her eyelashes swept up and down when she blinked.

"That was . . ." he finally murmured.

"That was . . ." she echoed.

He smiled. He couldn't help it. "It definitely was."

Her face broke into an echoing grin, and the sheer joy of the moment was almost too much. "Your hand is still on my head," he said, feeling his smile turn lopsided and teasing.

She looked up, as if she needed to actually see it to believe it. "Do you think your hat is safe?" she asked.

"We might be able to risk it."

She took her hand away, and the motion changed her entire position, trebling the space between them. Richard felt almost bereft, which was madness. She sat less than a foot away on the wagon bench, and it felt as if he'd lost something infinitely precious.

"Perhaps you should tie your bonnet more tightly," he suggested.

She murmured some sort of assent and did so.

He cleared his throat. "We should be on our way."

"Of course." She smiled, first hesitantly, then determinedly. "Of course," she said again. "Who will we be seeing first?"

He was grateful for the question, and the necessity of forming an answer. He needed something to prod his brain back into motion. "Ehrm . . . I think the Burnhams," he decided. "Theirs is the largest farm, and the closest."

"Excellent." Iris twisted in her seat, peering at the pile of gifts in the back of the wagon. "Theirs is the wooden box. Cook packed extra jam. She said young Master Burnham has a sweet tooth."

"I don't know that he still qualifies as young," Richard said, giving the reins a flick. "John Burnham must be twenty-two now, maybe twenty-three."

"That's younger than you are."

He gave her a wry smile. "True, but like me, he is the head of his family and farm. Youth departs quickly with such responsibility."

"Was it very difficult?" she asked quietly.

"It was the most difficult thing in the world." Richard thought back to those days right after his father's death. He'd been so lost, so overwhelmed. And in the middle of it all, while he was supposed to pretend he knew how to run Maycliffe and be a parent to his sisters, he was grieving. He'd loved his father. They may not have always seen eye to eye, but there had been a bond. His father had taught him to ride. He'd taught him to read—not the actual letters and words, but he'd taught him to love reading, to see value in books and knowledge. What he hadn't taught him—what no one had dreamed was yet necessary—was how to run Maycliffe. Bernard Kenworthy had not been an old man when he'd taken ill. There had been every reason to believe that Richard would have years, decades even, before he needed to take the reins.

But truthfully, there wouldn't have been much for his father to teach. Bernard Kenworthy had never bothered to learn it himself. He had not been a good steward of the land. It had never interested him, not deeply, and his decisions—when he bothered to make them—had been poor. It wasn't that he was greedy, it was just that he tended to do whatever was convenient, whatever required the least time and energy on his part. And Maycliffe had suffered for it.

"You were just a boy, really," Iris said.

Richard let out a short, one-note laugh. "That's the funny part. I thought I was a man. I'd gone to Oxford, I'd—" He caught himself before he said he'd slept with women. Iris was his wife. She did not need to know about the benchmarks by which stupid young men measured their virility.

"I thought I was a man," he said with a rueful twist of his lips. "But then . . . when I had to go home and *be* one . . ."

She placed her hand on his arm. "I'm so sorry."

He shrugged, but with his opposite shoulder. He did not want her to remove her hand.

"You've done a remarkable job," she said. She looked around, as if the verdant trees were evidence of his good stewardship. "By all accounts, Maycliffe is thriving."

"By all accounts?" he said with a teasing grin. "How many accounts, pray tell, have you heard in your lengthy time in residence?"

She gave a gigglish snort and bumped her shoulder against his. "People talk," she said archly. "And as you know, I listen."

"That you do."

He watched as she smiled. It was a satisfied little turn of her lips, and he loved it.

"Will you tell me more about the Burnhams?" she asked. "All the tenants, actually, but we should begin with the Burnhams, as they are our first visit."

"I'm not sure what you wish to know, but there are six of them. Mrs. Burnham, of course, her son John, who is now head of the family, and then four other children, two boys and two girls." He thought for a moment. "I can't remember how old they all are, but the youngest, Tommy—he can't be much more than eleven."

"How long has it been since the father passed?"

"Two years, maybe three. It was not unexpected."

"No?"

"He drank. A great deal." Richard frowned. He did not wish to speak ill of the dead, but it was the truth. Mr. Burnham had been too fond of ale, and it had ruined him. He'd grown fat, then yellow, and then he died.

"Is his son the same way?"

It was not a silly question. Sons took their cues from their fathers, as Richard well knew. When he had inherited Maycliffe, he, too, had done what was convenient, and he'd packed his sisters off to live with their aunt while he continued his life in London as if he had no new responsibilities at home. It had taken him several years before he realized how empty he had become. And even now, he was paying the price for his poor judgment.

"I don't know John Burnham well," he said to Iris, "but I don't think he drinks. At least not more than any man does."

Iris didn't say anything, so he continued. "He will be a good man, better than his father was."

"What do you mean?" she asked.

Richard thought for a moment. He'd never really taken the time to think about John Burnham, other than the fact that he was now the head of Maycliffe's largest tenant farm. He liked what he knew of him, but their paths did not often cross, nor would anyone expect them to.

"He is a serious fellow," Richard finally replied. "He's done well for himself. Finished school, even, thanks to my father."

"Your father?" Iris echoed, with some surprise.

"He paid the fees. He took a liking to him. Said he was very intelligent. My father always valued that."

"It is a good thing to value."

"Indeed." It was, after all, one of the many reasons he valued her. But this was not the time to say so, so he added, "John probably could have gone off and read law or something of the sort if he hadn't returned to Mill Farm."

"From a farmer to a barrister?" Iris asked. "Really?"

Richard gave a shrug. "No reason why it can't be done. Assuming one wanted to."

Iris was silent for a moment, then asked, "Is Mr. Burnham married?"

He gave her a quizzical look before returning his attention to the road. "Why such interest?"

"I need to know these things," she reminded him. She shifted a little in her seat. "And I was curious. I'm always curious about people. Perhaps he had to return home to support his family. Perhaps that is why he was not able to study law."

"I don't know if he did want to study law. I merely said he was intelligent enough to do so. And no, he's not married. But he does have a family to support. He would not turn his back on his mother and siblings."

Iris laid her hand on his arm. "He is much like you, then."

Richard swallowed uncomfortably.

"You take such good care of your sisters," she continued.

"You have yet even to meet them," he reminded her.

She gave a little shrug. "I can tell that you are a devoted brother. And guardian."

Richard briefly settled the reins in one hand, relieved that he could point ahead and change the subject. "It's just around the corner."

"Mill Farm?"

He looked over at her. There had been something in her voice. "Are you nervous?"

"A bit, yes," she admitted.

"Don't be. You are the mistress of Maycliffe."

She let out a little snort. "That is precisely why I feel nervous."

Richard started to say something, then just shook his head. Didn't she realize that the Burnhams were the ones who would be nervous to meet *her*?

"Oh!" Iris exclaimed. "It's much bigger than I expected."

"I did say it's the largest holding at Maycliffe," Richard murmured, bringing the wagon to a halt. The Burnhams had been farming the land there for several generations and over time had built quite a nice house, with four bedrooms, a sitting room, and an office. They'd once employed a maid, but she'd been let go when the family had fallen on hard times before the elder Mr. Burnham's death.

"I've never gone visiting with my cousins," Iris said self-consciously.

Richard hopped down and then offered her his hand. "Why do you sound so unsure all of a sudden?"

"I suppose I'm realizing how little I know." She motioned to the house. "I had assumed all tenant farmers lived in little cottages."

"Most do. But some are quite prosperous. One does not need to own the land to do well."

"But one does need to own the land to be considered a gentleman. Or at least have been born into a landowning family."

"True," he acceded. Even a yeoman farmer would not be considered gentry. One needed larger holdings for that.

"Sir Richard!" came a shout.

Richard grinned as he saw a young boy running toward him. "Tommy!" he called out. He tousled the boy's hair when he bounced into place in front of him. "What has your mother been feeding you? I believe you've grown a foot since our last meeting."

Tommy Burnham beamed. "John's got me working in the fields. Mum says it's the sunshine. I must be a weed."

Richard laughed, then introduced Iris, who earned Tommy's everlasting devotion by treating him like an adult and offering her hand for a shake.

"Is John in the house?" Richard asked, reaching into the wagon for the correct box.

"With Mum," Tommy replied, with a jerk of his head toward the house. "We're taking a break to eat."

"Is this the one?" Richard murmured to Iris. At her nod, he lifted the box out and motioned for her to begin walking toward the house. "You've other men working with you in the fields, though, don't you?" he asked Tommy.

"Oh, yes." Tommy looked at him as if he were daft to even consider that they might not. "We couldn't do it ourselves. Don't even need me, really, but John says I've got to do my part."

"Your brother is a wise man," Richard said.

Tommy rolled his eyes. "So he says."

Iris let out a little laugh.

"Watch out for her," Richard said with a tick of his head toward Iris. "Like you, she's got far too many siblings, and she's learned to be quick."

"Not quick," Iris corrected. "Devious."

"Even worse."

"He is the oldest," she told Tommy meaningfully. "What he achieved with brute force, we've had to manage with our wits."

"She's got you there, Sir Richard," Tommy chortled.

"She always does."

"Really?" Iris murmured, her brows high.

Richard just smiled secretively. Let her make of that what she will.

They entered the house, Tommy calling ahead to his mother that Sir Richard was here with the new Lady Kenworthy. Mrs. Burnham bustled out immediately, wiping floury hands on her apron. "Sir Richard," she said, bobbing a curtsy. "This is indeed an honor."

"I have come to introduce my wife."

Iris gave a pretty smile. "We've brought you a gift."

"Oh, but we should be giving gifts to you," Mrs. Burnham protested. "For your wedding."

"Nonsense," Iris said. "You are welcoming me into your home, onto your land."

"It is your land now, too," Richard reminded her, setting the box of treats on a table.

"Yes, but the Burnhams have been here a century longer than I have. I still must earn my place."

And just like that, Iris won the everlasting loyalty of Mrs. Burnham, and by extension, all the tenants. Society was the same no matter the sphere. Mrs. Burnham was the matron of the largest of the local farms, and this made her the leader of Maycliffe society. Iris's words would have reached the ears of every soul at Maycliffe by nightfall.

"You see why I married her," Richard said to Mrs. Burnham. The words flowed naturally from his smiling lips, but once said, a little prick of guilt sparked in his gut. It *wasn't* why he'd married her.

He wished it was why he'd married her.

"John," Mrs. Burnham said, "you must meet the new Lady Kenworthy."

Richard hadn't realized that John Burnham had entered the small foyer. He was a quiet man, always had been, and he was standing near the door to the kitchen, waiting for the others to notice him.

"My lady," John said with a little bow. "It is an honor to meet you."

"And you," Iris replied.

"How fares the farm?" Richard asked.

"Very well," John replied, and the two of them spoke for a few minutes about fields and crops and irrigation while Iris made polite conversation with Mrs. Burnham.

"We must be on our way," Richard finally said. "We've many more stops to make before heading back to Maycliffe."

"It must be quiet with your sisters gone," Mrs. Burnham said.

John turned sharply. "Your sisters are gone?"

"Just to visit our aunt. She thought we could do with some time alone." He gave John a man-to-man sort of smile. "Sisters don't add much to a honeymoon."

"No," John said, "I imagine not."

They made their farewells, and Richard took Iris's arm to lead her out.

"I think that went well," she said, as he helped her up into the wagon.

"You were splendid," he assured her.

"Truly? You would not just say that?"

"I would just say that," he admitted, "but it is true. Mrs. Burnham adores you already."

Iris's lips parted, and he could tell she was about to say something like "Truly?" or "Do you really think so?" but then she just smiled, her cheeks flushing with pride. "Thank you," she said softly.

He kissed her hand in reply, then gave the reins a flick.

"This is a lovely day," she said, as they drove away from Mill Farm. "*I'm* having a lovely day."

As was he. The loveliest in memory.

Chapter Fourteen

Three days later

SHE WAS FALLING in love with her husband. Iris didn't know how it could possibly be more obvious.

Wasn't love supposed to be confusing? Wasn't she supposed to lie in bed, agonizing under the weight of her tortuous thoughts—*Is this real? Is this love?* Back in London she'd asked her cousin Sarah about it—Sarah, who was so thoroughly and obviously in love with her husband, and even *she* had said that she hadn't been sure at first.

But no, Iris always had to do things her own way, and she simply woke up in the morning and thought to herself, *I love him.*

Or if she didn't yet, she would soon. It was

only a matter of time. Her breath caught whenever Richard walked into the room. She thought about him constantly. And he could make her laugh—oh, how he could make her laugh.

She could make him laugh, too. And when she did, her heart leapt.

The day they had visited the tenants had been magical, and she knew he'd felt it, too. He had kissed her as if she were a priceless treasure—*no*, she thought, not like that. That would have been cold and clinical.

Richard had kissed her as if she were light and warmth and rainbows all rolled into one. He'd kissed her as if the sun were shining down with a single beam of light, just on them, only on them.

It had been perfect.

Pure magic.

And then he hadn't done it again.

They spent their days together, exploring Maycliffe. He gazed warmly into her eyes. He held her hand, he even kissed the tender skin of her wrist. But he never brought his lips to hers.

Did he think she would not welcome his advances? Did he think it was still too soon? How could it be too soon? They were married, for heaven's sake. She was his wife.

And why didn't he realize that she would be too embarrassed to ask him about it?

So she kept pretending that she thought this was normal. Lots of married couples kept to their own bedchambers. If her own parents ever slept in the same bed, she didn't know about it.

Nor, she thought with a shudder, did she want to.

But even if Richard was the sort of man who felt that married couples should maintain their own chambers, surely he would wish to consummate the union? Her mother had said that men *liked* to do . . . that. And Sarah had said that women could like it, as well.

The only explanation was that Richard did not desire her. Except she thought . . . maybe . . . he did.

Twice she had caught him watching her with an intensity that made her pulse leap. And just this morning he'd almost kissed her. She was sure of it. They had been walking the winding path to the orangery, and she tripped. Richard had twisted as he caught her, and she'd fallen against him, her breasts pressed flat against his chest.

It was the closest she had ever been to him, and she looked up, straight into his eyes. The world around them had slipped away, and she saw nothing but his beloved face. His head dipped toward hers, and his gaze dropped to her lips, and she sighed . . .

And he stepped back.

"Forgive me," he'd murmured, and they were once again on their way.

But the morning had lost its magic. Their conversation, which had grown so easy and free, was once again stilted, and Richard did not touch her, not even casually. There was no hand at her back, no arm looped with hers.

Another woman—one who had more experience with the male sex, or maybe one who could read minds—might understand why Richard was acting as he did, but Iris was mystified.

And frustrated.

And sad.

Iris groaned and turned back to the book she was reading. It was late in the afternoon, and she'd found an old Sarah Gorely novel in Maycliffe's library—presumably the purchase of one of Richard's sisters. She could not imagine he would ever have bought it. It wasn't very good, but it was dramatic, and most importantly, it was distracting. And the blue sofa in the drawing room was exceedingly comfortable. The fabric had been worn down just enough to make it soft, but not quite so much as to render it careworn.

She liked reading in the drawing room. The afternoon light was excellent, and here, at the heart of the house, she could almost convince herself that she belonged to this place.

She'd managed to lose herself in the story for a chapter or so when she heard footsteps in the hall that could only belong to Richard.

"How are you this afternoon?" he asked from the doorway, greeting her with a polite dip of his head.

She smiled up at him. "Very well, thank you."

"What are you reading?"

Iris held up the book even though it was unlikely he could read the title from across the room. *"Miss Truesdale and the Silent Gentleman.* It's an old Sarah Gorely novel. Not her best, I'm afraid."

He came fully into the room. "I have never read anything by that author. But I believe she is quite well-known, is she not?"

"I don't think you would like it," Iris said.

He smiled—that warm, languid smile that seemed to melt across his face. "Try me."

Iris blinked and looked down at the book in her hands before holding it out toward him.

He laughed merrily. "I could not take it away from you."

She glanced up at him with surprise. "You wish for me to read to you?"

"Why not?"

Her brows rose into doubtful arches. "Don't say I didn't warn you," she murmured, and she scooted over a little on the sofa, trying to quash the sting of disappointment when he instead sat in a chair across from her.

"Did you find it in the library?" he asked. "I imagine it was Fleur's purchase."

Iris nodded as she took note of her place before turning back to the beginning. "You have the entire Gorely oeuvre."

"Really? I had no idea my sister was such a devotee."

"You did say she likes to read," Iris remarked. "And Mrs. Gorely is a very popular author."

"So I'm told," he murmured.

Iris looked over at him, and he regally inclined his head, signaling for her to begin. "*Chapter One,*" she read. "*Miss Ivory Truesdale was orphaned on—*" She looked back up. "Are you sure you want me to read this? I cannot imagine you will enjoy it."

He regarded her with a deeply amused expression. "You realize you must read it now, after all your protestations."

Iris shook her head. "Very well." She cleared her throat. *"Miss Ivory Truesdale was orphaned on a Wednesday afternoon, when her father was struck through the heart by a poison-tipped arrow, shot from the quiver of a Hungarian master archer, brought to England for the sole purpose of bringing about his gruesome and untimely demise."*

She looked up.

"Grim," Richard said.

Iris nodded. "It gets worse."

"How can it possibly?"

"The Hungarian archer meets *his* demise in a few chapters."

"Let me guess. A carriage accident."

"Far too pedestrian," Iris scoffed. "This is the author who pecked a character to death with pigeons in another book."

Richard's mouth opened, then closed. "Pigeons," he finally said, blinking several times in rapid succession. "Remarkable."

Iris held up the book. "Shall I continue?"

"Please," he said, with the particular expression of a man who is not at all certain he is treading the right path.

Iris cleared her throat. *"For the next six years, Ivory was unable to face a Wednesday afternoon without remembering the silent swish of the arrow as it swept by her face on its way to her father's doomed heart."*

Richard muttered something under his breath. Iris could not make out the exact words, but she was fairly certain *crapulence* was among them.

"Each Wednesday was torture. To rise from her

meager bed required energy she rarely possessed. Food was unpalatable, and sleep, when she found it, was her only escape."

Richard snorted.

Iris looked up. "Yes?"

"Nothing."

She turned back to the book.

"But really," he said with indignance, "Wednesdays?"

She looked back up.

"The woman is afraid of Wednesdays?"

"Apparently."

"Only Wednesdays."

Iris shrugged.

"What happens on Thursdays?"

"I was about to say."

Richard rolled his eyes at her impertinence and motioned for her to continue.

Iris gave him a deliberately patient stare, signaling her preparation for another interruption. He returned the expression with equal irony, and she turned back to the text.

"Thursdays brought hope and renewal, although one could not say that Ivory had reason to hope, nor could one say that her soul was renewed. Her life in Miss Winchell's Home for Orphaned Children was tedious at best and wretched at worst."

"Tedious might be the first apt word of the novel," Richard scoffed.

Iris raised her brows. "Shall I stop?"

"Please. I do not think I can bear to go on."

Iris bit back a smile, feeling just a little bit wicked for enjoying his distress.

"But I still want to know how the Hungarian archer dies," Richard added.

"That will spoil the story for you," Iris countered, adopting a prim expression.

"Somehow I doubt that."

Iris chuckled. She hadn't meant to, but Richard had a way of saying things with a sly undertone that never failed to amuse her. "Very well. The archer was shot in the head."

"That's not terribly interesting." At her look he added, "In a literary sense, of course."

"The gun was fired by a dog."

Richard's face went slack.

"And we now have another silent gentleman," Iris said with a superior smile.

"No, really," Richard said. "I must protest."

"To whom?"

That seemed to flummox him. "I don't know," he finally said. "But a protest must be lodged nonetheless."

"I don't think the dog *meant* to shoot him," Iris demurred.

"You mean the author does not make the canine's motivations clear?"

Iris assumed a scrupulously even expression. "Even she lacks such talent."

This was met by a snort.

"I did tell you that this was not one of her better novels," she reminded him.

Richard appeared to be incapable of response.

"I could read from one of her other books," she said, not even attempting to disguise her amusement.

"Please, no."

Iris laughed merrily.

"How is it possible," Richard opined, "that she is one of the most popular authors of our time?"

"I find her stories quite diverting," Iris admitted. It was true. They were not terribly well written, but there was something about them that was impossible to put down.

"A diversion from sanity, perhaps," Richard scoffed. "How many novels has Miss Gorely written? Or is it Missus?"

"I have no idea," Iris admitted. She looked at the front and back pages. "There is nothing here about her. Not even a sentence."

He shrugged nonchalantly. "That is to be expected. If you were to write a novel, I should not want you to use your real name."

Iris looked up, startled by the brief flash of pain behind her eyes. "You would be ashamed of me?"

"Of course not," he said sternly. "But I should not want your fame to intrude upon our private lives."

"You think I would be famous?" she blurted out.

"Of course." He regarded her dispassionately, as if the conclusion were so obvious as not to merit discussion.

Iris considered this, trying not to allow her entire body to suffuse with pleasure. She was fairly certain she was unsuccessful; already she could feel the skin on her cheeks growing warm. Her lower lip caught between her teeth; it was so strange, this bubble of joy, all because he'd thought that . . . that she was . . . well, clever.

And the mad thing was, she *knew* she was

clever. She didn't need him to say so for her to believe it.

She looked up with a shy smile. "You truly would not mind if I wrote a novel?"

"Do you *want* to write a novel?"

She thought about this. "Not really."

He chuckled. "Why are we having this conversation?"

"I don't know." Iris smiled, first at him and then to herself. *Miss Truesdale and the Silent Gentleman* still lay in her lap, so she held it up, and asked, "Do you wish for me to continue?"

"No!" he said forcefully, rising to his feet. He held out a hand. "Come. Let us go for a walk instead."

Iris placed her hand in his, trying to ignore the shiver of pleasure that swept across her skin at his touch.

"How did the dog pull the trigger?" Richard asked. "No, don't tell me, I don't want to know."

"Are you sure? It's actually very clever."

"Are you planning to teach our hounds?"

"We have hounds?"

"Of course."

Iris wondered what else she didn't know about her new home. Loads, probably. She tugged him to a halt in the middle of the hall, gazed up into his eyes, and solemnly said, "I promise not to teach any of our dogs how to fire a weapon."

Richard hooted with laughter, prompting more than one servant to poke his head into the hall. "You are a treasure, Iris Kenworthy," he said, guiding her once again toward the front door.

A treasure, Iris thought with a touch of angst. *Really?*

"Do you like your new name?" he inquired idly.

"It does roll off the tongue with a bit more ease than Smythe-Smith," she allowed.

"I think it suits you," he said.

"I should hope so," she murmured. It was difficult to imagine a name more unwieldy than the one she'd been born with.

Richard pulled Maycliffe's heavy front door open, and a chilly burst of wind swirled forth. Iris immediately hugged her arms to herself. It was later than she'd thought, and the air had a bite to it. "Let me run up to my room for a shawl," she said. "It was silly of me to wear short sleeves."

"Silly? Or optimistic?"

She laughed. "I'm rarely optimistic."

"Really?"

Iris was already halfway up the steps before she realized he was following her.

"I don't believe I've ever heard someone declare themselves a pessimist with such a merry laugh before," he mused.

"I'm not that, either," she said. At least she didn't think she was. She didn't live her life anticipating disaster and disappointment.

"Not an optimist or a pessimist," Richard said when they reached the top of the stairs. "What, then, I wonder, are you?"

"Not a wife," she muttered.

He went still. "What did you say?"

Iris gasped at the retort that had escaped unbidden from her lips. "I'm sorry," she blurted. "I didn't mean . . ." She looked up, then wished she hadn't. He was regarding her with an inscrutable expression, and she felt awful. Embarrassed and angry and sorry and wronged and probably eight other things she really didn't have the inclination to discern.

"I beg your pardon," she mumbled, dashing off to her room.

"Wait!" he called out.

But she didn't.

"Iris, wait!"

She kept going, her feet moving as fast as they possibly could without switching from a walk to a run. But then she tripped—over what, she did not know—and just barely managed to catch her balance.

Richard was at her side in a heartbeat, his steadying hand at her arm. "Are you all right?"

"I'm fine," she said in a clipped voice. She tugged at her arm, but he held firm. She nearly laughed. Or maybe she nearly cried. *Now* he wanted to touch her? *Now* he wouldn't let go?

"I need to get my shawl," she mumbled, but she no longer wished to go for a walk. All she wanted to do was crawl into her bed and pull the covers up tight.

Richard regarded her for several seconds before releasing his grip. "Very well," he said.

She tried for a smile but couldn't manage it. Her hands were shaking, and she suddenly felt ill.

"Iris," he said, concern evident in his eyes, "are you sure you're well?"

She nodded, then changed her mind and shook her head. "Perhaps I had better lie down."

"Of course," he said, ever the gentleman. "We shall take our walk another time."

She tried for that smile again—and failed again—and instead made do with a jerky curtsy. But before she could escape, he took her arm again to guide her to her room.

"I don't need help," she said. "I'm fine, really."

"It would make *me* feel better."

Iris gritted her teeth. Why did he have to be so *nice*?

"I shall send for a doctor," he said, as they crossed the threshold.

"No, please don't." Good God, what was a doctor going to say? That she had a broken heart? That she was mad to think her husband would ever care for her?

He let go of her arm and let out a sigh as his eyes searched her face. "Iris, clearly something is wrong."

"I'm just tired."

He did not say anything, just looked at her with a steady gaze, and she knew what he was thinking. She had not seemed the least bit tired in the drawing room.

"I'll be fine," she assured him, relieved that her voice was starting to sound more like its usual matter-of-fact self. "I promise."

His lips pressed together, and Iris could see that he did not know whether to believe her. Finally, he said, "Very well," and he placed his hands gently on her shoulders and leaned down—

To kiss her! Iris's breath caught, and in one deluded moment of bliss she closed her eyes, tilting her face toward his. She longed for this, for his lips on hers, for the hot touch of his tongue on the soft skin at the corner of her mouth.

"Richard," she whispered.

His lips touched her forehead. It was not the kiss of a lover.

Humiliated, she wrenched herself away, turning toward the wall, the window, anywhere but him.

"Iris . . ."

"Please," she choked out, "just go away."

He did not speak, but nor did he leave the room. She would have heard his footsteps. She would have felt his loss.

She hugged her arms to her body, silently begging him to obey her.

And then he did. She heard him turn, heard the unmistakable sound of his boot on the carpet. She was getting what she wanted, what she'd asked for, but it was all so wrong. She needed to understand. She needed to *know*.

She whirled around.

He stopped, his hand already on the door handle.

"Why?" she said brokenly. "Why?"

He did not turn around.

"Don't pretend you didn't hear me."

"I'm not," he said quietly.

"Then don't pretend you do not understand the question."

She stared at his back, watching as his posture grew ever more rigid. The hand at his side tensed into a claw, and if she had any sense, she would not have pushed him. But she was tired of being sensible, so she said, "You chose me. Out of everyone in London, you chose me."

He did not move for several seconds. Then, with precise motions, he shut the door and turned around to face her. "You could have declined," he said.

"We both know that isn't true."

"Are you so unhappy, then?"

"No," she said, and she wasn't, not really. "But that does not negate the fundamental truth of our marriage."

"The fundamental truth," he repeated, his voice as dull and hollow as she'd ever heard it.

Iris turned away. It was too difficult to locate her courage when she could see his face. "Why did you marry me?" she choked out.

"I compromised you."

"*After* you had already proposed," she snapped, startled by her own impatience.

His voice, when he spoke, was tightly controlled. "Most women would consider a proposal of marriage to be a *good* thing."

"Are you telling me I should consider myself lucky?"

"I said no such thing."

"Why did you marry me?" she demanded.

"I wanted to," he said with a shrug. "And you said yes."

"I had no choice!" she burst out. "You made sure I had no choice."

Richard's hand shot out, circling her wrist like steel. It did not hurt; he was far too gentle for that. But it was clear she could not escape.

"If you *had* had a choice," he said, "if your aunt

had not come in, if no one had seen my lips on yours . . ." He paused, and the silence was so heavy and tight that she had to look up.

"Tell me, Iris," he said softly, "can you say that your answer would have been different?"

No.

She would have asked for time. She *had* asked for time. But in the end, she would have accepted him. They both knew it.

The pressure of his hand on her wrist softened, and it felt almost like a caress. "Iris?"

He was not going to allow her to ignore his question. But she would not give voice to her answer. She glared at him mutinously, her teeth clamped together so tightly she shook. She would not back down. She didn't know why it was so important that she not answer his question, but it felt as if her very soul hung in the balance.

Her soul.

Her *very* soul.

Good God, she was as bad as the fictitious Miss Truesdale. Was this what love did? Turned one's brain to melodramatic rot?

A pained bubble of laughter burst from her throat. It was a horrible sound, bitter and raw.

"Are you *laughing*?" Richard asked.

"Apparently," Iris replied, because she could not quite believe it herself.

"Why on earth?"

She shrugged. "I don't know what else to do."

He stared at her. "We were having a perfectly pleasant afternoon," he finally said.

"We were," she agreed.

"Why are you angry?"

"I'm not sure that I am," she replied.

Again, he just stared at her in disbelief.

"Look at me," Iris said, her voice rising with passion. "I am Lady Kenworthy, and I hardly know how it happened."

"You stood before a priest, and—"

"Don't patronize me," she snapped. "Why did you force the wedding? Why did we need to rush?"

"Does it matter?" he shot back.

She took a step back. "Yes," she said quietly. "Yes, I think it does."

"You are my wife," he said, his eyes blazing. "I have pledged to you my fidelity and my support. I have granted you all my worldly possessions, I have granted you my name."

Iris had never seen him so angry, had never imagined his body so tightly coiled with fury. Her hand itched to slap him, but she refused to demean herself in such a fashion.

"Why does it matter how it happened?" Richard finished.

Iris's lips had come together to form words, but the crack in his voice stopped her. Something was not right. She forced her gaze to his face, her eyes meeting his with uncompromising intensity.

His eyes held hers . . . and then slid away.

Chapter Fifteen

HE WAS THE worst sort of bastard.

Richard knew this, but still he turned for the door. He *could* tell her the truth. There was no reason he couldn't except that he was selfish and he was a coward, and damn it all, he wanted just a few more days before her displeasure descended into outright hatred. Was that really so much to ask?

"I will leave you," he said stiffly. And he would have done. If nothing had happened, if she'd not said a word, he would have opened the door and taken himself across the house. He would have shut himself in a room with a bottle of brandy and walls thick enough so that he could not hear her cry.

But then, just as his hand pressed down on the handle of the door, he heard her whisper, "Did I do something wrong?"

His hand stilled. But his arm trembled.

"I don't know what you mean," he said. But of course he knew exactly what she meant.

"It's—I—"

He forced himself to turn around. Dear God, it *hurt* to watch her like this, so awkward and pained. She couldn't get the sentence out, and if he were any sort of man, he'd figure out some way to spare her this humiliation.

He swallowed convulsively, searching for words that he knew would not be enough. "You are everything I could ask for in a wife."

But the look in her eyes was distrustful.

He took a long breath. He could not leave her like this. He crossed the room and reached for her hand. Perhaps if he brought it to his lips, if he kissed her . . .

"No!" She jerked her hand back, her voice as raw as her eyes. "I can't think straight when you do that."

Under normal circumstances, he would have delighted in such an admission.

Iris looked away, her eyes squeezing shut for a second, just long enough for her head to give a little jerk. "I don't understand you," she said in a very low voice.

"Do you need to?"

She looked up. "What sort of question is that?"

He forced a shrug, trying to look casual. "I don't understand anyone." Himself, least of all.

She stared at him for so long he had to fight the urge to shift his weight from foot to foot. "Why did you marry me?" she finally asked.

"Didn't we just have this conversation?"

Her mouth came together in an implacable line.

She did not speak. She did not speak for so long that he was compelled to fill the silence.

"You know why I married you," he said, not meeting her eyes.

"No," she said, "I really don't."

"I compromised you."

She gave him a withering glance. "We both know it started long before that."

He tried to calculate how long he might be able to feign ignorance.

"Oh, for the love of God, Richard, please do not insult my intelligence. You kissed me that night with the express purpose of being seen by my aunt. You demean me by insisting otherwise."

"I kissed you," he said hotly, "because I wanted to." It was the truth. Not the whole truth, but by God, it was part of the truth.

But Iris snorted with disbelief. "Maybe you did, but the question is *why* you wanted to."

Good God. He raked his hand through his hair. "Why does any man want to kiss a woman?"

"I really wouldn't know, now would I?" she practically spat. "Because my husband finds me repulsive."

He took a step back, shocked into silence. Finally, because he knew he had to say something, he said, "Don't be absurd."

It was the wrong thing. Her eyes widened as they filled with outrage, and she turned on her heel and stalked away from him.

But he was faster, and he caught her by the wrist. "I don't find you repulsive."

Her eyes flicked up as she dismissed this. "I

may not have the kind of experience you do, but I know what is meant to go on between a husband and wife. And I know that we have not—"

"Iris," he cut in, desperate to put a stop to this, "you're upsetting yourself."

Her eyes blazed with icy fury as she yanked her hand away. "Don't patronize me!"

"I'm not."

"You *are*."

He was. Of course he was.

"Iris," he began.

"Do you fancy men? Is that it?"

His mouth fell open, and he would have taken a breath, except it seemed his throat was no longer connected to his belly, which felt as if it had been punched.

"Because if you do—"

"No!" he practically howled. "How do you even know of such a thing?"

She gave him a flat stare, and he had the uncomfortable impression that she was trying to decide if she believed him. "I know someone," she finally said.

"You *know* someone?"

"Well, *of* him," she mumbled. "My cousin's brother."

"I don't fancy men," Richard said tightly.

"I rather wish you did," she muttered, glancing off to the side. "At least it would explain—"

"Enough!" Richard roared. Dear God, how much was a man meant to endure? He did not fancy men, and he *did* desire his wife. Quite urgently, as a matter of fact. And if he were living anyone's life but his own, he would make sure she knew that, in every way possible.

He stepped in close. Close enough to make her uncomfortable. "You think I find you repulsive?"

"I-I don't know," she whispered.

"Allow me to demonstrate." He took her face in his hands and brought his lips down to hers, burning with all the torment in his heart. He'd spent the past week wanting her, imagining every delicious thing he was going to do with her once he could finally take her to his bed. It had been a week of denial, of torture, of punishing his body in the most primitive way possible, and he had reached his limit.

He might not be able to do everything he wanted, but by God, she would know the difference between desire and disdain.

His mouth plundered hers, sweeping, tasting, devouring. It was as if every moment of his life had coalesced into this one kiss, and if he broke contact, even for a moment, even to breathe, it would all disappear.

The bed. It was all he could think, even though he knew it was a mistake. He had to get her to the bed. He had to feel her under him, to imprint himself upon her body.

She was his. She had to know that.

"Iris," he groaned against her mouth. "My wife."

He nudged her backward, and then he did it again, until she was edged up against the bed. She was so slender, such a wispy little thing, but she was kissing him back with a fire that threatened to consume them both.

No one else knew what lay beneath her placid surface. And no one else would, he vowed. She might give others her breathtaking smile, or even a taste of her sly, subtle wit, but *this* . . .

This was his.

He brought his hands behind her, and then under her, cupping the delightful curve of her bottom. "You are perfect," he said against her skin. "Perfect in my arms."

Her only response was a heated moan, and with a stunningly quick motion, he lifted her skirt and jerked her up so that her hips were level against his. "Wrap your legs around me," he commanded.

She did. It was nearly his undoing.

"Do you feel this?" he rasped, pressing his arousal hard against her.

"Yes," she said desperately.

"Do you? Do you really?"

He could feel her nodding against him, but he did not ease the pressure until she whispered once again, "Yes."

"Do not *ever* accuse me of not wanting you."

She pulled back. Not her hips; he was holding her far too tightly for that. But she pulled back her head, just far enough so that he was forced to look into her eyes.

Blue. So pale but so blue. And so full of confusion.

"You will find many things of which to accuse me," he growled, "but this will never be one of them."

He tumbled them both to the bed, reveling in the soft gasp that flew from her lips as he came down onto her.

"You are beautiful," he whispered, tasting the salty skin below her ear.

"You are exquisite," he murmured, running his tongue down the arched length of her throat.

His teeth found the scalloped edge of her bodice, and his hands made short work of it, yanking it down until he could see the surprisingly luscious shape of her breasts through the thin silk of her chemise. He cupped them, plumping her in his hands, and he shuddered with desire.

"You are mine," he told her, and he bent down to take one bud in his mouth.

He kissed her through silk, and then when that wasn't enough he kissed her skin, hot satisfaction rolling through him when he saw the cherry blush of her nipple.

"You're not pale here," he said, his tongue dancing a naughty circle around the tip.

She gasped his name, but he only chuckled. "You're so pale," he said huskily, trailing his hand up the length of her leg. "It was the first thing I noticed about you. Your hair . . ."

He took one thick lock and tickled it across her breastbone.

"Your eyes . . ."

He leaned down, brushing his lips against her temple.

"Your skin . . ."

This last was said with a moan, because her skin, all milky white and smooth, was bared beneath him, in stark contrast to the luscious pink tip of her breast.

"What color are you here, I wonder?" he murmured, trailing his fingers up the length of her thigh. She quivered beneath him, let out a gasp of pleasure as he ran one digit along the intimate crease where her leg met her hip.

"What are you doing to me?" she whispered.

He grinned wolfishly. "I'm making love to you." Then, spurred by some devilish bit of humor, he leaned down until his lips were warm at her ear. "I should have thought it was obvious."

She let out a surprised chuckle, and he could not help but grin at her expression. "I can't believe I just laughed," she said, one hand covering her mouth.

"And why not?" he drawled. "This is meant to be enjoyable."

Her mouth opened, but no sound came out.

"*I'm* enjoying myself."

Iris let out another astonished giggle.

"Are you?" he murmured.

She nodded.

He pretended to consider this. "I'm not convinced."

Her brows rose. "You're not?"

He shook his head slowly. "You're wearing far too many clothes to be truly enjoying yourself."

Her chin tucked in as she glanced down at herself. Her gown had been pushed down and pulled up in all the best ways, and she looked thoroughly decadent.

He liked her this way, he realized. He did not want her on a pedestal. He wanted her rumpled and earthy, pinned beneath him and flushed with pleasure. He brought his lips back to her ear. "It gets better."

Her dress had already been undone; it required little work to divest her of the garment completely.

"This has to go, too," he said, grasping the hem of her chemise.

"But you—"

"Are completely dressed, I know," he said with a low chuckle. "We'll have to do something about that, too." He sat up, still straddling her, and stripped off his coat and cravat. His eyes never left her face. He saw her tongue dart out to moisten her lips, and then he saw her catch her lower lip between her teeth, as if she was nervous about something, or maybe just trying to reach a decision.

"Tell me what you want," he commanded.

Her eyes went from his torso to his face and then back again, and Richard sucked in his breath as her trembling fingers reached for the buttons on his waistcoat.

"I want to see you," she whispered.

Every nerve in his body was screaming for him to rip off the last of his clothing, but he forced himself to remain still, unmoving except for the rapid rise and fall of his chest. He was mesmerized by her small hands, shaking as they fumbled with his buttons. It was taking her so long; she could barely force the disc through the buttonhole.

"I'm sorry," she said sheepishly. "I—"

His hand covered hers. "Don't apologize."

"But—"

"*Don't* . . ."

She looked up.

He tried to smile. " . . . apologize."

Together they managed the buttons, and Richard was soon pulling his shirt over his head.

"You're beautiful," she whispered. "I've never seen a man before. Not like this."

"I should hope not," he tried to joke, but then her fingers came to rest on his chest, and it felt as if his breath were being sucked from his body. "What you do to me," he gasped, and he came back down to cover her, hoping she had not noticed that he had not removed his breeches.

He could not. He'd stepped far too close to the fire as it was. Somewhere in the feverish recesses of his mind he knew that if he removed this last barrier, he would not survive it.

He would take her. Make her his in truth.

And that he could not do.

Not yet.

But nor could he leave her. She was temptation itself, lying beneath him, but that wasn't what kept him rooted to the spot.

He could not take what he so desperately desired, but he could give it to her.

She deserved that.

And something inside him said that maybe, just maybe, her pleasure would be almost as good as his own.

He rolled to his side, pulling her with him as he captured her mouth in another burning kiss. Her hands were in his hair, then on his back, and as he kissed his way down her neck, he felt her pulse beating beneath her skin. She was so aroused, maybe even as much as he was. She might be a virgin, but by God he was going to give her pleasure.

His hands dipped lower, gently parting her legs before resting over her mound. She stiffened, but he was patient, and after a moment of gently stroking she relaxed enough for him to dip into her folds.

"Shhhh," he crooned, bringing his face back to hers. "Let me do this for you."

She gave a jerky nod, even though he was fairly certain she had no idea what "this" was. It was humbling, the trust she'd placed in him, and he forced from his mind all the reasons he did not deserve it.

He showered her face with gentle kisses as his fingers worked their magic at her core. She felt so good, all warm and wet and womanly. He was nearly to bursting, but he ignored it, kissing her deeply before whispering, "Does this feel good?"

She nodded again, her eyes almost bewildered with desire.

"Do you trust me?"

"Yes," she whispered, and he made his way down her body, pausing at each breast before descending even farther.

"Richard?" Her voice was panicky, barely more than breath.

"Trust me," he murmured, the words sinking into the soft skin of her belly.

Her hands grasped the bedsheets beside her, but she did not halt his sensual progress.

He kissed her then, right at the very heart of her, softly making love with his lips and tongue. His hands spread over her thighs, holding them in place, holding her open for his erotic invasion.

She began to squirm beneath him, and he kissed her harder, sliding a finger inside and groaning with desire as he felt her muscles draw him in. He had to pause for a moment just to take a steadying breath. When he kissed her again, she strained against him, her hips coming off the bed with the force of her need.

"I'm not letting you go," he said, and he had no idea if she heard him. He pushed her legs farther apart, and he kissed and sucked and tickled until she cried out his name and shattered beneath him.

And still he drank of her, holding himself to her until she came back down to earth.

"Richard," she gasped, her hand frantically batting against the bed. "Richard . . ."

He slid himself up along her body, hovering above her so that he could gaze upon her passion-glazed face.

"Why did you do that?" she whispered.

He gave her a lazy smile. "Didn't you like it?"

"Yes, but . . ." She blinked rapidly, clearly at a loss for words.

He settled beside her, kissing her ear. "Was it enjoyable?"

Her chest rose and fell several times before she answered, "It was, but you—"

"I found it very enjoyable," he cut in. And he did, even if he was now frustrated as hell.

"But you . . . you . . ." She touched the waist of his breeches. He did not know if her passion had left her beyond words or if she was simply too embarrassed to speak of their intimacies.

"Shhhh." He put a finger to her lips. He didn't want to talk about it.

He didn't even want to think about it.

He held her until she fell asleep. And then he slipped from the bed and staggered back to his own room.

He could not fall asleep in her bed. He did not trust himself to awaken in her arms.

Chapter Sixteen

Iris awakened a bit before supper, just as she always did—slowly and with apathetic eyelids. She felt marvelously languorous, her limbs heavy with sleep and something more . . . something sensual and lovely. She found herself rubbing her feet against the sheets, wondering if they had ever felt so silky. The air was sweet, like fresh flowers and something else, something earthy and lush. She breathed in deeply, her lungs filling as she rolled onto her side and burrowed her face into her pillow. She did not think she had ever slept so well. She felt—

Her eyes snapped open.

Richard.

She glanced about the room, her head twitching back and forth. Where was he?

Clutching the sheet to her naked body, Iris sat

up, turning her attention to the other side of the bed. What time was it? When had he left?

She stared at the other pillow. What did she think she was going to see? An imprint of his face?

What had they done? He had . . .

She had . . .

But he definitely *hadn't* . . .

She closed her eyes in agony. She didn't know what was going on. She didn't *understand*.

He could not have consummated the union. He hadn't even removed his breeches. She might be ignorant when it came to the marriage bed, but she knew that much.

Her stomach rumbled, reminding her that it had been much too long since her last meal. Good heavens, she was hungry. What time was it? Had she missed supper?

She glanced over at her window, trying to figure out how late it was. Someone had pulled the heavy velvet curtains shut. Probably Richard, she thought, since the corner was caught on itself. A housemaid would never leave them askew like that.

It was dark out, but perhaps not yet pitch-black, and—oh, *bother*. She might as well just get up and look.

With a bit of a grunt she yanked the sheet free so that she could wrap herself with it. She didn't know *why* she felt this strange compulsion to know the time, but she certainly wasn't going to get her answer staring at a tiny triangle of window peeping out from behind her disheveled curtains.

Tripping over the edge of the sheet, she stumbled to the window and peered out. The moon shone brightly, not quite full, but round enough to lend the air a pearly glow. It was definitely well past dusk. How long had she been asleep?

"I wasn't even tired," she muttered.

She wrapped the sheet more tightly around her, grimacing when she realized how difficult she'd made it to walk. But she didn't rewrap herself—that would have been far too sensible. Instead she hopped and jumped herself over to her mantel clock. She gave it a little turn so that it better faced the moonlit window. Almost half nine. So that meant she'd been asleep . . . what . . . three hours? Four?

To know precisely would mean she knew how long she'd spent with Richard, doing . . .

That.

She shivered. She wasn't the least bit cold, but she shivered.

She needed to get dressed. She needed to get dressed, and get some food, and—

The door opened.

Iris shrieked.

So did the housemaid in the doorway.

But only one of them was wrapped like a mummy, and Iris's lurch of surprise landed her in a heap on the floor.

"Oh, my lady!" the housemaid cried. "I'm sorry, I'm so sorry." She rushed over, thrust her hand out, then pulled it back, clearly unsure of the proper behavior when faced with a nearly naked baronet's wife on floor.

Iris almost asked for help, then decided against it. Arranging herself with as much poise as she could manage, she looked up at the maid and tried to school her features into a coolly dignified expression.

In her head, at that moment, she rather thought she resembled her mother.

"Yes?" she intoned.

"Ehrm . . ." The maid—who looked supremely uncomfortable, there really was no other way to describe it—bobbed an awkward curtsy. "Sir Richard was wondering if you wished to take supper in your room."

Iris gave a regal nod. "That would be lovely, thank you."

"Have you any preference?" the maid asked. "Cook made fish, but if that is not to your choosing, she can make something else. She told me to tell you that."

"Whatever Sir Richard has chosen," Iris said. He would have eaten over an hour earlier; she did not wish to force the kitchen staff back to their ovens to cater to her whims.

"Right away, then, my lady." The maid curtsied again and practically ran from the room.

Iris sighed, then started to laugh because really, what else could she do? She gave this five minutes before every soul in the house knew of her mortifying—and mortifyingly dressed—tumble. Except her husband, of course. No one would dare breathe a word of it to *him*.

It was a very small shred of dignity, but she decided to cling to it.

Ten minutes later she'd donned one of her new silk nightgowns and covered it with a less revealing robe. She braided her hair for bed; it was where she intended to go just as soon as she finished eating. She could not imagine she would sleep right away, not after the nap she'd just taken. But she could read. It wouldn't be the first time she'd stayed up half the night with a book and a candle.

She walked over to her side table to look through the stack of books she'd pulled from the library earlier that afternoon. She'd left *Miss Truesdale and the Silent Gentleman* down in the drawing room, but she'd lost her taste for Hungarian archers.

And pathetic heroines who spent their time dithering and crying and wondering who might come to the rescue.

She'd read ahead. She knew what was coming.

No, she was not going to spend any more time with the piteous Miss Truesdale.

Picking up the books one by one, she examined her options. Another Sarah Gorely novel, a bit of Shakespeare, and a history of Yorkshire.

She took the history. She hoped it was boring.

But no sooner had she settled on her bed than she heard another knock at her door.

"Enter!" she called out, eager for supper.

The door that opened, however, was not the one that led to the hall. Instead it was the connecting door, the one that led to her husband's bedchamber. And the person who entered was her husband.

"Richard!" she squeaked, scrambling off the bed.

"Good evening," he said, his voice smooth as brandy. Not that she drank brandy, but everyone said it was smooth.

Good God, she was nervous.

"You're dressed for supper," she blurted out. Rather splendidly, too, in a bottle green superfine coat and pale yellow brocaded waistcoat. She now knew firsthand that his coats needed no padding. He'd told her once that he often helped his tenants in his fields. She believed him.

"You're not," he said.

She looked down at her tightly belted robe. It covered her up more than most ball gowns, but then again, most ball gowns could not be undone by a single tug of a sash.

"I intended to eat in my room," she said.

"As do I."

She looked at the open doorway behind him.

"Your room," he clarified.

She blinked. "My room?"

"Is that a problem?"

"But you've already eaten."

One corner of his mouth tipped up. "Actually, I have not."

"But it's half nine," she stammered. "Why haven't you eaten?"

"I was waiting for you," he said, as if it was the most obvious thing in the world.

"Oh." She swallowed. "You didn't have to do that."

"I wanted to."

She tightened her arms around her body, feeling strangely as if she had to protect herself, or cover herself, or *some*thing. She felt utterly out of her element. This man had seen her naked. Granted, he was her husband, but still, the things he'd done to her . . . and the way she'd reacted . . .

Her face flushed crimson. She didn't have to see it for herself to know just how deeply red she'd gone.

He quirked a brow. "Thinking of me?"

That was enough to strike her temper. "I think you should leave."

"But I'm hungry."

"Well, you should have thought of that earlier."

This made him smile. "I'm to be punished for waiting for my wife?"

"That's not what I mean, and you know it."

"And I thought I was being a gentleman by allowing you your slumber."

"I was tired," she said, and then she blushed again, because they both knew why.

She was spared further embarrassment by a knock at her door, and before she knew it, two footmen entered with a small table and chairs, followed by two maids carrying trays.

"Good heavens," Iris said, watching the flurry of activity. She'd been planning to take her tray in bed. But, of course, she could not do that now, not if Richard insisted upon dining with her.

The footmen set the table with quick precision, stepping back to allow the maids to bring forth the food. It smelled heavenly, and as the servants filed out Iris's stomach growled.

"One moment," Richard murmured, and he walked to the door and peered down the hall. "Ah, here we are. Thank you." When he stepped back into the room, he was holding a tall, narrow vase.

With a single iris.

"For you," he said softly.

Her lips trembled. "Where did you—they're not in season."

He shrugged, and for the briefest second he looked almost apprehensive. But that could not be true; he was never nervous. "There are a few left," he said, "if you know where to look."

"But it's—" She stopped, her lips parted in an astonished oval. She looked to the window, even though the curtains were now drawn tight. It was late. Had he gone out in the dark? Just to pick her a flower?

"Thank you," she said. Because sometimes it was best not to question a gift. Sometimes one simply had to be glad for it without knowing why.

Richard placed the vase at the center of their small table, and Iris stared at the bloom, mesmerized by the thin inner streaks of gold, delicate and bright in the soft violet petals.

"It's beautiful," she said.

"Irises are."

Her eyes flew from the flower to his face. She couldn't help it.

He held out his hand. "Come," he said. "We should eat."

It was an apology. She saw it right there in his outstretched hand. She just wished she knew what he was apologizing for.

Stop, she told herself. *Stop questioning everything.* For once she was going to let herself be happy without needing to know why. She'd fallen in love with her husband, and that was a good thing. He'd brought her unimaginable pleasure in bed. That was a good thing, too.

It was enough. It had to be enough.

She took his hand. It was large and strong and warm and everything a hand ought to be. *Everything a hand ought to be?* She let out a little burst of absurd laughter. Good gracious, she was growing melodramatic.

"What is so funny?" he asked.

She shook her head. How was she to tell him that she had been measuring the perfection of hands, and his topped the list?

"Tell me," he said, his fingers tightening around hers. "I insist."

"No." She kept shaking her head, her thoughts making her voice round and full of mirth.

"Tell me," he growled, pulling her closer.

Her lips were now pressed together hard, the corners desperately fighting a smile.

His lips drew close to her ear. "I have ways of making you talk."

Something wicked jumped within her, something greedy and lush.

His teeth found her earlobe, softly scraping the tender skin. "Tell me, Iris . . ."

"Your hands," she said, barely recognizing her own voice.

He stilled, but she could feel his smile against her skin. "My hands?"

"Mmm."

They spanned her waist. "These hands?"

"Yes."

"You like them?"

She nodded, then gasped as he slid them lower, cupping the gentle curve of her bottom.

He brushed his mouth against her jaw, along her neck, and then back to the corner of her lips. "What else do you like?"

"Everything." The word spilled forth without warning, and she probably should have felt embarrassed, but she didn't. She couldn't. Not with him.

Richard chuckled, the sound full and solid with male pride. His hands moved to the front of her body, each one grasping a dangling end of the bow knot she'd tied in the belt of her dressing gown.

His lips touched her ear. "Are you my present?"

Before she could respond, he gave a sharp tug, staring down at her with hot desire as the robe came loose.

"Richard," she whispered, but he had already moved on, sliding those wonderful wonderful hands up along her body, pausing for an agonizing moment on her breasts before reaching her shoulders and pushing the robe away. It felt to the floor in a cloud of pale blue silk.

Iris stood before him in another one of her decadent trousseau nightgowns. It was not a practical garment; it would not even pretend to keep her warm at night. But she could not remember ever feeling so womanly, so desirable and daring.

"You are so beautiful," Richard whispered, skimming his hand back down to her breast. His palm teased the tip, moving in a slow circle over the silk of her gown.

"I'm—" She cut herself off.

Richard look down at her, one finger touching

her chin until her eyes met his. His brows rose in question.

"It's nothing," Iris murmured. She'd almost protested, almost said that she wasn't beautiful, because she wasn't. A woman did not reach the age of one-and-twenty without knowing if she was beautiful or not. But then she'd thought—

No. *No.* If he thought she was beautiful, she damn well wasn't going to contradict. If he thought she was beautiful, then she was beautiful, at least on this night, in this room.

"Kiss me," she whispered.

His eyes flared with heat, and his face dipped toward hers. When their lips touched, Iris felt a jolt of desire at the very core of her womanhood. He'd kissed her there just a few hours before. She let out a little moan. Just the thought of it made her weak.

But this time he was kissing her lips. His tongue swept in, tickling the sensitive skin at the roof of her mouth, daring her to respond in kind. She did, her desire making her bold, and when he groaned and pulled her more tightly against him, her body thrilled with power. She moved her hands to his chest and shoved his coat from his shoulders, tugging it down as he yanked his arms from the sleeves.

She wanted to feel him again. She was beyond wanton; it had been mere hours since the last time, and already she wanted to pull him down to her bed, to feel his weight pinning her against the mattress.

This couldn't be normal, this incredible, unearthly need.

"*My* present," she said, bringing her fingers to

the snowy white cravat at his throat. It had been tied simply, thank heavens; she didn't think her trembling fingers could have managed one of those intricate knots that was all the rage among the London dandies.

She then turned her attention to the three buttons at the neck of his shirt, her lips parting as his throat was revealed to her, his pulse beating with a hard, strong rhythm.

She touched his skin, loving the way the muscles jumped beneath her fingers.

"You're a witch," he groaned, yanking his shirt over his head.

She just smiled, because she felt like one, as if she had new powers. She had touched his chest the last time, felt the hard muscles flexing beneath his skin, but she hadn't been able to do anything more. He'd been so quick to make everything about her. When his hands had run up and down her body, she'd lost control, and when his mouth covered her most private place she'd lost all thought.

But not this time.

This time she wanted to explore.

She listened to the heavy rasp of his breath as her fingers trailed along his taut abdomen. A thin line of hair, dark and crisp, trailed from his navel to the waist of his breeches. When she touched it his entire belly sucked in, almost enough for her to slide her hand under the fabric.

She didn't, though. She was not that audacious. Not yet.

But she would be. Before the night was through, she vowed that she would be.

The food was forgotten as Richard swept her

into his arms and carried her to the bed. He laid her down—not roughly, but not gently, either—and Iris felt a frisson of feminine glee as she realized how close he was to the edge of his control.

Emboldened, she let her hand drift back down toward his breeches. But just before her fingertips slid under the waistband, his hand landed heavily on hers.

"No," he said roughly, holding her still. And then, before she could voice her questions, he said, "I can't."

She smiled up at him, some flirtatious inner demon finally waking up in her soul. "Please?" she murmured.

"I'll make you feel good." His free hand moved to her leg, squeezed her thigh. "I'll make you feel so good."

"But I want to make *you* feel good."

He closed his eyes, and for a moment Iris thought he was in pain. His teeth were gritted together, and his face was a harsh, tense mask. She reached up to smooth his brow, sliding her fingers along his cheek as he turned his head into the cradle of her hand.

She felt him acquiesce, felt a little bit of the tension slide from his body, and her other hand, the one resting so dangerously on his belly, edged under his breeches. She did not go far, just to the springy hair that lay on his flat abdomen. It surprised her, although she didn't really know why, and she caught her lower lip in her teeth and looked up at him.

"Don't stop there," he groaned.

She didn't want to, but his breeches were flat-fronted and snug, with barely enough room for her whole hand. She moved to the fastening, then slowly set him free.

She gasped.

This was not what she'd seen on the statue at the museum.

A lot of what her mother had said began to make sense.

She looked up him with a question in her eyes, and he gave a jerky nod. Holding her breath, she reached out and touched him, gingerly at first, pulling back when his member twitched beneath her fingers.

He rolled over to his side, and Iris fell with him, only just realizing that he still had his boots on.

She didn't care. And he didn't seem to, either.

She pushed him until he was on his back, then crouched next to him, just looking. How had it grown so big?

Yet another thing in her world she did not understand.

She touched it again, this time letting her fingers drift along the surprisingly silky skin. Richard sucked in his breath, and his body jerked, but she knew it was with pleasure, not pain.

Or if it was pain, it was a good kind of pain.

"More," he groaned, and this time she wrapped her hand lightly around him, glancing back up to his face to make sure she was doing the right thing. His eyes were closed, and he was breathing fast and hard. She moved her hand, just a little bit, but before she could do more, his fingers wrapped over hers, holding her still.

For a moment she thought she'd hurt him, but then his grip tightened, and she realized he was showing her what to do. After a few strokes his hand fell away, and she was left in control, thrilled by the seductive power she held over him.

"My God, Iris," Richard groaned. "What you do to me . . ."

She caught her lower lip between her teeth as she felt a proud smile rising within her. She wanted to take him over the edge, as he had done for her. After so many lonely nights, she wanted proof that he desired her, that she was woman enough to satisfy him. He would not be able to hide behind a chaste kiss on her forehead again.

"Can I kiss you?" she whispered.

His eyes flew open.

"Like you did to me?"

"No," he said quickly, the word hoarse and wrenched from his throat. "No," he said again, and he almost looked a little panicked.

"Why not?"

"Because . . . because . . ." He swore and scooted himself up, not quite to a sitting position, but enough so that he could rest on his elbows. "Because I won't—I can't—"

"Will it hurt you?"

He groaned, closing his eyes. He looked so distressed. Iris touched him again, watching his face as his body jerked beneath her. The sound of his breath electrified her, and he looked like . . . he looked like . . .

He looked the way she felt. Overcome.

His head fell back, and she knew the moment

he gave in. The tension did not leave his body, but something told her he was through fighting himself. She peeked back up at his face to make sure his eyes were still closed—somehow she wasn't brave enough to do this if she knew he was watching—and she bent over and placed the lightest of kisses on the tip of his manhood.

He gasped, his belly sucking in with his breath, but he did not stop her. Emboldened, Iris kissed him again, allowing her lips to linger a bit longer. He twitched, and she drew back, glancing at his face. He didn't open his eyes, but he must have sensed her hesitation, because he gave a brief nod, and then with one single word, he made her soul sing.

"Please."

It was so strange to think that just a few weeks ago she was Miss Iris Smythe-Smith, hiding behind her cello at her family's awful musicale. Her world had changed so much; it was as if the earth had flipped on its axis, landing her here, as Lady Kenworthy, in bed with this glorious man, kissing him on a part of his body she hadn't even known existed before. Or at least not in its present state.

"How does it do that?" she murmured to herself.

"What?"

"Oh, sorry," she mumbled, blushing. "It was nothing."

His hand found her chin, turning her to face him. "Tell me."

"I was just, well, wondering . . ." She swallowed, utterly mortified, which was ludicrous. She was about to kiss him *there* again, and she was embarrassed to be wondering how it all worked?

"Iris . . ." His voice was like warmed honey, melting through her bones.

Not quite looking at him, she motioned to his member. "It's not like this all the time." And then, second-guessing herself, she added, "Right?"

He let out a hoarse laugh. "God, no. It would kill me."

She blinked in confusion.

"It's desire, Iris," he said in a husky voice. "Desire makes a man like this. Hard."

She touched him gently. He was indeed hard. Under the softest of skin, he was hard as granite.

"Desire for you," he said, then admitted, "I've been like this all week."

Her eyes widened with shock. She did not speak, but she rather thought he saw the question in her eyes.

"Yes," he said with a self-mocking chuckle. "It hurts."

"But then—"

"Not pain like an injury," he said, stroking her cheek. "Pain like frustration, like unfulfilled need."

But you could have had me. The words hovered unspoken in her mind. Clearly he hadn't thought she was ready. Maybe he'd thought he was being considerate. But she did not wish to be treated like a fragile ornament. People seemed to think she was delicate and frail—it was her coloring, she thought, and her slight frame. But she wasn't. She never had been. On the inside she was fierce.

And she was ready to prove it.

Chapter Seventeen

Richard didn't know if he was in heaven or hell.

His wife, whom he had not even properly bedded, was . . . She was kissing his . . . Good Lord, she had her mouth on his cock, and what she lacked in skill she was making up for in enthusiasm, and—

What the hell was he saying? She wasn't lacking in skill. Did skill even matter? This was every man's erotic dream. And this wasn't some courtesan, this was his wife. His *wife*.

He should stop her. But he couldn't, dear God he couldn't. He'd been aching for her for so long, and now, as she knelt between his legs, kissing him in the most intimate way imaginable, he found himself enslaved by his desire. With every hesitant flick of her tongue, his hips arched off the bed, and he was brought treacherously closer to release.

"Do you like it?" Iris whispered.

She sounded almost shy. Good God, she sounded almost *shy*, and yet she was taking him in her mouth.

Did he like it? The innocence of the question nearly unmanned him. She had no idea what she was doing to him, didn't know that he'd never even dared to dream she might give of herself in such a way.

"Richard?" she whispered.

He was a beast. A cur. A wife wasn't meant to do such things, at least not before she'd been given time to be gently initiated into the ways of the marriage bed.

But Iris had surprised him. She was always surprising him. And when she cautiously took him into her mouth he was lost to all sanity.

Nothing had ever felt so good.

Never had he felt so loved.

He froze. *Loved?*

No, that was impossible. She didn't love him. She couldn't. He did not deserve it.

But then an awful little voice from deep inside—a voice he could only conclude was his wayward conscience—reminded him that this had been his plan. He would use their brief honeymoon at Maycliffe to seduce her, in heart if not in body. He had been *trying* to get her to fall in love.

He should not have done that. He should not have even contemplated it.

And yet, if she did . . . if she did love him . . .

It would be *wonderful*.

He closed his eyes, allowing pure sensation to wash over him. His wife's innocent lips were bringing him unimaginable pleasure. It shot through him with electric intensity, and at the same time bathed him in a warm, contented glow. He felt . . .

Happy.

Now there was something he wasn't used to experiencing in the throes of passion. Excitement, yes. Desire, of course. But happiness?

And then it hit him. It wasn't that Iris was falling in love with him. *He* was falling in love with *Iris.*

"Stop!" he cried, the word wrenching itself from his throat. He could not let her do this.

She backed away, looking up at him with bewilderment. "Did I hurt you?"

"No," he said quickly, moving away from her before he changed his mind and gave in to the harsh need raging through his body. She had not hurt him. Far from it. But he was going to hurt her. It was inevitable. Every single thing he'd done since that moment he'd first seen her at her family's musicale . . .

It had all been leading to one moment.

How could he let her give of herself so intimately when he knew what was about to happen?

She would hate him. And then she would hate herself for having done this, for having all but *serviced* him.

"Was I doing it wrong?" she asked, her pale blue eyes steady on his.

Good God, she was direct. He'd thought that was what he loved so much about her, but right now it was killing him.

"No," he said. "You weren't . . . that is to say . . ." He could not tell her that she'd been so utterly perfect, he thought he might lose his mind. She'd made him feel things he'd never imagined possible. The touch of her lips, her tongue . . . the soft whisper of her breath . . . It had been transcendent. He had been clenching the sheets beneath him just to keep himself from flipping her over and burying himself inside her warmth.

He forced himself to sit up. It was easier to think that way, or maybe it just put a little more space between them. He pinched the bridge of his nose, trying to figure out what to say. She was staring at him like a lost little bird, waiting with an almost preternatural stillness.

He pulled the sheet up, covering his arousal. There was no reason he could not tell her the truth now, no reason except his own cowardice. But he did not want to. Was it so very weak of him to want just a few more days of her good opinion?

"I don't expect you to do such a thing," he finally said. It was the worst sort of evasion, but he didn't know what else to say.

She regarded him with a blank stare, followed by a soft furrowing of her brow. "I don't understand."

Of course she didn't. He sighed. "Most wives don't do"—he waved a pathetic hand in the air—"*that.*"

He face instantly flushed. "Oh," she said, her voice achingly hollow. "You must think—I didn't know—I'm so—"

"Stop, *please*," he begged, grasping her hand. He did not think he could bear it if she actually apologized. "You did nothing wrong. I promise. Quite the opposite," he said before he thought to censor himself.

She scrambled off the bed, but not before he saw the confusion on her face.

"It's just . . . it's quite a lot . . . so early in our marriage . . ." He let his words trail off. It was the only thing to do. He had no idea how to complete the sentence. Good God, he was an ass.

"This is all too much," he said, hoping she did not hear the slight pause before he added, "for you."

He jerked himself to his feet, cursing as he hastily refastened his breeches. What kind of man was he? He'd taken the worst sort of advantage. For the love of God, he still had his bloody boots on.

He looked at her. Her lips were parted, still swollen from his kisses. But the desire was gone from her eyes, replaced by something he could not quite name.

Something he did not want to identify.

He raked his hand through his hair. "I think I should go."

"You didn't eat," she said. Her voice sounded flat. He hated that.

"It doesn't matter."

She nodded, but he was fairly certain neither of them knew why. "Please," he whispered, allowing himself one last touch. His fingers gently caressed her brow, then paused to cup her cheek in his hand. "Please know one thing. You have done nothing wrong."

She did not speak. She just stared at him with those huge blue eyes, not even looking confused. Just . . .

Resigned. And that was even worse.

"It's not you," he said. "It's me." He had a feeling he was making this worse with every word, but he couldn't seem to stop himself. He swallowed, waiting again for her to say something, but she did not.

"Good night," he said softly. He bowed with his head and left the room. Never in his life had he felt so awful doing the right thing.

Two days later

RICHARD WAS SITTING in his study, nursing a second glass of brandy, when he saw a carriage coming up the drive, its windows glinting in the late-afternoon sun.

His sisters?

He'd sent word to his aunt that Fleur and Marie-Claire could not be permitted to stay the full two weeks, but still, he wasn't expecting them today.

Setting his glass down, he walked over to the window and peered out for a closer look. It was indeed his aunt's carriage. He closed his eyes for a moment. He wasn't sure why they were back early, but there was nothing he could do about it now.

It was time.

He could not decide whether to greet them alone or with Iris, but in the end it did not matter; Iris was reading in the drawing room, and she called out to him as he walked by.

"Is that a carriage in the drive?"

"My sisters," he confirmed.

"Oh."

That's all she said. Oh. He had a feeling she'd soon be saying quite a bit more.

He paused in the doorway, watching as she slowly set her book down. She'd been curled on the blue sofa with her legs tucked under her, and she had to pause to put her feet back in her slippers before standing.

"Do I look all right?" she asked, smoothing her dress.

"Of course," he said distractedly.

Her lips pressed together.

"You look lovely," he said, taking in her green-striped frock and softly pinned hair. "Forgive me. My mind is elsewhere."

She seemed to accept his explanation and took his arm when he offered it. She did not quite meet his eyes. They had not spoken of what had happened in her room the two nights before, and it appeared they were not going to do so anytime soon.

When Iris had come down for breakfast the previous morning he had been sure their conversation would be stilted, if they spoke at all. But as always, she had surprised him. Or maybe he had surprised himself. Whatever the case, they had spoken of the weather, and of the book Iris was reading, and a problem the Burnhams were having with flooding in one of their fields. It had all been very smooth.

But it had not felt right.

When they spoke, it felt almost . . . careful. As long as they restricted their conversation to trivialities, they could pretend that nothing had changed. They both seemed to recognize that eventually they would run out of impersonal topics, and so they measured their words, doling them out like treasures.

But that was all about to end.

"I did not think they were expected until Thursday," Iris said, allowing him to lead her from the room.

"Nor did I."

"Why do you sound so grim?" she asked, after a brief pause.

Grim did not even begin to cover it. "We should wait for them in the drive," he said.

She nodded, ignoring the fact that he did not answer her question, and they headed out the front door. Cresswell was already standing at attention in the drive, along with Mrs. Hopkins and the two footmen. Richard and Iris took their places just as the carriage pulled up behind his aunt's prized team of dappled grays.

The door to the carriage was opened, and Richard immediately stepped forward to assist his sisters. Marie-Claire bounced down first, giving his hand a little squeeze as she descended. "She is in a beastly mood," she said without preamble.

"Wonderful," Richard muttered.

"You must be Marie-Claire," Iris said brightly. She was anxious, though. Richard could see it in the way her hands were clasped tightly together in front of her. He'd noticed that she did that to keep herself from bunching the fabric of her dress in her fingers when she was nervous.

Marie-Claire gave a small curtsy. At fourteen she was already taller than Iris, but her face still held the roundness of childhood. "I am. Please forgive us for returning early. Fleur wasn't feeling well."

"No?" Iris inquired, peering toward the open carriage door. There was still no sign of Fleur.

Marie-Claire looked over at Richard while Iris wasn't watching and made a retching motion.

"In the carriage?" he could not help but ask.

"Twice."

He winced, then stepped up on the stool that had been laid beside the carriage door and peered inside. "Fleur?"

She was huddled in the corner, miserable and pale. She *looked* like she'd been sick twice in the carriage. Smelled like it, too.

"I'm not talking to you."

Bloody hell. "So it's like this, then."

She turned away, her dark hair obscuring her face. "I would prefer to have one of the footmen assist me from the carriage."

Richard pinched the bridge of his nose, trying to stave off the raging headache he knew would soon have his skull in a vise. He and Fleur had been at odds about this for well over a month. There was only one acceptable solution. He knew this, and it infuriated him that she refused to accept what must be done.

He sighed wearily. "For the love of God, Fleur, put aside your irritation for one minute and let me help you out of the carriage. It smells like a hospital in here."

"I'm not *irritated*," she spat.

"You're irritating *me*."

She drew back at the insult. "I want a footman."

"You will take my hand," he ground out.

For a moment he thought she would hurl herself out the opposite door just to vex him, but she must have retained at least an ounce of the sense she'd once displayed, because she looked up, and snarled, "Fine." With a purposeful lack of grace, she slapped her hand onto his and allowed him to assist her out of the carriage. Iris and Marie-Claire were standing side by side, pretending not to watch.

"Fleur," Richard said in a dangerous voice, "I would like to introduce you to your new sister. My wife, Lady Kenworthy."

Fleur looked at Iris. There was an awful silence.

"It's lovely to meet you," Iris said, holding out her hand.

Fleur did not take it.

For the first time in his life, Richard almost hit a woman. "*Fleur*," he said warningly.

With a disrespectful purse of her lips, Fleur made a curtsy. "Lady Kenworthy."

"Please," Iris said, her eyes flicking nervously to Richard before settling back on Fleur. "I hope you will call me Iris."

Fleur gave her a withering stare, then turned to Richard. "It isn't going to work."

"Don't do this here, Fleur," he warned her.

She jerked her arm out toward Iris. "Look at her!"

Iris took a little step back. Richard had a feeling she did not even realize she'd done it. Their eyes met, hers bewildered, his exhausted, and he silently pleaded with her not to ask, not yet.

But Fleur wasn't done. "I've already said—"

Richard grabbed her by the arm and hauled her away from the others. "This is not the time or the place."

She stared at him mutinously, then yanked her arm free. "I'll be in my room, then," she said, and stalked off toward the house. But she stumbled on the bottom step and would have fallen if Iris had not leapt forward to catch her.

For a moment the two women remained frozen as if in a tableau. Iris kept her hand on Fleur's elbow, almost as if she realized that the younger woman was unsteady, that she'd been unsteady for weeks and needed some sort of human contact.

"Thank you," Fleur said grudgingly.

Iris took a step back, her hands returning to their tightly clasped position in front of her. "It was nothing."

"Fleur," Richard said in a commanding voice. It was not a tone he'd often used with his sisters. Perhaps he should have done.

Slowly, she turned.

"Iris is my wife," he stated. "Maycliffe is her home now, as much as it is ours."

Fleur's eyes met his. "I could never overlook her presence here. I assure you."

And then Richard did the strangest thing. He reached out and took Iris's hand. Not to kiss it, not to lead her somewhere.

Just to hold it. To feel her warmth.

He felt her fingers lace through his, and he tightened his grip. He did not deserve her. He knew it. Fleur knew it, too. But for this one awful moment, with his entire life crashing around him, he was going to hold his wife's hand and pretend she would never let go.

Chapter Eighteen

For MUCH OF her life, Iris had made a conscious choice to keep her mouth shut. It wasn't that she had nothing to say; put her in a roomful of cousins and she'd run on at the mouth all night. Her father had once said she was a born strategist, always looking two steps ahead, and maybe this was why she had always recognized the value of choosing *when* to speak. Never, however, had she been truly rendered speechless. Truly, flabbergastedly, she-could-not-even-*think*-in-complete-sentences, speechless.

But now, as she watched Fleur Kenworthy disappear into Maycliffe, Richard's hand still improbably twined with her own, all Iris could think was—*Whhaaaaa?*

No one moved for at least five seconds. The first to wake up was Mrs. Hopkins, who mumbled something about making sure Fleur's room was ready before hurrying into the house. Cresswell, too, made a swift and discreet exit, ushering the two footmen along with him.

Iris held herself totally still, her only movement her eyes as they darted back and forth between Richard and Marie-Claire.

What on *earth* had just happened?

"I'm sorry," Richard said, releasing her hand. "She is not usually like that."

Marie-Claire snorted. "It would be more accurate to say she's not *always* like that."

"Marie-Claire," he snapped.

He looked exhausted, Iris thought. Utterly wrecked.

Marie-Claire crossed her arms over her chest and leveled a dark stare at her brother. "She's been awful, Richard. Just awful. Even Aunt Milton lost her patience with her."

Richard turned sharply toward her. "Does she . . ."

Marie-Claire shook her head.

Richard exhaled.

Iris kept watching. And listening. Something strange was going on, some sort of hidden conversation beneath their scowls and shrugs.

"I don't envy you, Brother." Marie-Claire looked at Iris. "Or you."

Iris started. She'd almost thought they'd forgotten her presence. "What is she talking about?" she asked Richard.

"Nothing," he bit off.

Well, *that* was clearly a lie.

"Or me, really," Marie-Claire continued. "I'm

the one who has to share a room with her." She groaned dramatically. "It's going to be a long year."

"Not now, Marie-Claire," Richard warned.

The siblings shared a look that Iris could not even begin to interpret. They had the same eyes, she realized, the same way of narrowing them to make a point. Fleur, too, although hers had a greenish hue, where Richard's and Marie-Claire's were dark and brown.

"You have lovely hair," Marie-Claire said suddenly.

"Thank you," Iris said, trying not to blink at the sharp change of subject. "So do you."

Marie-Claire let out a little laugh. "No I don't, but it's very kind of you to say so."

"But it's just like your brother's," Iris said, darting a mortified look at Richard when she realized what she'd said. He was looking at her strangely, as if he didn't know what to make of her accidental compliment.

"You must be weary after your journey," Iris said, trying to salvage the moment. "Would you like to rest?"

"Er . . . yes. I suppose so," Marie-Claire said, "although I'm not sure my bedchamber will be very restful just now."

"I'll talk to her," Richard said grimly.

"Now?" Iris asked. She almost suggested that he wait until Fleur had had time to calm down, but what did she know? She hadn't a clue what was happening. A quarter of an hour ago she'd been peacefully reading a novel. Now she felt as if she were living in one.

And she was the only character who did not seem to know the plot.

Richard stared up at the house, his expression stark. Iris watched as his mouth flattened into a hard, forbidding line. "It's got to be done," he muttered. Without further farewell, he stalked off into the house, leaving Iris and Marie-Claire alone in the drive.

Iris cleared her throat. This was awkward. She smiled at her new sister, the kind where you can't quite manage to show your teeth, but it's not really insincere because truly, you're *trying*.

Marie-Claire smiled back in precisely the same way.

"It's a nice day," Iris finally said.

Marie-Claire nodded slowly. "Yes."

"Sunny."

"Yes."

Iris realized she was rocking on her feet, up to her toes and back to her heels. She clamped herself back into place. What on earth was she supposed to say to this girl?

But in the end she didn't have to say anything. Because Marie-Claire turned and looked at her with an expression that Iris greatly feared was pity.

"You don't know, do you?" the younger girl said softly.

Iris shook her head.

Marie-Claire glanced over her shoulder, staring at absolutely nothing before turning back to Iris. "I'm sorry."

Then she, too, walked into the house.

And Iris just stood in the drive.

Alone.

"Open the door, Fleur!"

Richard pounded his fist against the wood, oblivious to the shock reverberating down his arm.

Fleur made no response, not that he'd thought she would.

"Fleur!" he roared.

Nothing.

"I'm not leaving this spot until you open the door," he growled.

At that he heard footsteps, followed by, "Then I hope you don't need to use the chamber pot!"

He was going to kill her. Surely no older brother had ever been pushed quite so far.

He took a breath, then let it out in a lengthy exhale. Nothing would come of his bad temper. One of them needed to act like an adult. He flexed his fingers, straight out, then back into fists. The bite of his nails in his palms had a paradoxically calming effect.

Calming. But he was not calm, not by any stretch.

"I cannot help you if you will not speak to me," he said, his voice tightly controlled.

No response.

He had half a mind to head down to the library, where he could access the secret staircase that led to her room. But knowing Fleur, she would have already thought of that. It wouldn't be the first time she dragged her vanity table in front of the hidden door to block access. Besides, she'd know what he was about the instant he abandoned his current post.

"Fleur!" he yelled, slamming the door with the

flat of his hand. It stung, and he swore viciously. "I will saw off the bloody doorknob!"

Again, nothing.

"I will do it!" he bellowed. "Do not think I won't!"

Silence.

Richard closed his eyes and leaned back against the wall. He was appalled at what he'd been reduced to, screaming like a madman outside his sister's bedroom door. He didn't even want to think about what the servants were saying belowstairs. They had to know something was amiss; no doubt each would have his own lurid theory.

He didn't care, just as long as no one guessed the truth.

Or rather, what would be the truth.

He hated himself for what had to happen. But what else could he do? When his father had died, he had been entrusted with the care and well-being of his sisters. He was only trying to protect her. And Marie-Claire. Was she really so selfish that she could not see that?

"Richard?"

He nearly jumped a foot. Iris had sneaked up on him while his eyes were closed.

"I'm sorry," she said in a quiet voice. "I did not mean to give you a fright."

He choked back irrational laughter. "You're the least frightening thing in the house, I assure you."

Wisely, she did not respond.

But her presence made him only more determined to speak to his sister. "Forgive me," he said to his wife, then once again bellowed, "Fleur!"

He pounded on the door so hard, the wall shook. "God help me, I will kick this door down!"

"Before or after you saw off the doorknob?" came Fleur's taunting response.

He ground his teeth together, taking a shuddering breath through his nose. "Fleur!"

Iris laid a gentle hand on his arm. "Can I be of help?"

"It's a family matter," he bit off.

She drew her hand back, and then she drew her body back. "Forgive me," she said sharply. "I thought I was family."

"You met her three minutes ago," he snapped. It was a cruel comment, and completely uncalled for, but he was so furious just then, he couldn't possibly temper his words.

"I'll leave you to it, then," Iris said haughtily. "Since you're managing so well."

"You know nothing about this."

Her eyes narrowed. "A fact of which I am quite aware."

Dear God, he couldn't fight both of them right now. "Please," he said to her, "try to be reasonable."

Which was *always* the wrong thing to say to a woman.

"Reasonable?" she demanded. "You want me to be *reasonable*? After everything that has happened in the last fortnight, it's a wonder I am even sentient!"

"Hyperbole, Iris?"

"Do not patronize me," she hissed.

He did not bother to contradict.

Her eyes blazing, she stepped forward, almost close enough to touch. "First you drag me into a marriage—"

"I did not drag you."

"You might as well have done."

"You weren't complaining two days ago."

She flinched.

He knew he had gone too far, but he'd lost all of his reserves. He didn't know how to stop now. He moved closer, but she did not budge an inch. "For better or for worse, you are my wife."

Time seemed to stop. Iris's jaw clenched with the effort of containing her rage, and Richard could not take his eyes off her mouth, pink and lush. He knew what she tasted like now. He knew it as well as he knew his own breath.

With a curse, he jerked his head and turned away. What sort of monster was he? In the middle of all this, all he could think of was kissing her.

Consuming her.

Making love to her before she despised him.

"I want to know what is going on," Iris said, her voice clipped with fury.

"Right now I must deal with my sister," he said.

"No, right now you will tell me—"

He cut her off. "I will tell you what you need to know when you need to know it."

Which would probably be in the next few minutes, assuming Fleur ever opened her damned door.

"This has something to do with why you married me, doesn't it?" Iris said.

He turned sharply to face her. She was pale, even paler than normal, but her eyes were blazing.

He couldn't lie to her any longer. Maybe he wasn't ready to tell her the truth, but he couldn't lie.

"Fleur!" he bellowed. "Open the damn—"

The door slammed open, and there she was, wild-eyed and shaking with fury. Richard had never seen his sister thus. Her dark hair had come half-loose from its pins and was sticking out at odd angles. Her cheeks were high with color.

What happened to the sweet, biddable sister he'd once known? He'd sat through *tea* parties with her, for God's sake.

"You wished to speak with me?" Fleur voice's dripped with disdain.

"Not in the hall," he said viciously, grabbing her arm. He tried to pull her into the bedchamber she shared with Marie-Claire, but she dug in her heels.

"She comes, too," she said, jerking her head toward Iris.

"*She* has a name," Richard ground out.

"So sorry." Fleur turned to Iris and batted her lashes. "Lady Kenworthy, your presence is humbly requested."

Richard saw red. "Do not speak to her in that tone of voice."

"How do mean, like she's family?"

Richard did not trust himself to speak. Instead he hauled his sister back into her room. Iris followed, although she did not look convinced that she was doing the right thing.

"We're going to be very close, I know," Fleur said to Iris, her smile sickeningly sweet. "You have no idea how close."

Iris eyed her with well-deserved apprehension. "Perhaps I should come anoth—"

"Oh, no," Fleur cut in. "You should stay."

"Close the door," Richard ordered.

Iris did so, and he tightened his grip on Fleur, trying to pull her farther into the room.

"Let go of me," Fleur hissed, trying to shake him off.

"Will you be reasonable?"

"I have never been unreasonable," she shot back.

That was open to debate, but he released her arm. He despised the madman she was turning him into.

But then Fleur whipped around to face Iris, her eyes glittering dangerously. "Did Richard tell you about me?"

Iris did not reply immediately. She swallowed, the motion shuddering down her delicate throat, and her eyes flicked to Richard's before she finally said, "Some."

"Just some?" Fleur looked over at Richard, one brow curved in a sardonic arch. "You omitted all the good parts, didn't you?"

"Fleur . . ." he said warningly.

But Fleur had already returned her attention to Iris. "By any chance, did my brother happen to tell you that I'm pregnant?"

Richard felt his heart drop. He shot a desperate look at Iris. She'd gone positively bloodless. He wanted to go to her, to hold her and protect her, but he knew the only thing she needed protection from was him.

"I'll be showing soon," Fleur said, her voice a mockery of decorum. She smoothed her dress down over her body, pressing the pale pink fabric against her belly. "Won't that be a lark?"

"For the love of God, Fleur," Richard spat, "have you no tact?"

"None," Fleur said unrepentantly. "I'm a fallen woman now."

"Don't say that," Richard bit off.

"Why not? It's true." Fleur turned to Iris. "You wouldn't have married him if you'd known about his wretched ruined sister, now would you?"

Iris was shaking her head, little movements back and forth as if she could not recognize her own thoughts. "Did you know this?" she asked him. She held up a hand, almost as if to ward him off. "No, of course you did."

Richard stepped forward, trying to meet her eyes. "Iris, there's something I need to tell you."

"I'm sure we can come up with a solution," Iris said, her voice taking on a strange, almost frantic tinge. She looked at Fleur, she looked at the wardrobe, she looked anywhere but at her husband. "It's not a good situation, to be sure, but you're not the first young lady to find herself like this, and—"

"Iris," Richard said quietly.

"You have the support of your family," she told Fleur. "Your brother loves you. I know he does, and you do, too. We'll think of something. There's always something."

He spoke again. "I've already thought of something, Iris."

Finally, she looked at him.

She whispered, "Why did you marry me, Richard?"

It was time to tell the truth.

"You will pretend to be pregnant, Iris. And we will raise Fleur's baby as our legitimate child."

Chapter Nineteen

Iris STARED AT her husband with mounting disbelief. Surely he did not mean . . . He would never . . .

"No," she said. *No*, she wouldn't do this. *No*, he couldn't possibly be asking it of her.

"I'm afraid you have no choice," Richard said grimly.

She gaped at him. "I have no *choice*?"

"If we do not do this, Fleur will be ruined."

"I think she's already managed that quite well herself," Iris snapped before she could even think of tempering her words.

Fleur let out a bark of harsh laughter, looking almost amused at Iris's insult, but Richard stepped forward with a hot look in his eyes, and warned, "You are speaking of my sister."

"And you are speaking *to* your wife!" Iris cried. Horrified by the agonized catch in her voice, she clapped her hand to her mouth and twisted away. She could not look at his face. Not right now.

She'd known he was hiding something. Even as she was falling in love and trying to convince herself it was all in her head, she had known there had to be a reason behind their hasty marriage. But she had never imagined something like this. She *could* never have imagined it.

It was madness. Madness, and yet it explained everything. From the rushed wedding to his refusal to consummate the marriage . . . it all made perfect, hideous sense. No wonder he'd had to find a bride so quickly. And, of course, he could not risk getting Iris pregnant before Fleur had her baby. Iris would like to see him explain *that*.

As it was, they would have to claim that Iris delivered the child a month—or maybe even two months—early. And then, when the babe emerged perfectly healthy and large, everyone would assume it had been a forced marriage, that Richard had seduced her before the wedding.

Iris let out a harsh laugh. Dear God, nothing could be further from the truth.

"You find this funny?" Richard demanded.

She wrapped her arms around her body, trying to contain the painful bubble of hysteria ballooning within her. Turning around so that she could look straight at his face, she replied, "Not even one bit."

He had the good sense not to ask for further clarification. Iris could only imagine the wild look in her eyes.

After a few moments, Richard cleared his throat, and said, "I realize that you have been put in a difficult situation . . ."

Difficult? Her jaw came unhinged. He wanted her to feign a pregnancy and then claim another woman's child as her own? And he called that *difficult*?

" . . . but I think you will see that it is the only solution."

No. She shook her head. "That cannot be possible. There must be some other way."

"Do you really think I came to this decision lightly?" Richard said, his voice rising with temper. "Do you imagine I did not consider every possible alternative?"

Iris's lungs grew tight, and she fought the need to suck in great big gulps of air. She couldn't breathe. She could barely *think*. Who *was* this man? He'd been almost a stranger when they married, but she had thought he was at heart a good and honest person. She had let him kiss her in the most mortifyingly intimate way imaginable, and she did not even *know* him.

She'd thought she might even be falling in love.

And the worst part was, he could force her to do this. They both knew that. In marriage, the man's word was law, and the woman's lot was to obey. Oh, she could run to her parents, but they would just send her back to Maycliffe. They might be shocked, they might think Richard was mad to consider such a scheme, but in the end, they would tell her that he was her husband, and if this was his choice, she must go along with it.

"You deceived me," she whispered. "You deliberately tricked me into marriage."

"I am sorry."

And he probably was, but that did not excuse him.

Then she asked the most terrifying question of all. "Why me?"

Richard blanched.

Iris felt her blood drain from her body, and she stumbled back, the force of his unsaid reply a punch to her gut. He didn't need to say anything; the answer was right there on his face. Richard had chosen her because he *could*. Because he'd known that with her modest dowry and unremarkable looks she would not have suitors clamoring for her hand. A girl like her would be eager for marriage. A girl like her would never refuse a man like him.

Good Lord, had he *researched* her? Of course. He must have done. Why else would he have attended the Smythe-Smith musicale, if not to seek an introduction?

Winston Bevelstoke's face suddenly flashed in her mind, his smile so practiced and suave as he introduced them. Had he helped Richard to choose a bride?

Iris nearly choked with the horror of it. Richard must have asked his friends to draw up lists of the most desperate women in London. And she had topped the charts.

She had been judged. And she had been pitied.

"You have humiliated me," she said, barely able to find her voice.

No one would call Sir Richard Kenworthy a fool. He had known exactly what he needed in a bride—someone so pathetic and grateful for a marriage proposal that she'd roll over and say *yes, please* when he finally revealed the truth.

That was what he thought of her.

Iris gasped, clapping her hand to her mouth to stifle the cry that rose from her throat.

Fleur regarded her with a disconcertingly steady gaze before saying to Richard, "You really should have told her the truth before you asked her to marry you."

"Shut *up*," he snarled.

"Don't tell her to shut up," Iris snapped.

"Oh, now you're on her side?"

"Well, nobody seems to be on *mine*."

"You should know that I have told him I will not agree to the scheme," Fleur said.

Iris turned to look at her, to really look at her for the first time that afternoon, to try to see something beyond the petulant, hysterical girl who'd stepped down from the carriage. "Are you mad?" she demanded. "What do you propose to do? Who is the baby's father?"

"It's obviously no one you know," Fleur snapped.

"The younger son of a local baron," Richard said in a flat voice. "He seduced her."

Iris whirled to face him. "Well, then, why don't you force him to marry her?"

"He's dead," he replied.

"Oh." Iris felt as if she'd been punched. "Oh." She looked at Fleur. "I'm sorry."

"I'm not," Richard said.

Iris's eyes widened with shock.

"His name was William Parnell," he spat. "He was a bastard. Always has been."

"What happened?" Iris asked, not sure that she wanted to know.

Richard glanced over at her with an arched

brow. "He fell over the side of a balcony, drunk and waving a pistol. It's a miracle no one was shot."

"Were you there?" Iris whispered. Because she had the most awful feeling he might have had something to do with it.

"Of course not." He looked at her with a disgusted expression. "There were a dozen witnesses. Including three prostitutes."

Iris swallowed uncomfortably.

Richard's face was a ravaged mask as he said, "I tell you this only so you will know what sort of man he was."

Iris nodded dumbly. She didn't know what to say. She didn't know what to *feel.* After a few moments, she turned to Fleur—her new sister, she reminded herself—and took her hands. "I'm so sorry." She swallowed, keeping her voice careful and soft. "Did he hurt you?"

Fleur turned away. "It was not like that."

Richard lurched forward. "Do you mean to tell me you *let*—"

"Stop!" Iris cried out, yanking him back. "There is nothing to be gained by making accusations."

Richard gave a curt nod, but he and Fleur continued to watch each other warily.

Iris swallowed. She hated to be insensitive, but she had no idea how far along Fleur was— her dress was loose enough to conceal an early pregnancy—and she rather thought they hadn't many moments to spare.

"Is there another gentleman who will marry her?" she asked. "Someone who—"

"I'm not going to marry a stranger," Fleur said hotly.

I did. The words came unbidden to Iris's mind. Unbidden, but undeniably true.

Richard's eyes made a disdainful roll. "I haven't the money to buy her a husband, in any case."

"Surely you could find someone—"

"Willing to take her babe as his heir, should it be a boy? That takes a hefty bribe indeed."

"And yet you're prepared to do it," she stated.

Richard flinched, but he said, "The child will be my niece or nephew."

"But not yours!" Iris turned away, hugging her arms to her body. "And not mine."

"You cannot love a child not of your body?" His voice was low, accusing.

"Of course I can. But this is deceptive. It's wrong. You know it is!"

"I wish you luck convincing him of that," Fleur said.

"Oh, for heaven's sake, be quiet!" Iris snapped. "Can't you see I'm trying to help you?"

Fleur lurched back, startled by Iris's display of temper.

"What will you do when we have a boy," Iris asked Richard, "and your son—your firstborn son—cannot inherit Maycliffe because you have already given it away?"

Richard said nothing, his lips pressed so tightly together they were nearly gone white.

"You would deny your own child his birthright?" Iris pressed.

"I will make arrangements," he said stiffly.

"There are no arrangements that can be made," Iris cried. "You cannot have thought this through.

If you claim her son as ours, you cannot make a younger child your heir. You—"

"Maycliffe is not entailed," Richard reminded her.

Iris drew an angry breath. "That's even worse. You would allow Fleur's son to believe he is your firstborn and then hand Maycliffe to his younger brother?"

"Of course not," Richard nearly hissed. "What sort of man do you think I am?"

"Honestly? I don't know."

He recoiled, but he continued speaking. "I will divide the property in two if necessary."

"Oh, that will be fair," Iris drawled. "One child will get the house and the other the orangery. No one is going to feel slighted at *that*."

"For the love of God," Richard exploded, "will you just *shut up*?"

Iris gasped, flinching at his tone.

"I shouldn't have said that if I were you," Fleur said.

Richard snarled something at his sister; Iris didn't know what, but Fleur took a step back, and all three of them hung frozen in an uneasy tableau until Richard drew a loud breath, and said in an emotionless voice, "We will all travel to Scotland next week. To visit cousins."

"We have no Scottish cousins," Fleur said flatly.

"We do now," he told her.

Fleur looked at him as if he'd gone mad.

"Just recently discovered on the family tree," he said, with enough false cheer to indicate that he was making the whole thing up. "Hamish and Mary Tavistock."

"Now you're inventing relations?" Fleur scoffed.

He ignored her sarcasm. "*You* are going to enjoy their company so much you decide to stay." He gave her a sickly smile. "For months."

Fleur crossed her arms. "I won't do it."

Iris looked at Richard. The raw pain in his eyes was almost too much to bear. For a moment she wanted to go to him, to lay her hand on his arm and comfort him.

But no. *No.* He did not deserve her comfort. He had lied to her. He had deceived her in the worst possible way.

"I cannot stay here," she said suddenly. She could not remain in this room. She could not look at him. Or his sister.

"You will not leave me," Richard said sharply.

She turned, not sure if her face belied her disbelief. Or her contempt. "I am going to my room," she said slowly.

He shifted his weight slightly. He was embarrassed. Good.

"Do not disturb me," Iris said.

Neither Richard nor Fleur said a word.

Iris stalked to the door and wrenched it open, only to find Marie-Claire, tripping over her feet as she jumped back, trying to look as if she hadn't been blatantly eavesdropping.

"Good afternoon," Marie-Claire said with a hasty smile. "I was just—"

"Oh for God's sake," Iris snapped, "you already *know.*"

She brushed past her, beyond caring that she'd made the younger girl stumble. When she got to her room, she did not slam the door. Instead she shut it with a careful click, her hand remaining frozen on the handle. With a strange detachment, she watched as her fingers began to tremble and then shake. And then her legs were shaking, and she had to lean against the door for support, and then she was sliding down, down to the floor where she bent into herself and began to weep.

IRIS WAS GONE for a full minute before Richard could bring himself to look at his sister.

"Do not blame this on me," Fleur said with low fervor. "I did not ask this of you."

Richard tried not to respond. He was so damned weary of arguing with her. But he could not see anything but the shattered look on Iris's face, and he had an awful sense that he'd broken something within her, something he could never repair.

He began to feel chilled, the hot fury of the last month replaced by a devastating frost. His eyes settled hard on Fleur's. "Your lack of gratitude astounds me."

"I am not the one who demanded that she commit such an immoral fraud."

Richard clenched his teeth until his jaw shook. Why could she not see reason? He was trying to protect her, to give her a chance at a happy, respectable life.

Fleur gave him a scornful glance. "Did you really think she was going to smile, and say, 'As you wish, sir?'"

"I will deal with my wife as I see fit," he bit off.

Fleur snorted.

"My God," he exploded. "You have absolutely

no—" He cut himself off, raking a hand through his hair as he wrenched himself away, turning to face the window. "Do you think I like this?" he nearly hissed. He clutched the sill with whitened fingers. "Do you think I enjoyed deceiving her?"

"Then don't."

"The damage is done."

"But you can fix it. All you have to do is tell her she doesn't have to steal my child."

He whirled around. "It's not steal—" He caught the triumphant look on her face, and said, "You're enjoying this, aren't you?"

Fleur gave him a stony stare. "I assure you, I enjoy nothing about this."

He looked at her then, really looked at her. Behind her eyes she was just as broken as Iris. The pain in her face . . . Had he put it there? No. *No.* He was trying to help her, to save her from the ruined existence with which that bastard Parnell had left her.

His hands curled into fists. If that bloody rotter hadn't gone and died, he would have killed him. No, he would have marched him to the church with Fleur and *then* killed him. He thought of how his sister had once been, full of dreams and romance. She used to lie in the grass by the orangery and read in the sunshine. She used to *laugh.*

"Make me understand," he pleaded. "Why do you resist this? Don't you realize this is your only hope for a respectable life?"

Fleur's lips trembled, and for the first time that afternoon, she looked unsure of herself. He saw in her face the child she'd once been, and it broke his heart anew.

"Why can you not set me up somewhere as a young widow?" she asked. "I can go to Devon. Or Cornwall. Somewhere where we don't know a soul."

"I haven't the money to provide you with a proper household," Richard said, shame at his financial constraints making his voice hard. "And I will not allow you to live in poverty."

"I don't need much," Fleur said. "Just a little cottage, and—"

"You think you don't need much," Richard cut in. "But you don't know. You've lived your whole life with servants. You've never had to shop for your food or stoke your own fires."

"Neither have *you*," she shot back.

"This isn't *about* me. I'm not the one who will be off in a leaky cottage, worrying over the price of meat."

Fleur looked away.

"I'm the one," he said in a softer voice, "who will have to worry about you, wondering what I will do if you fall ill, or are taken advantage of, and I can't even help you because you're half a country away."

Fleur did not speak for some time. "I cannot marry the baby's father," she finally said. "And I will not give up my child."

"It will be with me," he reminded her.

"But it won't be *mine*," she cried. "I don't want to be its aunt."

"You say that now, but what happens in ten years when you realize that no one will marry you?"

"I realize that now," she said sharply.

"If you have this child and raise it yourself, you

will be lost to respectable society. You won't be able to stay here."

She went still. "You would cut me off, then."

"No," he said quickly. "Never. But I cannot keep you in the house. Not while Marie-Claire is yet unmarried."

Fleur looked away.

"Your ruin is her ruin. Surely you know that."

"Of course I know that," she said hotly. "Why do you think I—"

But she stopped, clamping her mouth shut.

"What?" he demanded. Why did he think she *what*?

She shook her head. And in a voice low and sad, she said, "We will never agree on this."

He sighed. "I am only trying to help you, Fleur."

"I know." She looked up at him, her eyes tired and sad and maybe even a little wise.

"I love you," he said, choking on the words. "You are my sister. I vowed to protect you. And I failed. I *failed*."

"You did not fail."

He threw out an arm, motioning to her still-flat belly. "You mean to tell me you gave yourself to Parnell willingly?"

"I told you, that's not what—"

"I should have been here," he said. "I should have been here to protect you, and I wasn't. So for the love of God, Fleur, give me the opportunity to protect you now."

"I cannot be my child's aunt," she said with quiet determination. "I cannot."

Richard rubbed his face with the heel of his

hand. He was so tired. He didn't think he'd ever been so tired in his life. He would talk to her to-morrow. He would make her see.

He walked to the door. "Do not do something rash," he said quietly. And then he added, "Please."

She gave a single nod. It was enough. He trusted her. It was the damnedest thing, but he trusted her.

He let himself out of the room, pausing only briefly to acknowledge Marie-Claire's presence in the hall. She was still standing near the door, her fingers nervously clasped together. He could not imagine she'd needed to eavesdrop; most of the conversation had been amply loud.

"Should I go in?" she asked.

He shrugged. He had no answers. He kept walking.

He wanted to talk to Iris. He wanted take her hand in his and make her understand that he hated this, too, that he was sorry he'd tricked her.

But not sorry he married her. He could never be that.

He paused outside her door. She was crying.

He wanted to hold her.

But how could he be of comfort, when he was the one who had done this to her?

So he kept walking, past his own bedroom door and down the stairs. He went to his study and he shut the door. He looked at his half-drunk glass of brandy and decided he hadn't had nearly enough.

That was a problem easily remedied.

He downed the dregs and refilled the glass, raising it in a silent toast to the devil.

Would that all his problems had such easy an-swers.

Chapter Twenty

Never had Maycliffe been such a cold and quiet house.

At breakfast the next morning, Richard sat in silence, his eyes following Fleur as she selected her food from the sideboard. She sat across from him, but they did not speak, and when Marie-Claire entered the room, their greetings were nothing but grunts.

Iris did not come down.

Richard did not see her all day, and when the dinner gong sounded, he lifted his hand to knock at her door, but he found himself frozen before he made contact with the wood. He could not forget the look on her face when he'd told her what she must do, could not erase the sound of her tears after she'd fled to her room.

He'd known this would happen. He'd been dreading it since the moment he slid his ring on her finger. But it was so much worse than his imaginings. The foreboding sense of guilt had been replaced by soul-deep loathing, and he truly wasn't sure he'd ever feel at ease with himself again.

He used to be a good person. Maybe not the *best* person, but he'd been fundamentally good. Hadn't he?

In the end, he did not knock at Iris's door. He went down to the dining room by himself, stopping only to instruct a maid to have supper brought up to her on a tray.

Iris did not come down to breakfast the next day, either, prompting Marie-Claire to proclaim herself jealous. "It's so unfair that married women can take their breakfast in bed, and I can't," she said as she stabbed her knife in the butter. "There's really no—"

She stopped talking, Richard's and Fleur's twin expressions of ire enough to silence anyone.

The following morning Richard resolved to speak to his wife. He knew she deserved her privacy after such a shock, but she had to know as well as anyone that time was not their friend. He had given her three days; he could not give her any more.

Once again he breakfasted with his sisters, not that any of them spoke a word. He was trying to decide the best way to approach Iris, attempting to arrange his words into coherent and persuasive sentences, when she appeared in the doorway. She was wearing a frock of the palest blue—her favorite color, he'd deduced—and her hair had been dressed into an intricate twist of braids and loops and honestly, he didn't know how to describe it except that she looked more done-up than he'd ever seen her.

She'd donned armor, he realized. He could not blame her.

Iris hovered in place for a moment, and he shot to his feet, suddenly aware that he'd been staring. "Lady Kenworthy," he said with full respect. It was perhaps too formal, but his sisters were still at the table, and he would not have them think he held his wife in anything but the highest regard.

Iris glanced at him with icy blue eyes, dipped her chin in a small nod of recognition, and then busied herself at the sideboard. Richard watched as she spooned a small portion of eggs onto her plate, then added two pieces of bacon and a slice of ham. Her movements were steady and precise, and he could not help but admire her composure as she took her seat and greeted them one by one: "Marie-Claire," then "Fleur," and finally, "Sir Richard."

"Lady Kenworthy," Marie-Claire said in polite greeting.

Iris did not remind her to use her Christian name.

Richard looked down at his plate. He had just a few bites of food left. He wasn't really hungry, but it felt as if he ought to be eating if Iris was, so he took a slice of toast from a plate at the center of the table and began to butter it. His knife scraped too hard against the bread, the sound grating and loud in the overwhelming silence.

"Richard?" Fleur murmured.

He looked at her. She glanced rather pointedly at his toast, which, it had to be said, was looking very sad and mangled.

Richard gave her a glare, for no logical reason whatsoever, and took a savage bite. Then coughed. Bloody hell. It was dry as dust. He looked down.

All the butter he'd attempted to spread had scraped up onto the knife, all curled up like some sort of tortured dairy ribbon.

With a growl he slapped the now rather soft butter onto the toast and took another bite. Iris stared at him with a disconcertingly steady gaze, then said, with no inflection whatsoever, "Jam?"

He blinked, the sound of her voice startling in the silence. "Thank you," he said, taking the small dish from her fingers. He had no idea what flavor it was—something crimson, so he'd probably like it—but he didn't care. Other than his name, it was the first word she'd spoken to him in three days.

After another minute or so, however, he was beginning to think that it would be the *only* word for the next three days as well. Richard did not quite understand how silence could have varying degrees of awkwardness, but this four-person silence was infinitely more awful than the one he'd endured with just his sisters for company. A frigid mantle had come over the room, not of temperature but of mood, and every clink of fork against dish was like the crack of ice.

And then suddenly—thankfully—Marie-Claire spoke. It occurred to Richard that perhaps she was the only one who could. She was the only one who wasn't playing a role in this macabre farce that had become his life.

"It is good to see you downstairs," she said to Iris.

"It is good to be down," Iris said with barely a glance in Marie-Claire's direction. "I am feeling much better."

Marie-Claire blinked. "Were you ill?"

Iris took a sip of her tea. "In a manner of speaking."

Out of the corner of his eye, Richard saw Fleur's head snap around.

"And are you well now?" he asked, staring at Iris until she was forced to meet his gaze.

"Quite." She turned her attention back to her toast, then set it down with an oddly deliberate motion. "If you will all forgive me," she said, rising to her feet.

Richard stood immediately, and this time so too did his sisters.

"You haven't eaten a thing," Marie-Claire said.

"I'm afraid my stomach is somewhat unsettled," Iris replied in a voice that Richard found far too composed. She placed her napkin on the table next to her plate. "It is my understanding that it is a malady common to women in my condition."

Fleur gasped.

"Shall you wish me joy?" Iris said tonelessly.

Richard realized he couldn't. He'd got what he wanted—no, not what he *wanted,* it had never been what he *wanted.* But he'd got what he asked for. Iris might not be smiling about it, but for all intents and purposes she had just announced her pregnancy. To three people who knew full well it was a lie, but still, she'd signaled that she would do what Richard had demanded of her. He'd won.

But he could not wish her joy.

"Excuse me," Iris said, exiting the room.

He stood frozen. And then—

"Wait!"

He somehow came to his senses, or at least as much sense as was needed to force his legs into motion. He strode from the room, well aware that his two sisters were gaping at him like landed fish. He called out Iris's name, but she was nowhere to be seen. His wife was fast, Richard thought wryly. Either that, or she was hiding from him.

"Darling?" he called out, past caring if the entire household could hear him. "Where are you?"

He peered in the drawing room, then the library. Bloody hell. He supposed she had the right to make this difficult for him, but it was beyond time they talked.

"Iris!" he called again. "I really need to speak with you!"

He stood in the center of the hall, frustrated beyond measure. Frustrated, and then extremely embarrassed. William, the younger of the two footmen, was standing in a doorway, watching him.

Richard scowled, refusing to acknowledge the moment.

But then William started to twitch.

Richard could not help but stare.

William's head began to jerk to the right.

"Are you quite all right?" Richard could no longer avoid asking.

"M'lady," William said in a loud whisper. "She went into the drawing room."

"She's not there now."

William blinked. He took a few steps and poked his head into the room in question. "The tunnel," he said, turning back to face Richard.

"The . . ." Richard frowned, peering over William's shoulder. "You think she went into one of the tunnels?"

"I don't think she went out the window," William retorted. He cleared his throat. "Sir."

Richard stepped into the drawing room, his eyes lighting on the comfortable blue sofa. It had become one of Iris's favorite spots to read, not that she'd ventured outside her bedchamber in the past few days. At the far wall was the cleverly camouflaged panel that hid the entrance to the most well used of Maycliffe's secret tunnels. "You're sure she entered the drawing room," he said to William.

The footman gave a nod.

"Then in the tunnel she must be." Richard shrugged, crossing the room in three long strides. "I thank you, William," he said, his fingers easily working the hidden latch.

"It was nothing, sir."

"All the same," Richard said with a nod. He peered into the passageway, blinking into the darkness. He'd forgotten how cold and damp it could get in there. "Iris?" he called out. It was unlikely she'd got very far. He doubted she'd had time to light a candle, and the tunnel grew black as night once it twisted away from the house.

There was no answer, however, and so Richard lit a candle, placed it in a small lantern, and then stepped into the hidden passageway. "Iris?" he called again. Still no answer. Maybe she hadn't entered the tunnel. She was angry, but she wasn't stupid, and she wasn't going to hide out in a pitch-dark hole in the ground just to avoid him.

Holding his lantern low enough to light the way, he stepped carefully forward. The Maycliffe tunnels had never been laid with stone, and the ground was rough and uneven, with loose rocks and even the occasional tree root snaking through. He had a sudden vision of Iris taking a tumble, twisting her ankle or worse, hitting her head . . .

"Iris!" he yelled once again, and this time he was rewarded with the tiniest sound, a cross between a sniffle and a sob. "Thank God," he breathed. His relief was so quick and sudden he couldn't even manage regret over the fact that she was obviously trying not to cry. He rounded a long, shallow corner, and then there she was, sitting on the hard-packed dirt, huddled like a child, her arms wrapped round her knees.

"Iris!" he exclaimed, dropping to her side. "Did you fall? Are you injured?"

Her head was buried against her knees, and she did not look up as she shook it in the negative.

"Are you certain?" He swallowed awkwardly. He'd found her; now he didn't know what to say. She'd been so magnificently cool and composed in the breakfast room; he could have argued with *that* woman. He could have thanked her for agreeing to mother Fleur's child, he could have told her that it was past time they made plans. At the very least he could have formed *words*.

But seeing her like this, forlorn and curled up tight . . . he was lost. He brought a tentative hand to her back and patted, painfully aware that she'd hardly want comfort from the man who had made her so miserable in the first place.

She didn't pull away, though, and somehow that left Richard feeling even more awkward. He set the lantern down a safe distance away and rested on his haunches beside her. "I'm sorry," he said, aware that he had no idea what he was apologizing for—there were far too many transgressions to choose just one.

"I tripped," she suddenly said. She looked up at him with defiant eyes. *Wet* defiant eyes. "I *tripped*. That's why I'm upset. Because I tripped."

"Of course."

"And I'm fine. I'm not hurt at all."

He nodded slowly, holding out his hand. "May I still help you to your feet?"

For a moment she didn't move. Richard watched her jaw set defiantly in the flickering light, and then she put her hand in his.

He stood, nudging her along with him. "Are you certain you can walk?"

"I said I wasn't injured," she said, but there was a rough, forced quality to her voice.

He did not respond, just tucked her hand in the crook of his arm after reaching down to retrieve the lantern. "Would you like to return to the drawing room or head outside?" he inquired.

"Outside," she said, her chin quivering through her regal tone. "Please."

He nodded and led her forward. She did not seem to be limping, but it was hard to tell for sure; she was holding herself so stiffly. They had walked together so many times during that brief period he had come to think of as their honeymoon; never had she felt like this, all glassy and brittle.

"Is it far?" she asked.

"No." He'd heard the swallow in her voice. He didn't like it. "The exit is near the orangery."

"I know."

He didn't bother to ask how. It had to be the servants; he knew she hadn't spoken to either of his sisters. He'd meant to show her the tunnels, he'd been looking forward to it. But there hadn't been time. Or maybe he hadn't made time. Or forced her to take the time.

"I tripped," she said again. "I would have been there already if I hadn't tripped."

"I'm sure," he murmured.

She stopped hard enough for him to stumble. "I would!"

"I wasn't being sarcastic."

She scowled, then looked away so quickly he knew her ire was self-directed.

"The exit is just up ahead," he said, a few moments after they resumed their pace.

She gave a terse nod. Richard led her along the final stretch of the tunnel, then released her arm so that he could push open the door in the ceiling. He always needed to crouch in this part of the tunnel. Iris, he noted with a wry amusement, could stand straight, the top of her blond head just skimming the ceiling.

"It's up there?" Iris asked, looking up at the hatch.

"It's at a bit of a slant," he replied, working the latching mechanism. "From the outside it looks a bit like a shed."

She watched for a moment, then said. "It latches from the inside?"

He gritted his teeth. "Could you hold this?" he asked, holding out the light. "I need two hands."

Wordlessly, she took the lantern. Richard winced as the latch pinched his index finger. "It's a tricky thing," he said, finally snapping it free. "You can open it from either side, but you have to know how to do it. It's not like a regular gate."

"I would have been trapped," she said in a hollow voice.

"No you wouldn't." He pushed the door open, blinking as the sunlight assaulted them. "You would have turned around and gone back to the drawing room."

"I closed that door, too."

"It's easier to open," he lied. He supposed he'd have to show her how to do it eventually, for her own safety, but for now, he was going to let her think she'd have been fine.

"I can't even run away properly," she muttered.

He held out his hand to steer her up the shallow steps. "Is that what you were doing? Running away?"

"I was making an exit."

"If that's the case, then you did a fine job."

Iris turned to him with an inscrutable expression, then deftly pulled her hand from his. She used it to shade her eyes, but it felt like a rejection.

"You don't need to be nice to me," she said bluntly.

His lips parted, and it took him a moment to mask his surprise. "I don't see why I shouldn't."

"I don't *want* you to be nice to me!"

"You don't—"

"You are a monster!" She put a fist against her mouth, but he heard the choked sob all the same. And then, in a much smaller voice, she said, "Why can't you just act like one and let me hate you?"

"I don't want you to hate me," he said softly.

"That's not your choice."

"No," he agreed.

She looked away, the dappled morning light playing along the intricate braids she wore like a crown. She was so beautiful to him it hurt. He wanted to go to her, wrap his arms around her and whisper nonsense against her hair. He wanted to make her feel better, and then he wanted to make sure no one ever hurt her again.

That, he thought caustically, was his honor.

Would she ever forgive him? Or at least understand? Yes, this was a mad thing he'd asked of her, but he'd done it for his sister. To protect her. Surely Iris, of all people, could understand that.

"I would like to be alone right now," Iris said.

Richard was quiet for a moment before saying, "If that is your wish." But he didn't leave. He wanted just one more moment with her, even in silence.

She looked up at him as if to say, *what now?*

He cleared his throat. "May I escort you to a bench?"

"No thank you."

"I would—"

"Stop!" She lurched back, holding her hand out as if to ward off an evil spirit. "Stop being *nice*. What you did was reprehensible."

"I'm not a monster," he stated.

"You *are*," she cried. "You have to be."

"Iris, I—"

"Don't you understand?" she demanded. "I don't want to like you."

Richard felt a glimmer of hope. "I'm your husband," he said. She was supposed to like him. She was supposed to feel so much more than that.

"If you are my husband, it is only because you tricked me," she said in a low voice.

"It wasn't like that," he protested, even though it was *exactly* like that. But the thing was, it had *felt* different, at least a little. "You have to understand," he tried, "the whole time . . . In London, when I was courting you . . . All the things about you that made you seem a good choice were the things I liked so well about you."

"Really?" she said, and she didn't sound snide, just disbelieving. "You liked me for my desperation?"

"No!" God above, what was she talking about?

"I know why you married me," she said hotly. "You needed someone who would need *you* even more. Someone who could overlook a suspiciously hasty proposal and be desperate enough to *thank* you for your hand."

Richard recoiled. He hated that those very thoughts had once sounded in his head. He could not remember thinking them specifically about Iris, but he had certainly thought them before he met her. They were the reason he'd gone to the musicale that first fateful evening.

He'd heard about the Smythe-Smiths. And *desperate* was the very word he'd heard.

Desperate was what had drawn him in.

"You needed someone," Iris said with devastating quiet, "who would not have to choose between you and another gentleman. You needed someone who would choose between you and loneliness."

"No," he said, shaking his head. "That's not—"

"But it was!" she cried. "You can't tell me that—"

"Maybe at the beginning," he cut in. "Maybe

that's what I thought I was looking for—No, I'll be honest, that's what I *was* looking for. But can you blame me? I had to—"

"Yes!" she cried. "Yes, I blame you. I was perfectly happy before I met you."

"Were you?" he said roughly. "Were you really?"

"Happy enough. I had my family, and I had my friends. And I had the possibility that I might someday find someone who—" Her words shattered, and she turned away.

"Once I met you," he said quietly, "I thought differently."

"I don't believe you." Her voice was small, but her words were tight and perfectly enunciated.

He held himself still. If he moved, if he so much as extended a finger in her direction, he did not know that he would be able to contain himself. He wanted to touch her. He wanted it with a fervor that should have terrified him.

He waited for her to turn around. She did not.

"It is difficult to have a conversation with your back."

Her shoulders tensed. She turned to face him with slow intensity, her eyes gleaming with fury. She wanted to hate him, he could see that. She was clinging to it. But for how long? A few months? A lifetime?

"You chose me because you pitied me," she said in a low voice.

He tried not to flinch. "That's not how it was."

"Then how was it?" Her voice rose in anger, and her eyes somehow darkened. "When you asked me to marry you, when you just *had* to kiss me—"

"That's exactly it!" he cried. "I wasn't even going to *ask* you. I never thought I might find someone I could ask in such a short time."

"Oh, thank you," she choked, clearly insulted by his words.

"That's not what I meant," he said impatiently. "I assumed I would have to find the right woman and put her in a compromising position."

Iris looked at him with such disappointment it was almost too much to bear. But he kept talking. Because he had to keep talking. It was the only way he might get her to understand.

"I'm not proud of that," he said, "but it was what I thought I had to do to save my sister. And before you think the worst of me, I would never have seduced you before marriage."

"Of course not," she said with a bitter laugh. "You couldn't very well have your wife and sister pregnant at the same time."

"Yes . . . No! I mean, yes, obviously, but that wasn't what was going through my head. God!" He raked his hand through his hair. "Do you really think I would take advantage of an innocent after what had happened to my own sister?"

He saw her throat work. He saw her fighting her own words. "No," she finally said. "No. I know you wouldn't."

"Thank you for that," he said stiffly.

She turned away again, hugging her arms to her body. "I don't want to talk to you right now."

"I'm sure you don't, but you will have to. If not today, then soon."

"I already said I would agree to your ungodly plan."

"Not in so many words."

She whipped back around to face him. "You're going to make me say it out loud? My little announcement at breakfast wasn't enough?"

"I need your word, Iris."

She stared at him, and he couldn't quite tell whether it was with disbelief or horror.

"I need your word because I trust your word." He paused for a moment to let her reflect upon *that*.

"You are my husband," she said without emotion. "I will obey you."

"I don't want you to—" He cut himself off.

"Then what do you want?" she burst out. "Do you want me to *like* this? To tell you I think you're doing the right thing? Because I can't. I will lie to the entire world, apparently, but I won't lie to you."

"It is enough that you will accept Fleur's baby," he said, even though it wasn't. He wanted more. He wanted everything, and he would never have the right to ask her for it.

"Kiss me," he said, so impulsively, so suddenly that even he did not believe he'd done it.

"What?"

"I will make no more demands on you," he said. "But for now, just this once, kiss me."

"Why?" she asked.

He stared at her in incomprehension. Why? *Why?* "Does there have to be a reason?"

"There is always a reason," she said with a

quiet choke in her voice. "More fool me, for letting myself forget that."

He felt his lips move, trying and failing to find words. He had nothing, no sweet poetry to make her keep forgetting. The light morning wind swept across his face, and he watched as one lonely tendril of her hair broke free of its braid, catching the sunlight until it sparkled like platinum.

How was she so lovely? How had he not seen it?

"Kiss me," he said again, and this time it felt like begging.

He didn't care.

"You are my husband," Iris said again. Her eyes burned into his. "I will obey you."

It was the fiercest of blows. "Don't say that," he hissed.

Her mouth clamped into a defiant line.

Richard closed the distance between them, his hand thrusting forward to grab her arm, but at the last minute he stilled. Slowly, gently, he reached out to touch her cheek.

She was so rigid, he thought she might break, and then, he heard it—a tiny whisper of breath, a small sob of acquiescence, and she turned, allowing his hand to cradle her cheek.

"Iris," he whispered.

She brought her eyes to his, pale, blue, and impossibly sad.

He didn't want to hurt her. He wanted to cherish her.

"Please," he whispered, his lips coming within a feather's breadth of hers. "Let me kiss you."

Chapter Twenty-one

Kɪss ʜɪᴍ?

Iris almost laughed. The very thought of it had consumed her for the past few days, but not like this. Not when she was wet-cheeked and dusty and her elbow felt bruised from when she'd tripped over her own feet because she couldn't even run away with dignity. Not when he hadn't said a word of reproof in the tunnel, and he was being so bloody *kind*.

Kiss him?

There was nothing she wanted more. Or less. Her anger was the only thing holding her up, and if he kissed her . . . if *she* kissed *him* . . .

He would make her forget. And then she would lose herself, all over again.

"I've missed you," he murmured, and his hand was so lovely and warm at her cheek.

She should pull away. She knew she should, but she could not bring herself to move. There was nothing in that moment but him and her and the way he was looking at her as if she were the very air he breathed.

He was a consummate actor; she knew that now. He had not fooled her completely—she took some pride in the fact that she'd known that he'd been hiding something—but he'd been good enough to make her think she could fall in love with him. And for all she knew, he was faking this now.

Maybe he didn't want her. Maybe all he wanted was her compliance.

But she wasn't sure that mattered. Because she wanted him. She wanted the touch of his lips and the soft brush of his breath on her skin. She wanted the *moment.* That sacred, suspended moment before they touched, when they only stared, wanting.

Needing.

Anticipation. It was almost better than a kiss. The air between them was heavy and expectant, warm and thick from the heat of their breaths.

Iris held herself still, waiting for him to gather her into his arms, to kiss her and make her forget, if only for a moment, that she was the world's biggest fool.

But he didn't. He was still as a statue, his dark eyes never leaving hers. He was going to make her say it, she realized. He would not kiss her until she granted him permission.

Until she admitted her desire.

"I can't," she whispered.

He did not say a word. He did not even move.

"I *can't,*" she said again, nearly choking on the short sentence. "You have taken everything from me."

"Not everything," Richard reminded her.

"Oh, yes." She nearly laughed at the irony. "You've left my innocence intact. Very kind of you."

He stepped away. "Oh, for God's sake, Iris, you know why—"

"Stop," she cut in. "Just stop. Don't you understand? I don't want this conversation."

And she didn't. He would only try to explain himself, and she didn't want to listen. He would tell her that he'd had no choice, that he was acting out of love for his sister. And maybe all that was true, but Iris was still so damned *angry.* He didn't deserve her forgiveness. He didn't deserve her understanding.

He had humiliated her. He didn't get the opportunity to talk her out of her fury.

"It's just a kiss," he said softly, but he was not that naive. He had to know it was more than a kiss.

"You took my freedom," she said, hating how her voice trembled with emotion. "You took my dignity. You will not take my self-respect."

"You know that was not my intention. What can I do to make you understand?"

Iris shook her head sadly. "Maybe after . . ." She glanced down at her belly, where her empty womb hid beneath her clothes. "Maybe I will fall in love with Fleur's baby. And maybe then I'll decide that this was all worth it, even that it was God's plan. But right now . . ." She swallowed, trying to find compassion for the innocent child at the heart of it all. Was she so unnatural that she couldn't even manage that? Or maybe she was just selfish, too hurt by Richard's manipulation to let herself ponder what might be the greater good.

"Right now," she said softly, "it doesn't feel like it."

She took a step back. It felt as if she were snapping a rope in two. She felt empowered. And infinitely more sad.

"You should talk to your sister," she said.

His eyes flicked toward hers.

"Unless you have finally gained her agreement," Iris said, answering his unspoken question.

Richard seemed to be vaguely perturbed that she was questioning this. "Fleur has not argued with me about it since the day she arrived."

"And you perceive that to be acquiescence?" Really, men could be so stupid.

He frowned.

"I would not be so sure that she has come around to your way of thinking," she told him.

Richard looked at her sharply. "Have you spoken to her?"

"You know very well I have spoken to no one."

"Then perhaps you should not speculate," he said in what Iris found to be an unbecomingly snippy voice.

She shrugged. "Perhaps not."

"You do not know Fleur," he persisted. "Your interaction has been limited to a single conversation."

Iris rolled her eyes. "Conversation" was not the word she would have used to describe that awful scene in Fleur's bedroom. "I don't know why she is so determined to keep the baby," Iris said. "Perhaps it is the sort of thing only a mother could understand."

He flinched.

"That was not meant as a blow," she informed him coolly.

Richard's eyes met hers, then he murmured, "Forgive me."

"Regardless," Iris continued, "I don't think you should consider yourself secure until Fleur gives you her explicit consent."

"She will."

Iris raised her brows doubtfully.

"She has no choice."

Again, so *stupid.* She gave him a pitying look. "So you think."

He looked at her assessingly. "You disagree?"

"You already know that I don't approve of your scheme. But that hardly matters."

"I meant," he said through clenched teeth, "do you think she can raise the baby on her own?"

"It doesn't matter what I think," Iris said, even though in *this*, she agreed with him. Fleur was mad to think she could withstand the hardship and scorn she would suffer as an unwed mother. Almost as mad as Richard was to think he could pass off her child as his and not have it rain unhappiness later. If it was a girl, they might make it work, but if Fleur had a boy . . .

Clearly they needed to find that girl a husband. Iris still didn't understand why no one else seemed to see this. Fleur flat out refused to consider marriage, and Richard kept saying that there was no one suitable. But Iris had trouble believing this. Perhaps they lacked the funds to buy Fleur a well-connected husband who would be willing to accept her child, but why couldn't she wed a vicar? Or a soldier? Or even someone in trade?

This was no time for snobbery.

"What matters," Iris continued, "is what Fleur thinks, and she wants to be a mother."

"Stupid, stupid girl," Richard said harshly, the words a bitter hiss on his lips.

"I cannot disagree there," Iris said.

He looked at her in surprise.

"You did not marry a paragon of Christian charity and forgiveness," she said sardonically.

"Apparently not."

Iris was silent for a moment, then she said, almost dutifully, "I will still support her. And I will love her as a sister."

"Like you do Daisy?" he quipped.

Iris stared. Then she laughed. Or maybe she snorted. Either way, it was indisputably the sound of humor, and she brought one of her hands to her mouth, barely able to believe herself. "I do love Daisy," she said, bringing her hand back down to the flat plane of her collarbone. "Truly."

A faint smile played across Richard's face. "You have the capacity for more charity and forgiveness than you give yourself credit."

Iris snorted again. Daisy *was* vexing.

"If Daisy has given you something about which to smile," he said softly, "then I must love her, too."

Iris looked at him and sighed. He looked tired.

His eyes had always been deeply set, but the shadows beneath them were more pronounced. And the crinkles at the corners . . . the ones that formed so merrily when he smiled . . . now they were weary grooves.

This hadn't been easy for him, either.

She looked away. She didn't want to feel sympathy.

"Iris," Richard said, "I only wanted—*damn*."

"What is it?" She turned back around, following his gaze toward the path from the house. "Oh . . ."

Fleur was approaching, storming toward them with angry strides.

"She doesn't look happy," Iris said.

"No, she does not," Richard said quietly, and then he sighed. It was a sad, exhausted sound, and Iris cursed her own heart for breaking.

"How dare you!" Fleur cried, as soon as she was close enough to be heard. Two more steps and it was clear which of them she was accusing.

Iris.

"What the devil do you think you were doing at breakfast?" Fleur demanded.

"Eating," Iris retorted, even though that was barely true. She'd felt so panicked, knowing she was about to commit to the biggest lie of her life. She'd barely been able to eat anything.

Fleur scowled. "You might as well have come right out and announced that you are with child."

"I *did* come right out and announce it," Iris said. "I *thought* that was what I was supposed to do."

"I'm not giving you the baby," Fleur seethed.

Iris turned to Richard with a look that quite clearly said, *this is your problem.*

Fleur stepped between them, practically spitting at Iris in her rage. "Tomorrow you will announce that you have miscarried."

"To whom?" Iris retorted. It had been only family in the room when she'd made her cryptic statement.

"She will do no such thing," Richard snapped. "Have you any compassion? Any sense for all that your new sister is giving up for you?"

Iris crossed her arms. It was about time someone acknowledged her sacrifice.

"I didn't ask this of her," Fleur protested.

But Richard was implacable. "You are not thinking clearly."

Fleur gasped. "You are the most patronizing, hateful—"

"I am your brother!"

"*Not* my keeper."

Richard's tone turned to ice. "The law begs to differ."

Fleur drew back as if struck. But when she spoke, it was with seething intensity. "Forgive me if I have difficulty trusting your sense of obligation."

"What the hell is that supposed to mean?"

"You *left* us," Fleur cried. "When Father died. You left."

Richard's face, which had been red with fury, suddenly drained white.

"You could not wait to be rid of us," Fleur went on. "Father wasn't even cold in his grave before you had us packed up and living with Aunt Milton."

"I could not take care of you," Richard said.

Iris bit her lip, watching him with wary concern. His voice was shaking, and he looked . . .

Wrecked. He looked positively wrecked, as if Fleur had found the one festering wound deep in his soul and jammed her thumb into it.

"You could have tried," Fleur whispered.

"I would have failed."

Fleur's mouth tightened. Or maybe it trembled. Iris could not tell what she was feeling.

Richard's throat worked, and several seconds passed before he spoke. "Do you think I am proud of my behavior? I have spent every moment of the last few years trying to make up for it. Father might as well have been gone after Mother died. And then I—" He swore, raking his hand through his hair as he turned away. When he continued, his voice was more even. "I am constantly trying to be a better man than I was, a better man than *he* was."

Iris felt her eyes go wide.

"I feel so bloody disloyal, and—" Richard stopped, quite suddenly.

Iris went still. Fleur, too. It was almost as if Richard's lack of movement was a contagious thing, and they all stood there, tense and waiting.

"This is not about Father," Richard finally said. "And it's not about me, either."

"Precisely why it should be my decision," Fleur said sharply.

Oh, Fleur, Iris thought with sigh. She'd pulled

out her claws just when things were starting to settle down.

Richard looked over at Iris, saw her dejected posture, and then turned back to his sister with furious eyes. "*Now* look what you've done," he snapped.

"Me?" Fleur shrieked.

"Yes, you. Your behavior has been unfathomably selfish. Don't you realized I might have to give Maycliffe to the son of Willam Parnell? Have you any idea how abhorrent I find that?"

"You said you would love the child," Iris said quietly, "regardless of his parentage."

"I will," Richard practically exploded. "But that doesn't mean it's easy. And she"—he flung his arm toward Fleur—"is not helping."

"I did not ask this of you!" Fleur cried. Her voice was shaking, but it didn't sound like rage anymore. She sounded, Iris realized, like a woman about to shatter.

"That's enough, Richard," Iris suddenly announced.

He turned to her with irritated bewilderment. "What?"

Iris put her arm around Fleur. "She needs to lie down."

Fleur let out a few wretched gasps and then crumpled against Iris's side, sobbing.

Richard looked dumbstruck. "She was just yelling at me," he said to no one in particular. And then to Fleur, "You were just yelling at me."

"Go away," Fleur sobbed, her words echoing through Iris's body.

Richard stared at the two of them for a long moment, then cursed under his breath. "Now you're on her side, I see."

"There aren't any *sides*," Iris said, despite the fact that she had no idea which of them he meant was on the other's side. "Don't you understand? This is a horrible situation. For everyone. *No one* will emerge with heart intact."

Their eyes met; no, their eyes clashed, and Richard finally turned on his heel and stalked away. Iris watched him disappear over the rise, then let out her breath in a long, shaky whoosh.

"Are you all right?" she asked Fleur, who was still hiccuping in her arms. "No, don't answer that. Of course you're not all right. None of us is."

"Why won't he listen to me?" Fleur whispered.

"He believes that he is acting in your best interest."

"But he's not."

Iris sucked in her breath, trying to keep her voice even as she said, "He's certainly not acting in his own best interest."

Fleur pulled back and looked up at her. "Nor yours."

"Certainly not mine," Iris said, her agreement caustic at best.

Fleur's mouth flattened into a sullen line. "He does not understand me."

"I don't either," Iris admitted.

Fleur touched her hand to her flat abdomen. "I love—I'm sorry, I *loved* the father. The baby is born of that love. I can't just give him up."

"You *loved* him?" Iris asked. How was that possible? If even half of what Richard said was true, William Parnell had been a terrible person.

Fleur looked toward her feet, mumbling, "It is difficult to explain."

Iris just shook her head. "Don't even try. Come, shall we head back to the house?"

Fleur nodded, and they began walking. After a few minutes she said, completely without fervor, "I still hate you, you know."

"I know," Iris said. She reached out and gave the younger girl's hand a squeeze. "I still hate you, too, sometimes."

Fleur looked over at her with an almost hopeful expression. "You do?"

"Sometimes." Iris reached down and plucked a blade of grass. She put it between her thumbs, trying to make a whistle. "I don't really want to have your baby, you know."

"I can't imagine why you would."

They resumed walking, Iris taking about six steps before saying, "You're not going to ask me why I'm doing it?"

Fleur shrugged. "Doesn't really matter, does it?"

Iris thought about that for a moment. "No, I suppose not."

"I know you mean well."

Iris nodded absently, keeping the pace up the hill.

"Aren't you going to return the sentiment?" Fleur asked.

Iris turned her head sharply. "That you mean well?"

Fleur's lips pressed peevishly together.

"I suppose you do," Iris finally capitulated. "I will confess I find your motives utterly baffling, but I suppose you *mean* well."

"I don't want to marry a stranger."

"I did."

Fleur stopped in her tracks.

"Well, almost one, anyway," Iris allowed.

"You weren't pregnant with another man's child."

Good heavens, the girl was exasperating. "No one is saying you should deceive your bride-groom," Iris told her. "I'm sure there is someone who will leap at the chance to align himself with Maycliffe."

"And I shall be made to feel *grateful* for the rest of my life," Fleur said bitterly. "Have you considered that?"

"No," Iris said quietly. "I had not."

They reached the edge of the west lawn, and Iris squinted up at the sky. It was still overcast, but the clouds had grown thinner. The sun might well yet make an appearance. "I'm going to stay outside," she said.

Fleur looked up, too. "Won't you want a shawl?"

"Yes, I suppose I will."

"I can have one of the maids bring one down."

It was as clear a gesture of friendship as Iris had ever seen. "That would be most helpful, thank you."

Fleur nodded and entered the house.

Iris walked over to bench and sat down, waiting for the sun.

Chapter Twenty-two

By NIGHTFALL IRIS was a bit more at ease. She had spent the rest of the day in her own company, feeling only the tiniest pang of guilt when she elected to take her evening meal in her room. After the morning's interactions with Richard and Fleur, she rather thought she'd earned the right to abstain from conversation for a day or so. The entire exchange had been exhausting.

But sleep proved elusive, no matter how weary she felt, and sometime after midnight she gave up the attempt, threw back her covers, and padded across her bedchamber to the petite writing desk Richard had had brought up the week before.

She looked down at the small selection of books lying on the desktop. She'd finished them all except the history of Yorkshire, which had stubbornly refused to get the least bit interesting, even in the chapter about the War of the Roses. How the author managed to make that dull she'd never know, but she had given up trying to find out.

Gathering the books in her arms, she shoved her feet in her night slippers and headed for the door. She wouldn't wake anyone if she tiptoed down to the library.

The servants had long since retired, and the house was very quiet. Still, Iris stepped gently, grateful for the soft carpets that muffled her footsteps. At home she'd known every creaky board and squeaky door hinge. She hadn't had a chance yet to learn the same for Maycliffe.

She paused in her steps, frowning. That was not right. She had to stop thinking of her parents' house as home. Maycliffe was her home now. She needed to get used to that.

She supposed she was starting to feel that way, at least a little bit. Even with all the drama—and heavens, there was a *lot* of drama—Maycliffe was starting to settle into her heart. The sofa in the drawing room was *her* sofa now, no question about that, and already she'd grown accustomed to the unique song of the yellow-bellied birds that nested near her window. She wasn't sure what they were called, only that they didn't have them in London.

She was starting to feel at home here, strange as that seemed. At home with a husband who would not bed her, a sister who hated her (sometimes) for trying to save her from ruin, and another sister who . . . who . . .

She thought about that. There really wasn't

much to say about Marie-Claire. Iris hadn't shared more than two words with her since that first day. She ought to rectify that. It'd be nice if at least one of Richard's sisters didn't (sometimes) see her as the devil incarnate.

At the bottom of the stairs Iris turned right toward the library. It was just down the hall, past the drawing room and Richard's study. She rather liked his study, she decided. She hadn't had much occasion to enter the masculine sanctuary recently, but it was warm and comfortable and with the same southerly view she had from her bedroom.

She paused for a moment to adjust her grip on her candleholder, then squinted. Was that a light down the hall or just her own candle, throwing off flickers and shadows meant to tease and deceive? She held still, held her breath, even, then moved forward again, stepping lightly.

"Iris?"

She froze. There was nothing for it. She nudged herself forward and peered into Richard's study. He was sitting in a chair by the fire, a half-filled glass of something alcoholic in his hand.

He tipped his tousled head in her direction. "I thought that might be you."

"I'm sorry. Did I disturb you?"

"Not at all," he said, smiling up at her from his comfortable spot. Iris thought he might be a little bit drunk. It was very unlike him not to rise when a lady entered a room.

It was also a little odd that he was smiling at her. Given the way they'd parted and all.

She clutched her small pile of books to her chest. "I was getting something to read," she said, motioning toward the library.

"I'd assumed."

"I couldn't sleep," she said.

He shrugged. "Nor I."

"Yes, I see."

His mouth curled into a lazy half smile. "Witty conversationalists, we two."

Iris let out a little laugh. Strange that they could find their humor again now that the house was abed. Or maybe not so strange. She'd been in a contemplative mood all day, ever since her unexpected rapprochement with Fleur. They had not agreed on anything, not really, but Iris thought they had been able to find the good in each other nonetheless.

Surely she ought to be able to find the same with Richard.

"Penny for them," the man in question said.

Iris looked up with arched brows. "I have enough pennies, thank you."

He clutched his hand to his heart. "Wounded! And with coin."

"Without coin, actually," Iris corrected. Because it was the sort of thing she could never let pass.

He grinned.

"It's important to be precise in all things," she said, but she was grinning, too.

He chuckled at that, then held up his glass. "Drink?"

"What is it?"

"Whiskey."

Iris blinked in surprise. She'd never heard of a man offering a woman a sip of whiskey.

Immediately, she wanted some.

"Just a little," she said, setting her books down on a table. "I don't know if I'll like it."

Richard chuckled as he poured a finger of the amber liquid into a glass. "If you don't like this, you don't like whiskey."

She gave him a questioning glance as she took a seat in the straight-backed chair across from him.

"It's the best there is," he said without modesty. "It's not hard to get the really good stuff here, as close to Scotland as we are."

She peered down at her glass and took a little sniff. "I did not realize you were such a connoisseur."

He shrugged. "I seem to be drinking a lot of it lately."

Iris looked away.

"Didn't say that to blame you, by the way." He paused, presumably to take a drink. "Believe me when I say that I know this is a quagmire of my own making."

"And Fleur's," Iris said quietly.

His eyes found hers, and the corner of his mouth tipped up. Just a bit. Just enough to thank her for recognizing that. "And Fleur's," he agreed.

They sat in silence for several minutes, Richard downing his glass of whiskey while Iris carefully sipped hers. She liked it, she decided. It was hot and cold at the same time. How else could one describe something that burned until it made you shiver?

She spent more time looking at her drink than at her husband, allowing herself to study his face only when his eyes closed and he leaned his head against the back of the chair. Was he asleep? She didn't think so. No one could fall asleep that quickly, especially upright.

She raised her glass to her lips, experimenting with trying a larger sip. It went down even more smoothly, although that could be the result of all the whiskey that had gone down before it.

Richard still had his eyes closed. He was definitely not asleep, she decided. His lips pressed together and relaxed, and she realized she recognized the expression. He did that when he was thinking. Well, of course he was always thinking, that's what humans did, but he did that when he was thinking about something particularly vexing.

"Am I such a bad person?" he asked, his eyes remaining shut.

Iris's lips parted in surprise. "Of course not."

He let out a little sigh and finally opened his eyes. "I didn't used to think so."

"You're not," she said again.

He regarded her for a long moment, then nodded. "Good to know."

Iris wasn't sure what to say to that, so she took another sip of her whiskey, tipping it back to get the last few drops.

"More?" Richard inquired, holding up the decanter.

"I probably shouldn't," she said, but she held out her glass all the same.

He poured, this time two fingers.

She regarded her glass, holding it up level with her eyes. "Will this make me drunk?"

"Probably not." He cocked his head, his mouth twisting as if he were doing arithmetic in his head. "But I suppose it could do. You're small. Did you eat supper?"

"I did."

"You should be all right, then."

Iris nodded and looked back down at her glass, giving it a little swirl. They sipped in silence for another minute, then she said, "You should not think you are a bad person."

He quirked a brow.

"I'm enormously angry with you, and I think you're making a mistake, but I do understand your motives." She looked down at her whiskey, momentarily mesmerized by the way it seemed to flicker and glow in the candlelight. Her voice, when she found it again, was pensive. "No one who loves his sisters so well could ever be a bad person."

He was quiet for a moment, and then—"Thank you."

"It does you credit, I suppose, that you are willing to make such a sacrifice."

"I am hoping," he said quietly, "that it will not feel like such a sacrifice once the babe is in my arms."

Iris swallowed. "I am hoping the same."

He leaned forward quite suddenly, resting his forearms on his knees. The motion brought his head lower than hers, and he looked up at her through his thick, dark lashes. "I really am sorry, you know."

She didn't say anything.

"For what you've been forced to do," he needlessly clarified. "It probably won't matter, but I dreaded telling you."

"I should think so," she retorted before she could think to temper her tone. Of course he would dread it. Who on earth would enjoy such a thing?

"No, I mean, I knew you would hate me." He closed his eyes. "It wasn't the telling that I dreaded. I didn't really even think about the actual telling. I just didn't want you to hate me."

She sighed. "I don't hate you."

He looked up. "You should."

"Well, I did. For a few days, at least."

He nodded. "That's good."

Iris couldn't help but smile.

"It would be rather churlish of me to deny you that," he said wryly.

"My anger?"

He held up his glass. A salute? Maybe. "You deserve it," he said.

Iris nodded slowly, then thought, *what the hell*, and raised her glass a little, too.

"What are we toasting?" he asked.

"I have no idea."

"Fair enough." He cocked his head. "To your health, then."

"My health," Iris said with a choked laugh. Good heavens, what a thing.

"It shall surely be the least dangerous pregnancy in history," she remarked.

His eyes met hers with a flash of surprise, and then his lips curved into a half smile. "No childbirth fever for you," he agreed.

She took a gulp of her whiskey. "I shall regain my figure with supernatural speed."

"The other ladies will be envious," he said solemnly.

Iris laughed, her eyes closing briefly with mirth before returning to Richard's face. He was watching her, studying her almost, and his expression . . . it wasn't amorous or lustful, it was just . . .

Grateful.

She looked down, wondering why gratitude seemed so disappointing. He *should* be grateful for all she was doing, and yet . . .

It didn't feel right.

It didn't feel like enough.

She swirled her whiskey. There wasn't much left.

Richard's voice, when she heard it, was soft and sad in the darkness. "What shall we do, Iris?"

"Do?"

"We have a lifetime of marriage ahead of us."

Iris stared at her drink. Was he asking her to forgive him? She wasn't sure she was ready to do that. And yet, somehow she knew she would. Was that what it meant to fall in love? That she would forgive the unforgivable? If such a thing had happened to one of her sisters or cousins, Iris would have never forgiven the husband, never.

But this was Richard. And she loved him. In the end, that was all that would matter.

In the end.

But maybe not yet.

She let out a little snort. How like her that was. To know that she *would* forgive him but to refuse to do it just yet. It wasn't about making him suffer, though. It wasn't even about holding a grudge. She just wasn't ready. He'd said she deserved her anger, and he was right.

She looked up. He was watching her patiently.

"It will be all right," she said. That was all she could give him. She hoped he would understand.

He nodded, then rose to his feet and held out his hand. "May I walk you to your room?"

Part of her longed for the warmth of his body near hers, even just the touch of her hand on his arm. But she didn't want to fall more in love with him. At least, not tonight. She gave him a regretful smile as she stood. "I'm not sure that would be such a good idea."

"Then may I walk you to the door?"

Iris's lips parted as she stared up at his face. The door was barely three yards away. It was as unnecessary a gesture as she could imagine, and yet she could not resist. She placed her hand in his.

He gave it a little squeeze and then lifted it a few inches, as if he were going to bring her fingers to his lips. But then he seemed to change his mind, and instead he twined their hands and led her to the door.

"Good night," he said, but he didn't release her hand.

"Good night," she said, but she didn't try to pull away.

"Iris . . ."

She looked up. He was going to kiss her. She could see it in his eyes, hot and heavy with need.

"Iris," he said again, and she did not say no.

His warm fingers touched her jaw, tipping her face toward his. Still, he waited, and finally she could do nothing else but dip her chin, barely a nod, really, but he felt it.

Slowly, so slowly she was certain the world had time to turn twice on its axis, his face moved toward hers. Their lips met, the touch soft and electric. He brushed against her, the light friction sending ripples of sensation to the very center of her being.

"Richard," she whispered, and maybe he could hear the love in her voice. Maybe in that moment she didn't care.

Her lips parted, but he did not deepen the kiss. Instead he rested his forehead on hers.

"You should go," he said.

She allowed herself one more moment, then stepped back.

"Thank you," he said.

She nodded, placing her hand on the doorframe as she moved around him.

Thank you, he'd said.

Something in her heart shifted. *Soon,* she thought. Soon she would be ready to forgive.

RICHARD WATCHED HER GO.

He watched her glide down the hall and disappear around the corner to the stairs. There was little to light the darkened hallway, but what there was seemed to catch on her pale hair like spun starlight.

She was such a contradiction. So ethereal in looks and so pragmatic in mind. He loved that about her, the way she was so relentlessly sensible. He wondered if perhaps that was part of what had initially drawn him to her. Had he thought that her innate rationality would allow her to get over the fundamental insult of their marriage? That she'd just shrug and say, *Quite right, that makes sense.*

What a fool he'd been.

Even if she did forgive him, and he was beginning to think that she might, he could never forgive himself.

He had wounded her deeply. He had chosen her for his wife for the most reprehensible of reasons. It was only fitting that now he should love her so ardently.

So hopelessly.

He did not see how she could ever love him, not after what he'd done. But he had to try. And maybe it would be enough that he loved her.

Maybe.

Chapter Twenty-three

The following morning

"Iris? Iris?"

Iris pried open an eye. Just one, mind you; the other was firmly closed and pressed hard into her pillow.

"Oh, good, you're awake!"

Marie-Claire, Iris thought with her usual morning-induced irritability. Good Lord, what time was it, and why was she in Iris's room?

Iris closed her eye.

"It's half ten," Marie-Claire said cheerily, "and it's uncommonly warm out."

Iris could not imagine what this might have to do with her.

"I thought we might go for a walk."

Ah.

The mattress dipped under Marie-Claire's weight as she perched on the end. "We really haven't had a chance to get to know each other."

Iris let out a sigh, the sort that would have been accompanied by the closing of eyes if she weren't already facedown in her pillow. She had been thinking this very thing the night before. She just hadn't meant to do anything about it before noon.

"Shall we?" Marie-Claire asked, just bursting with annoyingly chippy energy.

"Mmphghrglick."

A very small silence, and then—"I beg your pardon?"

Iris growled into her pillow. She really didn't know how she could have been more clear.

"Iris? Are you unwell?"

Iris finally rolled her body over and forced herself to enunciate as she said, "I am not at my best in the morning."

Marie-Claire just stared at her.

Iris rubbed her eye. "Perhaps if we depart—what?" The last bit was not much more than a snap, really.

"Ehrm . . ." One corner of Marie-Claire's mouth stretched out in a bizarre approximation of a grimace. "Your cheek."

Iris let out an aggrieved sigh. "Pillow crease?"

"Oh. Is that what that is?" Asked with enough perkiness to make Iris want to reach for a weapon.

"Have you never seen one before?" she asked instead.

"No." Marie-Claire frowned. "I always sleep on my back. I suppose Fleur does, too."

"I sleep in many positions," Iris grumbled, "but mostly . . . I sleep late."

"I see." Marie-Claire swallowed, but that was her only sign of awkwardness before she added, "Well, you're awake now, so you might as well get up and meet the day. I don't think there is any breakfast left in the dining room, but I'm sure Mrs. Hopkins can put together a cold collation. You can bring it with you."

Iris looked longingly at her bed. She imagined this bed, tidy and sweet with a breakfast tray on it. But Marie-Claire had made a friendly gesture, and Iris knew she must accept. "Thank you," she said, hoping her face did not belie the effort required to pry the words from her mouth. "That would be lovely."

"Wonderful!" Marie-Claire beamed. "Shall I meet you in the drive, say in about ten minutes?"

Iris was about to bargain for fifteen, or better yet twenty, but then she thought—she was already awake. In for a penny, in for a pound. Ten minutes. Good Lord.

To Marie-Claire, she said, "Why not?"

TWENTY MINUTES LATER Iris and Marie-Claire were trudging across the western fields of Maycliffe. Iris still wasn't entirely certain where they were going; Marie-Claire had said something about picking berries, but it seemed far too early in the year for that. Either way, Iris didn't much care. She had a warm, buttery scone in her hands, and she was fairly certain it was the best thing she had ever eaten. Someone in the kitchens *had* to be from Scotland. It seemed the only explanation.

They didn't say much as they made their way down the hill. Iris was busy savoring her breakfast, and Marie-Claire seemed happy enough swinging her basket as she skipped along. But once they reached the bottom and turned onto a well-worn path, Marie-Claire cleared her throat, and said, "I don't know if anyone has properly thanked you."

Iris went still, forgetting for a moment even to chew. She had not the pleasure of many conversations with Marie-Claire, and this . . . Well, frankly it surprised her.

"For . . ." Marie-Claire motioned toward Iris's midsection, her hand making an awkward little circle in the air. "For that."

Iris returned her eyes to the walking path. Richard had thanked her. It had taken him three days, but in all fairness, she had not given him the opportunity to do so before their conversation the night before. And even if he had tried, if he had banged her door down and insisted that she listen to him, it wouldn't have mattered. She would not have heard anything he said. She had not been ready to allow him a true conversation.

"Iris?"

"You're welcome," Iris said, pretending to be absorbed in extracting a currant from her scone. She really didn't feel like talking about this with Marie-Claire.

But the younger girl had other ideas. "I know Fleur seems ungrateful," she persisted, "but she will come around. Eventually."

"I'm afraid I cannot agree with your assess-ment," Iris said. She still had no idea how Rich-ard thought he was going to pull this off without Fleur's cooperation.

"She's not stupid, no matter how she might be acting right now. In fact, most of the time she's not this—well, not *quite* this emotional." Marie-Claire's lips came together, pursing into a thought-ful frown. "She was very close to our mother, you know, more so than either Richard or me."

Iris hadn't known that. Richard had not said much of his mother to her, just that she'd died, and he missed her.

"Perhaps that made Fleur more motherly," Marie-Claire continued. She looked over at Iris and gave a little shrug. "Perhaps that's why she feels so attached to the baby."

"Perhaps," Iris said. She sighed, glancing down at her own belly. She was going to have to start padding herself soon. The only reason she had not yet done so were the three hundred miles between Yorkshire and London. Ladies were not quite so relentlessly fashionable here, and she could get away with wear-ing last year's frocks. Waistlines were dropping in the capital; the forgiving billows of the Regency style were giving way to something far more structured and uncomfortable. By 1840, Iris predicted, women would be corseted into nothingness.

They walked on for a few quiet moments, then Marie-Claire said, "Well, *I'm* thanking you."

"You're welcome," Iris said again, this time turning to Marie-Claire with a small, rueful smile. The younger girl was trying. The least she could do was be gracious.

"I know that Fleur says she wants to be a mother," Marie-Claire went on blithely, "but it's really quite selfish of her. Do you know she has not apologized to me even once?"

"To you?" Iris murmured. Because really, she rather thought *she* deserved one first.

"She'll ruin me," Marie-Claire said. "You know she will. If you weren't doing what you're doing—"

Doing what you're doing, Iris thought. *What a lovely euphemism.*

"—and she went ahead and had this baby out of wedlock, no one would have me." Marie-Claire turned to Iris with an expression that was almost belligerent. "You'll probably say I'm being selfish, but you know it's true."

"I know," Iris said quietly. Perhaps if Richard gave Marie-Claire a season in London . . . They could probably find someone for her, someone who lived far from this corner of Yorkshire. Gossip traveled, but usually not that far.

"It's so unfair. *She* makes a mistake, and *I'm* the one who would have to pay the price."

"I hardly think she would find herself getting off scot-free," Iris pointed out.

Marie-Claire pressed her lips together impatiently. "Yes, well, *she* would deserve it, not me."

It was not the most becoming of attitudes, but Iris had to admit that Marie-Claire had a point.

"Trust me when I tell you there are girls here who are just *dying* for a reason to cut me." Marie-Claire sighed, and a little bit of bravado seemed to seep out of her. She looked over at Iris with a slightly forlorn expression. "Do you know girls like that?"

"Quite a few," Iris admitted.

They walked about ten more paces, and then Marie-Claire suddenly said, "I suppose I can forgive her a little."

"A little?" Iris had always thought that forgiveness was an all-or-nothing sort of thing.

"I'm not completely unreasonable," Marie-Claire said with a sniff. "I do recognize that she's in a difficult situation. After all, it's not as if she can marry the father."

That was true, but Iris still thought Fleur was being extremely shortsighted about the whole thing. *Not* that she thought that Richard had the right of it. Any fool could see that the only solution was to find a husband for Fleur. She could not expect a gentleman of high standing; Richard had already said he didn't have the blunt to purchase a husband willing to overlook her condition. But surely there would be *some*one in the area eager to align himself with the Kenworthys. A vicar, perhaps, who didn't have to worry about his land and property passing along to another man's son. Or a new-to-the-area landowner looking to improve his standing.

Iris reached out to touch a delicate white flower blooming in the hedge. She wondered what it was. She'd not seen it in the south of England. "It is difficult to marry a dead man," she tried to quip. But it wasn't easy to quip with so much bitterness in one's voice.

Marie-Claire only snorted.

"What?" Iris turned and looked at her with

narrowed eyes. There was something in Marie-Claire's tone . . .

"Please," Marie-Claire scoffed. "Fleur is *such* a liar."

Iris froze, her hand going still in the leaves of the hedge. "I beg your pardon?"

Marie-Claire caught her lower lip nervously between her teeth, as if she'd only just realized what she said.

"Marie-Claire," Iris said, grabbing her arm, "what do you mean, Fleur is a liar?"

The younger girl swallowed and looked down at Iris's fingers. Iris did not relax her grasp.

"Marie-Claire!" she said sternly. "Tell me!"

"Why does it even matter?" Marie-Claire retorted. She pulled hard with her arm. "She's pregnant, and she's not going to get married, and in the end, that's all anyone will care about."

Iris fought the urge to scream. "What did she lie about?"

"The father, of course," Marie-Claire grunted, still trying to break free. "Will you let go of me?"

"No," Iris said baldly. "It wasn't William Parnell?"

"Oh, please. Even Fleur is smart enough to stay away from him." Marie-Claire's eyes flicked up to the sky. "God rest his soul." She thought about that. "I suppose."

Iris tightened her grasp. "I don't care how William Parnell's soul is resting," she growled. "Or where. I want to know why Fleur lied. Did she tell you this? That he wasn't the father?"

At this, Marie-Claire looked almost insulted. "Of course not."

"Then who is?"

Marie-Claire chose that moment to adopt a prim expression. "It's not for me to say."

Iris yanked her sister-in-law hard and fast, giving Marie-Claire barely enough time to breathe before they were nose to nose. "Marie-Claire Kenworthy," Iris hissed, "you will tell me the name of the father this instant or so help me God the only reason I will not kill you is because it is a hanging offense."

Marie-Claire could only stare.

Iris's hand tightened on Marie-Claire's upper arm. "I have four sisters, Marie-Claire, one of whom is extraordinarily vexing. Trust me when I tell you that I can make your life a living hell."

"But why does it—"

"Tell me!" Iris roared.

"John Burnham!" Marie-Claire shrieked.

Iris dropped her arm. "What?"

"It was John Burnham," Marie-Claire said, rubbing her bruised flesh. "I'm almost certain."

"Almost?"

"Well, she was always running off to meet him. She thought I didn't know, but really—"

"Of course you knew," Iris muttered. She knew how it was between sisters. There was no way Fleur could have been sneaking off to meet a man without Marie-Claire's knowing.

"I'm going to need a sling," Marie-Claire said petulantly. "Look at these bruises. You didn't need to be so rough."

Iris ignored this. "Why didn't you say something?"

"To whom?" Marie-Claire demanded. "My brother? He would hardly have liked this more than William Parnell."

"But John Burnham is alive," Iris cried out. "Fleur could marry him and keep her baby."

Marie-Claire looked over at her with a disdainful expression. "He's a farmer, Iris. And not even a yeoman. He does not own his land."

"Are you really such a snob?"

"And you're not?"

Iris recoiled at the accusation. "What does that mean?"

"I don't know," Marie-Claire shot back with a frustrated growl. "But tell me, how would *your* family have liked it if you married a tenant farmer? Or does it not count because *your* grandfather was an earl?"

That was it. Iris had had it with her. "Shut your mouth," she snapped. "You have no idea what you're talking about. If my grandfather's title gave me leave to misbehave with impunity, I'd hardly have married your brother."

Marie-Claire gaped at her.

"Richard *kissed* me, and I found myself trussed up at the altar," Iris burst out. She hated remembering that, how she'd thought *maybe* he'd wanted her, maybe he'd been so overcome with desire that he could not help himself. But the truth was nothing so romantic. The truth, she was learning, never was.

She turned to Marie-Claire with what felt like an unbearably hard glint in her eyes. "I can assure you that if I had somehow got myself pregnant by a tenant farmer, I would have married him." She paused for a moment. "Assuming, of course, that the intimacy had been consensual."

Marie-Claire didn't say anything, so Iris added, "From what you have said of your sister and Mr. Burnham, I assume their relations were consensual."

Marie-Claire gave a terse nod. "I wasn't *there*, of course," she muttered.

Iris ground her teeth together and flexed her fingers, hoping the motion would be enough to quell the urge to wrap them around Marie-Claire's neck. She could not believe she was having this conversation. It wasn't just that Marie-Claire *knew* that John Burnham was the true father of Fleur's baby. It wasn't even that she had chosen not to say anything. What absolutely galled Iris was that Marie-Claire seemed to think she had done the right thing by not saying anything.

Good God, was she living among idiots?

"I need to go back to the house," Iris announced. She turned and began marching up the hill. The sun was inching to the top of the sky, and the air was lovely and warm, but she wanted nothing more than to shut herself in her room, lock the door, and speak to absolutely no one.

"Iris," Marie-Claire said, and something in her voice gave Iris pause.

"What?" she asked wearily.

Marie-Claire stood stock-still for several seconds, blinking rapidly. Then she said, "Richard didn't . . . That is to say, he would never . . ."

"Of course not!" Iris exclaimed, horrified by the mere suggestion. Richard might have surprised her with his advances, but he had not forced himself upon her. He could never do such a thing. He was far too fine a man.

Iris swallowed. She did not wish to dwell upon her husband's good qualities.

"And you love him," Marie-Claire said softly. "Don't you?"

Iris pressed her lips together, breathing furiously through her nose. She could not deny it, but nor would she say it aloud. She *had* to have more pride than that.

"I'm tired," she said.

Marie-Claire nodded, and they turned toward home. But they had barely taken ten steps before Iris suddenly thought of something. "Wait a moment," she said. "Why hasn't Fleur said anything?"

"I'm sorry?"

"Why did she lie?"

Marie-Claire shrugged.

"She must care for Mr. Burnham," Iris pressed.

Marie-Claire shrugged again. Iris wanted to hit her.

"You said that she sneaked out to see him," Iris said. "That would seem to indicate some level of caring."

"Well, I didn't ask her about it," Marie-Claire responded. "She was obviously trying to hide it. Wouldn't you?"

Iris let out a frustrated breath. "Do you have an opinion on the matter?" she asked, with a slowness that was almost insulting. "Might you have some hypothesis as to why your sister lied about the identity of the father of her unborn child?"

Marie-Claire stared at her as if she were an idiot. "He's a *farmer*. I told you that."

Iris *really* wanted to hit her. "I understand that he is not the sort of man she might have been expected to wed, but if she cares for him, surely it is better to marry him than to raise their child out of wedlock."

"But she's not going to do that," Marie-Claire pointed out. "She's giving the baby to you."

"I wouldn't be so sure of that," Iris muttered. Fleur had never actually come out and agreed to Richard's scheme. *He* might think her silence was assent, but Iris was not so trusting.

Marie-Claire sighed. "I'm sure she realized that she can't possibly marry John Burnham, no matter how strongly she might feel about him. I don't mean to sound unsympathetic. Truly, I don't. But you're not from here, Iris. You don't know how it is. Fleur is a Kenworthy. We have been the main landholding family of Flixton for centuries. Do you have any idea what sort of scandal would ensue if she married a local farmer?"

"It can't be worse than the alternative," Iris pointed out.

"Obviously *she* thinks so," Marie-Claire said. "And hers is the opinion that matters, don't you think?"

Iris stared at her for a long moment, then said, "You're right," and turned and stalked away. Heaven help Fleur when she found her.

"Wait!" Marie-Claire yelled, hitching up her skirts so that she could catch up. "Where are you going?"

"Where do you think?"

"I don't know." Marie-Claire sounded almost sarcastic, which was enough to give Iris pause. When she glanced over her shoulder, Marie-Claire asked, "Are you going to Fleur or to Richard?"

Now Iris really did pause. It had not even occurred to her to take this information straight to Richard. But perhaps it should have done. He was her husband. Should not her first priority lie with him?

It should . . . but this was Fleur's secret to reveal, not hers.

"Well?" Marie-Claire demanded.

"Fleur," Iris said curtly. But if Fleur didn't do the right thing and tell Richard the truth, Iris would be bloody well happy to do it for her.

"Really?" Marie-Claire said. "I thought surely you'd go straight to Richard."

"Then why did you ask?" Iris snapped, resuming her trek up the hill.

Marie-Claire ignored this. "Fleur won't tell you anything, you know."

Iris stopped for just long enough to spear Marie-Claire with a raging glare. "You did."

Marie-Claire froze. "You're not going to tell her I told you, are you?"

Iris turned and stared in disbelief. Then she said a word she'd never uttered before and resumed her strides.

"Iris!" Marie-Claire yelled, running up alongside her. "She'll kill me!"

"Really? *That's* what you're worried about?"

Marie-Claire slumped. "You're right." And then she said it again. "You're right."

"Damned right I am," Iris said under her breath. She marched on. It was amazing how empowering a bit of profanity could be.

"What will you say to her?"

"Oh, I don't know. Maybe *'Are you out of your bloody mind?'*"

Marie-Claire's mouth fell open. And then, skipping forward to catch up, she asked, "Can I watch?"

Iris turned, measuring the malevolence in her eyes by the degree to which Marie-Claire drew back. "I am about one step away from clubbing you with a cricket bat," she hissed. "No you may not watch."

Marie-Claire's expression took on an almost reverential touch. "Does my brother know you're so violent?"

"He might by the end of the day," Iris muttered. She picked up her speed.

"I'm coming with you!" Marie-Claire shouted from behind her.

Iris snorted. She didn't bother to respond.

Marie-Claire drew up next to her. "Don't you want to know where she is?"

"She's in the orangery."

"What—how do you know?"

"I saw her walking down the path when we left," Iris snapped. And then, because she felt a ridiculous need to defend herself, she added, "I notice things. It's what I *do.*"

But not very well, apparently. Or maybe Fleur was simply a spectacular liar. But that was neither here nor there. The truth was out. And Iris was about to get to the bottom of it.

Chapter Twenty-four

Richard had not slept. Or at least he thought he hadn't. His eyes had closed once or twice during the night, but if he'd found any slumber, it had been fitful at best. He reckoned he must have dozed once dawn had broken; it was nearly half ten by the time he finally hauled himself from his bed and eleven before he was ready to head downstairs.

His valet had managed to wrestle his appearance into something approaching that of a gentleman, but one look in the mirror told Richard that he looked almost as bad as he felt, which was to say, tired.

Dejected.

And most of all, bleak.

The door to Iris's bedroom was open as he walked past, and he heard the maids moving about inside, indicating that she had already risen.

But when he reached the breakfast room, his wife was nowhere in sight.

Neither was breakfast, but this was less of a disappointment.

He tapped his hand against the sideboard, wondering what he should do next. The accounts, he supposed. His stomach was rumbling, but he could last until the midday meal. He didn't really *feel* like eating, anyway.

"There you are, lad!"

He glanced over at the door that led to the kitchens. "Mrs. Hopkins. Good morning." He smiled. She only called him *lad* when they were alone. He liked it. It reminded him of his childhood.

She gave him a vaguely scolding look. "Morning? Barely. I've not known you to lie abed so late in years."

"Trouble sleeping," he admitted, ruffling his hand through his hair.

She nodded knowingly. "Your wife, too."

Richard's heart leapt at the mention of her, but he forced himself not to react visibly. "You've seen Lady Kenworthy this morning?"

"Briefly. She went out with your sister."

"Fleur?" This he found difficult to believe.

Mrs. Hopkins shook her head. "Marie-Claire. I got the impression that Lady Kenworthy had not perhaps intended to be up and about so early."

Early? Iris?

"Not early to *me*, mind you," Mrs. Hopkins went on. "It was gone past ten before I saw her. She did miss breakfast."

"She didn't take a tray in her room?"

Mrs. Hopkins clucked disapprovingly. "Marie-Claire was rushing her out the door. I made sure to give her something to eat on the walk, though."

"Thank you." Richard wondered if he ought to make a comment about a woman in Iris's "condition" needing to eat properly. It seemed the sort of thing a caring husband might do.

But instead he heard himself saying, "Did they mention where they might be going?"

"Just for a walk, I think. It does my heart good to see them acting like sisters." The housekeeper leaned in, her smile warm and maternal. "I do like your lady, sir."

"I like her, too," Richard murmured. He thought about the evening they had met. He had not originally been planning to attend her family's musicale; he had not even been invited. It was only when Winston Bevelstoke had described the event to him that he'd thought it might be a good opportunity to look for a bride.

Iris Smythe-Smith was surely the happiest accident of his life.

When he had kissed her the night before, he had been consumed with the most exquisite sense of longing. It wasn't merely desire, although that had certainly been present in abundance. He had been nearly overcome with the need to feel the warmth of her body, to breathe the same air.

He wanted to be near her. He wanted to be *with* her, in every sense of the word.

He loved her. He loved Iris Kenworthy with every last drop of his soul, and he might well have destroyed their only chance at lasting happiness.

He had been so sure that he was doing the right thing. He had been trying to protect his sister. He had been willing to sacrifice his very birthright to save Fleur's reputation.

But now Fleur seemed hell-bent on her own destruction. He did not know how he could save a woman who did not want saving. He had to try, though. He was her brother, blood-sworn to protect her. But maybe there was another way.

There had to be another way.

He loved Iris far too much for there not to be another way.

IRIS HAD CROSSED the fields of Maycliffe in record time, but when she reached the orangery, Fleur was nowhere to be found. This was probably for the best. It took Iris the better part of an hour to rid herself of Marie-Claire, who had clearly not found the threat of a cricket bat sufficient deterrence to leave well enough alone.

When Iris finally did find Fleur, she was methodically pruning roses in the small briar at the southern edge of the estate. She had clearly dressed for the task; her brown dress was worn and serviceable, and her hair had been pinned back haphazardly, several pieces already falling around her shoulders. A blue plaid blanket lay folded on a stone bench, along with three not-quite-ripe oranges and a chunk of bread and cheese.

"You found my secret place," Fleur said, glancing up only briefly as Iris entered. She examined the bramble with narrowed eyes and a critical expression before reaching in with a long-handled pair of shears. With a savage swish, the blades came together and snipped off a branch.

Iris could see how one might find this a most satisfying endeavor.

"My mother built this place," Fleur said, using the shears to grasp the dead branch and pull it from the twisted mass of vines.

Iris looked around her. The roses had been trained to grow in a circle, creating a small, hidden space. They were not yet in full bloom; Iris could only imagine how lush and fragrant it would be in a few months. "It's lovely," she said. "Very peaceful."

"I know," Fleur said flatly. "I often come here to be alone."

"How nice for you," Iris said. She gave Fleur a bland smile as she stepped fully inside the bower.

Fleur looked over at her, her lips flattening into a tense line.

"We need to have a talk, you and I," Iris said bluntly.

"Do we?" *Snip snip.* "On what topic?"

"The father of your baby."

Fleur's hands stilled, but she recovered quickly, reaching to take out a particularly nasty branch. "I don't know what you mean."

Iris didn't say anything. She knew better than that.

Fleur didn't turn around, but sure enough, barely ten seconds had passed before she repeated herself. "I *said* I don't know what you mean."

"I heard you."

The snipping sounds sped up. "Then what did you— Ow!"

"Thorn?" Iris inquired.

"You might show a little sympathy," Fleur growled, sucking her injured finger.

Iris snorted. "You're barely bleeding."

"It still hurts."

"Really?" Iris regarded her dispassionately. "I'm told childbirth is a great deal more painful."

Fleur glared at her.

"Not for me, of course," Iris said lightly. "My first birth shall be painless. Not too difficult to pass a pillow, I imagine."

Fleur froze. Slowly she took her injured finger from her mouth. When she spoke, her words were unswerving and fierce.

"I'm not giving you my baby."

Iris met this with equal intensity, hissing, "Do you really think I want it?"

Fleur's lips parted with surprise, although not, Iris imagined, at her words. Iris had already made it plain that she was a most reluctant participant in Richard's scheme. But Iris's tone . . . well, it could not have been described as kind. Quite honestly, she was not sure she could manage a kind voice for this particular conversation.

"You are a cold person," Fleur accused.

Iris nearly rolled her eyes. "On the contrary, I would be a very warm and loving aunt."

"We want the same thing," Fleur cried out. "For me to keep the baby. Why are you arguing with me?"

"Why are *you* making this so difficult?" Iris shot back.

Fleur thrust her chin out defiantly, but she was starting to lose some of her bravado. Her eyes flicked to the side and then down, her gaze settling somewhere on the grass near her feet.

"I want the truth," Iris demanded.

Fleur said nothing.

"The *truth*, Fleur."

"I don't know what you mean."

"Stop lying," Iris snapped. "Marie-Claire told me everything."

Fleur's head jerked up, but she looked more wary than anything else. It was then that Iris remembered that Fleur did not know that Marie-Claire knew about Mr. Burnham. And Iris wasn't going to get any answers without being more specific in her questions.

"Marie-Claire told me about the father of your baby," Iris said. "She knows. And now I do, too."

Fleur paled, but still she did not admit to anything. One almost had to admire her fortitude.

"Why didn't you tell Richard that John Burnham is the father?" Iris demanded. "Why on earth would you want him to think it was a scoundrel like William Parnell?"

"Because William Parnell is dead!" Fleur burst out. Her skin flushed to an angry pink, but her eyes were hopeless, almost lost. "Richard can't very well make me marry a dead man."

"But Mr. Burnham is *alive*. And he is the father of your baby."

Fleur was shaking her head, although not as if she were denying it. "It doesn't matter," she kept saying. "It doesn't matter."

"Fleur—"

"I can go somewhere else." As if to indicate direction, Fleur flung her arm out in a wide, hysterical circle. She did not notice when Iris was forced to hop back to avoid the tip of the shears. "I can pretend to be a widow. Why won't Richard let me do that? No one will know. Why would anyone know?"

Iris ducked as the clippers swung toward her once again. "Put down the damned shears!"

Fleur sucked in a breath, staring at the shears with horror. "I'm sorry," she stuttered. "I'm so—I—I—" With shaking hands she set the shears down on the bench. Her movements were slow and careful, as if she were measuring them out in her head. "I'm going to go away," she with quiet hysteria. "I shall become a widow. It will be best for everyone."

"For the love of—" Iris cut herself off, trying to control her temper. She took a breath, and then another, letting the air out in a slow tight stream. "You are not making sense," she said. "You know as well as anyone that if you wish to be a true mother to this child, you ought to be married."

Fleur hugged her arms to her body, looking away, through the bower's opening toward the distant horizon.

Iris finally voiced the question that had to be asked. "Does he even know?"

Fleur grew so stiff she trembled. With the tiniest of motions, she shook her head.

"Don't you think you should tell him?"

"It would break his heart," Fleur whispered.

"*Because* . . . ?" Iris prompted. And if she sounded derisive, well, she hadn't much patience when she'd entered this conversation. Now it was bloody well gone.

"Because he loves me," Fleur said simply.

Iris closed her eyes, summoning patience and an even demeanor as she asked, "Do you love him?"

"Of course I do!" Fleur cried. "What sort of woman do you think I am?"

"I don't know," Iris said plainly. And when Fleur drew back with an affronted glare, she added, somewhat irritably, "Do *you* know what sort of woman *I* am?"

Fleur stood stiff as a board, then finally dipped her chin with a curt, "Fair enough."

"If you love Mr. Burnham," Iris said with patience that was more forced than felt, "surely you see that you must tell him about the baby so that he may marry you. I realize that he is not what your family hoped for you—"

"He is a good man!" Fleur interrupted. "I won't have you denigrating him."

Lord help me, Iris thought. How could she talk sense when Fleur's every sentence contradicted the last?

"I would not dream of speaking ill of Mr. Burnham," Iris said carefully. "I was saying only that—"

"He is a wonderful man." Fleur crossed her arms belligerently, and Iris wondered if she'd even noticed that no one was arguing with her. "Honorable and true."

"Yes, of course—"

"Better than any of the *so-called*"—she sneered the last—"gentlemen I see at local assemblies."

"Then you should marry him."

"*I can't!*"

Iris took a long, steadying breath through her nose. She was never going to be the sort of woman who cradled distraught friends and sisters in her arms and murmured, "*There, there.*"

She decided she was at ease with that.

Instead, she was the plainspoken, occasional termagant who yelled, "For the love of *God*, Fleur, what the devil is wrong with you?"

Fleur blinked. And stepped back. With real concern in her eyes.

Iris forcibly unclenched her teeth. "You already made one mistake. Don't compound it with another."

"But—"

"You *say* you love him, but you don't respect him enough even to tell him he is to be a father."

"That is not true!"

"I can only deduce that your refusal has to do with his social status," Iris said.

Fleur gave a small, bitter nod.

"Well, if that's the case," Iris snapped, shaking a finger perilously close to Fleur's nose, "you should bloody well have taken that into consideration before you gave him your virginity."

Fleur's jaw jutted out. "It wasn't like that."

"As I was not there, I will not argue with you. *However,*" Iris said pointedly when she saw Fleur open her mouth to argue, "you did lie with him, and now you're pregnant."

"Do you think I don't know that?"

Iris decided to ignore this utterly superfluous question. "Let me ask you this," she said instead. "If you are so concerned about your position, *why* are you fighting Richard about adopting the baby? Surely you see that it's the only way to protect your reputation."

"Because it's *my* baby," Fleur cried. "I can't just give it away."

"It's not as if it would go to strangers," Iris said as callously as she could manage. She had to push Fleur to the edge. She could think of no other way to make her see sense.

"Don't you see that that is almost worse?" Fleur's face fell into her hands, and she began to weep. "To have to smile when my child calls me his aunt Fleur? To have to pretend it doesn't kill me every time he calls you his mama?"

"Then marry Mr. Burnham," Iris pleaded.

"I can't."

"Why the bloody hell not?"

Iris's foul language seemed to give Fleur a momentary jolt, and she blinked.

"Is it Marie-Claire?" Iris asked.

Fleur slowly raised her head, her eyes red and wet and so heartbreakingly bleak. She did not nod, but she did not need to. Iris had her answer.

Marie-Claire had said it all earlier that morning. If Fleur married her brother's tenant farmer, the local scandal would be stupendous. Fleur would no longer be welcome in any of the better homes in the area. All the families with whom she'd socialized would turn their heads and pretend not to see her when they crossed paths in the village.

"We British do not think warmly of those who dare to trade one social class for another," Iris said with wry inflection, "whether the movement be up or down."

"Indeed," Fleur said, her smile small, wobbly, and humorless. She touched a tightly furled rosebud, her fingers sliding across the pale pink petals. She turned abruptly, regarding Iris with an expression that was disconcertingly devoid of emotion. "Did you know that there are over one hundred species of roses?"

Iris shook her head.

"My mother bred them. She taught me a great deal. These"—Fleur trailed her hand along the leaves of the climbing vines behind her—"are all centifolia roses. People like them because they have lots of petals." She leaned forward and gave a sniff. "And they are quite fragrant."

"Cabbage roses," Iris murmured.

Fleur's brows rose in a small salute. "You do know about roses."

"That is about the extent of it," Iris admitted. She didn't know where Fleur was going with this line of conversation, but at least she had stopped crying.

Fleur was quiet for a moment, glancing at the blooms. Most were still buds, their petals packed into darker pinks than the ones that had begun to open. "Consider these," she said. "These are all Bishop roses. Every last one. They all bloom to precisely the same shade of pink." She glanced over at Iris. "My mother liked uniformity."

"It's very beautiful," Iris said.

"It is, isn't it?" Fleur took a few aimless steps, stopping to give a sniff. "But it's not the only way to grow a beautiful garden. I could choose five different sorts of centifolias. Or ten. I could have purples. Different shades of pink. There is no reason it has to be the same."

Iris just nodded. It was fairly clear that Fleur was no longer talking about roses.

"I could plant a moss rose. Or a gallica. It would be unexpected here in a cultivated garden, but they would grow."

"They might even thrive," Iris said softly.

Fleur turned sharply to look at her. "They might," she repeated. And then, with a tired sigh, she sank onto the small stone bench. "The roses aren't the problem. It's the people who look at them."

"It usually is," Iris said.

Fleur looked up, all traces of wistfulness banished from her eyes. "Right now my younger sister is Miss Kenworthy of Maycliffe, sister to Sir Richard Kenworthy, baronet. She might not attract much attention were she to go to London, but here in our corner of Yorkshire, she will be one of the most sought-after young ladies when she comes of age."

Iris nodded.

Abruptly, Fleur stood. She turned away from Iris, hugging her arms to her body. "We have parties here, too, you know. And balls and assemblies. Marie-Claire will have the opportunity to meet dozens of eligible young gentlemen. And I hope she will fall in love with one." She glanced just far enough over her shoulder for Iris to see her face in profile. "But if I marry John . . ."

"You have to marry John," Iris said gently.

"If I marry John," Fleur said, louder this time, as if she could forcibly contradict Iris with nothing but the tone of her voice, "Marie-Claire will be the sister of *that Kenworthy girl*, the one who married a peasant. She will not receive invitations, and she will have no opportunity to meet those eligible young gentlemen. If she marries, it will be to some fat old merchant who wants nothing but her name."

"I daresay that several of those eligible gentlemen will also be fat and old," Iris said, "and they will certainly want her for her name."

Fleur turned sharply around, her eyes flashing. "But she wouldn't *have* to marry them. It's not the same. Don't you see? If I marry John—no, let's be honest, if I *choose* to marry John, Marie-Claire will have no choices at all. My freedom for my sister's— what kind of person would that make me?"

"But you don't have a choice," Iris said. "At least not the one you think. You can either marry Mr. Burnham or let us pretend the baby is ours. If you steal away and pretend to be a widow, you will be found out. Do you really think no one will discover what you've done? And when they do, you will ruin Marie-Claire far more thoroughly than if you were Mrs. Burnham."

Iris crossed her arms and waited for Fleur to consider this. In truth, she had probably been exaggerating. England was a big country, maybe not as big as France or Spain, but it took the better part of a week to travel from one end to the other. If Fleur settled in the south, she might be able to live her whole life as a fake widow without anyone near Maycliffe learning the truth.

But surely that couldn't be the best solution.

"I wish . . ." Fleur turned with a rueful smile. "I wish that . . ." She sighed. "Maybe if I were from your family, if my cousin were an earl and my other cousin had married one . . ."

It wouldn't make a difference, Iris thought. Not for a gently born lady wishing to marry a tenant farmer. Still, she said, "I will support you."

Fleur looked up with a puzzled expression.

"Richard, too," Iris said, praying that she was right to speak for him in this. "There will be a scandal, and there will be some who will no longer acknowledge you, but Richard and I will stand by you. You and Mr. Burnham will always be welcome in our home, and when we entertain, you will be our most honored guests."

Fleur smiled at her gratefully. "That is very sweet of you," she said, but the look on her face was gently condescending.

"You are my sister," Iris said plainly.

Fleur's eyes grew bright, and she gave a little nod, the sort one made when one didn't trust one's voice. Finally, just when Iris was wondering if their conversation had come to a close, Fleur looked up with renewed clarity, and said, "I've never been to London."

Iris blinked, confused by the sudden change of subject. "I beg your pardon?"

"I've never been to London," Fleur repeated. "Did you know that?"

Iris shook her head. London was so crowded, so full of humanity. It seemed impossible that someone might never have stepped foot in its boundaries.

"I never really wanted to." Fleur shrugged, looking over at Iris with a knowing expression. "I know you think I'm a thoughtless, frivolous girl, but I don't need silks and satins and invitations to the best sorts of parties. All I want is a warm home, and good food, and a husband who can provide all that. But Marie-Claire—"

"Can go to London!" Iris blurted, her head snapping up. "Good heavens, why didn't I think of it before?"

Fleur stared at her. "I don't understand."

"We'll send Marie-Claire to my mother," Iris said excitedly. "She can give her a season."

"She would do that?"

Iris waved this away as the ridiculous question it was. By the time Marie-Claire was of a proper age, Daisy would be married and out of the house. Iris's mother would be bored beyond tears without a daughter to shepherd through the marriage mart.

Yes, Marie-Claire would do nicely.

"I would have to go down with her for part of the season," Iris said, "but that's hardly a difficulty."

"But surely people would gossip . . . Even in London . . . if I actually married John . . ." Fleur did not seem able to complete a sentence, but for the first time since Iris had met her, there was hope in her eyes.

"They'll know what we tell them," Iris said firmly. "By the time my mother is done, your Mr. Burnham will be lauded as a minor but respectable landowner, just the sort of sober and serious young man a girl like you should marry."

And maybe he *would* be a landowner by then. Iris rather thought that Mill Farm would make an excellent dowry. John Burnham would go from being a tenant farmer to a yeoman, and with the former Fleur Kenworthy as his bride, he would be well on his way to the status of gentleman.

There would be a scandal, there was no getting around that. But nothing so permanent as Fleur's giving birth to a bastard, and nothing that Marie-Claire could not weather two hundred miles away in London, with the full weight of Iris's family behind her.

"Go tell him," Iris urged.

"Now?"

Iris almost laughed with happiness. "Is there any reason to wait?"

"Well, no, but—" Fleur looked at her with an almost desperate expression. "Are you sure?"

Iris reached out and squeezed her hands. "Go find him. Go tell him he is to be a father."

"He will be angry," Fleur whispered. "That I didn't tell him. He will be furious."

"He has every right to be. But if he loves you, he will understand."

"Yes," Fleur said, sounding as if she were trying to convince herself. "Yes. Yes, I think he will."

"Go," Iris said, taking Fleur by the shoulders and pointing her toward the opening in the rose bower. "Go."

Fleur started to leave, then turned around suddenly and threw her arms around Iris. Iris tried to return the embrace, but before she could so much as move, Fleur was racing away, skirts hitched and hair streaming, ready to embark upon her new life.

Chapter Twenty-five

THERE WAS A certain irony at play, Richard thought. Here he was, ready to declare himself, to transform his life, to throw himself at the mercy of his wife, and he couldn't bloody *find* her.

"Iris!" he bellowed. He'd skidded down across the western fields after one of the grooms had said he'd seen her heading in that direction, but the only sign of her was a half-eaten scone near the hedgerow, currently under vicious attack by a small murder of crows.

More irritated than discouraged, he tramped back up the hill to the house, which he tore through in record time, crashing through doors and scaring the dickens out of no fewer than three housemaids. Finally, he came across Marie-Claire, who was sulking in the main hall. He took one look at her pose—arms crossed tight, toe tapping with angry irritation—and he decided he wanted no knowledge of whatever had brought her to that point.

He did, however, need her assistance. "Where is my wife?" he demanded.

"I don't know."

He let out a noise. It might have been a growl.

"I don't!" Marie-Claire protested. "I was with her earlier, but she ran away."

Richard felt his heart contract. "*She ran away?*"

"She *tripped* me," Marie-Claire said. With considerable affront.

Wait . . . *what?* Richard tried to make sense of this. "She tripped you?"

"She did! We were leaving the orangery, and she stuck out her foot and tripped me. I could have been seriously injured."

"Were you?"

Marie-Claire scowled. And said most grudgingly, "No."

"Where did she go?"

"Well, I don't exactly *know,*" Marie-Claire snipped, "as I was busy making sure I could still walk."

Richard rubbed his brow. It really shouldn't be this difficult to find one slip of a girl. "Why were you at the orangery?" he asked.

"Looking for Fle—" Marie-Claire clamped her mouth shut, although Richard couldn't imagine why. Normally he'd be suspicious. Right now he simply didn't have the patience.

"What did she want with Fleur?"

Marie-Claire's mouth clamped firmly into a line.

Richard let out an impatient exhale. Really, he didn't have time for this nonsense. "Well, if you see her, tell her I'm looking for her."

"Fleur?"

"*Iris.*"

"Oh." Marie-Claire let out an affronted sniff. "Of course."

Richard nodded curtly and strode out the front door.

"Wait!" Marie-Claire called out.

He didn't.

"Where are you going?"

He kept walking. "To the orangery."

"But she's not there," Marie-Claire's voice was a little breathless. He assumed she had to run to keep up with him.

"She's not in the hall," he said with a shrug. "I might as well try the orangery."

"Can I come with you?"

That was enough to stop him. "What? Why?"

Marie-Claire's mouth opened and closed a few times. "I just . . . Well, I have nothing to do."

He stared at her in disbelief. "You are a terrible liar."

"That's not true! I'm a very good liar."

"Is this really a conversation you wish to have with your elder brother and guardian?"

"No, but—" She gasped. "There's Fleur!"

"What? Where?" Richard followed her gaze to the left, and sure enough, there was Fleur, flat out sprinting across the field. "What the devil has got into her?" he muttered.

Marie-Claire gasped again, this one a longer,

more gossipy sound. Rather like a deflating accordion.

Richard shaded his eyes as he squinted down toward Fleur. She looked upset. He probably should go after her.

"Bye!"

Before Richard could blink, Marie-Claire had taken off at a run after Fleur.

Richard turned back toward the orangery, then thought the better of it. Iris was probably wherever Fleur had just been. Revising his course to the south, he headed down the hill and once again bellowed Iris's name.

HE DIDN'T FIND her. He checked the strawberry patch he knew Fleur liked down near the stream, doubled back to his mother's rose briar, which did show signs of recent occupancy, and then finally gave up and headed back to the house. His ridiculous route had leached some of the urgency from his search, and by the time he entered his bedroom and shut the door behind him, he was more exasperated than anything else. He reckoned he'd walked three miles at least, half of it along the same path, and now here he was, back in his bedroom with nothing to—

"Richard?"

He swung around. "Iris?"

She was standing in the doorway that connected their bedrooms, her hand resting nervously on the frame. "Mrs. Hopkins said you were looking for me?"

He almost laughed. *Looking for her.* Somehow that seemed a monstrous understatement.

Her head tilted as she watched with a mix of curiosity and concern. "Is something wrong?"

"No." He stared at her, wondering if he'd ever regain his ability to speak in multisyllabic words. It was just that when she stood there, the soft rosy hues of her bedroom like a morning cloud behind her, she was so beautiful.

No, not beautiful. Beautiful didn't come close.

He didn't know the word. He didn't know if there was a word to describe what he felt in that moment, how he saw the lines of his own heart when her eyes met his.

He wet his lips, but he could not seem able even to *try* to speak. Instead he was gripped by the most disconcerting urge to kneel before her like some medieval knight, to take her hand and pledge his devotion.

She took a step into his room, and then another, but there she paused. "Actually," she said, the word tumbling quickly from her lips, "I needed to speak with you, too. You won't believe wh—"

"I'm sorry," he blurted out.

She blinked in surprise, and her voice was tiny and bewildered when she said, "What?"

"I'm sorry," he said, choking on the words. "I'm sorry. When I came up with the plan, I didn't think . . . I didn't know that . . ." He raked his hand through his hair. Why was this so hard? He'd taken the time to think out his words. The whole time he'd been crisscrossing the fields and bellowing her name he'd been practicing them in his head, testing them out, measuring each syllable. But now, faced with the clear blue eyes of his wife, he was lost.

"Richard," she said, "I must tell—"

"No, please." He swallowed. "Let me continue. I beg you."

She went still, and he could see in her eyes that she was startled to see him so humbled.

He said her name, or at least he thought he did. He had no recollection of crossing the room, but somehow he was there before her, taking her hands in his.

"I love you," he said. It wasn't what he had meant to say, not yet anyway, but there it was, more important and more precious than anything.

"I love you." He dropped to his knees. "I love you so much it hurts sometimes, but even if I knew how to make it stop, I wouldn't because the pain is at least *some*thing."

Her eyes shone bright with tears, and he saw her tender pulse fluttering in her throat.

"I love you," he said again, because he wasn't sure how to stop saying it. "I love you, and if you will allow me, I will spend the rest of my life proving it to you." He stood, never letting go of her hands, and his eyes met hers in a solemn vow. "I will earn your forgiveness."

She licked her trembling lips. "Richard, you don't—"

"No, I do. *I hurt you*." It pained him to say it out loud, such a stark, bleak acknowledgment. "I lied to you, and I tricked you, and—"

"Stop," she pleaded. "Please."

Was that forgiveness he saw in her eyes? Even a shred of it?

"Listen to me," he said, taking one of her hands tightly in his. "You don't have to do it. We'll find some other way. I'll convince Fleur to marry someone else, or I'll scrape together the funds, and we'll find a way for her to pass herself off as a widow. I won't be able to see her as often as I'd like, but—"

"Stop," Iris cut in, placing a finger against his lips. She was smiling. Her lips were quivering, but she was most definitely smiling. "I mean it. Stop."

He shook his head, not understanding.

"Fleur lied," she said.

He froze. "What?"

"Not about the baby, but about the father. It wasn't William Parnell."

Richard blinked, trying to make sense of this. "Then who?"

Iris caught her lower lip between her teeth, her eyes shifting to the side with hesitation.

"For the love of God, Iris, if you do not tell me—"

"John Burnham," she blurted out.

"What?"

"John Burnham, your tenant."

"I *know* who he is," he said, far more sharply than he'd meant. "I just—" His brow furrowed, and his mouth went slack, and he was sure he looked like some bloody idiot about to be fitted with a dunce cap, but—"John Burnham? Really?"

"Marie-Claire told me."

"*Marie-Claire* knew?"

Iris nodded.

"I'm going to throttle her."

Iris gave a hesitant frown. "To be fair, she wasn't *sure* . . ."

He looked at her in disbelief.

"Fleur didn't tell her," she explained. "Marie-Claire figured it out on her own."

"She figured it out," he said, feeling more like that dunce-capped idiot than ever, "and I didn't?"

"You're not her sister," Iris said, as if that ought to explain everything.

He rubbed his eyes. "Dear God. John Burnham." He looked at her, trying to blink the disbelief from his face. "John. Burnham."

"You will let her marry him, won't you?"

"I don't see how I have any choice. The baby needs a father . . . The baby *has* a father." He looked up sharply. "He did not force himself on her?"

"No," Iris said. "He did not."

"Of course he didn't." He shook his head. "He would not do that. I know him that well at least."

"Then you like him?"

"I do. I've said as much. It's just . . . he has . . ." He sighed. "I suppose this is why she did not say anything. She thought I would not approve."

"That, and she feared for Marie-Claire."

"Oh, God," Richard groaned. He had not even thought of Marie-Claire. It would be impossible for her to make a good match after this.

"No, no, don't worry," Iris said, her entire face perking with excitement. "I've taken care of that. I figured it all out. We'll send her to London. My mother will sponsor her."

"Are you sure?" Richard could not identify this strange, clenching in his chest. He was utterly humbled by her, by her brilliance, her caring heart. She was everything he had not even realized he needed in a woman, and somehow, miraculously, she was his.

"My mother has not been without an unmarried daughter of marrying age since 1818," Iris said with wry grin. "She's not going to know what to do with herself once Daisy is gone and out of the house. Trust me, you don't want to see her when she's bored. She's an absolute nightmare."

Richard laughed.

"I'm not joking."

"I did not think you were," he told her. "I've met your mother, you recall."

Iris's lips curved in a rather sly manner. "She and Marie-Claire will do well together."

He nodded. Mrs. Smythe-Smith would surely do a better job than he ever had. He looked back over at Iris. "You do realize I'm going to have to kill Fleur before I let her marry him."

His wife smiled at such nonsense. "Just forgive her. I have."

"I thought you said you were not a model of Christian charity and forgiveness."

She shrugged. "I'm turning over a new leaf."

Richard took her hand and brought it to his lips. "Do you think you might be able to forgive me?"

"I already have," she whispered.

Relief washed over him with such force it was a wonder he remained able to stand. But then he looked into her eyes, her pale lashes still wet with tears, and he was gone. He took her face in his hands and brought her to him, kissing her with all the urgency of a man who has faced the precipice and survived.

"I love you," he said roughly, his words kisses in themselves. "I love you so much."

"I love you, too."

"I never thought I would hear you say that."

"I love you."

"Again," he ordered.

"I love you."

He brought her hands to his mouth. "I worship you."

"Is this a contest?"

Slowly, he shook his head. "I'm going to worship you right now."

"Right . . . now?" She glanced at the window. The afternoon sun was streaming in, relentlessly bright and cheerful.

"I've waited far too long," he growled, sweeping her into his arms. "And so have you."

Iris let out a little squeal of surprise as he dropped her onto the bed. It was only a few inches to the mattress, but it was enough to give her a little bounce, and enough for him to take the moment to cover her body with his, reveling in the primitive sensation of having her pinned beneath him.

She was at his mercy.

She was his to love.

"I adore you," he murmured, nuzzling his face into the crook of her neck. He kissed the delicate hollow over her collarbone, reveling in her soft mewl of pleasure. His fingers found the lacy edge of her bodice. "I have dreamed of this."

"So have I," she said tremulously, gasping when she heard the unmistakable sound of ripping fabric.

"Sorry," he said, glancing cursorily at the small tear at the bodice of her frock.

"No you're not."

"I'm not," he agreed cheerfully, taking the edge of the fabric between his teeth.

"Richard!" she nearly shrieked.

He looked up. God, he was like a dog with a bone, and he didn't care one bit.

Her lips quivered with unspent laughter. "Don't make it worse."

He grinned wolfishly, tugging gently with his teeth. "Like this?"

"Stop!"

He released the fabric and used his hands to push her dress down, revealing one perfect breast. "Like this?"

Her only answer was the quickening of her breath.

"Or like this?" he asked huskily, taking her into his mouth.

Iris let out a keening cry, and her hands sank into his hair.

"Definitely like this," he murmured, teasing her with his tongue.

"Why do I feel that . . . ?" she whispered helplessly.

He looked up in bemusement and echoed, "Why do you feel it?"

Her flush spread from her cheeks to her neck and down. "Why do I feel it . . . down . . . *there*?"

Maybe he was a rogue. Maybe he was just very very wicked, but he could only lick his lips and whisper, "Where?"

She shuddered with desire, but did not speak.

He slid her slipper from her foot. "Here?"

She shook her head.

His hand slid up her slender calf to the inside of her knee. "Here?"

"No."

He smiled to himself. She was enjoying their game, too. "What about"—he brought his fingers higher, resting them at the soft crease between her hip and her thigh—"here?"

She swallowed, and her voice was barely audible when she whispered, "Almost."

He moved closer to his goal, trailing the tips of his fingers through the soft thatch covering her womanhood. He wanted to look at her again, see the impossibly blond curls in light of day, but that would have to wait. He was too busy watching her face as he slid his finger inside her.

"Richard," she gasped.

He groaned. She was so wet and ready for him. But she was tiny, and as they both well knew, still a virgin. He would have to make love to her with great care, moving slowly and with a gentleness at complete odds with the raging fire burning within.

"What you do to me," he whispered, taking a moment to regain at least a portion of his composure.

She smiled up at him, and there was something so sunny and open in her expression . . . He felt it echo across his own face until he was grinning like a loon, almost laughing with the sheer joy of her company.

"Richard?" she said, her grin right there in her voice.

"I'm just so happy." He sat up to yank his shirt over his head. "I can't help it."

She touched his face, her small hand light and delicate along the line of his jaw.

"Stand up," he said suddenly.

"What?"

"Stand up." He eased himself off the bed, then tugged at her hand until she followed suit.

"What are you doing?"

"I believe," he said, sliding her dress down over her hips, "I'm disrobing you."

Her eyes fell to the front of his breeches.

"Oh, I'll get to that," he promised. "But first . . ." He found the delicate ties to her chemise and pulled, catching his breath when it fell to the floor in a cloud of white silk. She was still wearing her stockings, but he wasn't sure he could wait long enough to divest her of those, and at any rate, her hands were at his waist, urgently slipping the buttons undone.

"You're too slow," she muttered, practically yanking his breeches down.

The threads of his desire stretched impossibly taut.

"I'm trying to be gentle."

"I don't want you to be gentle."

He grabbed her under her buttocks, lifting her to meet him, and they both tumbled to the bed. Her legs slid open, and without even trying he found himself at her entrance, using every ounce of his control to keep himself from plunging forward.

He looked at her, his eyes asking—*Are you ready?*

She grabbed his bottom and let out a frustrated cry. It might have been his name. He didn't know; he couldn't hear anything beyond the blood rushing through his body as he surged forward, sheathing himself within her.

It was all so fast. He felt her tense, and he lifted himself up as best he could. "Are you all right? Did I hurt you?"

"Don't stop," she growled, and then all speech was lost. He plunged into her, over and over, driven by an urgency he did not fully comprehend. All he knew was that he needed her. He needed to fill her, to be consumed by her. He wanted to feel her legs wrapped around him, to feel the thrust of her hips as she rose to meet him.

She was hungry, maybe even as hungry as he was, and it only served to inflame his desire. He was close, so close, he could barely keep himself from exploding. And then—thank God because he didn't think he could have lasted another second—he felt her clench around him, tight as a fist, and she cried out. He came so fast, she was still pulsing around him when he was done.

He collapsed atop her, lying there for two breaths before sliding to the side so as not to crush her. They lay there for quite some time, just letting their bodies cool, and then, finally, Iris let out a little sigh.

"Oh my."

He felt himself smile, slow and satisfied.

"That was . . ." But she didn't finish.

He rolled to his side, propping himself up on his elbow. "That was what?"

She just shook her head. "I don't even know how to describe it. I don't know how to begin."

"It begins," he said, leaning down to kiss her lightly, "with 'I love you.'"

She nodded, her movements still slow and languid. "I think it ends with it as well."

"No," he said, his voice gentle but brooking no argument.

"No?"

"It doesn't end," he whispered. "It never ends."

She touched his cheek. "No. I don't think it does."

Then he kissed her again. Because he wanted to. Because he *had* to.

But mostly because he knew that even when his lips left hers, their kiss would still linger.

It, too, would never end.

Epilogue

Maycliffe
1830

"WHAT ARE YOU READING?"

Iris smiled at her husband as she looked up from her correspondence. "A letter from my mother. She says that Marie-Claire attended three balls last week."

"Three?" Richard shuddered.

"Torture for you, perhaps," Iris laughed. "But Marie-Claire is in heaven."

"I suppose so." He took a seat beside her on the little bench she used at her writing table. "Any potential suitors?"

"Nothing serious, but I have a feeling my

mother is not trying *quite* as hard as she might. I think she wants another season with Marie-Claire. Your sister is proving a far more cunning debutante than any of her own daughters were."

Richard rolled his eyes. "God help them both."

"And in other news," Iris said with a laugh, "Marie-Claire is taking viola lessons three days per week."

"Viola?"

"Perhaps the other reason my mother is reluctant to let her go. Marie-Claire has a spot in next year's musicale."

"God help *us* both."

"Oh, yes. There is no way we shall be allowed to miss it. I would have to be nine months pregnant to—"

"Then we should start right now," Richard said with enthusiasm.

"Stop!" Iris protested. But she was laughing, even as her husband's lips found a particularly sensitive spot just above her collarbone. He always seemed to know exactly where to kiss her . . .

"I'll shut the door," Richard murmured.

"It's open?" Iris squealed. She yanked herself away.

"I knew I shouldn't have said that," he muttered.

"Later," Iris promised. "We haven't the time now, anyway."

"I can be quick," Richard said hopefully.

Iris gave him a lingering kiss. "I don't want you to be quick."

He groaned. "You're killing me."

"I promised Bernie we would take him out to try his toy boat on the lake."

Richard acquiesced with a smile and a sigh, as Iris knew he would. Their son was now three, an adorable little butterball with plump pink cheeks and his father's dark eyes. He was the center of their world, even if *they* were not the center of his. That honor went to his cousin Samuel, who at age four was one year older, one year taller, and one year more wily. Fleur's second son Robbie was six months younger than Bernie and completed the mischievous trio.

The first year of marriage had not been easy for Fleur and John Burnham. As expected, their wedding had caused quite a scandal, and even though they now owned Mill Farm, there were still those who would not let John forget that he had not been born a gentleman.

But Fleur had spoken true when she'd said she had never wished for riches. She and John had made a very happy home, and Iris was grateful that her children would grow up with cousins just down the lane. It was still just Bernie, but she hoped . . . there had been a few signs . . .

Her hand went to her abdomen without her realizing it. She would know soon.

"Well, I suppose we have a ship to launch," Richard said, holding out his hand as he came to his feet. "I feel I should tell you, though," he said as Iris rose and took his arm, "I had a similar boat as a boy."

Iris winced at his tone. "Why do I think this does not end well?"

"Sailing is not in the Kenworthy blood, I'm afraid."

"Well, that's all right. I should miss you too much if you took to the sea."

"Oh, I almost forgot!" Richard dropped her hand. "I have something for you."

"You do?"

"Wait right there." He left the room, returning a moment later with his hands behind his back. "Close your eyes."

Iris rolled them, then closed them.

"Open!"

She did, and then gasped. He was holding a single long-stemmed iris, the most beautiful bloom she'd ever beheld. The color was brilliant—not quite purple, not quite red.

"It's from Japan," Richard said, looking inordinately pleased with himself. "We've been growing them in the orangery. We've had a devil of a time keeping you away."

"From Japan, though," Iris said, shaking her head in disbelief. "I can't believe—"

"I would go to the ends of the earth," Richard murmured, leaning down to brush her lips with his.

"For a flower?"

"For you."

She looked up at him with shining eyes. "I wouldn't want you to, you know."

"To go to the ends of the earth?"

She shook her head. "You'd have to take me with you."

"Well, that goes without saying."

"And Bernie."

"Oh, of course."

"And—" *Oops.*

"Iris?" Richard said carefully. "Is there something you wish to tell me?"

She gave him a sheepish smile. "We might need room for four on that journey."

His face broke into a slow smile.

"I'm not positive," she warned him. "But I think . . ." She paused. "Where *is* the end of the earth?"

He grinned. "Does it matter?"

She smiled back. She couldn't help it. "I don't suppose it does."

He took her hand, kissed it, and then led her out into the hall. "It will never matter where we are," he said softly, "just so long as we're together."